If you would like a Fnovella

THE ART OF THE CON

download it at

www.artonbaleci.com

To Kerry

Let the mesmerisation commence!

Anton

WITH THANKS

This book is partly about optimism, pessimism, and cynicism. In a world where the latter two are often easier defaults, thank you for being shining examples of people who, again and again, justify the first.

Stephen Ashcroft and Jonathan Frank, I'm truly grateful for your invaluable feedback on all versions of this. *Vielen Dank* and *muchas gracias*.

Stephanie Vernier and Mike Bullen, thank you for your feedback in the days when this was a pilot script.

Terell Cole, thank you for all our chats in which you helped me sort out some of my thoughts around this entire subject matter.

Lesley Higginbottom, thank you for your speedy last-minute proofread.

And saving the biggest thanks for last, Cally Higginbottom, thank you for being a sounding board on this since 2019, for your proofing, and for creating an incredible cover, as always.

First published in Great Britain in 2023

Copyright © 2023 Arton Baleci
www.artonbaleci.com

The moral right of Arton Baleci to be
identified as the author of this work has been
asserted in accordance with the
Copyright, Designs and Patents Act, 1988

All rights reserved. No part of this publication
may be reproduced or transmitted in any form
or by any means, electronic or mechanical,
including photocopy, recording, or any
information storage and retrieval system,
without permission in writing from the publisher.

All characters in this publication are fictitious and
any resemblance to living persons, living or dead,
is purely coincidental. Their thoughts, words and
actions do not represent those of the author.

ISBN 979-8-86566-478-9

Cover design by Cally Higginbottom

THE CANCER MAN

Arton Baleci

CHAPTER 1

She watched the smoke from her cigarette swirl and dissipate into the blood-red evening sky. Between the skyscape and the panorama of the valley of stone and woodland below her, all lit by the dying rays of the golden hour, the view was magnificent. She coughed so deeply it sounded like a lung may come up.

'Excuse me, madam,' called a man's voice from behind her. Still hacking violently, she turned towards him. The man, dressed in traditional butler's garb, stood in front of the rear of a vast Art Deco style mansion. 'Are you ready?'

Spluttering, she pulled a hankie out of her pocket and tried to hold the coughs in with it. As she eventually pulled it away, she accidentally caught the tubes feeding into her nose from the oxygen tank stationed on the ground. The woman was only in her forties, so the oxygen tank and the headscarf gave the world an easy guess at why she looked frail beyond her years. After adjusting her nose tube back into place, she checked the hankie and scrunched it up around the blob of blood sat in it. 'Let's hope not,' she replied with an ironic smile. She took one last look at the majestic landscape ahead of her, then a deep breath before flicking her almost-finished cigarette off the cliff edge she stood on.

Inside, she sat in an armchair, twiddling with her oxygen tube. Along one side of her was a wall of floor to ceiling windows looking out onto the vista she had been admiring. She turned her attention to the dominant feature on the wall the other side of her: a large replica painting of a Salvador Dali painting which depicted a series of strange melting clocks strewn across a barren landscape with its own cliff formation in its background. The almost molten form of the objects, usually so solid and perfectly shaped, oddly uneased her before the sound of footsteps along the marble floor roused her.

'Mr O'Shea,' she said, forcing herself up to standing to welcome her host, a towering middle-aged man wearing a decorative aubergine evening jacket over a black polo neck jumper. 'Thank you so much for agreeing to work with me. This is truly an honour.'

His icy blue eyes met hers as he raised his hand to signal her to stop. 'Please. Don't trouble yourself,' he replied in his soft, bassy Southern Irish accent.

'Thanks,' she said, lowering herself back into her chair. 'And thank you so much for fitting me in. You must have had such a long day?'

A polite, muted smile crept across his face. 'Something like that.' He reached down onto a small table beside her armchair and picked up a canvas garment, the buckles of its leather straps jangling. 'May I?'

'Of course,' she replied enthusiastically. 'Are you sure you don't need me up?'

He nodded and unfolded the garment – a straitjacket – then took one of her hands and fed it into one of its sleeves.

'My husband would have a field day if he saw this!'

The Irishman slipped her other hand into the free sleeve and wryly smiled. He then took one of the arm straps around her body and behind her before reaching for the other.

'It's quite soothing, actually,' she said as he fastened one of the straps into its buckle.

'The jacket or those Japanese Black Menthols?'

She flushed maroon. 'I'm so sorry. I…I guessed at this point it doesn't matter.'

'Allegra, dear,' he said as he gripped the other buckle. 'You misunderstand. The only judgement you're getting from me is for your fine taste in tobacco. They're a contraband delicacy.' He grinned as he moved her oxygen line aside, then fastened the second arm across her. 'And no, it doesn't matter at this point, but it never did. People live into their hundreds smoking. It's not about the substance so much as how you respond to it.'

She nodded uncertainly as he fastened a few more straps, then a look of confusion overcame her. 'How did you know I was smoking Japanese Black Menthols?'

He double tapped his nose.

She squinted as she thought. 'But there are lots of menthol brands in the world. How did you know it was the Japanese?'

'The same way I know you ate quail eggs earlier today rather than chicken eggs?'

Her jaw fell open in puzzlement.

He carried on without responding. 'Not too tight, no?'

She shook her head. 'It's fine, thank you.'

He threaded a strap originating from the armchair through those at the back of the straitjacket and fastened it to a buckle built into the chair, securing her to the seat. He then pulled over a plush, wheeled chair and positioned it close in front of her, slightly off to the side so that her thigh rested beside his. 'What do you think of my clocks?' he asked, nodding to the painting.

'I think they need new batteries,' she answered with a grin.

He flicked the brake lever down on his wheely chair to set it in place. 'You're right that something needs power, but it isn't the clocks, is it?'

'I suppose not,' she said with a wheeze, turning away slightly in an effort to hide welling up.

'You've been looking away too much, Allegra,' he continued. 'From so many things in your life. And it's drained you almost to a halt, hasn't it?'

She turned her gaze back to him as a tear fell. Choked up, she just nodded.

'Well, today we take your power back. Today we look. We face what's weakened you. What's divided you. And we get your mechanism moving again. We find you more time. Look,' he said, gesturing towards the painting, redirecting her gaze. 'And feel. Feel as you sit still, your gaze fixed on those clocks, that your chest still rises and falls, your eyelids still open and close, and your hands, as still as you feel they're resting, still pulsate against you, driven by the beat of your heart. Everything moves with time.' He made three ticking noises, popping his tongue off the roof of his mouth. 'And the more you pay attention to that movement, the more you sense that everything else moves. That gaze you hold on the painting, it wanders, doesn't it?'

Even holding her eyes in place, she noted that they constantly changed their point of focus and nodded.

'Listening to my words. Do those ears ever take them in from exactly the same place?'

She noticed the minute movement of her ears in space, even sensing the blood rushing round inside them.

'And even the silence between my words...' He paused. 'Doesn't that silence move? What is sound but the movement of air? And what can you feel in the silence, Allegra? And what can you hear as you watch those melting clocks?'

Her breathing stalled as her jaw fell open again, wider this time. *Tick tick tick.* The faint sound came from one of the clocks in the painting. Then another ticking began. Then another and another. 'I hear them!' she gasped.

'That's right, you hear them. And as you keep watching, what do you see?'

The ticking slowed. Everything slowed. Even the blink of her eyelids felt elongated. And then she saw it. One of the melting clocks was slowly oozing down. They were all running, stretching, deforming, millimetre by millimetre. She couldn't believe her eyes.

'That's right. Time moves, Allegra,' said the Irishman. 'And as you see that now, something else needs to move. This painting is called *The Persistence of Memory*. Which memory persists in you, Allegra? Which one ticks away and tears you apart inside second after second?'

The woman flinched violently.

'There it is. Now close your eyes.'

She clenched her eyes shut.

'Let it build in front of you, around you, as vivid as the moment it happened now,' he said, his voice ramping up its ferocity with each word. 'Let it pull you into it, subsume you. It fills your lungs…'

She gasped desperately as her body began shaking against the chair.

'…like the poison they have grown full of. It seems inescapable, asphyxiating…terminal…'

Her entire body convulsed. As she thrashed around in the chair, trying to escape it and her imagination, he leaned forward and with a firm hand across the top of her breastbone pinned her back. '…but there is one way out of your suffocating hell…and that is through it. Face your fear, Allegra. Tell me where you are.'

As she cried her imaginary location at him in sheer terror, her legs kicked out and raked the ground, trying to get purchase on anything they could to help her get out of the chair. As the two talked more and more, he slid his hand up just past her sternum and collar bones to sit at the bottom of her throat. An artery in her scrawny neck pounded against his palm like a jackhammer, its beats so fast they were barely separate.

Never stopping talking with her, he leaned further forward still, gripped her moaning head firmly between both hands, and examined her closely. As she answered his next question, an unrestrained grin spread across his face. Then he leaned whispered into her ear.

She shrieked and threw her head back with a freakishly powerful jolt, causing him to lose his grip. Wailing at the top of her lungs, her eyelids ripped open revealing nothing but the whites of her eyes.

CHAPTER 2

The darkness was pierced by a dazzling light display cutting through a cloud of stage smoke. It lit up the face of a strawberry blonde man sceptically scanning the thousands sat around him who had just burst into fanatical applause. Emet Gordon didn't want to be here. At the best of times, his energy never matched this frequency. This was bright lights, bold colours, and big dreams. He was happier hidden away in greys, blacks and browns, and dreams really weren't his thing as the rings under his eyes, resembling the stains on well-used coffee cups, attested to.

'Now leap to your feet and go meet 'n greet!' blared a preacher-esque American accent out of the hall's sound system. Upbeat motivational music kicked in as the house lights came up. The people on either side of Emet sprung to their feet, prompting him to labour up too and then wander out into the aisle where everyone was mixing. After avoiding eye contact with the swarming people for a few moments, he couldn't help his eyes flicker towards fast movement. Enthusiastically waving his way was a fat guy wearing a T-shirt that said "SEE THE GOOD, BE THE GOOD" on its front.

The man opened his arms, offering a hug. 'C'mon, spitfire! Spread the love. Let's leap into our better futures, starting right now!'

Emet tried to mask his cynical scoff and begrudgingly accepted the hug. As they parted, the man examined his face.

'A smile spreads a mile, you know, buddy.'

Emet forced his most sincere-looking smile, garnering a joyful thumbs up from his hugger before he left. Now to find the next violator of his personal space. He met eyes with a jolly old lady with no slogan-bearing T-shirt, who looked pleasant enough. They nodded to each other. As he opened his arms for her, a guy in his mid-twenties wearing shades indoors cut between them.

'Woooo! Top of the morning to ya, fellow Leaper!' He launched himself into a hug with Emet, gripping like an anaconda.

After a few seconds, with no sign of let up, Emet patted his back a few times. 'That's a lot of hug just for me.' *Take the hint.*

The guy gripped him even tighter. 'What're you talking about "just for you"? You're a legend, bro.'

Shit. Emet's face tightened in concern. *He hasn't recognised me?*

The guy slapped his back hard and popped open his grip. 'We're all legends in the making. Do you know how many people in here are gonna go down in history for doing revolutionary shit after the changes we make this weekend?'

Given the thousands of people surrounding them, the odds suggested that somebody there may do something remarkable with their lives, but judging by their Pollyannaish daft grins, Emet wasn't putting money on it.

'Mind-blowing, right?' asked the guy.

'Some minds are definitely blown.'

'Smash your day, bro!' said the guy, raising his fist with oomph.

Emet sarcastically raised his in kind and the two parted ways, allowing him to look for the jolly old lady he figured he could have a painless experience with. A hand landed on his shoulder. *What brand of glass-half-fullard awaits?*

He turned to find a doe-eyed bohemian woman with a nose ring, maybe a few years younger than himself, impishly smiling his way. He gulped.

'You look like he gave you a right huggering!' she said with a wide smile. 'Can I perhaps make it better wiiith…a hug?'

A genuine smile appeared on his face. 'I think I just exceeded my recommended weekly allowance, but what's one more?' He leaned his torso in for a stranger-of-the-opposite-sex hug, but she stepped in closer and embraced like a long-lost friend, laying her wavy hair and braids on his shoulder. Awkward at first, he softened into it.

'There, there,' she said. 'I won't let that shady man have his way with you again.'

He smirked. 'My hero.'

She released the hug and playfully skipped back from him.

'That I may be,' she said, gesturing to the surrounding thousands, 'but I can't save you from them all!'

He grinned, unable to take his gaze off her as she backed away into the crowd. The name on her badge was Skye. With a cute little wave to him, she turned away, showing the flouncy feathers and crystals woven into the back of her hair, which resembled a dreamcatcher, and then she was gone. His first genuine smile of the seminar fell away. An artificial one replaced it as the next stranger came for their hug.

CHAPTER 3

It's not often that smiles are described as powerful, but Emet, as much as he hated it, couldn't think of a better term for it. Jim Akachi-Rawlings, the American on stage leading this personal development seminar, had a powerful smile. His voice was powerful, and his physique – at least six-foot three and looking more like that of a thirty-year-old than a near fifty-year-old – was powerful. Commanding the stage, striding up and down it in his headset mic and purple polo shirt, Akachi-Rawlings was a motivational speaking machine.

'Belief,' stated Jim. 'Belief's what brings us here. Belief's what brought me up here. But it wasn't always that way. As a matter of fact, doubt was chapter one for me. A twenty-two-year long chapter. Heaven knows in this world it's easy to doubt. Where the right path often ain't clear and the natural order of the universe tends towards chaos and decay. Life is hard. Mine was hard. I doubted it could be otherwise. That doubt infected every thought, every action, every cell of my being. Even the things I did from a good place in my heart to try to get my family outta our neighbourhood were sick and riddled with fear. Have y'all had times when every thought you had felt eaten by doubt from the inside out?'

'Hell yeah!' the eight-thousand-strong audience boomed as loudly as a crowd at any rock gig.

'Well, my strongest moment of doubt and fear was when it all changed for me. I was twenty-two years old. My black ass had been up to no good for over a decade. I started with petty theft and pickpocketing when I was ten and only did worse from then. I used to justify it to myself that I was taking care of my people but, if I'm gonna be honest, it was more to make myself look like the man. I was doing a cash collection at an apartment on the top floor of some high rise in my hood. Hearing a scream in a place like that wasn't nothing outta the ordinary, but we started hearing a chorus of them. We pulled back the curtain and saw the upper three or four floors of the apartment block across the alley going up in smoke. Shit looked like a scene from Dante's Inferno. Anyway, for all the shouts we were hearing down below, with people running from their homes streaming into the street, my homie Tone said he could hear a kid screaming from the roof. The other dudes we were with said they couldn't hear shit and headed down to the street in case the blaze was gonna spread in the wind. Tone was adamant a young 'n was up on that roof. We had to go check, right? Well, your man here, *the man*, I was petrified of heights. Looking down a flight of stairs was enough to make me feel queasy. But Tone was ad-a-mant, so we took off up the stairs as everyone else in the building headed down and busted through the fire escape onto the roof. I hang back as Tone ran over towards the edge to take a look.

"'Yo, J!" he yells.

'I have to go see. Luckily, I can see what was going down well away from the edge. By the pigeon coops on that roof, a little girl, no older than four, is sobbing her little heart out. She's given up bawling by now. The fire escape door over on her side's open, but smoke's billowing through it. She has nowhere to go.

"'We gotta do something, J," says Tone.

"'We? What *we* gon do?" I say. "There's gotta be fifteen feet between these buildings and we twelve storeys up, G."

'This girl, she sees us. She comes running over towards the edge, crying her little heart out to us. She don't know what's going on but she's so scared, crying for her momma.

"'We gotta do something!" yells Tone.

"'Man. We can't do nothin,'" I say. I shout over to the little girl to ask her name. It's Tamika, she sobs. "Tamika. You stay right where you are. The fire fighters are gon be here real soon and they'll get you to your momma," But Tone nudges me. Maybe we ain't got time for that, he says. The flames are coming out through the exit now. The roof surface near it's starting to melt and warp.

'Tone spots a ladder laid by the pigeon coop. "One of us needs to get over there, get that ladder, and bring her across here."

'You know what my reply was? "Be my motherfucking guest." But I knew as soon as I'd said it that it wasn't even an option. Tone had been shot a few months before and was still limping bad.

"'I can't do that shit," I said to him.

'But I went through high school with Tone. "You was all-state long jump, J. You used to do that shit *before* the warm-up."

"'Not twelve motherfucking stories up, I didn't!" I say.

'He shoves me full force in the chest. "Shut the fuck up, man. That little girl over there probably gon die if we do nothing, and I really can't. You *have* to do this. And you can. All you do is you focus on that take off and run at it with everything you got."

'I go to argue back with him but homie shoves me again. "Yo!" He thrusts his hands out, his hands making a diamond-shaped viewfinder pointed just ahead of the ledge, just like I used to before my long jump run-up to focus myself on nothing but the pit. "Full belief!" he yells. That must have been some shove, because that shit knocked every doubt out of my mind. "Full belief, man." Tone shouts over to the girl to stand back, and I back up. "Full belief!"

"'Full belief!" I thrust my hands out and stare at my take-off point through them. Everything else was gone. "Full belief." And I started my run-up. I'd run track, I'd run crack, but I ain't never run like that. I hit that take-off point hard and I catapult myself through the air, not looking down once. Then bang! I hit the other roof top, and not with some smooth roll like one of those Parkour brothers. I stack it like some Evel Knievel shit gone wrong. But I'm there. And

I grab that ladder and put it back across the gap. I put little Tamika on my back and tell her to close her eyes. Tone pins the ladder down at the other side. "You flew, J. You can sure as shit crawl," he shouts over. Homie was right. I fixed my eyes so that the furthest I could see down was only so I could reach the next rung of the ladder, and I crawled across it with little Tamika on my back.'

The audience burst into rapturous applause. The story, which Emet assumed must be at least mostly true, given Jim's fame, had even temporarily disarmed his scepticism. He eventually joined in with a few luke-warm claps, but by this point Jim was begging the audience to stop.

'I ain't telling you this for your applause or to show off. I'm telling you this because it was this very experience that taught me to doubt the use of doubt itself. Now, there were sure as hell rational, justifiable reasons to doubt upon that rooftop, but where's the rationality in not fully committing to your actions once you've decided to go through with them? What good comes from doubting yourself and others once you've decided to act? I began to question what else I could do in my life if I replaced doubt and fear with belief. What could my future be like then?

'I got home that night, a Friday night, and I saw a different man in the mirror. My spirits were lifted. My soul elevated. But I knew that hadn't happened after the jump. The real leap had happened when I made the decision *to believe* I could jump. I asked myself what would happen if I chose to cast out all doubt out of my life that coming weekend and do nothing but believe. And that weekend my life took another leap forward and I've been leaping ever since. Belief brought me relief from lots of life's suffering and took me to places I never dreamed I could go.' The seminar's signature motivational music quietly began to build in the background. 'Now, it's your weekend to leap. Get on your feet, everybody.'

The eight-thousand-strong audience rose in almost perfect unison.

'I want you to copy me with everything you've got.' With his palms facing forward and his forefingers and thumbs held in a diamond shape, he thrust his hands out from his chest as far forward as they would go. 'Full belief!' he bellowed with unbridled power.

'Full belief!' came back the chorus, along with the whoosh of eight-thousand pairs of hands projecting out with full force. Emet went through the motions to avoid disapproving looks from those around him, although they were so pumped up, he wasn't sure they would notice.

'And again,' roared Jim with another thrust. 'Full belief!'

The audience somehow boomed back at him even louder. Buoyed by the energy, Emet was swept away, almost all in. It felt surprisingly good to him.

'One more time,' demanded the almighty man up on stage. 'From the bottom of your soul, with a little something extra at the end. Full belief!' he thundered, torpedoing his hands towards them, instigating the loudest response yet.

Emet put everything into this one, allowing himself to revel in the feeling of raw power that surged through him.

Jim beamed his winning smile into the crowd and jumped a few inches forward. 'Take the leap!' he yelled.

The entire audience echoed it back to him and the floor tremored as eight thousand pairs of feet landed on it.

'Excellent. Before you all sit down, give a full-belief high five to the people either side of you. That's right,' said Jim after giving the audience a few seconds to congratulate one another. 'Full energy. Full attention. Before we leap tomorrow, nothing else exists. Now, there's an assistant at the end of your row or one near you with a box. Please turn off your cell or your *mobile* as you guys say, take that little sticker with your mugshot and QR code off your name badge, stick it to the back of your phone, and pass it to that assistant. They'll swap you for one of our fancy tech bundles. You'll get your phones back at the end of the evening.'

A quiet frenzy swept the audience.

'I know it's a little surprise, but if this ain't for you - if you can't be all here while we're doing what we're doing - no hard feelings, but you ain't for this. If you head out the exit at the back, you'll be fully refunded and my wonderful team will help you arrange transport home.'

The stir continued. As most people began fishing their phones out and passing them along, a small percentage remonstrated loudly with assistants, and people here and there gathered their belongings.

Emet observed the unrest, looked down at his phone and badge, and then on stage to Jim; standing tall, earnestly waiting. The tech bundles being passed to those relinquishing their phones interested him. Phone off, sticker on, passed along. He was all in.

Eventually, the ninety-nine-plus percent of the remaining crowd settled. Jim proudly nodded out at them. 'Here we are, Leaple. All in. Let's begin.'

CHAPTER 4

The audience sat silently in the dim hall. The only sound was that of a metronome ticking away at sixty beats per minute.

'A major pillar of our work will be sensory sharpening,' explained Jim, lit by a single spotlight. 'First, we'll learn to monitor ourselves in finer and finer detail, and then we'll learn to regulate ourselves, from our most controllable actions to the hidden bodily functions you may have thought we can't learn to control.'

The metronome was extensively used over the coming few hours as a reference rhythm for breathing exercises. With the aid of a large-faced smart watch and a chest strap, that were part of the tech pack everybody exchanged their phones for, Emet could see how changing his breathing pattern could quickly and significantly change his heart rate and blood pressure. Deep breaths in and controlled breaths out, lasting as long as ten seconds, eventually reduced his heart rate to the mid-fifties, a range he'd always assumed was beyond the reach of his sedentary self, reserved for trained athletes like his beloved Warriors. With quick, shallow breaths, he saw in real time how he could rapidly spike his heart rate and blood pressure to birth sensations of anxiety and, even, panic out of nowhere.

After the breathwork exploration, the last item from the tech pack came into play – an inch wide plastic head band worn around the hat rim. After putting it on, the audience were asked to look at their smart watch and select a mode called EEG, which produced a screen with what looked like a real-time chaotic heart rate depiction on it.

'Ladies and gentlemen. meet your brainwaves,' said Jim.

A flash of doubt registered in Emet's mind, but no sooner than it had, he saw an erratic squiggle on his watch's display. He knew about electroencephalography from many years ago but had no idea that wireless lightweight devices with no need for a cap full of electrodes to be stuck with gel to the skin were available to the general public, albeit with lower accuracy than medical-grade models.

After a tutorial on using the breath to manipulate the brainwaves, making them erratic then smooth, pushing their frequency up and down, they changed watch mode again, selecting BGAME. A few minutes later, Emet was smiling like a bemused child, playing Pong with his mind as the controller. He improved quickly, too.

'Mastering your brain can be as simple and as fun as child's play,' said Jim as he concluded the section.

With the tech removed, next came a section on sensory sharpening for the outside world. Eyes closed, the audience cautiously felt their way around the rows and aisles, using their hands to steer them.

'Cleaner senses mean less need for defences,' said Jim. 'Doubt becomes obsolete when your trust in your gut's more concrete.'

Emet's face was hurting from smiling and chuckling after all the fumbling and bumps and trips from twenty minutes of blind wandering.

'OK. Stop where you are,' said Jim. 'Your next partner is standing in front of you. Open your eyes and show 'em some love.'

Emet looked. His smile widened further. There she was, smiling back radiantly.

'You survived!' said Skye.

'I didn't just survive,' he replied, doing a sarcastic impression of Akachi-Rawlings. 'I thrived.'

She smirked, her eyes flashing towards the stage as if checking if the great speaker had heard them, then whispered back his way. 'Hey! None of that, you. Are you all in or not?'

From all the sensory sharpening earlier, he became acutely aware of his heart fluttering. For a moment, he dropped all sarcasm and cynicism and answered her question, just not the way she'd meant it. 'I'm getting there.'

Jim tasked the audience with a series of basic physical mirroring exercises, all to aid in the building of rapport and empathy with others. Stood opposite each other, Emet's job was to move like a mirror image of Skye. She lifted her arm to the side. He immediately followed. She lifted her other. He followed. She bent both arms at the elbows. He followed. She flapped her arms like a chicken. He followed, them both bursting into laughter as he did.

The minutes melted away as the pair swapped the lead in variations of the exercises, reverse mirroring, mirroring the upper body with the lower and vice versa, making things more subtle as they struggled to stop giggling. Receiving new instructions from the stage, they coyly looked back at one another. She held aloft her palm. He stepped close to her and met it with his, then closed his eyes, almost breathing a sigh of relief that he could take a break from her beauty for a while. She began moving her hand, and his job was to keep their palms together. After a while of staying with her, she paused. 'Up a notch?'

'Bring it on.'

She sped up her movements, then began squatting down, and bending and twisting, challenging him to follow her in something like a blind game of Twister.

'I thought you were taking this up a notch?' he said, prompting a huge grin on her face and a further increase in her pace and scope of her movements. Mid squat, Emet's palm slid off hers and as he searched in his personal darkness for it, he bumped legs with her and fell. She landed beside him with her head on his shoulder. As he opened his eyes, hers were right there in front of them. He was almost nose to nose with her, having what felt like a moment before out of nowhere, they burst into howling laughter. She cuddled into him for a second, before jumping up to her feet and extending her hand down to help him up.

'Saving me again,' he said, grinning broadly. As he reached for her hand, his fingers noticed something: a ring on her wedding finger. *Fuck*. He did everything he could to hide his disappointment as he stood. Giddily, she offered her palm to play again. A grimace seized his face as he clutched his knee. 'I think I need a few minutes. Maybe best seeing if anyone's spare to sub in for me?'

Her expression dropped. 'Oh…right…yeh. Sit it out for a bit.'

'I might pop to the loo, actually,' he replied.

'Oh, OK. Come find me when you're ready?'

He nodded back but looking at his knee rather than her. She reluctantly began her search for a new partner as he hobbled off into the crowd.

CHAPTER 5

The pan Asian restaurant crackled with excitement, full of participants from the seminar. On a table buzzing with chatter about the day's teachings, Emet sat at the end of one of its benches, quietly munching down pork gyozas.

'I'm the same age as him,' said a middle-aged Canadian guy. 'The same age!'

'Yes,' chipped in Emet, 'but he probably bathes in emollient suspension, sleeps in a hyperbaric oxygen chamber, and gets massaged every morning like a Wagyu cow…before his Wagyu steak lunch.'

'Aren't you a dark horse?' replied the guy, a saccharine grin on his face. 'Not a peep out of you, then you hit us with a string of ten-dollar words!'

Emet shrugged and dipped his next dumpling in soy sauce, disengaging from the chat.

The Canadian turned back to the group, trying to remember what he'd been talking about. 'The same God damn age. That's twenty-five years of unflappable self-belief for you. No doubt. No stress. Healthy as a horse. Says he hasn't had a sniffle for decades.'

The rest of the table nodded away, impressed, as they refuelled with ramen and rice.

Rather than picking up the next gyoza between his chopsticks, Emet stabbed it. 'How can we know that, though?'

A host of chastising glares met him.

'Is this one killing the vibe?' Skye asked playfully, having approached the table from his blindside. She slid onto the end of the bench opposite him and pulled a menu over.

'I'd say your friend's…not enriching it,' replied the guy.

'What? Aren't I allowed to ask questions?' asked Emet, his eyes glancing at her ring on top of the menu.

'Not this weekend,' she said, catching where he was looking before he saw and looked her in the eye, 'One more day, Emet. All in.'

A few hours later, some the course-goers had taken the party to one of the nearby hotel bars. Emet and Skye had split off the main pack into a secluded corner, both near the bottom of their drinks.

'How low did you get yours, then?' she asked tipsily, flicking the left side of Emet's chest.

'The lowest I got was fifty-two,' he replied. 'You?'

'Snap!' she said, lightly slapping her hand off the table. 'You mirrored me.'

He chuckled. 'Nah. I don't believe you. Unless you're an endurance athlete or some sort of medical outlier, all the evidence shows that men have considerably lower heart rates than women. We're talking nearly ten beats per minute.'

'Fifty-two. Cross my freakish heart,' she said as she did it. After a moment, she raised her hand, non-verbally asking for his against it.

'I think I've hit the deck enough for today,' he replied.

'You won't. Guide's honour. Give it to me.'

He raised an eyebrow, then raised his palm to hers. Instead of the game they had played earlier, she softly grasped it and placed it against her chest, over her heart. He tensed up a little. She offered him a reassuring smile and laid her palm on top of his.

'I'll count a minute on that clock there, you count my beats,' she instructed, letting him look at the clock as the second hand ticked its last few steps towards the twelve.

'It's much better at the neck or the wrist,' he said.

He tried to move his hand, but she pinned it where it was. 'Here'll do, Dr Emet. Go.'

As he began a silent count of the thumps emanating from beneath her ribcage, she slowly drew a breath in, softly smiling his way. Everything inside him suddenly lost its sensation of weight and felt untethered, like it may drift off in any direction. Her smile was mesmerising. *It must be written all over my face.* As he caught himself losing track of her beat, which was slowing considerably as she began a protracted, deliberate exhale out of her pursed lips, he closed his eyes to focus himself. Her heartbeat was slower than he'd expected it to feel, and now with her beauty shut out literally if not out of his mind's eye, his relaxed a little too. *Bu-bum. Bu-bum. Bu—bum.* He didn't know if he'd ever felt a pulse rate so slow in somebody awake and healthy. She stroked his hand with her thumb.

'Open your eyes, you prat. I want you to see it's a minute.'

As he opened them, there she was, serenely smiling, maybe a touch closer than before. His breathing quickened, so he looked at the clock, which had ten seconds left to go. He turned his gaze back to her, part of him wanting the time to be up, part wishing for it to stretch out an eternity.

'Time,' she announced.

He removed his hand from her chest, her letting it go on its way.

'Well?' she asked.

He sheepishly screwed his mouth shut for a while. 'Forty-nine.'

Her hands shot up in the air in elation before she did a little seated dance. 'The evidence says blah blah blaahhh.'

'I concede. You beat me fair and square,' he said, holding his palms up.

'And that was under pressure too. Ice cold!'

He nodded as he raised his glass to her, then downed the rest of his drink. 'Frosty.' He stood. 'But at that, Ice Queen, I must bid you goodnight.'

'C'mooonnn,' she droned. 'You can't be that much of a sore loser...or a lightweight?'

He shrugged. 'Tell that to my immune system. Plus, I know I'll struggle to get to sleep in a strange bed, so unfortunately I need to get an early one. I'm gonna need some fully charged batteries if I want some spring in my legs come tomorrow.'

Skye downed her drink and popped up to her feet. 'I'll call it a night too, then. What floor are you on?'

The two stood by each other in tense silence as the elevator ascended. Out of the corner of his eye, he couldn't resist appreciating her, trying not to get caught, before remembering he probably shouldn't be looking and redirecting his gaze.

'So, why are you such a lightweight, lightweight?' she asked, breaking the quiet.

'I burned myself out at work a while back, so I've got to try to pace myself now, get plenty of R and R, watch my sleep, et cetera.'

She nodded along. 'Don't let them overwork you.'

'They don't.'

She smiled. 'Well, it sounds like some of that stuff we learned today'll be magic for you. There's nothing you can't make better by managing your own state.'

Not wanting to disagree outrightly, he searched for a placating reply. 'I'm sure it can help with some things.'

'Tell me one thing being less stressed won't help with,' she replied.

He was saved from having to answer by the ping of the elevator arriving at a floor. It stopped and its doors opened.

Skye bashfully glanced at him, then headed out and turned back his way. 'Sweet dreams,' she said with a little wave.

He smiled and nodded. The doors closed. He let out an almighty sigh and slouched back against the elevator wall. The doors suddenly reopened. Skye stood there; her smile glowing. 'How about a chamomile tea nightcap to help you drift off in that strange bed, lightweight?'

He couldn't contain his smile. He pushed himself up off the wall and walked out to her. They ambled along the corridor, their footsteps in sync, their fingers eventually touching.

'There's nothing the stuff we learned today can't help. If it can cure cancer, I'm sure it can help—'

Emet stopped dead in his tracks, his fingers abandoning hers. 'Did you just say "cure cancer"? he asked with a searing glare.

'Yes,' she replied, completely taken aback.

'Why would you say something so idiotic?' he hissed.

'Woah. Calm down,' she replied. 'And please don't call me an idiot.'

'I didn't. I said you said something idiotic. Why would you say something so stupid?'

'Hey. There's no need to be so angry,' she said, examining his expression, noticing a shadow of sadness behind his fury. She took a deep breath and composed herself. 'Look, I didn't mean anything by it. It's just something I'd heard. I'm sorry.' She extended her hand towards him. 'Can we just forget I said anything and get that nightcap on the boil?'

'Best we leave it,' he replied through gritted teeth. 'Goodnight.' He stormed off back towards the elevator.

She retracted her rejected hand and watched him get into the lift without even the slightest turn before its doors closed.

CHAPTER 6

The morning arrived. The crowd swarmed; their anticipation electric as they all exchanged full-bodied hugs to start their day. Emet's hug was more like two leaves of wet lettuce wrapping themselves around their recipient. Overnight, the coffee ring stains under his eyes had gone from latte to americano.

After the hugathon, he plonked himself onto his seat. The signature music began to build. Everybody around him rose and started clapping along. *Fuck my life.* He joined them, his wilted hands silently slapping against one another. Jim Akachi-Rawlings bounded onto the stage, igniting the audience into raucous ovation. Emet's droopy eyes fixated on the guru's gleaming smile. *And fuck his too.* As the celebration of the start of the day died down and Jim welcomed his audience back, Emet scanned around the elated faces and spotted a particularly joyous old lady fiddling with the end of her walking cane. Eventually, she screwed the duck-head handle of it, pulled out a small corked test tube filled with what looked like whisky, and took a sip. *Ah. At least I get why she's smiling.*

'Today's the day, Leaple! Tonight, some of you are gonna do something you'd never dreamed you were capable of. Tomorrow, you're all gonna have everything you need to live a life you'd never dreamed of living.'

As the audience broke into rapturous applause, Emet raked his hand down his mouth as he peered around at the euphoric faces.

'When you listen to what I say, do you have belief?'

'Full belief!' The audience boomed backed.

'I know it's early, but that ain't gonna cut it. Tell me again. What do you have?' asked Jim, charisma dialled up to eleven as he thrust his hands out from his chest and viewed his audience through them.

'Full belief!' came the even more resounding response with the whoosh of around eight thousand pairs of hands thrusting forward too. His fists balled up and remaining firmly on his lap, Emet clocked the side-eye from a few of his audience neighbours.

'Yes, my Leaple! I can feeeeel your belief. All that sensory sharpening and self-regulation work we did yesterday has turned y'all up a few notches, but we gonna take that energy right round as far as the dial goes. Yesterday, we worked primarily at the body level,' said Jim, laying his hands on his chest. 'Today, we're gonna focus primarily on the mind,' he explained, pointing at his temples, his muscular arms and the timbre of his voice adding to the gravity of his message. 'We learned how to influence our breathing, our heartbeat, even brain waves to put us in a better place to believe and to leap. Now, we're going to focus on the words we use and how to use 'em to ask better questions, give better answers, and tell more captivating stories to better influence the specific thoughts and actions of ourselves and others.'

Emet launched his hand up in the air with the gusto of a full-belief thrust, much to the surprise of those around him. As Jim continued his teaching, Emet stood up and began waving his raised hand. 'Excuse me.'

The surrounding participants looked on mortified. Nobody had shouted out like this during the previous day, where it had been made clear that questions were reserved for specific question sections to allow the seminar to flow maximally.

'Excuse me!' he yelled.

Jim finally saw his desperate waving, paused, and flashed him a winning smile. 'It seems one of us has something urgent to share. Can somebody get our brother a mic?'

One of the seminar assistants scampered along a nearby aisle with a microphone and passed it along the row to Emet, who took a deep breath and adjusted his glasses as he stared into the mic before eventually bringing his gaze back to Jim. 'What if you have no fucking right to influence anybody else?'

The audience gasped.

Jim smiled sympathetically. 'What's your name, brother?'

'I'm not your brother,' Emet seethed. 'Answer my question, please.'

Eight thousand pairs of eyes glowered at the blasphemer.

'Sir, I sense you're angry, but I don't know what about,' replied Jim, firmly yet carefully. 'If we can take this back a few steps and I can get a better sense of what you're asking, maybe I can answer you. Who has no right to influence who and why?'

'*You* have no right to influence *terminally sick people*, telling them that *your* coaching can help cure their *cancer* when it most certainly fucking cannot!' barked Emet.

The crowd gasped collective in horror. Jim looked on earnestly. 'Sir, I believe there's been a misunderstanding. I don't claim I can cure cancer. There's a guy I did a few days study with years back who I believe is doing that sort of thing now, but I cut that study short as even back then I didn't like where it looked like it was heading. I get why someone could be angry about claims like that, but I hope you won't hold me responsible for someone else's actions?'

The wind had been knocked out of Emet's sails. He ground his teeth against each other as he stared at the presenter. 'I won't.' Too embarrassed to apologise, he passed the microphone back along the row to the assistant, who just moments ago had been ready to push down the row to grab it from him, and then sat down, sweating in the heat of thousands of glares, whilst those around him leaned away from him as if he were a leper.

'Our friend raises a good point about ethics which we'll come back to,' said Jim solemnly before clapping his hands and smiling once again. 'Now let's take the powerful feelings that's brought up in us all and put them to use. Up on your feet, my Leaple.'

Everybody stood, even the hollowed-out Emet.

CHAPTER 7

During the break, the various coffee outlets in the conference centre were swamped with course-goers. As Emet reached the front of his queue and ordered a large black decaf, he peered across at the stall beside him, whose queue was triple the length with people waiting for Jim Akachi-Rawling's signature green drink, Juggerjuice. Full of vitamins, minerals, and phytonutrients, the powder mix juice took its name from the seminar that Jim had made his name with: Juggernaut. Judging by the number of people not only buying the juice but also signing up with iPad-holding seminar assistants for monthly subscriptions to receive the product by post, Emet suspected the juice business must be very lucrative for Jim. As he left the stall with his coffee and took a sip, an assistant handed him a leaflet for it. "Be Unstoppable. Juggerjuice." He scowled at his bitter-tasting java and wandered away from the crowds to a quieter spot, shaking his head at the leaflet and the queue.

'Good morning.'

Emet turned to the familiar voice. There stood Skye, cautiously smiling.

'Morning,' replied Emet, averting his gaze from hers almost as soon as it had met it.

'Are you okay?'

'I'll be fine. Just need to see the rest of this out.'

'That evil decaf or the seminar?' she asked, trying to prise a smile out of him.

It wasn't forthcoming. He was consumed by embarrassment and his conscience compelling him to apologise. 'Both.' An awkward moment of silence passed as he drummed up the courage to say something. 'Skye—'

'Good morning there, Leaple!' enthusiastically interrupted the assistant who had passed Emet the microphone for his outburst. 'Can I grab a word with you, sir?' signalling for Emet to step aside with him.

'Go on,' clipped Emet.

'Oh…' replied the assistant, uncomfortable they hadn't stepped to privacy. 'Jim was wondering if you'd do him the pleasure of joining him in his dressing room for a chat?'

Skye's eyes lit up like he was being granted an audience with the Pope.

'I'm good here, thanks,' replied Emet before taking a swig of coffee that made his nostrils flare.

Skye and the assistant were lost for words. After a moment, the assistant resumed his uber-positive air. 'He'd really love to chat with you in his dressing room, sir.'

Emet replied through gritted teeth. 'I'm chatting with my fellow Leaper right now. If he wants to speak, tell him to bring over a few bottles of that swamp water to my gaff any evening and we'll have a jolly old tête-à-tête. I'm in the one on the corner of Oakington Road, W9, next to the Juggerjuice-green shithole that's bringing my house price down ten grand.'

'I think he'd really like a conversation as soon as possible, sir,' pressed the assistant.

'And I'd really like people who can't take a hint to take a running jump, but tell Mr Collins, even on a seminar about jumping to success, we can't always get what we want.'

Flabbergasted and needing to stay professional, the assistant eventually responded as politely as he could. 'Righteo. Enjoy the rest of your session.' As he wandered off, Skye shook her head.

'I'm sorry for snapping at you last night,' Emet blurted out. 'It's just…it's just…they're such dangerous ideas to go around spreading.'

Skye surveyed his face with understanding eyes. 'OK.' She thought for a moment. 'If you want to talk to anybody about whatever it is…'

'Not now.'

'No, not now,' she replied, quickly scanning the vast crowd they were amongst. 'I work at a newish coffee shop on Ludgate called Crema The Crop. We can talk…or at least I can make you the decaf of your dreams instead of that sludge of your nightmares.' He was still lost in his sadness. 'Or if you're feeling super healthy…' She raised her bottle of Juggerjuice with a cheesy grin.

'I think I'll give that a miss,' he replied, casting a quick glance her way rather than at the bottle, with his eyes momentarily flickering towards her ring.

She studied him long and hard. 'I really, *really* need the little girls' room before we go back in. I'll catch you in there or for lunch, yes?'

He nodded unconvincingly.

'I don't believe you,' she said with a flatness replacing her usual sing song tone.

He half-heartedly thrust his hands out towards her, taking her in through them. 'Full belief,' he said with a small smile.

Half reassured, she smiled and left for the ladies' room. Emet downed the rest of his acrid coffee, crumpled up his cup, and returned to the seminar hall, where he found himself a new seat, far, far away from where he'd sat until then.

CHAPTER 8

'The time is nigh, Leaple. On your feet!' proclaimed Jim from the stage, raising his hands.

As the eight thousand participants rose, the house lights dimmed. The seminar's signature motivational music that had played at particularly rousing times over the last two days started slowly amping up as smoke billowed onto the stage and a spectacular light show dazzled from above.

'Feel that energy pulsating through the room. Isn't this the most powerful room you've ever been in?' asked Jim.

'Hell yeah!' boomed the crowd.

'What's that the energy of?' he asked, walking to the edge of the stage and cupping his ear.

'Full belief!' bellowed the audience, even louder, thrusting eight thousand sets of hands out front.

'One more time!'

'Full belief!' they roared, somehow louder still, their hands creating a current of air through the room. Emet had taken part in the high-energy antics for most of the day, partly because he'd grown sick of the scolding gazes of the Full Believers, and partly because he'd been swept up in the whole thing. Jim Akachi-Rawlings, although dishing out fairly simplistic, often cliché ideas, was a force of nature who seemed to genuinely care for people. It was hard to not be moved by him. Then there had been the atmosphere. It had dwarfed the largest concerts he'd been to. He'd seen gig-goers lose themselves in music they love, but it was nothing like the hysteria of a crowd screaming for a rockstar messiah who they believed was telling them how to hit the highest notes in their own lives. Plus, gigs generally last a few hours. Jim had been whipping this crowd up into a frenzy for two full days with mosh pits of hugs and intoxication by Juggerjuice.

'Yes!' celebrated Jim as the music built and more smoke drifted onto the stage. 'For two days we've been building to this moment, to the moment I hope you'll take your literal leap. You know what to do. You've trained your body and mind to power you. To focus. To fly. And while this leap will be impressive, I know to that to really impress yourselves, you'll have to make larger leaps ahead.' The smoke on the stage, which had continued to build, now submerged Jim. 'Leaps not just to rungs you want to grab a hold of, but to new heights in your life you want to jump to.' The music swelled. 'Leaps not cheered on by eight thousand new friends who believe like you do, but in the silence of the real world, sometimes actually to noise of the naysayers and the doubters.' Jim began to rise out of the stage smoke as the music built towards a crescendo. 'Leaps not just scary because of the inbuilt fear of heights we have even when we know safety is assured, but leaps in the real world with no metaphorical safety nets and serious consequences.' Lifted by a one-square-metre podium growing out of the stage, he fully transcended the smoke and kept going. Ten feet, fifteen feet, stopping at twenty feet up from stage in time with the music climaxing. Then, as silence fell, the crowd gasped as they saw it. As Jim stopped his ascent, something had begun its descent from the rigging in the ceiling: a single ladder rung. It lowered until stopping at Jim's eye level way out to the right of him and his podium. Some of the crowd murmured in concern over what it looked like their guru was going to try.

The steely look in Jim's eyes intensified. He thrust his hands out towards his audience. 'Full belief. Take the leap.' He turned ninety degrees on the tiny podium to face the rung hanging in the middle of nowhere. The smoke was clearing. There was no safety net. The stage was bare and hard. 'Say it with me, Leaple.' He diamonded his hands in front of this chest and thrust them out to eye level to focus on the rung as eight thousand strong incanted 'Full belief. Take the leap' with him. He thrust them again, the chant deafening now.

'And again!' he yelled.

'Full belief,' Emet screamed along with the thousands of other energised, possibly petrified people. 'Take the l…'

Jim swung his hands violently back from their viewfinder pose, then flung them forward once more, launching himself off the platform into flight as half of the audience got the word 'leap' out and the other half gasped. The silhouette he cut, angled like a ski jumper as he sliced through the swirling smoke in the single spotlight twenty feet above certain injury or worse, was breathtaking.

Emet's hands involuntarily rushed towards his face, not knowing whether they would cover his gaping mouth or his bulging eyes. The hand of somebody next to him clenched his shoulder.

Jim soared. The spotlight burned the gap between his reaching hands and that rung. His athletic body stayed fully extended, his open hands willing that rung into them. Eight thousand souls willing that rung into them.

The clang of flesh against metal. The reflexive curling of fingers gripping. A roar from another dimension shook the building as Jim slowed his pendulum swing from the rung to a stationary hang. As the rung lowered from the ceiling taking Jim towards solid ground, the audience continued their pandemonium as the seminar's signature music blared out. With his feet half a yard from the stage, Jim let go of the bar and landed, blowing kisses to numerous sections of the audience and joining his hands in gratitude for them. 'It has been my honour to lead you towards your own leap. Now it's your turn, first outside and then back in your lives. Just remember, wherever you are, it all starts right here.' He thrust his hands out from his chest one last time, then blew a massive kiss to the audience. 'Love and leaps, my incredible peeps!' he yelled before jumping down off stage and running down the middle aisle towards the main exit. 'Follow me.'

A sea of people poured out of the hangar doors at the back of the seminar space. Swept along in the crowd through the main conference centre hallway towards its exit, motivational music pumping throughout the vast space, Emet, who had thought the seminar's climax for the participants was a silly gimmick, just a one-up on the typical motivational seminar finish with a board break or a walk across hot coals, was now on his way to it with his excitement burgeoning. He scanned around him. Mostly, he saw euphoric faces and his fellow Leaple geeing each other up. Some wore a steely focus with eyes fixed straight ahead. 'Full belief. Take the leap,' was their mantra. Through so many mirroring exercises over the weekend to help develop rapport and empathy with others, just watching them say it made the words almost fall out of his mouth like an automaton. He caught himself, embarrassed his actions had almost been hijacked by a bunch of simplistic, pseudoscientific methods.

As the march towards the exit continued, through the crowd ahead of him his gaze fixated on a couple, both around his age, hand in hand, the man raising his partner's hand and kissing it in proud encouragement. There was trepidation on her face, but she was clearly trying to override it with a smile. She leaned over towards her man and pursed her lips, receiving an enthusiastic smacker of a kiss.

Emet scanned the crowd for Skye. *You should've taken her hand while you had the chance. You should've been warmer with her earlier, regardless of what she'd said or her ring. She wanted you and you avoided her. You fucking muppet.*

His self-castigation ceased as he finally reached the conference centre exit. The hazy purple dusk sky shimmered above the swarm of people as now they made their way towards the steps to the roof of the building. Speakers lined the route, keeping the atmosphere buzzing even in the open air. As he climbed the concrete staircase and turned its first corner, his progress almost came to a standstill.

Everyone ahead of him was peering out to the side of the building, eyes wide. He joined them. *Wow*. They'd been gearing up for the leap and here it was.

CHAPTER 9

One side of the concrete rooftop of the conference centre they had spent the last couple days in, which must have been as long as five or six football pitches laid end to end, was rigged out like nothing Emet had ever seen. Metal frames spanned most of the length of the rooftop and extended out around forty metres off the side of the building and around twelve metres down to ground level. The rigging housed a row of around fifty zip wires side by side. Beside the building, spanning its entire length, sat a gargantuan inflatable slide, the soft sort used for movie stunts, that started at around half of the building's height and descended to ground level. From the edge of the rooftop, which had been levelled off to make a flat surface from which to leap, down to the inflatable slide must have been a drop of two storeys. In addition to the hefty drop height, the slide was almost entirely transparent, creating the illusion when looking down from the roof's edge that it wasn't there; that there was no safety net. The scale of the set up was spectacular. But then the real spectacle began.

The first of the Leaple appeared on the rooftop's edge and was given the all-clear by an assistant beside him. He stood for a moment, looking out at the rung dangling around six feet ahead of him from the colossal rig above and around him. All he must have been able to see was the rung hanging from the early evening sky, the Thames River in the distance, and, from the bottom of their field of vision, the colour of the concrete floor way down below.

Somebody chanted from the crowd, pumping his fist towards the man on the ledge. 'Full belief. Take the leap.' Hundreds around them on the steps joined in the next chant. Then thousands behind them lent their lungs to the next chorus, most not even being able to see what they were chanting for. The man on the ledge softened his knees to ground himself. Then came the thrust of the hands in the viewfinder shape out to the front they'd done so many times. Then the man flung his arms back and reversed them to propel himself off the rooftop. The mass chant quietened for half a second as he soared through the air. Emet's breathing stalled. Would he catch the rung?

He did. The onlooking crowd erupted in celebration as the man hung from the rung kicking his legs jubilantly before it began to move. The giant mechanical arm the rung was attached to extended down towards the slide below, allowing the Leaper a small drop of a couple of feet to the inflatable crashmat-cum-slide rather than a two-storey fall. He slid off victoriously down to ground level.

As Emet turned his gaze back towards the ledge, it was lined with Leaple now. The chant continued. The next to leap was a woman who looked to be in her sixties to one of the rungs set much closer to the building's ledge. As she grabbed her rung and her audience exploded jubilantly again, tens more people took flight. It was an utterly surreal spectacle that reminded Emet of lemmings taking fabled flight off a cliff edge. Most of these people caught their rungs and descended gently down to the crash slide, but a few fell the two-story drop. Maybe the loudest cheer yet came for the faller who upon hitting the crash slide exuberantly double thumbs-upped the crowd. Jim had said time and time again that the success was in taking the leap, not necessarily making the leap. How you responded to not making what you were aiming for immediately would mean everything to how likely you were to keep leaping your life forward. While this clichéd line of thought passed through Emet's mind, he couldn't help but think that the faller, who revelled in his failure, probably would get up and go again in a heartbeat.

Emet finally stepped onto the rooftop. The crowd swept him forward, although the sheer number of bodies meant he couldn't see how close he was to the ledge. He stood on the foot of somebody beside him. 'Sorry,' he said, looking their way. For a split second, he thought the woman he saw was Skye. As she accepted his apology and vanished into the bodies, he couldn't help but wonder if Skye had taken the leap yet, or if he would end up on the ledge at the same time as her, the next rung along.

A few minutes later, the sea of bodies parted. He had washed up to the ledge with just a three people ahead of him to jump, supervised by an assistant. He scanned to his left in hope to see a familiar face. As he turned to face forward again, one of those ahead of him jumped. He had now seen tens of people do this on his way up the steps and had seen Jim do it with no safety contingency earlier, but that split second when somebody took flight was still breathtaking. People weren't meant to fly, yet here they were doing their best imitation. The adrenaline fizzed and crackled through his veins. As he stepped forward to be next in line, he looked right. This wasn't an assistant setting people off, it was Jim Akachi-Rawlings himself, larger and more impressive up close. With his bright, infectious smile, he waved his next leaper forward. 'What's your name, sister?'

Emet's head hopefully snapped round as a woman strode out of the bodies. Disappointment instantly morphed into shock. The woman, smiling from ear to ear, was eyebrowless and donning a floral headscarf, almost covering her entirely smooth scalp. Emet watched on in horror as she hugged the charismatic leader before hanging on his every word as he prepared her for her jump on the edge.

'C'mon forward, sir. It's time for your life to take a leap forward.'

Emet looked at the assistant ahead of him with pure disdain. 'This is sick. This whole thing.' As the woman in the headscarf thrust her hands out into the night sky, he turned away before she jumped, and barged his way through the zealous crowd behind him.

'How was your leap, sir?'

'Just give me my phone, please,' said the utterly washed-out Emet to the assistant at the phone collection desk.

'Sure thing, sir. I'll just need to scan the QR code on your bad...'

Before the assistant could finish his sentence, Emet tore the badge off his shirt and stuck it to the desk, carelessly creasing the code.

'It's OK, sir. Let me take care of that for you,' said the assistant with a smile, trying to cover his nervousness as he fumbled with the sticker, trying to straighten the code out so that his scanner could read it. The beep brought palpable relief. 'Just give me one minute, sir,' he said before scurrying away.

As he waited, Emet scanned around the room. There were smiles as far as the eye could see between seminar assistants and the first batch of euphoric Leapers. He felt sick to his stomach.

'Here you go, sir.'

Emet grabbed his phone from the assistant and mumbled a thanks.

'Thank you, sir,' said the assistant with a massive grin. 'And don't worry. There are many successful leaps ahead for you. Of that, I have full belief!'

'Oh, piss off,' groaned Emet before turning and heading out of the Inspire Centre as quickly as he could.

CHAPTER 10

As he jiggled his key in the sticky lock of his front door, he stared across at the house next door. He'd never hated its Juggerjuice-green façade so much. The lock was trying his last nerve. He really didn't have any more fight left to give today, although today had technically run into tomorrow now. The Leap had taken him right across the weekend.

He finally got in his front door and slammed it behind him, partly out of anger and partly exhaustion. After stepping over the pile of padded envelopes on his doormat and kicking off his shoes, he headed past the living room, catching a glimpse of the painting above his fireplace. It was clearly a homage to a famous René Magritte piece called *Golconda*, in which an array of almost identical men dressed in dark overcoats and bowler hats look to be falling from or floating up into the sky ahead of a block of houses in front of a pale sky. In Emet's version, the men were all identical – a bohemian, ponytailed, artsy fellow dressed in white and beige – and instead of the suburban backdrop, they hovered between a bright, pearlescent heaven and a bleak, fiery hell. He had seen enough people in mid-air for the day. Bed beckoned.

His air con set to cool the room on what was a warm summer evening, he pulled his blackout curtains shut, unfolding an edge so that no light whatsoever could leak in, and set his sunrise alarm clock. A thorough search of his bag for his phone charger proved unsuccessful, meaning he'd probably left it at the hotel and would be without charge until tomorrow. Although it meant he wouldn't be able to play the ambient sound he usually would to help him get to sleep, it wasn't a bad thing to have no connection to others right now. As he collapsed onto his luxurious mattress and pulled the cover over himself, the weight of his limbs fell away. The only heaviness that remained now was in his eyelids.

A few minutes had gone by when the gentle whisper of the wind beckoned him out of the depths of his rest. *Fuck.* He must have left the window open, and he knew that now he was aware of it, he wouldn't sleep until he'd rectified it. Even just a few minutes in bed had his body feeling lighter. He breezed over to the window and slid his hand under the bottom of the curtains to pull it closed. The light that came in surprised him, resembling dusk or dawn more than the darkest of night. It wasn't the wind that had woken him. It was actually the bass of music through the wall. *At this time?* He pulled on a T-shirt, trotted downstairs, and opened the front door. The music thumped louder outside, and he must have been asleep longer than a few minutes because the sky was a light, hazy purple rather than a dark navy.

He turned immediately towards the source of the music, the green house, but instead of jumping the short wall that separated his front steps from theirs, he froze. Hovering with disconcerting stillness in the sky as far as the eye could see, like a snapshot of raindrops mid fall, were people, every one of them with that Pollyannaish smile he had seen so much over the last few days. It was the sort of smile meant to visit a face fleetingly over a lifetime but that would make an odd and painful full-time resident. He ran down the stairs out onto the path and tried to pull one of the low-hanging people back to earth. They would not budge. Their unflinching grin made it look as if there was nowhere they'd rather be. He ran to another and another, his tugs futile. The music was louder now. It was The Leap's signature track. He recognised one of the low hangers. It was Shades Guy who'd given him a huggering at the seminar. Then it dawned on him. Many of the low hangers were younger. Ones hanging a little higher were generally a little older. The higher he looked, the older the floaters generally appeared. The music continued building as red began to bleed up into the sky from the horizon. 'Red sky at morning. How did that rhyme go again?' Emet mumbled to himself as his growing dread spiked. 'Skye! Skye!' he yelled.

His next yell was drowned out by a disembodied, booming chorus of 'Full belief. Take the leap.' The hands of every floater thrust out in uncanny unison.

'No,' he cried, begging those around him to come to their senses.

'Full belief. Take the leap,' the chorus boomed again.

As the floaters all drew their arms back in lockstep, Emet spotted the headscarved, eyebrowless lady high, high up. Surrounding her were droves of others who looked no stranger to a cancer ward. 'No, please! Come down! You don't understand!' he yelled in futility.

Red blotted the entire sky now. The music reached its climax. 'Full belief…'

Riddled with panic, Emet clasped his hands behind his head, tipping it back slightly to see one man hovering way above all. 'No!' he shrieked in bloodcurdling despair.

'Take the leap.'

The music cut. The bodies fell like raindrops, smashing into the pavements and rooftops below, bones crunching and blood exploding ever more violently from those falling from further up. Where their faces remained intact enough, those landing face up still smiled that Pollyanna smile. Everywhere around him littered by broken, bloodied bodies, one body still whistled down through the air. After all the carnage he had seen, Emet could not watch this last one.

He snatched his eyelids open just in time. It was still the black of night. But he wasn't going back to sleep anytime soon.

CHAPTER 11

Having bought a new phone charger en route, he was across the road from his office when another purchase called out to him: a packet of Sterling Superkings. He rued the day packs of ten had been outlawed. A fall off the wagon wouldn't have been as costly back then and with ten instead of twenty, he would have been far more likely to be able to jump back on the wagon before it sped off without him. He just needed a little lift after his abysmal night's sleep. Instead of heading to the newsagent's, he walked over to a familiar face outside his office. 'Happy Monday!'

Louise, who was known for her number of cigarette breaks and her protectiveness of "her" desk in an office of hot desks, took a drag on her current smoke and raised an eyebrow. 'If you say so.'

He nodded to her ciggy. 'Can I bum one from you?'

She examined him for a moment. 'I didn't know you smoke.'

'I don't. I'm trying not to buy a packet so I can keep it that way.'

She reluctantly took her packet from her jeans and lit him one.

'You're a star.' He took his first blissful puff in years.

'I am. Don't you be a black hole, trying to suck more in from me.'

'I won't. Scout's honour. This will scratch the itch sufficiently.' After savouring his nicotine rush in the morning sunshine and exchanging some low-energy, non-Leaple level chitchat with her, he headed inside.

The bustling newsroom of The Globe assaulted the senses. People scrambled from desk to desk, writers clattered away on keyboards with the force necessary for typewriters, and between phone conversations, writers dictating to their computers, and colleagues calling across sections of the room to each other, the place resembled a financial trading floor more than a den of journalistic excellence. After receiving a few nods from busy colleagues and a quick caffeination pit stop, Emet headed to his editor's office. As he walked in, his editor smiled like a hyena, his eyes disappearing into thin slits behind his jam-jar glasses lenses.

'Here he is, looking unstoppable, ready to leap into his week!' said Felix Riley with gleeful sarcasm.

'How about you take a running jump out of your window there?' replied Emet dryly.

Felix caressed his pot belly. 'That sounds a little too energetic to me. The closest I'd get is a walking fall.'

'I can live with that.'

'So, come on then. With you being the blinding, radiant picture of sunshine and sweetness I'm accustomed to, it's hard to tell if you're shining any brighter. How was it? Was it "transformative"?'

Emet sardonically smiled, set his coffee cup down on the desk, and sat. 'Did you want one, by the way?' he asked, noticing Felix's gaze flitter towards his cup.

'I've got a proper one coming, thanks. Come on, the suspense is killing me.'

'Well.' Emet leaned forward and took a sip to draw the faux suspense out even longer. 'It was certainly...something.'

'It's prose like that that keeps your readers flocking,' replied Felix amusedly.

'Thank you,' said Emet, taking a little bow. 'Seriously, though, it was a spectacle. I'll give Rawlings that. The man is an utter machine. He stayed turned up to eleven and whipped eight thousand people into a motivational frenzy for an entire weekend. He's bigger than a rockstar to them. Forget Mick Jagger; he's Mick Jugger. Even you'd have had your knickers up on stage for him.'

Felix winked at him. 'You're making quite the assumption there.'

Emet winced. 'That's way too much info.'

'We're the news, dear boy. There's no such thing.'

Emet leaned back in his chair. 'Hmm. I'm not too sure about that. You can take eight thousand suggestible souls, charismatically pepper them with "info" in a controlled environment for a couple of days, and they will literally jump off a rooftop for you.'

'What was it like?'

'What?'

'Taking the leap?' asked Felix.

'You'd have to ask one of the lemmings, or the Leaple as he calls them.'

'Leaple?' Felix asked in amused disbelief.

'I kid you not,' replied Emet. 'That was his term of affection for the audience he used all weekend without a hint of irony. And it wasn't just the roof he shepherded them off. God knows how many of them he corralled into signing up for his flagship course in Hawaii. He conditioned them with lights and music and trigger words like Pavlov's sheep for the best part of two days so that when he made his pitch, a salivating herd of them ran, bleating to the back of the room waving their credit cards in their hooves.'

'So, it wasn't all bad, then?' chuntered Felix.

Emet smiled wryly. 'Look. It wasn't *all* bad. Some of the stuff on stress reduction had merit. His biofeedback gizmos were cool. Gimmicky but cool. The standard personal development stuff on developing rapport and making friends was fine.'

'I hope you made good notes on that stuff,' interjected Felix.

Emet replied with a middle finger. 'Goal setting, a bit of stuff on self-belief. It was all fine. Nothing paradigm shattering, I can see how it could be helpful to some, but they dress it up as something special so they can charge through the nose for what is essentially common sense. Setting the exorbitant fee aside, if you can, Rawlings seems very likeable and genuine, he's a whirlwind of charisma and infectious energy, but I'm worried he's a bit of a Pied Piper. He starts bringing the audience along with useful titbits of wisdom and harmless, light-hearted fun, but then leads people up an airy-fairy, happy-clappy garden path until eventually they're somewhere quite vulnerable and dangerous. That said, he doesn't do much apart from sell them his health gunk or the next course. I don't think he's the real story. I think I found a much meatier one to serve up.'

'Meatier?' asked Felix. 'Your readers don't want meatier. You're one of those massive dessert parlours where you get the sprinkles and the sauce on top of the gelato on top of the cookie dough that sits on top of the Belgian waffle that sits on top of the milkshake. You're a crowd pleaser, packed to the rafters. You give the people what they crave. You don't wanna get into meaty. We have steak chefs for that. And they don't get a tenth of the punters in that you do. And it's bloody work, butchering those meaty ones. Stick to a nice warm ice cream scoop and those delicious, creamy stories just slide right out of the tub.'

'Don't you even want to know what it is?' asked Emet.

'I'd prefer either a five-star review waxing so lyrically it's like Madame Tussauds' John Lennon model, or a one-star Razzie-nominee evisceration that your readers will gorge themselves on until they have brain freeze and diabetes, and I want it by three.' Felix saw the disappointment on his writer's face. 'In your inimitable, invaluable style, of course. With just the right amount of sourness and heat to make it a real zinger.' He paused for a moment, noticing Emet's bloodshot eyes and the dark circles beneath them. 'And take it easy. We don't need you running through walls. We need you here in one piece.'

Emet listlessly rose from his chair. 'Anything else you need?'

Felix leaned back in his chair and opened his phone. 'A piece of cake with that coffee order, but it's probably too late to change it now.'

CHAPTER 12

Halfway down his second coffee of the morning, he wrote the final line of his review of The Leap. He would leave sending it for edit a little while. Letting them know he wrote so quickly would only increase his workload in the long run. And Felix was right. He should take it easy. He'd been well for a while now and wanted to keep it that way. He turned off the tilt lock on his chair, lounged back for a few moments, and thought about what to do next. Holidays. His mum had said he should get away when the weather turns, but he didn't want to go too far or for too long given the amount of absence he'd had last year. He'd done Spain and Portugal too many times in recent years, popping out to the latter to see one his old footballing heroes, Gunnar Magnusson, in his first management job before returning to England and falling a long, long way from grace. Southern Italy was meant to be gorgeous, but maybe that was a destination to share with another. He pulled up a map and looked further east. Turkey. His mum had been a few times during the last decade. She'd had nothing but good things to say about it, especially the cuisine. He searched 'best food instanbul' on YouTube and clicked the top video, transporting him straight to one of the city's top charcoal grills, where rows of skewers of succulent kofte and shish sizzled away. He closed his eyes and took a deep breath in, almost smelling the smoky meat. Turkey was a goer. But upon opening his eyes, the video had changed. One of the chef's was proudly filleting a lamb, showing the camera the quality of the meat as he carved flesh from bone, the white cutting board below stained pink in places from blood. A surge of revulsion shot through Emet's body. He couldn't click the tab off fast enough. He downed the rest of his coffee to help break the feeling of sickness and shuddered to rid himself of the disgust. Unsettled, he tapped lightly on his keyboard. What next?

'jim akachi rawlings' he cautiously typed. His fingers danced atop the keys, wanting to type more but knowing they shouldn't as the cursor in the search box continued to blink. He checked over his shoulders. *Fuck it.* 'cancer mentor'. He hit return. He thought he may have to do some digging but there it was at the top of the organic search results. 'Un-fucking believable,' he muttered to himself. thecancerman.com. His finger hovered over his touchpad for a long moment. *Do I really need to see this? Will it make my day better?* Definitely not, he told himself. Then he clicked. A slick homepage opened, white with Art Deco patterned borders. Above a video sat the phrase 'Your brain is the key that sets you free'. He unravelled a pair of earphones from his pocket, plugged them in, and hit play.

Evocative piano music began as a well-dressed, middle-aged woman appeared on screen, tears streaming down her face. 'They told me there was nothing they could do, and that I had twelve to eighteen months at best. They always say to get a second opinion, and so I did. One outside of the medical establishment. Instead of their treatment, I met with Delancey. One month later, my tests were completely clear. They rescanned me twice because they couldn't believe their eyes. Delancey understands things these *experts* clearly don't. Delancey O'Shea saved my life.'

The video cut to an older man in his late sixties or early seventies, a cashmere sweater tied around his shoulders, his face beaming with gratitude. 'I'd been diagnosed with stage four lung cancer. I was counting down the days, withering away, realising I wouldn't be leaving my family with enough. Within days of my session with Delancey, my coughing had started to subside. Six weeks after it, the doctors said they could find no sign of the cancer. Thank you,

Delancey. You helped me heal the rift within myself and now I get the chance to leave the legacy I'll be proud of.' The video cut to two CT scan images side by side, on the left, a pair of lungs riddled with white masses, and on the right, no white masses to be seen.

The testimonial stories kept coming over the touching melody, many with before-and-after images of medical scans and test results showing what appeared to be radical reductions in the appearance of various stage three and four cancers. Then a man with icy blue eyes and a muted smile, wearing an extravagant patterned black evening jacket over a black turtleneck jumper took centre screen. *'Fáilte,'* he greeted the viewer in Gaelic. 'My name is Delancey O'Shea. Some people refer to me as "The Cancer Man". While I find the name a tad reductive, the likelihood is it probably brought you here. I work with people living with cancer. Through working with their deep-seated psychological turmoil that often predates their diagnoses by years, even decades, I've found a way to mobilise the unconscious healing wisdom of even those with the most developed conditions. Over the years, I've helped hundreds of people that medicine was having little to no effect for to cure their own cancers. The percentage of clients who've cured themselves of their cancers with our work together stands at over ninety-five percent. While my methods can help everybody, they won't help just anybody. To solve true suffering is not for the faint of heart and requires total commitment. Life is precious so I spend my time wisely, only with the truly committed. Research the materials on this site to decide if you have the total commitment required to work with me, eradicate your suffering, and move your life out of dis-ease. If you would like to work together, go to the Apply page to start the selection process. Here's to the committed. *Sláinte.'*

The video stopped. Emet's mouth hung agape. *Surely laws existed against such fraudulent claims and charlatanism? How can this man have the gall to end his video with the Gaelic cheers for health?* He devoured the rest of the content on the site, which was made up by more testimonials, some vague explanations of Delancey's methods – centred around facing one's deepest fears – and the Apply page. Other than filling that in and hitting submit, there was no other contact method listed. He also noticed that no price was mentioned for the service. Judging by the dress tastes, accents, and background locations of everybody in the video testimonials, along with his general knowledge of con artists, he expected it to be far from free.

'Oy, lemming,' came the call from across the office. Emet sprang out of his Cancer Man rabbit hole to see Felix in his office's doorway, pointing at his watch. 'Is this piece leaping into my inbox soon or what?'

'Any second now,' replied Emet, looking at his computer's clock to see that it was two forty-five already. With a disbelieving shake of his head, he hit send. 'It should splat into your inbox momentarily.'

'Good. I've been looking forward to a sugar high since this morning. Oh, and a nice grande cappuccino to wash it down with,' Felix said, pumping his fist as the delivery man approached him with his hotbox-backpack in his hands.

As the delivery man unzipped the box and took out Felix's order, Emet couldn't help but notice the hotbox wasn't the usual green or turquoise of one of the main delivery companies. The black box, in a stylish font, read "Crema The Crop". Ludgate was listed as one of its locations. And after his dive down the rabbit hole, he was long in need of some sustenance.

CHAPTER 13

The jagged buzz of coffee grinding greeted him as he entered. Crema The Crop was a bustling, stylised coffee shop, not fitting the normal white-wall, Scandi or industrially furnished, minimalist mould. The walls were matte black, and the furniture plush and comfortable. On the wall, a purple neon-sign outline of a coffee cup read "I RISE" in the bottom of it, before the words blinked off and were replaced at the top of the cup with the words "TO THE TOP". Emet eventually reached the head of the queue.

'What can I get you?' asked the busied barista, Skye, barely glancing over her shoulder away from the coffee machine.

'Have you got anything better than the sludge of my nightmares?'

The familiarity of the voice pulled her around. A smile filled her face before dampening. 'I thought you were giving it a miss?'

'Just that treacherous green juice.' He looked at the queue behind him and then at Skye's colleague before mouthing 'sorry' to her.

She nodded graciously. 'Decaf of your dreams?'

'I'm in the mood to live dangerously. I'll go for a full caffeine…latte.'

She raised her eyebrows in amusement. 'That jump's transformed you. I'll bring it over, lightweight.'

A few minutes later, Skye arrived at Emet's table and set down his latte, a heart etched in its froth. 'I didn't think I'd see you again after you dodged me yesterday.'

'Well, I was passing by so I—'

'You were *passing by?*' she smirked.

'I was in the vicinity.'

'Oh, *the vicinity,*' she echoed with a big grin.

'OK...I wanted to say sorry for being an utter arse.'

'Utter.'

'Utter. That...well, we needn't go into it now, but let's just say my buttons had been well and truly pushed, but that was nothing to do with you. So I'm sorry.'

'Thank you.'

'To be honest, I also didn't know how to be with you with the whole...' He nodded her wedding-ring finger.

She took a wooden coffee stirrer out of her apron and slashed the frothy heart on his latte.

'Sorry, but the weekend's over, and it's in my nature to ask questions,' he said.

She extended her fingers, taking a good look at her ring. 'Well, it's only an engagement ring...only...that sounds awful. I mean, it's not a wedding ring, and we've been separated for a while now. I didn't want to get into it at a positivity seminar with someone I...I just...' she stopped in thought. 'Taking it off is just so final. It's a leap I'm not quite ready to take yet.' She looked Emet straight in his eyes. 'But I'm obviously thinking about it.'

'OK,' he said. 'Thanks. It's good to know what's what.'

She nodded, drumming up the courage to say something else. 'While I'm figuring stuff out, I could really do with a friend. I'm new round here, and besides all the high-fliers in here telling me the ins-and-outs of biotech start-ups and portfolio management while I don't have a clue where my life's going, I don't really have anybody to talk to. I sound like I'm in bloody year one,' she said with a chuckle. 'What I'm asking is will you be my friend, please?'

'I'll be your friend,' he replied warmly.

From behind the coffee bar, Skye's colleague called for her. 'Hi ho, hi ho,' she said, stepping back from Emet's table.

'You wanna meet sometime this week?' he asked.

'I'm on twelve till ten every day until Sunday or next Monday, but if you pop in after seven any day before Friday, the place is dead, and we'll be able to have a good old natter at the bar. I could even do you a decaf expresso martini.'

'It's a date,' he replied. 'Well, not a *date* date. You know what I mean.'

'I know what you mean,' she replied with a coy smile. 'Better than the nightmarish sludge?' she asked as she backed away from the table.

He took a sip and looked straight into her big, beautiful eyes. 'Positively dreamy.'

Her cheeks reddened slightly as her smile shone back his way. As she retreated towards the bar, he watched her all the way until her crystals and feathers vanished from sight. He sighed blissfully, taking another sip of his coffee and melting back into his chair. After a few minutes of beatific contemplation of what might be, the loud clink of coffee cups and cocktail glasses alongside a chorus of *'salud'* from a nearby table brought him back to the room. The table of Spanish speakers appeared to be celebrating some sort of work deal, and they weren't the only foreign language speaking table in. He'd heard some French on the way in. There was a Japanese couple a few tables away. The place was packed, yet only a quarter or so of the customers looked to be there for pure socialising. The rest of the cosmopolitan crowd were formally dressed people having work catch-ups, doing presentations to prospective clients, and typing frantically. Everybody had work to do. Even though his assignment for the day was wrapped up, his bliss evaporated as he remembered he did too.

CHAPTER 14

He looked above the mantelpiece. The floating men on his *Golconda*-inspired painting were barely visible anymore. Darkness had fallen hours ago, and he had been oblivious to it. The light from his laptop was all he had noticed as he dug away to unearth some contact details for Delancey O'Shea. Outside of The Cancer Man website, there was little mention of the man online. No social media, no podcasts, no advertisements, no news articles. Aside from a few threads on Reddit and other forum sites, talking about Delancey like he was an urban myth – it was these threads that mentioned Rawlings's brief association with the Irishman and must have led to Emet's search turning up a result – O'Shea was a digital nonentity.

Emet rubbed his red-raw eyes and glanced at the time. He could already hear his mum's lecture about looking after himself. He folded his laptop shut, placed it next to all the envelopes that he'd put on the table but not yet bothered opening, and headed upstairs, where he readied himself for bed in total darkness. His mind was still whirring from the search, and the monitor's blue light he'd been staring at for the last five hours was the enemy of the restful sleep he needed. After hitting play on some ambient wind and storm sounds to help him sleep, finally, snuggly under his duvet, he relinquished the weight of his head fully to his memory foam pillow, and forcibly closed his tired yet wired eyes. After a few moments of blackness, his mind quickly drifted to feathers and crystals, and the bliss he'd bathed in for a few fleeting moments while following them. If he followed them a few more times in his mind's eye, repeating the scene over and over like a mental mantra, maybe he could programme himself to have a night of blissful dreams. But no sooner than he had that thought, his own mind interrupted him with the loud clink of cups and glasses. *'Salud!'* He took a few breaths and ran the memory back from the start. Her eyes. *Positively dreamy.* That beaming smile. It had been a while since somebody had smiled at him like that. He followed the feather, her wiggle, her glide back towards the—

'Salud!'

For fuck's sake, he thought. *These personal development courses like The Leap where people pay through the nose to master their minds and their lives, when the reality is most of us can't master a single fucking thought one second to the next. Breathe, Emet. Relax. Give yourself a chance. Positively dreamy.* Before she could even smile this time, the clank and the *'salud!'* rankled him. 'Will you shut the fuck up?' he snapped at the Spanish-speaking table, who peered at him seriously for a few seconds before returning to their animated celebrations. He turned back to Skye, to apologise for another outburst, but she had gone.

'Salud!'

His gaze shot back round to the Spaniards. 'Are you taking the piss?'

'Salud!' they cheered again, clinking their glasses and cups together even louder than before.

'You think this is something to fucking cheers to?' he growled at them.

The Japanese couple appeared beside the Spanish speakers. 'Kanpai!' they cheered, raising their cups.

'Kanpai!' echoed back the Spanish speakers, raising their drinks again.

'This is nothing to fucking cheers to!' roared Emet as a launched himself at the nearest Spaniard, tackling him to the ground.

Instead of intervening, this only escalated the celebratory mood of the others. As Emet tussled with an insanely joyful Spaniard on the ground, more people ran over to the table. A woman clinked her coffee cup and everybody in the shop stopped, including the mid-struggle Emet.

'*À votre santé!*' she called out in French, raising her cup.

The entire coffee shop raised their drinks, clinked, and called it back her way except for Emet, who screamed out at them with tonsil-shredding ferocity, 'This is nothing to fucking cheers to!' waking himself in the process.

Soaked with sweat, he got out of bed and checked the time. What felt like a few minutes had been hours. He needed to calm his thumping heart before trying to get back to sleep. He could do with another cig. And the potential location of one he'd stashed long ago sprang to mind.

Five minutes later, he was sat on his front steps watching smoke swirl into the black, starry night sky. There was something deeply soothing about not just the nicotine hit itself, but the act of watching something burn away into nothing. Two in a day. It was just a blip after an odd weekend, not the slippery slope his mum would claim it to be if she found out, but she wouldn't because this would be the last one. He took it from between his lips and raised it in his mother's honour. 'To my health,' he ironically cheers'd, watching the orange burn creep and crackle from the end of the cigarette towards him. '*Sláinte!*' he yelled to himself as he popped up to his feet, threw the cigarette down his steps, and rushed inside.

All those toasts in different languages had made him think that maybe his online search wasn't over yet. And half an hour later, he struck gold. A search of 'Cancer Man' in various languages across various social media hadn't just turned up results, it had struck gold. He had found a woman posting a hopeful message in German about seeing The Cancer Man the next day, asking her friends to pray for her. And he knew exactly where it was going to happen.

CHAPTER 15

Accustomed to waking to the gently intensifying light of his sunrise alarm clock, on this morning, Emet woke to its full glow and the screech of its alarm, the full half an hour after the light began brightening. Returning to sleep after his epiphany had taken an age.

Instead of getting his usual Tube towards the city, a bus from near the end of his road would take him to where the story was today. As he sat on the half-full top deck watching the surrounding streets grow busier as the bus trawled forward, he listened to a track from one of Akachi-Rawlings's audio courses. His review of The Leap was out this morning or the next, so in a sense the story was done and dusted, but with his tangential mission this morning, he still felt a need to know more about the man and his teachings.

He alighted on Park Lane, just past the luxury car dealerships, and walked past The Dorchester Hotel with his head on a swivel until he reached the café opposite. With a treble shot flat white in hand, he sat on one of the outside tables and hawkishly observed The Dorchester's entrance.

A couple of hours later after slurping down the last of his second strong flat white, Emet lowered his cup at the rev of a sports car. It was at least the fifth he'd heard that morning, so beyond a customary glance at the car – another Lamborghini – it wasn't going to hold his attention beyond half a second, but as it subsided, he suspected he'd found what he'd came for. A vintage Rolls Royce, possibly a century old, was pulling in towards the grand hotel. Emet shot up out of his seat, power walking over whilst trying not to draw attention from the hotel doormen.

The car rolled up outside the hotel. First, a security man climbed out of the passenger side front seat. He walked to the door behind him, opened it, and out stepped Delancey O'Shea, even taller than Jim Akachi-Rawlings, dressed much like he had been in his website video, in an extravagant jacket over a turtleneck.

Emet made a beeline for him. 'Mr O'Shea.'

The security guard spun round, with Delancey turning much more slowly and deliberately after him.

'Mr O'Shea,' repeated Emet as the guard stepped towards him. 'I'm Emet Gordon,' he followed up, pulling out his news agency card. 'I work for The Globe newspaper.'

Delancey's icy blue eyes fixed on him as the beginnings of a smile manifested on the Irishman's face.

Emet shuffled forward eagerly and put out his hand to shake, only for the security guard to practically square up to him, causing him to retract his hand. 'I've tried to contact you through your site. I'd love to interview you about your work.'

Delancey stared at him for a long moment, his smile never quite breaking out.

'Nothing to be scared of, I promise. I don't bite,' said Emet, raising him palm to show he had nothing in it.

'It's OK, Giles,' Delancey said to his guard. 'He doesn't bite,' he continued, the smile creeping slowly across his lips.

The guard moved aside but Delancey held his ground.

'Your work sounds very impressive. When might we organise a time to speak on it?'

'Mr Gordon, you said?' asked Delancey in his smooth Irish lilt.

'That's right,' replied Emet.

Delancey extended his hand to shake. 'A pleasure to make your acquaintance.'

Emet grinned and took his hand.

Delancey's smile broadened. 'Nothing to be scared of.'

'Pardon?' asked Emet.

'If there's nothing to be scared of...' Delancey abruptly halted their hands mid-shake. '...what is it you're so scared of, Mr Gordon?'

Caught between his shock at the hands and the odd question, Emet was dumbfounded for half a second as he returned to the blue abyss of Delancey's gaze. 'What are you so...?'

An unmistakable rush of pride. The envelope. Panic. A hand on the wardrobe's doorknob. Opening it. Blood. Ashes.

His hand fell away from his face allowing the morning light to overexpose his vision for a couple of seconds. It took a moment to regain his equilibrium. He was still in front of The Dorchester. But Delancey and his guard were gone. A glance over his shoulder showed him the old-fashioned car was too. He frantically scanned around. His coffee cups were just being cleared from his table across at the café, so not long had passed. He peered back at the two doormen. They stared back his way, their eyes offering no comfort or answers. He strode towards the entrance.

They stepped across as a human barricade. 'I'm sorry, sir. I'm going to have to ask you to leave,' said one of them.

'Why?' clipped Emet. 'I just want to find my friend.'

'Mr O'Shea has told us you're harassing him...'

'Harassing him? Are you blind? He just did something to me,' replied Emet, full of incredulity. 'Didn't you see what he did?'

'We're going to need you to leave now, sir, or we're calling the police,' the doorman stated.

'Calling the police? I'm with the press! I write for The Globe. I demand to speak to your manager.'

'Are you a guest of the establishment, sir?'

He was taken aback. Usually mentioning he was press was enough for people to buckle. 'No, but...'

'Then this is a security issue, not a guest issue, and we're authorised to deal with it as we see fit. Please leave now, sir.'

Emet eyeballed them. They returned his gaze unfazed, stepping out of the way to let some guests out. 'Good morning, sir, madam.'

Emet saw a gap present itself but just as quickly saw one of the doormen spot his intention to dart at it and pull out his phone with a promissory look.

The doormen watched him all the way until he was out of sight. Flustered, he marched up towards Marble Arch. What on earth had just happened to him? One minute, Delancey was there. The next, he was gone. And those visions. They were like he'd been transported back in time. He couldn't shake the residue of them, or the panic of not knowing what had just happened. Something to his right caught his attention: a newsagent's. His feet carried him in on autopilot. 'A pack of Benson and Hedges, please.'

CHAPTER 16

Emet nudged around the uninspiring hospital canteen lasagne on his plate before washing some of the taste of it out of his mouth from a glass bottle of sparkling water.

'Sonny.'

Responding to the warm Scotch accented call from behind him, he pushed himself away from his half-eaten lunch and stood to greet his mum, Dr Leigh Gordon – a rotund, red-haired woman – with a hug.

'You smell nice,' he said. 'What is that?'

'Just my washing powder, sonny. You smell like an ash tray.'

'There's a bloody crowd of them at the entrance, puffing away like chimneys. I nearly got lost in the mist,' he replied.

'Course you did,' she said, shaking her head as she pulled away a little to look at him. 'You're a sight for sore eyes, anyway,' she said, squeezing him tighter.

'It hasn't even been two weeks,' he replied as they separated.

'Hasn't it? Well, anyway, lots can change in a fortnight.'

As she stepped back and pulled out a seat across the table, putting her lunch Tupperware down, he examined her. 'Oh wow. You're not bloody joking. How much more are you down?'

'Seven pounds in the last fortnight,' she said as she sat, delighted he'd noticed.

'Jesus. What's that now?' he asked.

'Nearly four stone,' she replied as she opened her Tupperware, revealing a substantial chicken salad inside.

'Wow. That's incredible, Maw,' he replied. 'I'm so proud of you. They're not pushing you too hard, are they?'

'No, not at all. I'm doing all the pushing. They're just supplying the structure and a few motivational words. Look at you, looking out for your maw,' she said, half-mocking his sweetness.

'Hey. I've seen those classes. How hard they, let's say, "encourage" folks to push themselves. And I know how people can get caught up in the atmosphere of something like that, with everyone else going for it, and the music, and some jumped-up wannabe cult leader willing you on from the front, going way beyond what you should.'

'Oh, sonny,' she said sympathetically. 'You sound like you're about to MeToo Mr Motivator.' She grinned her son's way as she cut into her chicken breast.

'I just worry is all,' he said, a blueness having descended over him. 'I want you to be around.'

She stopped raising her fork to her mouth and locked eyes with him. 'I know, sonny. I know. I want that too. I should have done this a long time ago, and I'm sorry it took being filmed to snap me into action, but here we are.'

'Here we are,' he said, forcing a smile. 'Any news on when you'll be making your small screen debut yet?'

'No. Apparently these documentaries can take years, but I'm sure I'll be notified. Or maybe you'll find out about it before I do.'

He nodded and returned to the original subject. 'Anyway, whatever got you going, you're doing really well.'

'Thank you, my dear,' she warmly replied.

'And the food's alright?'

'Better than yours, I suspect,' she said, eating the forkful of chicken whilst nodding at his plate. 'Although I do miss the chocolate. Enough about me. How are you?'

'I'm fine,' he said.

'You know what they say "fine" stands for on the psych ward here?'

'Enlighten me,' he said.

'Fucked up, insecure, and neurotic,' she replied.

'How very witty of them.'

She tilted her head, unimpressed. 'It's less about the wit of it, Mr Writer. It's more the accuracy. You look shattered, my wee lad. Are you sure you're alright?'

'I am. I've just had a bad few nights' sleep?'

'Are you doing all the—'

'Sleep hygiene stuff,' he cut in. 'Yep. I'm on it. Scout's honour.'

'Good,' she replied. 'And work aren't putting too much on you?'

'They aren't,' he said before cutting off a chunk of his sloppy lasagne and taking a short eternity to eat it.

'But?' she asked, sensing more.

He tapped his cutlery on his plate, watching some grease seep out of the pasta bake. 'It's nothing.'

'If it's nothing, just tell your maw.'

'It's just a story I think I've stumbled across. I don't wanna boil your blood,' he said.

'Ever the writer, drawing us into the story with deliberate vagaries,' she smiled. 'Come on. I'm a big besom. Lay it on me.'

He set his cutlery down. 'It's not a review, but in the course of doing one I've come across this nasty piece of work. Some vile charlatan who openly advertises he can cure cancer…sorry, can help you "cure your own cancer".'

Leigh pushed her tongue around her inner bottom lip and turned her gaze away, staring off through the far canteen wall.

'It's so brazen. His web address is literally The Cancer Man dot com.'

After a few moments, still looking away, she eventually responded. 'There are some bawbags in the world. What nonsense is he peddling? Organic poultices? Crystals? Homeopathy?'

'None of the above. He's hawking his own super-duper brand of talking therapy. One or two sessions of resolving your most toxic inner conflicts and abracadabra, cancer be gone. He's claiming nearly one hundred percent success rate with all cancers.'

'Bloody hell,' she said, shaking her head before resting it in her hands for a moment. 'Well, at least when he ends cancer, I'll be able to take the time off to do that motorhome pilgrimage I've always wanted.'

'Silver linings,' replied Emet. 'Is there some sort of regulator I can report him to?'

'If it's his own "method", I doubt there's any sort of professional body he falls within to regulate him.' She swirled the matter around her mind for a moment. 'Maybe there's some sort of advertising watchdog he falls afoul of. Or, very possibly, you can find the families of some patients he didn't deliver for who want their pound of flesh.'

Watching more oil ooze out of his lasagne, he lowered his cutlery, his appetite gone. 'Maybe. Anyway, I have to go for him. I have to stop him spreading his poison.'

She observed his scowl. 'Em, I get it. I really do. You want to watch fuckers like this burn. But you won't. If you write about him, you'll probably just help him burn his beacon brighter. If you want to do some good, write about the good work people are doing in the field. Educate people on the credible possibilities. Leave him be.'

'I can't leave him be. He's killing people with his lies, and I can't educate those people. They're desperate, or they're stupid, or both, and they don't want the truth anymore.' Emet's face flushed as his voice degenerated into a growl. 'They want to believe they're special cases the truth doesn't apply to. The only way to stop them falling victim to the likes of him is by ending him publicly, so there's no coming back from it, and so that the others like him see what can happen to them too.'

Leigh reached her hand across the table and rested it on his. 'Em. Breathe, darling. You've got a steady few months under your belt.

We both know this isn't a good one for *you* to chase. And this sort of thing isn't yours to write, anyway.'

He snatched his hand away from under hers and knocked his sparkling water off the table, smashing it on the floor. 'Bollocks!' He bent down to pick up the pieces.

'Leave it, treasure. We'll get a dustpan.' As she got up to look for a member of staff, Emet picked up a few shards of glass and put them on his tray. As we went to bend back down, he caught a glimpse of his hand shining red with blood, then everything faded to black.

CHAPTER 17

As if a dimmer had been dialled all the way back around, the blackness returned to light. Emet saw a familiar, grinning face stood over him, holding his feet in the air.

'And heee's back in the room!' said Clyde, his university friend turned biomedical scientist who worked in the hospital's pathology lab, jangling his raised legs to force some circulation back towards his head. 'You're lucky I was passing then. You were just about to faceplant into a pile of glass. It was like Quad Vod Tuesdays all over again. Classic!'

Emet felt somebody grabbing his hand and instinctively looked to see who it was.

'No no no, mate. Don't you look. We don't need the lights going out again. It's just Dr Mum checking it for glass and giving you a tissue. Just squeeze tight and don't look till we get it properly wrapped up.'

After the humiliation of having a crowd of lunch-eating medics checking in on him only to realise he had fainted over the sight of blood, he scampered back to his mum's office with her and Clyde, holding his bloody hand out of sight all the way. Leigh opened her first-aid kit and asked for his hand. 'I can do it,' he grumbled.

'I know but it's easi—'

'I'll do it,' he said, even shorter.

'Just let me check for any more glass.'

He silently and reluctantly passed her his hand.

'Well, that livened up my lunchtime,' said Clyde, trying to change the tone. 'Back in the trenches instead of sat on the sidelines.'

'Clyde,' said Leigh as she let her son's hand go, satisfied it was clear of glass. 'There's nothing sideline about what you do. None of us here can do our jobs without each other,' she said.

Emet retracted his hand and, with his gaze locked away from it, wiped the stinging cut with a sterile wipe.

'Leigh. You properly get your hands dirty with people, up close and personal. I look at life under a lens, and that's on an exciting day. Clyde turned to Emet. 'Maybe I can at least stop subjecting myself to the risk of every infectious disease that comes through the lab and get a job at your place? Surely my microscopically trained eyes can take a good photo. Your attention-grabbing headlines, my snaps. What do you say?'

Still with his gaze locked as far away from his hand as possible, Emet finished gauzing the wound dry and expertly wrapped his hand with a roll of dressing. 'I say they'd be as lucky to keep the Freckle and Clyde off the front page as they were to keep us out of the wards.'

'Freckle and Clyde. Classic,' said Clyde, grinning ear to ear.

'Is this hypoallergenic?' Emet asked his mum, nodding to the surgical tape in the first-aid kit.

'I think it all is now,' she replied.

He pulled some off the roll with his teeth, ripped it off to a perfectly straight edge, and stuck the dressing down with the speed and precision of a packing robot.

'Look at him,' said Clyde with a smile, nodding to Emet's hand dressing, then to Leigh. 'He said they were lucky to keep us off the wards, but he's still got it.' He turned back to his friend. 'Maybe Freckle and Clyde can still boss it here.'

'Aye,' replied Emet. 'I'm sure there are plenty of openings for a blood-phobic doctor.' He stood hastily. 'I've got to go. I'll catch you both soon.' He set off towards the door, only stopping when his mum called after him.

'No hug for your maw?'

He looked at his watch, then at her. He wandered back her way, meeting her halfway for a hug.

'You look after yourself, sonny.'

He responded with nothing but a kiss on her cheek, then peeled away and exited.

After the door closed, Clyde gave Leigh an enquiring look. 'What was that about?'

'Nothing, I hope.'

CHAPTER 18

By the time most mortals woke up, Jim Akachi-Rawlings had done more exercise than most would in their entire week. That morning in his apartment's custom-built fitness suite, he had done a high-energy aerobics-style session in a pair of Kangoo boots, which are like ski boots with a large spring mechanism on the bottom of each, allowing him to bounce into squat, lunges, and all manner of movements all over the exercise studio like it was a giant trampoline. Next had been an intense hot yoga session on a grounding mat, an accessory designed to mimic the benefits of being stood on the soil, directly connected to the Earth's electromagnetic field. Believing that the entire skin as an organ didn't get enough of the contact it needed with the outside world during the course of a day, Jim's yoga, as always when alone, had been performed fully naked. The recovery phase of his session had taken place stood in a cryotherapy pod, experiencing liquid nitrogen-cooled extreme cold to enhance physical rejuvenation, whist incanting gratitude mantras.

Now laid on a lounger with a Juggerjuice in hand, he reached for a morning paper from the stack beside him to speed read. A few pages into The Globe, he coughed and spluttered on his nutrient-dense juice.

Emet felt the powerful pull of an ethereal tobacco-scented hand as he walked by the newsagent's near his office. After a sleep crammed full of odd dreams, nicotine was alluring, but after being caught in a lie to his mum about it so soon after falling off the wagon, he found the willpower to continue past it.

Outside The Globe's office, a group of twenty or thirty demonstrators chanted and waved homemade signs around. This wasn't all that uncommon, and Emet enjoyed the occasional game of 'Guess the cause', his understrength glasses only adding to the suspense of it. As the crowd's chant changed, the guessing game ended. 'Gordon, take a leap. Gordon, take a leap. Gordon, take a leap.'

'For fuck's sake,' he mumbled to himself, bowing his head and increasing his walking speed whilst tucking in closer to the building. He fished his security pass out of his pocket, ready to wave it at one of the guards on the door.

'That's him! He wrote it!' yelled somebody in the mob, triggering them, Emet, and the security guards into action. As Emet rushed towards the door, somebody stepped across him, blocking his way.

'Bro! Why are you trying to infect something so positive with your negativity and lies?' asked Shades Guy from the seminar. As the security guards shoved past him and grabbed Emet, from somewhere out of the crowd, somebody swilled the journalist with a bucket of Juggerjuice.

Half of his white shirt stained his least favourite shade of green, Emet sat across from his editor.

'For such an enlightened, tolerant bunch, these happy clappers are vicious when you say something they don't like!' said Felix, grinning like the Cheshire Cat. 'At least we don't have to worry about acid attacks with all that hyper-alkalising green stuff.'

Emet smiled sarcastically. 'Nice to know you're looking out for me, chief.'

'You may want to hold your horses on that praise, there. Have you seen Akachi's Tweet at us?' asked Felix.

Emet quizzically shrugged.

'He said we're coming at this with an agenda. That you've misrepresented his course, and he questions the integrity of a journalist that turned down a chance to interview the subject of his piece.'

'He didn't even know we were writing a piece – that's the bloody point of a secret, impartial review,' declared Emet.

'But you still had a chance to speak with him one-to-one, right?' asked Felix.

Emet looked away and nodded.

'So, this time you're going to. He's offered us an interview and you're doing it. Correctly this time.' The editor pointed at the shiny black landline telephone on his desk. 'The last thing I need is upstairs on the Batphone giving me grief.

'What happened to me taking it easy?'

Felix snickered. 'Trying to play that card now? I've temporarily revoked it given you were robust enough to make this mess. Anyway, what's the worst Baloney Robbins can do to you?'

Emet smirked, accepting his fate.

Leigh sat in a moment of silence at her desk opposite a couple. The man anxiously twiddled with an unopened Kinder Bueno.

'What're our options, then?' asked the woman.

'As we're at stage three, our best approach is a combination of chemotherapy and radiotherapy,' replied Leigh. 'We could maybe use surgery instead of radiotherapy, but I'd need to discuss that with a colleague. If we go that route, we'd need to act fast before the tumour spreads further.'

Silence hung again as the couple absorbed the news. The woman looked to her husband, who remained in a world of his own, then turned back to Leigh. 'How quickly can he begin chemo?

'We can make a start in the next—'

The man snapped in his wife's direction. 'Why are you speaking about me like I'm not here? I'm right here!'

'Honey, I know you are,' said the wife with full sympathy. 'I could see you were processing it all. I was just asking about the best way forward.'

'The best way forward?' he asked incredulously. 'What? You mean poisoning me and blasting me with radiation?'

An enormous sigh of disappointment filled Leigh's lungs, but she let it out slowly and noiselessly to hide it from the couple as she had with numerous patients down her decades in practice. She sat tall in her chair and regarded her patient. 'Sir, let me assure you that what I'm proposing is your best way forward.'

'Best way forward?' he asked rhetorically. 'You're just hammering everything that looks like a nail cos all you have is a hammer. Bash me down, hope you've crushed the cancer but not me in the process. Best way forward,' he scoffed. 'According to your biased opinion.'

His wife glared his way, mortified. 'Jesus, Joe! She's a doctor. She's trained and worked for God knows how long. Apologise to her right now. She's not some bloody Big Pharma shill from one of those idiotic YouTube or Wildfire "documentaries".'

'How do you know?!' he asked.

Leigh interjected to stop the conversation going off the rails. 'Sir, I appreciate your concerns about your general health. The interventions aren't without their side-effects and their own risks, but they are still the very best—'

'If you're really trying to help me, as a human,' he interrupted in wide-eyed desperation, 'then surely you've got to present me with some less toxic, more natural options?'

His wife sat, her hands clasped on her lap, as if trying to hold in her tornado of feelings.

Leigh weighed her next words carefully. 'Sir, unfortunately, there's nothing natural about eradicating cancer. At this stage, the only thing natural, if we let things run their course, is the end of your life.'

All the stubborn tension in the man's face fell away.

'Every tool we use is derived from natural phenomena,' she continued. 'The compounds medicines are based on exist in nature. Radiation exists in nature. All we do is adjust their potencies and target them as best we can.'

He shuffled in his chair and cast his wife an embarrassed glance.

'I've been in the cancer treatment field for a very long time,' continued Leigh, 'and hand on heart, I can honestly say, without any outside interference, that I would suggest this exact course of treatment to my very nearest and dearest.'

As she teared up, the wife leaned across and kissed her husband's face. A tear rolled down her cheek and nestled in his stubble. His lips quivered.

Leigh took the scene in and then focused on the husband. 'Please. Let me help you.'

A few minutes later, Leigh peered through her fingers at the two vacated chairs and sighed, this time as loudly as she could. She lowered her hands and reached into her top drawer for her mid-afternoon snack: a hard-boiled egg with smoked paprika and smoked salt. Beside the small Tupperware containing it laid a framed photo of a much slimmer, younger her on a sun-drenched beach with a mid-teen Emet and a man with a top knot wearing a white lace-up neck t-shirt, everybody smiling warmly. The man, Pierre, was her late husband. She put her snack on the desk, carefully slid the drawer closed, and zoned out for a few moments. After snapping out of her reverie, she opened the plastic container, but something across the room past the chairs caught her eye. Her patient had left his unopened chocolate bar. Leigh surveyed her healthy snack, then turned her eyes back to the Bueno.

CHAPTER 19

As Tower Bridge station approached, Emet scratched at the dressing on his hand. When he changed it that morning, the wound from the glass looked fine, and he used a hypoallergenic tape again, but he had been scratching for most of the journey.

Stepping off the escalator, he pulled out his bank card, ready to tap at the exit barrier, and removed his earphones, stopping Rawlings programme he had been making notes on through the train journey. Ten yards before the barrier, *whack*. He stumbled forward from a hard barge to the back, and his earphones and bank card were gone, snatched from his hand. As soon as he regained his equilibrium and shouted after the young mugger, they were airborne, clearing the barrier with the grace of a freerunner who gravity was more of a suggestion to than a law. 'Little fucker,' Emet yelled after them, a miniscule part of him admiring their athleticism as he pulled out his phone to cancel his card. His cheap earphones and debit card weren't the only thing gone. The dressing from his hand was too. And if the tape he had used was hypoallergenic, his hand hadn't acted like it. The skin the tape had been stuck to was red and covered with tiny blisters, leaving strips of irritated bubble-wrap-like flesh on the back of his hand.

After one of the Tube guards, having seen the snatch, let Emet out of the barriers, his following five-minute walk was a distracted preparation for his interview, mostly spent focused on rubbing the blisters enough to relieve the itch without popping the grotesque, shiny growths.

He arrived at the foot of the towering, dazzling block that was his destination. Two huge doormen dressed in well-cut black suits stood either side of the entrance, examining him as he approached.

'Good morning, sir. Who is it you're visiting?' asked one of them.

'Jim Akachi-Rawlings.'

'Excellent, sir,' the doorman replied as the double doors slid open, Emet presumed at the push of a button by him as he hadn't advanced any further to trigger a sensor yet. 'Speak to reception and they'll send up for you.'

A minute later, Emet was in a spacious elevator floating up and up and up. It cushioned to a stop but after a moment, the doors still hadn't opened. As he reached to push the door-open button, as if by telekinesis, they separated, revealing Jim Akachi-Rawlings, arms open, smile beaming. 'Welcome, Mr Gordon.'

'It's Emet.'

'Emet. I feel that. Mr Rawlings always feels like they're asking for my Pops and, hell, they're more likely to know where he is than I am,' said Jim, seeing his smile and joke brought nothing from his guest. 'Call me Jim. The American offered Emet his hand to shake but the journalist gladly declined with a raise of his hand, showing the cut and the outbreak. 'No can do.'

'That doesn't look too great, man. Can I get you anything for it?' asked Jim.

'I'm fine,' replied Emet. 'Some anti-histamine cream later and I'll be dandy.'

'Dandy,' repeated Jim, enjoying the English turn of phrase. 'OK, then. Come on in.'

As Emet stepped out of the elevator, he realised they weren't in a hallway because there wasn't one. The elevator door was in Jim's apartment, which spanned the entire top floor of the high rise. Emet had been in some flashy London apartments but none like this. Marble floors, sofas so big a man could get lost down the side of one like a remote control, a wall aquarium to rival a sea life centre. And then there was the view. One wall of the apartment, glass from floor to ceiling, looked out over the Thames and Tower Bridge.

'Quite something, isn't it?' asked Jim as Emet gazed out at the bridge, whose centre was lifted to allow one of the scheduled boats on its way along the river. 'Royal history everywhere you look in this beautiful city of yours. That family did so much for the place and its people.'

Emet broke his admiring gaze away from the bridge and turned it towards his American host. 'That's certainly one way to look at it.'

Jim smiled back his way cordially. 'Take a seat when you're ready, brother.' As he took a seat on one of the oversized sofas, the journalist still stood at the window for a while before coming over to join him. 'Thank you for accepting my invitation to meet.'

'Second time lucky,' said Emet with a dollop of sarcasm.

'Yes, indeed,' replied Jim with a glint in his eye. 'Second time lucky.'

'I mean, it wasn't so much me accepting *your* invitation as accepting *my boss'* decision, but I guess that's by the by,' added Emet.

'I guess so,' replied Jim, sizing up his guest. 'Can I get you a drink? Some water? A Juggerjuice?'

'How about some Kool-Aid?'

Jim snickered. 'Now there's a home comfort. You think all us *Yanks* bring that stuff on the road with us?'

Emet shook his head. 'No. Just American Jims like you are pretty bloody famous for it.'

Jim understood the barb and smiled curiously his guest's way. 'Is this an English journalism thing?'

'What's that?' asked Emet obtusely.

'That right there,' said Jim with amusement. 'It's like the British sense of humour, just with an edge of…what's the word?'

'Dry wit?'

'Dry wit,' echoed Jim, his smile growing wider at Emet's intentional misinterpretation. 'I like it. Let's go with that.'

'So, to what do I owe the pleasure of your invitation?' asked Emet as he pulled a dictaphone out of his pocket and scratched his blistered skin. 'You don't mind if I record our chat, do you?'

'Not at all,' replied Jim, noticing his guest hadn't waited for his approval before hitting record. 'Well, I thought your article on the seminar was a little unfair, Emet.'

'Oh, really?' asked Emet, feigning surprise. 'Which part, specifically?'

Jim grinned. 'Specifically. Very good, sir. I just can't decide whether you're putting into practise the questioning techniques from our weekend together or that's that dry wit, as you called it.'

'With you being a sensory-sharpening Jedi, I have full belief you get it.'

Jim smiled wryly and nodded. 'I like you, Emet. Specifically, let's start with your headline.'

'I wouldn't call it *my* headline. I'm not too sure what the newsroom went with in the end.'

Jim opened a folder on the coffee table in front of him to reveal yesterday's edition of The Globe. 'Review. Jim Akachi-Rawlings's *The Leap.*' He moved on from the innocuous small heading to the much larger subheading headline. 'A leap of faith or the fall of all rationality?'

'Ah, yes,' replied Emet with a proud nod, breaking his playing-dumb act. 'They went with mine.'

With his eternal smile, Jim studied his guest for a long moment. 'OK, Emet. Would I be right that the animosity—'

'Dry wit,' interjected Emet.

'Dry wit,' continued Jim with a grin, 'undertone running throughout your catchy headline and trending article—'

'It's trending, is it?' Emet interrupted again with a smirk.

'Emet,' levelled Jim. 'You can keep playing these games, but I can see you're hurting. I'm guessing you're still holding me responsible by association to the guy I did a few days of training with once upon a time, and that cancer has touched the life of somebody dear to you.'

'Or maybe your senses aren't as sharp as you think, and I just thought your seminar was cliché, derivative drivel that makes no real difference to anybody except you,' Emet replied, signalling with his hands to the luxurious penthouse they sat in.

Jim raised his eyebrows. 'Wow. With that on too,' he said as he nodded at the dictaphone before taking a breath and studying his guest for a moment. 'I'm truly sorry for your loss, Emet,' he continued sincerely.

'I have no loss, so you can quit with your cold reading bullshit,' replied Emet, realising how loud his voice had raised halfway through his sentence and quietening it. 'But I know people who work in cancer treatment, who try to save lives, and I know how damaging people like you can be to that.'

'Emet. I told you, I ain't saying I can cure cancer, so how am I damaging anybody?' asked Jim.

'By saying that you even tried to,' replied Emet. 'You're a charismatic, influential man, *Jim*. The fact that you even tried means you believed in the charlatanism, and if you believed and your audience knows that, some of them are believing now.'

'I think you're giving me too much credit, Emet,' said Jim. 'I ain't denying I can be persuasive but I ain't brainwashing folks like Manchurian Candidates to pull the trigger on regular medical cancer treatment.'

'As much as I know you'll refute it, Mr Personal Responsibility, there are desperate, suggestible, vulnerable people in your audiences who literally jump off a rooftop because you tell them to. Do you think in a dire health situation, none of them would search out the dangerous charlatan you yourself believed could cure cancer?'

Jim turned his eyes to the dictaphone and drummed his fingers on his lap. 'I think we're done here.'

'Don't tell me the man who'll leap onto a burning building is scared of a little voice recorder?' asked Emet, scratching his hand before picking up his dictaphone and tossing it his host's way. 'It's not on, anyway.'

Jim examined the device and chuckled to himself. 'And here was me thinking you were tryna commit professional suicide. Fun trick.' The American fiddled with the recorder in his hand. 'You want some real talk, Emet? Off the record?'

'Go on.'

'I would never promote what Delancey O'Shea does,' said Jim, shaking his head as he set the recorder down on the table in front of him. 'But that's on me.'

'What do you mean?' asked Emet.

Jim paused, his entire body freezing. 'I saw him doing things…the man…well…he ain't no charlatan.'

Emet dropped his head and shook it.

'Yo. Don't you think I know how that sounds?' asked Jim. 'I'm tryna be real with you here. We met sick, sick people. We saw their medical records and their scans. Then we saw them months down the line, healthy with clear scans and blood.'

'And here was me thinking it was just gullible people in your audience,' replied Emet.

'Hey.' Jim's voice was stern. 'My audience is full of good people trying to better their lives. If you're going to belittle anybody, belittle me. I'm the one too cowardly to tell them about something I *know* works because of how it sounds.'

'You *know works?*' hissed Emet. He signalled with his hand for his dictaphone back before scratching it again. 'You're only lucky I've already written my piece, Mr Rawlings. We are done here.'

Jim went to give the recorder back but hesitated. 'I can show you if you want? On the record.'

Emet cackled with incredulity. 'What? Are you going to cure *my* cancer?!'

'No, Emet. I can't cure cancer. I didn't learn how to do it all. I didn't have the stomach for it. But maybe I can help with that hand of yours.'

'What are you? Human antihistamine?'

'Something like that,' replied Jim. 'Your little breakout there is just an overreaction of your immune system. I learned a little about how to dial that up and down. What've you got to lose, my man? Either you walk out of here knowing even more than you do now that I'm full of shit, or you go home with your hand looking a whole lot better with a serious story to investigate. And maybe, at some point, a little retraction to write about yours truly.'

Emet observed Jim's seriousness, then shook his head, smiling to himself disbelievingly. 'Dial away,' he said defiantly. 'On the record.' He took the dictaphone back from his host, hit record, and set it on the table before Jim invited him to sit back and relax.

CHAPTER 20

'What is it you had that reaction to?' asked Jim.

'Just the adhesive on some surgical tape,' replied Emet.

'OK. And have you had these reactions before?'

'Yeah, a few.'

'Do you remember the first?'

Emet hesitated momentarily. 'I can't say I do. Is this where you pull out the pocket watch and start swinging it back and forth?'

'Us American savages don't carry such gentlemanly timepieces,' Jim said as he tapped his smartwatch, triggering Emet to glance at the time on his own watch. 'I've seen you looking at the aquarium a few times. How about you rest your eyes on that?'

Emet shot his gaze at the aquarium and locked it tightly there.

'You guys sure have a different interpretation of resting this side of the pond,' commented Jim. 'Anyway, you got a favourite fish in there?'

Emet scanned around his options, unimpressed by the childish question. 'I'll go for that blue one there that looks like that forgetful fish, whatever her name is, from that Disney film.'

Jim smiled curiously. 'Excellent choice. Follow the forgetful fish as she glides through that serene blue water, navigating her way through all her neighbour fish, her blue and yellow…going,' he said as the fish passed behind another, 'and coming,' as it re-emerged, 'just like your vision as you notice your eyes opening,' he said, timing his words perfectly with Emet's eyes opening after blinking, 'and, at some point closing again.'

Emet's mouth furrowed as he strained to keep his eyes open longer than they naturally would stay between blinks before he eventually gave in to the next one.

'That's right,' remarked Jim. 'And as you watch the bubbles rise from her mouth, floating up through the blue until they pop at the very top,' his word coincided with a bubble bursting into nothingness, 'I want you to notice your own breathing, and that point between having breathed out and having to pull that next breath in.'

'It's clever stuff, this, *Jim,*' said Emet, still following his fish. 'Remarking on physical inevitabilities as they happen, so I get the impression you have some sort of control over me.'

'I ain't got control over you, Emet,' insisted Jim. 'But you don't have the control you'd like over yourself. You couldn't hold out on blinking for more than a few seconds, you couldn't hold out on the next breath for more than a moment, and you couldn't quite remember your first reaction to the adhesive…'

An inkling of a grin appeared on Emet's face, relaxing his entire demeanour.

'…or at least you couldn't quite convince me you'd forgotten it.'

His entire body tightened as the grin fell away.

'And I don't need to know what happened. You don't need to tell me at all if no part of you wants to. But you have no idea how much control you can have over yourself, and I want to give you an experience of that, so if any part of you is curious to see what you're really capable of, there's just one thing you need to do for yourself, brother.'

Emet's eyes still followed the fish. After a long moment, he spoke. 'What's that?' Inexplicably, from behind, a pair of arms wrapped around his torso and ripped him out of his seat, so powerful they pulled his body like a rag doll along the marble floor and slung him up in the air.

'Take the leap.'

With those words, he was launched from the ceiling into the aquarium. He flapped around in the water, desperately trying to make it to the glass walls, screaming for help with nothing but silence escaping in the bubbles rushing out of his horrified mouth. The more frantically he paddled, the further away the walls seemed to be. Then he noticed all around him, the fish hung motionlessly in the luminescent blue waters, all oriented his way. Directly in front of him hovered the bluest of them all, the forgetful fish. Its mouth opened. The cluster of bubbles that emerged looked familiar, somehow forming a face he hadn't seen for years, before they disbanded into the calm blue. Emet wailed for them to come back, but again no sound came. And having breathed everything he had out, the feeling of needing to pull the next breath in strengthened and strengthened until finally he had no choice. But all there was to pull in was water. He coughed and spluttered like his life depended on it, trying to expel the water with everything he had. And then the air came. His feet were back on the floor. The blue no longer submerged him; it merely filled the wall ahead of him.

'Woah. It's OK, Emet. You're perfectly safe.'

He continued to cough his guts up as a hand landed on his dry shoulder.

'You're here. I'm here. You just came to with a jump is all.'

'With a fucking jump?' asked Emet, swiping Jim's hand off his shoulder. 'What the fuck did you do to me?'

'I've done nothing apart from talk to you,' replied Jim. 'But check out what you've done to yourself,' said the American, directing Emet's attention down with a nod.

The journalist peered down at his cut hand. *No.* The swelling was down and the blisters all but gone. 'What…you've put something on my hand!'

'Emet. I promise you I haven't,' replied Jim. 'I've been sat across from you this entire time. I ain't touched you before this very moment.'

'Bullshit! You've spiked me or something.'

'No, Emet. I know it's hard to believe, but listen to the recording,' Jim said, pointing to the dictaphone.

Emet snatched it off the table. It had been recording. For forty-three minutes. He pressed stop. 'You've tampered with this. There's somebody else here!'

Jim held his hands up. 'Please. Check the rooms. It's just us.'

'You really think I'm gullible enough to be conned by some happy-clappy, pound shop, pseudo-psychologist?'

'Emet. I spoke to you. Your subconscious mind did the rest.'

'Like magic, yeh?'

'It ain't magic,' replied Jim. 'It's just powerful.'

'Fuck you and your powerful. It's cheap sleight of hand, is what it is. You've just put some antihistamine on it.'

'Touch your hand, Emet. It's bone dry,' urged Jim.

Emet stormed off towards the door. 'You may be too smart to advertise cancer cures, but I will bury this bullshit you and this fucking idol of yours peddle.'

'Emet. Please.'

The journalist smashed the elevator button repeatedly, hitting it a few times after the door immediately opened.

'Listen to the recording, Emet.'

'Enjoy the view from up here,' said Emet as the doors began to close. 'It's gonna be a long fucking way down.'

CHAPTER 21

'Good evening, Drumma Mummas!' welcomed the lithe, well groomed, middle-aged Frenchman from behind the leisure centre's reception desk as Leigh and four Lycra-clad ladies approached.

'Good evening, Davide,' the quartet sing songed back.

'Good evening,' he said to Leigh, drawing her eyes back his way.

'Good evening, Davide,' she replied, breaking eye contact almost as soon as she'd made it.

'You ladies are looking more and more delicious every week.'

'You say that every week,' replied one of the ladies.

'Because I mean it every week,' he said. 'Today is my long shift, so I remember your little bit of sweetness that gets me through.'

The ladies cooed as Davide smiled their way. Leigh felt his eyes linger on her and turned hers away again.

'Are you ready to work up a sweat?' he asked.

'We're ready to drum one up!' replied one of the ladies.

'Do you have any requests?' another asked Davide.

He considered his answer for a moment. 'You need something with a good beat, yes?'

'Yep.'

'I've got it. Chaka Khan, *Ain't Nobody*,' he replied.

'Ooo. That's a bit leftfield,' answered one of the ladies. 'We mostly do rock.'

'I know,' he replied as another of the ladies scanned her membership card on the reader and passed through the turnstile.

'So, where'd it come from?'

'Well, I thought you might like something new,' he said, his eyes eventually finding their way to Leigh. 'And who does it better?'

She snatched her gaze away as she swiped her card and carried on past the desk.

'Have a fantastic session, ladies,' called Davide after them.

'We will!' a few called back in a chorus.

'He's hilarious,' said one of the women. 'A proper ladies' man.'

'Oh, I don't know about that,' said another. 'I think he's just trying to make us all feel included. It's less a plural than a singular lady he has his eye on,' she said, grinning Leigh's way.

'What're you looking at *me* for?' asked Leigh.

'Come on, Dr Leigh. You don't need to be an ophthalmologist to see how he's looking at you,' said one of the ladies.

'Nooo. The man's just a flirt,' Leigh replied. 'Smooth talking to pass the time.'

'In that velvety accent of his. Even the word *sweaty* sounds exquisite out of his mouth,' said one of the ladies, losing herself in a daydream.

'Hey. Back to the point of discussion, you,' said one of the others. 'We're talking about his eyes – *sez yeux* – and how they're only for one of us.'

Leigh shook her head as they walked into the studio.

'Leigh, what's so hard to believe? You're fabulous. You're beautiful. Sexier by the week. And you're a bloody doctor, for God's sake. All you do is look after everyone else. You deserve something nice for yourself too.'

Another pitched in. 'She's right. You're absolutely smoking, Leigh. Let *Davide* take your temperature.'

They all chuckled as they picked the fluorescently coloured weighted drumsticks out of the bucket.

'You lot are shocking,' said Leigh, tamping her amusement down. 'And delusional, obviously. That's my medical diagnosis.

Right, time to work out some bigger muscles than yer jaws. See you on the other side.'

'Drumma Mummas! Is everybody ready to get a pump to the thump tonight?!' enthusiastically roared the instructor in her red headband, Black Sabbath vest, and Lycra leggings from the front of the studio as everybody spread out to find space.

Leigh limbered herself up as the class went back and forth with the instructor for a while.

'Before we get pounding those pounds away, anybody got any requests for tonight's set-list? Speak now or forever hold your peace.'

In Leigh's peripheral vision, a hot pink drumstick shot up in the air.

'Chaka Khan, *Ain't Nobody*,' called out one of Leigh's crew.

With a grin and a shake of her head, the doctor side eyed her friend and banged her sticks together, as if to smash the memory of the last few minutes into pieces before washing it away with sweat. But as *Ain't Nobody* came on forty minutes later, as ferociously as she'd squatted and lunged and flung her weighted sticks around throughout the class so far, redlining herself more than any of the other class-goers, her friends' words and Davide's gaze had gone nowhere, and the only thing at threat of being washed away was some of the perspiration on her cheeks by some of the hot tears welling up in her eyes.

CHAPTER 22

Jim peered through the gargantuan Art Deco gates at the period mansion ahead of him. After a long moment, two security men showed up and manually opened the gates, welcoming him into the vast place. His electric Lotus hypercar crept up the long driveway.

After being let into the mansion by a butler, the traditionally dressed helper led him along a lengthy dark-wood, dimly lit hallway towards some distant music. Peculiar paintings watched down on him from the walls as his footsteps echoed off the shiny black and gold marble underfoot. He reached a large pair of golden double doors, their pattern much like the gates he drove in through; the only thing now separating him from the tinny female vocals. The butler opened the doors for Jim before turning away and striding back along the long hallway. The American stood for a moment and closed his eyes. 'Full belief,' he whispered to himself before entering.

A fire blazed away from an impressive fireplace on one side of the room, with the only other light from some stylised geometric fixtures uplighting the corners. Aside from the fireplace, the room was a library. Leather and canvas-bound books lined shelves from ceiling to floor, with only room for one piece of art above the fireplace: a large black-and-white photograph of a smartly dressed man bound by shackles and draped in chains connected to two weighty cast iron balls sat ahead of his feet.

Jim walked towards the empty velvet sofa. Across the coffee table from it on another, wearing a set of ornate silk pyjamas, lounged Delancey O'Shea. As the visitor took a seat, there was no indication that the host was aware of his presence. His eyes were closed, and he was basking in the antiquated music playing from the gramophone on the side table next to his sofa. Jim turned to watch the fire flicker as the song played itself out until nothing remained but crackles.

'Ethereal, isn't it, Jimmy?' asked Delancey, his eyes still closed.

'Yeah. Beautiful stuff.'

'You can't beat the fragility of shellac for a sound so beautiful it deserves to live forever,' mused Delancey as he opened his eyes.

'Shellac?'

'Yes,' replied Delancey, seeing after a moment that his guest had no idea what he was talking about. 'Vinyl's predecessor. It's ever rarer to get the discs in good condition now, and they cost a pretty penny too.'

'I bet. A real niche collectible,' said Jim before a nostalgic smile spread across his face. 'Hell, my son used to look at me like I was some kinda dinosaur if I dared play some vinyl. "Can't fit ten thousand of those in your pocket can you, Pops?"'

'No. That's today's world. Abundance. The abandonment of the singular, the special. And they call it progress,' said Delancey, the corners of his mouth turned down sourly as he glanced at the still-revolving record. 'Anyway, to what do I owe the pleasure of your visit, Jimmy? This isn't a transatlantic leap to borrow some sugar, is it?'

'Don't you wanna stop that?' asked Jim, nodding to the gramophone.

'It'll stop when it wants to,' replied Delancey.

'OK. Well, no. Not transatlantic. I'm in town for a few months. Had a seminar the other day at the Inspire.' He paused. Delancey's slight smile didn't change. 'Nearly ten thousand people.'

'Can't fit those in your pocket,' replied Delancey, his expression and tone not making it clear whether he was making an impressed light quip or something with more edge to it.

'No. You can not. But yeah, I'm here for a few months, actually. I've got some corporate gigs, FTSE 100s, some very well-known clients. I've even got your guy Sharpa, who's giving Silicon Valley a run for its money. We could have sold the event at the weekend out two or three times over, so I might even do another one.'

Delancey nodded to acknowledge he'd heard his guest but didn't reply.

Jim eventually filled the silence. 'How about you? What've you been up to?'

'Much the same as always, Jimmy,' replied the Irishman. 'One to ones. Enjoying my own company when I get the chance.'

'Sorry for interrupting your me time,' said the American. 'No, not at all,' was the response Jim hoped for. Instead, he received another impassive nod. 'Rather than take up any more of your time, I'll get to what I came here for,' he continued. 'Did you catch the piece about my seminar in the paper the other day?'

'I don't think we're on the paper boy's round up here, Jimmy,' replied Delancey.

'No, sure,' replied Jim with a polite smile. 'Well, basically, a fairly prominent critic did a bit of a hit piece on The Leap and rather than judging the event on its own merits, he tore it a new one because of my link to you.'

Delancey picked up a glass of red wine from the coffee table between them. 'What link would that be?'

'Exactly,' replied Jim. 'A few days the best part of a decade ago doesn't constitute much of a link now, does it?'

Delancey had closed his eyes and was taking in the aroma of his wine.

'Anyway, I met the guy. I wanted to get where he was coming from, maybe straighten some things out with him, but I think I've only fuelled his fire. And I think he may try burning you next.'

Delancey blindly sipped his wine, then downed the large glass, popped his icy blue eyes open, and grinned. 'Jimmy. I know the sun's out now but before you know it, the nippy autumn mists will descend on these bleak shores. I'll take whatever heat I can get.'

Not knowing what to make of his host's response, Jim smiled back. 'His name's Emet Gordon. He works for The Globe.'

Delancey nodded again. The silence hung between them with the Irishman's gaze drifting to his empty glass. 'I so seldom have people here socially that I didn't think to ask.' Still lounging, he reached forward and took the bottle of wine from the table. 'Would you like a glass? It's a twenty-six Rothschild.'

'That's very kind, but no thanks,' replied Jim.

Delancey poured himself a large glass and put the bottle back on the table. 'I'm sorry to hear about the new one you were torn, as you put it, but it's a delight to see an old student.' He raised his glass. *'Sláinte agus táinte.'*

'Cheers,' replied Jim before watching Delancey steadily down the whole glass then stare at the empty vessel.

'Of course, you needn't remain an old student,' said the Irishman as he weighed up whether to pour himself another glass.

Jim's eyes narrowed. 'What's that?'

'You've gained a lot of experience over the last decade. Maybe you're ready now.'

'Nah,' Jim blurted out. 'I mean, I'm sure I could, but I don't think that's my path now, you know?'

'I don't know, Jimmy. Maybe our paths are reconverging for a reason.' Delancey picked up the bottle and began pouring another glass. 'You want to help people. Is there a more profound way to do that?'

Jim hurriedly pushed himself to standing. 'I'm blessed to help like I do, but thanks for the vote of confidence. I just wanted to give you the heads up. I got to go. Busy week ahead.'

'I'm sure you have,' said Delancey as he picked his glass up, now more focused on that than his guest.

'OK, then. You take care of yourself, Delancey.'

Already drinking, Delancey gave a thumbs up and pointed right back at him. Jim returned an awkward thumbs up and set off across the large room. As he reached the door, the Irishman called his name, and he turned.

'*Profound* good. Think about it.'

Jim nodded placatingly, then closed the heavy door behind him. A full thirty seconds passed before he turned away from it and set back off along the marble floor.

CHAPTER 23

The sound of the hot blood rushing throughout his head filled his ears as he sprinted into the bedroom. He tossed the note onto the bed as he ran around it, smashing his shin off the bedframe with an ungodly thud as he went, not slowing a shred as he reached for the wardrobe doors. But before he could yank the white shutter doors open, his gaze shot up to the top of the door, waiting for red to seep down the white wooden slats. But it didn't. Confusion seized him. He removed his hands from the doorknobs and wiped them along the slats frantically. Where was it? Then agony throbbed from his shin up his entire self, so strongly he gagged and glanced down at its source. As he turned his eyes back up to the shutter-panelled doors, thick burgundy blood oozed down them. He grabbed the doorknobs, disgusted by the gore that would inevitably meet them any second, full of dread for what he knew laid in the wardrobe. But another emotion also filled him: relief.

Emet startled awake like a drowning man buoyed above the surface. His sunrise alarm clock was dimly glowing. It was twenty-five minutes before he was due up, but not wanting an encore, he jumped out of bed, threw on some clothes out of the summer side of his wardrobe, and got ready to go early. Gathering the last of his things before leaving, he turned into the living room. On a shelf by the Floating Men painting sat his dictaphone. He took a deep breath, picked it up, and fetched, from amongst a tangle of cables in an electronics drawer, a bulky pair of headphones. As he picked them up, he noticed his hand again as he had while getting ready. It was almost as if the blisters had never been there.

Out of the house, onto the bus, and settled, he closed out the ambient rumbling of the engine and hit play on his recorder, ready to listen as the early London roads rolled by.

JIM
What is it you had that reaction to?

EMET
Just the adhesive on some surgical tape.

JIM
OK. And have you h…

Emet fast forwarded the recording.

JIM
…you're really capable of, there's just one thing you need to do for yourself, Emet.

EMET
(long pause)
What's that?

JIM
Take the leap.
(pause)
There you go. Excellent. Boundless. Floating like a sea creature in an aquarium, unshackled from the gravity of life as we know it until this very point…watching your entire life stretched out through a tunnel underneath you outside of these relaxing

depths…unable to feel its effects because it's happening to the past Emet's out there. Fully in control of how much you engage with it. Of how much you want to watch or hear or feel of it. Only telling me as much about it as you want to…Do you know when you had your first reaction to the adhesive?……Excellent. Do you want to tell me how old *that* Emet down there, that younger Emet you're watching, was when it happened?

EMET
Twenty-one.

Emet's breath stalled as he listened to a disconnected version of his voice. He had no recollection of telling Jim anything.

JIM
Twenty-one. Thank you. And can you see where he was when it happened?…Very good. Do you mind sharing that with me?

EMET
He was at home.

JIM
Home. Thank you. Tell me about his home back then.

He listened on in amazement as his entranced self painted a detailed verbal portrait of his family home to this stranger, who he suspected was a huckster. After describing the entire place, garden studio to roof tiles, he set about recounting his mother's character and how she was much slimmer back then.

JIM
And was there anybody else who lived there with younger Emet?

EMET
Yes, my dad. He spent most of his time out in the—

Emet scrambled for the fast-forward button and skipped the recording ahead.

JIM
You're doing amazingly well. Now, you mentioned before that you remember first time younger Emet had this reaction to the adhesive. Where in the home was he, specifically?

EMET
He was in his bedroom.

JIM
And where on his body did he react?

EMET
On his hands. The palms.

JIM
Did he have some sort of plaster or taping on his palms?

EMET
Yes, he'd cut them pretty badly. Maw wrapped them for him. He wouldn't. He woke up the next morning

and his hands were swollen and completely covered with blisters. Classic irritant contact dermatitis.

> JIM
> Do you mind telling me how he cut them?

> EMET
> In the wardrobe. He ripped the clothes rail and top shelves down and snagged his hand on some screws.

Emet heard his transfixed, monotone voice wobble with emotion.

> JIM
> It's alright. We're all the way up here. Remember, we leapt outside of all that, where none of it can touch you. Where you have more control than you ever knew was possible.

During the next few minutes of the recording, Jim backed off the topic, revisiting safe descriptions of the house, eventually leading them back to the wardrobe.

> JIM
> That wardrobe where young Emet snagged his hand. You said he ripped some of it down. What was his intention in doing that?

> EMET
> (after a long pause)
> He wanted to destroy something.

> JIM
> Why's that?

EMET
(choking up tearfully)
He was angry.

Over the next minute, Jim backed off the topic again. Sick of the low, slow, hypnotic speech and the repetition of facile descriptions, Emet skipped the recording forward again to the final few minutes.

JIM
…and see those feelings outside of him again, swirling like a ribbon through the air, slowing, their colour fading to something calmer, cooler, it shrinking, slowing more, until nothing around it can feel its affect. How much cooler is it now, Emet?

EMET
It's slower. Smaller.

JIM
What colour is it now?

EMET
It's purple. But more blue than red.

JIM
Excellent. You said that red's the colour of anger. The colour of irritation. The colour of inflammation. If young Emet takes those feelings back in, can he feel how that's reduced and how everything's calmed now?

EMET
(pause) He can.

JIM
And do you think he'd like to completely resolve those feelings and for their effect to blow away like a purple ribbon in the wind?

EMET
Uhuh.

JIM
Super. Do you know what I think purple's the colour of? I think it's the colour of forgiveness. I think you, the older you, the more experienced you, whatever it is the younger Emet did that led to him feeling so angry, you have the perspective now to tell him he can forgive himself, don't you?

EMET
(a vicious growl) No!

JIM
It's OK, Emet. We're—

EMET
(barks) NO! It's not!

JIM
Breathe, Emet. Breathe. Remember you're floating in the aquarium, way above it. That's not you now. You can see and hear everything he did, but you have perspective. You can let that go.

EMET

>   (coughing and spluttering)
>
>   JIM
>   Breathe.
>
>   EMET
>   (choking)
>   I can't. The ribbon...the water...
>
>   JIM
>   (with more urgency)
>   The ribbon belongs down there. Let it go.

Emet listened on to one gut-wrenching cough, then a barrage of coughs and splutters over the sound of footsteps.

>   JIM
>   Woah. It's OK, Emet. You're perfectly safe.
>   (over continued coughing)
>   You're here. I'm here. You just came to with a jump is
>   all.

He hit stop, remembering exactly how the rest went. As he took his headphones off, he realised he was drenched in a cold sweat.

Forty-five minutes later, when the clamminess had just about dried out, he arrived at work and made a beeline for Felix's office, but it, like much of the rest of the office, was empty. One sad filter coffee and a cigarette break later, he focused himself enough to work on some non-urgent assignments. Eight thirty came and went. Then nine. Ten. Every ten minutes or so brought a new curse out of him until he finally checked his editor's calendar, only to see he was out of office for a conference for the day.

Barring a few caffeine and nicotine breaks, he hammered away at his keyboard for the rest of the day, crafting all the rest of the work he had due. Eighteen minutes past six. He was done for the day. He wearily closed his laptop, unplugged it from the hot-desk monitor, and pushed himself to his feet.

'If I go to a conference every day, maybe you'll write enough to start a side publication,' said Felix as he sipped a coffee, referring to the myriad of finished pieces he'd received by email.

'Maybe then you'd actually get the readership up,' replied Emet wryly. 'Have you got a few minutes?'

Felix panned around the graveyard of an office. 'I reckon I can fit you in.'

A few minutes later in his office, he watched his top critic pace up and down alongside his desk. 'How do you know he messed with it?'

'I can't *know* because he had me turn my recorder off, but there's obviously some chicanery going on. They're fraudsters. The only difference is that the guy above him is pulling this sort of shit with cancer patients. *Cancer*. He's a full-on snake oil salesman.'

Felix sighed as he studied his journalist's manner. 'I get it but look at you. Pacing up and down like a captive tiger waiting to be fed…or me waiting for the chippy to open. Except I can see it in your eyes that unlike me you don't just want meat, you want blood.'

Emet slowed his pacing and, in an attempt to hide his intensity, took a seat. 'Blood is the last thing I want. These con men just need to be stopped. They're hurting people.'

As vengeful and wound up as Emet was, Felix could also see a streak of sadness running through him. 'I know. We'll look into it. I'll get somebody great on it, one of the best investigative lot, I promise.'

'It needs to be me,' replied Emet, his tense throat strangling the words on their way out. 'I've got the context. I need to finish this.'

'I'm not having you finish it *or* it finish you,' said Felix sternly before recovering his smile and softening his tone. 'Now get yourself away from here, forget about it for the evening, and relax. You've done plenty enough for one day. We'll get somebody else moving on it tomorrow.' As he stood to signal they were done, Emet remained rooted to his seat, eyeballing him. 'Please, don't make me play the authoritarian card. I'm trying to look out for you.'

His journalist glared at him, unimpressed.

'For everyone,' continued Felix, holding his junior's stubborn gaze.

Emet eventually conceded, stood, and wished his editor a good evening.

Felix picked up his coffee cup and raised it, toast-like. 'Here's to one of those...if I ever get home.'

After his weary journalist left, he sat back down, downed half of his drink, and began replying to emails from the day, humming joyfully as he went.

Ring ring. The shiny black landline across his desk startled him. 'Bloody hell! Them upstairs must be paying themselves overtime.' He picked up the receiver. 'Aloha!' After listening to the caller's response, his jovial expression fell flaccid, and the eyes behind his jam-jar lenses completely defocused. Ten seconds later, like somebody had hit his off button, he dropped the receiver, and his body flopped to his desk. Gone was his humming. All that remained was the phone's line-dead tone.

CHAPTER 24

'I feel like a hipster James Bond getting one of these,' Emet said as Skye placed the espresso martini on a napkin in front of him. 'Only if it isn't decaf, I'll be the one shaken.'

'Hot nerd. Don't get too excited,' she said with a grin, noticing his reaction to being called 'hot'. 'They were just the first words that came to mind to finish the rhyme.'

'I think the psychological term for that is a Freudian quip,' he replied with an even wider grin. 'Thank you,' he continued, raising his glass. 'Cheers.'

'Wait there. It's bad luck to cheers without a drink.' She reached under the counter, emerged with a bottle of green juice, and nudged his glass with it. 'Cheers, me dears.'

'That's not what I think it...?' Emet asked, scrutinising her drink, trying to mask his disapproval with playfulness.

'My senses aren't sharpened quite to the level of Jedi mind reader yet but yes, it is. They were doing a big discount, and it's meant to be great for you. So sod off and drink your drink,' she said as she unscrewed her bottle's top.

He took a sip and nodded approvingly. 'That's a hell of a drink.'

She took a bow, the crystals on her hair tie jangling as she rose from it. Beyond that sound and the atmospheric ambient music, there was nothing else; the coffee shop was dead in the evening.

'These should be filling the place,' he said.

'We only opened last month,' she replied. 'I'm sure they will, eventually.'

He nodded. 'Still, it's nice that they don't yet.'

She smiled coyly and sipped her drink. He breathed through his irritation at it. 'Yep. It gives me a nice easy evening to enjoy your company. I wasn't sure you'd pop in.'

'I said it was a date, sort of, didn't I?'

'You did,' she replied. 'How was your day?'

'Best left forgotten,' he said, forcing a toothy smile.

'Oh. Sorry to hear that. Can I at least ask what you do? I never found out what you do in the real world.'

'In the real world…I'm a journalist for The Globe.'

'Ooo, get you,' she replied. 'What do you write about?'

'Entertainment, the arts, and culture.'

'Oh what? So you're, like, a reviewer?' she asked excitedly.

'Slash critic and commentator, yes.'

'I can see the critic part,' she said, poking her tongue out a little at him. 'What would your review headline be for my cocktail?'

He took another sip as he ruminated on it. 'A coffee cocktail so good, words can't espresso it.'

She jovially rolled her eyes his way. 'You know, I remember one of my art lecturers at uni used to despise critics, and I mean *despise*. He had a list of sayings as long as his arm about how they were the devil's spawn. I remember one of his monologues about how,' she deepened her voice, '"it's not the critic who counts, but the man in the arena, marred with sweat and dust and blood". And I'm sure he had one, "Don't care what they write about you. Just measure it in inches."'

Emet smirked. 'Your lecturer sounds like a hack who probably didn't pack all that many inches.'

She giggled. 'That didn't stop him trying it on with half the class.'

'Give a narcissist who loves the sound of his own voice a stage and an audience and he'll try to fuck them all, one way or another,' he said.

'That sounds like another of his quotes,' she said. 'Does that make me your audience?' she asked with a twinkle in her eye.

He nearly choked on a sip of his cocktail, chuckling and coughing in equal measure. 'No comment. So, you're an artist?'

'A latte artist, perhaps.' She picked up a nearby milk frothing jug and put on a posh voice. *'Milk is my canvas, darling.'*

He chuckled. 'And do you art outside of here?'

'Noooo. It's been forever since I did a piece. It's been a while since I've even doodled, actually,' she said, a glumness underpinning her smile.

'Why's that?'

She glanced down at her ring. 'Dunno. Just life, I guess.'

'Well,' a wistful expression washed over his face, 'a life devoid of art is a life devoid of life.'

'Are you sure you don't know my old lecturer?'

'I doubt it. That's just from another of the many bullshitters painted by the same brush,' he replied, looking away. 'But really, you should get back to it. If you loved it once, that love'll still be there, just buried under life's rubbish. And if you paint or whatever it is as well as you make coffee and cocktails, I reckon as long as you aren't creating, you're depriving the world of some masterpieces.'

She reached over the counter and put her hand on his. 'That's very sweet, lightweight.'

He savoured the silkiness of her thumb as it stroked his skin.

Bxxxt bxxxt. Something vibrated loudly against the underside of the counter. She reached under for it with her free hand and emerged with her phone, an old-fashioned, brick-like Nokia. Upon seeing the caller ID, her entire demeanour changed, and she instinctively withdrew her hand from his. Emet knew exactly who it must be. And she knew he knew. She grimaced, utterly torn, not knowing the next move to make.

'Take it,' he said, smiling bittersweetly.

'But I—'

'Take it.'

She clenched her teeth together. 'I'll just be two minutes.'

'Take as long as you need,' he insisted, to which she nodded appreciatively, her expression thoroughly fraught.

He watched her scurry away to accept the call in the back, her feathers and crystals dancing out of sight. When she returned a few minutes later, all that remained was his empty cocktail glass beside her bottle of Juggerjuice.

CHAPTER 25

The ringing pierced Felix's sleep. His body felt lead heavy. He heaved his head up from the hard, uncomfortable surface it rested on, his mouth brining a string of drool with it. Where the hell was he? His eyes found some focus through his thick lenses. Why was he in his office? He turned on his desk lamp, wiped the slobber off his face, and pulled his mobile from his pocket, missing the call that had woken him. It had just gone nine fifteen. He shook his head to himself, dazed and bemused. The mobile rang again. A private number. He answered. 'Hello.' A few moments later, he looked at his phone, tapped the screen a few times, and dropped it to the floor. He sprang to his feet and out of his office door, then took off through the newsroom at full tilt.

A full thirty seconds had passed before Emet realised he'd been staring at the crystals in the toothpaste on his brush. He finally brushed his teeth, put on his bedtime boxers and T-shirt, and closed out the world with his blackout curtains. As he climbed under his covers and pressed play on a stormy sleep soundtrack, he took a few deep breaths to get rid of the tension of the day; a day of doors closing in his face. But he hated now that the idea to take deep breaths seemed to belong to Jim Akachi-Rawlings and the shysters. They had taken common sense strategies collective humanity had known about since the dawn of time to make themselves feel a little better and commoditised them, turning them into magical "methods" and "technologies" to be exclusively learned on their costly courses, claiming them to be panaceas. He breathed through the thought until it was no longer splashing around on the surface of his consciousness, just barely causing a ripple, and his mind, without him knowing it, began to drift.

Riiiiiiiing. The doorbell rattled him awake. They've either got the wrong house or it's somebody pissing around, he thought to himself, wanting to stay under the covers. *Riiiiiiiiiiiiiiiiiinnnnggg.* 'Fucking bastard!' He threw the covers back and trampled down the stairs to his front door, where the bell was ringing again. 'Hey! Give that a fucking rest, will you?' He opened the door a crack, keeping it on the chain. Stood with his finger jammed into the doorbell, glistening with sweat that had drenched his work shirt through was a gasping Felix. 'What're you doing here? What's wrong?'

'I came to tell you something,' replied Felix, the life sucked out of his usual singsong delivery. And it wasn't just his voice that was flat. Behind those jam-jar specs, the light in those bright eyes of his was out. Nobody looked home. 'Delancey O'Shea wants you to interview him. Do you understand?'

'One second, mate.' As Emet closed the door to take it off the chain, his boss immediately jammed his finger back into the doorbell again. 'Felix, stop it! I'm right here,' he said as he reopened the door. His boss took the order but was far from right there with him. Beyond the glazed look on his boss' face, Emet was also worried about his breathing, which made him look as if he was ready to drop. 'Mate, come in. You need to sit down.'

'Delancey O'Shea wants you to interview him. Do you understand?'

'I understand what you're saying but you need to—'

Felix swivelled and took off at pace, down the steps and along the street.

'Felix! Stop!'

The editor paid the shouted plea no heed, sprinting at a speed that looked beyond his doughy body.

'Shit.' Emet dashed back inside, pulled on a pair of trainers and searched for his keys. As he fished around in a drawer, swearing he'd put them there less than an hour ago, the doorbell rang again. He stumbled over his untied lace as he rushed over to answer it, fumbled the chain off, then yanked the door open. Felix wasn't there.

'You weren't joking about the colour of next door.' Gesturing with a Juggerjuice in each hand to the neighbouring property as she turned to face Emet was Skye. Her radiant smile fell away upon seeing his wired expression and wardrobe choice. 'Bad time?'

CHAPTER 26

'Umm. I don't know how to answer that,' he said as he frantically scanned both ways along the street. 'Did a tubby bloke in thick specs just sprint past you on your way here?'

She chuckled bewilderedly but could see his concern. 'Umm, no. What's going on?'

After explaining the situation and inviting her to wait inside while he went to look for Felix, she insisted on helping and they headed off in opposite directions. Fifteen minutes later, he arrived back at the steps up to his door, where Skye was waiting. 'Sorry I kept you waiting. Any joy?'

She shook her head.

'Fuck,' he said, gripping his hands behind his head. 'I don't know what to do. He's not answering his phone. Somebody's done something to him, he's not in his right mind, and he's sprinting round the streets like a maniac. It's not gonna take much for him to run out into a road and get himself killed.'

'Is it worth calling the police?'

He blew out a sigh as his mind flipped through possibilities. 'I doubt it. There's no provable crime and we don't know where he is to direct them to.'

'Can we go to his house and see if he turns up there?'

'He only moved a few weeks ago. I don't know where he lives. I could try a few colleagues to see if they do. Thanks. My head's a mess.'

She shrugged. 'No problem.'

'Sorry. Not every night's like this. You want to come in?'

Fifteen minutes later, he'd attempted to reach all his colleagues that he thought might know Felix's new address. Of the two who took his call, neither knew it. He'd tried his best to keep the call from alarming them or sounding odd with a cover story, for their sake and Felix's, but wasn't sure how successful he'd been.

'There's nothing you can do,' she said before taking a sip of her Juggerjuice. 'Hopefully you roll into the office tomorrow and he's there, all in one piece.'

He carried on pacing up and down the length of the living room. 'I know you're right, but my mind won't stop racing, trying to think of another way. Let me try his mobile and his office one more time.'

She nodded understandingly. He dialled both; each rang through. He continued pacing and pulled a pack of cigarettes from his pocket.

'He'll call when he reaches his phone with all those missed calls from you.' She patted the sofa beside her. 'Come on. You're making me dizzy, and, more importantly, yourself. Sit.'

He came and sat beside her. His agitation, with no physical outlet, heightened.

'Put those away for a couple of minutes,' she said, nodding to the cigarettes, which he set down on the sofa. 'Still yourself. Slow your breathing,' she said. His face hardened with stubbornness. 'Hey. I'm not Rawlings. I'm not trying to sell you anything. I'm just trying to help. So breathe with me.'

He let out an almighty sigh, then began slowing his breathing.

'Widen your visual field and let any thoughts come and go as easily as your breath.'

His in-breath juddered as distress furrowed his brow.

'It's OK. Away as easily as the breath.' She shuffled over and laid her hand on his. 'We're here. Feel my hand. It's just you and me. Breathe.'

He closed his eyes and took a few more deep breaths.

'That's it,' she said, squeezing his hand comfortingly. 'It's just you and me.'

He relaxed even further. He felt her hand leave his. Then he felt her warm, delicate fingers against his face. Then he felt the moistness of her lips press against his cheek. He opened his eyes. She was there right in front of him. 'But your...situation?'

She showed him her hand and smiled. Her ring was gone. 'It's just you...and me.'

Finally, their lips came together.

A gentle jangling woke him. His sunrise alarm clock was lightless and his blackout curtains were fully drawn, but some light came from behind him. He rolled over to find the other side's bedside lamp must have been on all night. Even the tiniest hint of light usually disturbed his sleep, but he had been out for the count. And she still was, lying in the lamp's golden glow. He admired the sleeping beauty for a long moment, then reached over to lay his hand on hers. A few seconds later, she slid the hand away and rolled over. This was better; he could spoon her now. They had done nothing beyond kissing and caressing last night, but this was bliss, and it had been a long time since he'd felt such warmth in his house or his life. He could lie like this all day, but it was a weekday. *Oh shit. Work!*

He couldn't believe he'd forgotten about Felix. Usually even his dreams would be plagued by such a thing. Last night, he couldn't remember having any. He tried to slide his hand out from underneath Skye without disturbing her. It was nearly eight fifteen. He rolled over and grabbed his phone off his bedside table. He had missed calls and messages from colleagues who hadn't answered last night, but nothing from his boss.

'Good morning, lightweight,' she said with a yawn as she rolled over to face him.

'Good morning,' he replied, putting the phone down, then shuffling over to rest his hand on her hip. 'You sleep OK?'

'Fabulously, thanks,' she said with a pure smile. 'You?'

'Perfectly,' he replied, leaning forward and kissing her. 'And I could stay here with you all day,' he said as he eventually and reluctantly peeled away, 'but I have to try to find Felix.'

Just after nine thirty, they arrived outside of The Globe's office. It was near enough on Skye's way home, and she didn't start her shift until midday.

'I hope you walk in there and he's sat in his office, safe and sound,' she said.

He squeezed her hand as they turned to face one another. 'Thanks.'

'You'll keep me posted?'

He nodded.

'And you won't scarper again so I have to track you down with a juicy colour swatch?'

'As much as it's the only thing that swamp water's probably good for, no. I promise,' he replied, smiling warmly.

Like a jack-in-the-box, she popped towards him and planted a peck on his lips, back in her place just as quickly with a mischievous grin on her face.

'Is that all I get?' Emet asked.

'That's all you can handle right now, lightweight,' she replied, turning away, her feathers gliding as she walked off.

He joyfully watched her all the way to the corner, eventually receiving a flirtatious look over the shoulder and a little wave before she turned out of sight. His face ached from prolonged smiling, but as he snapped out of his infatuated state upon looking up at the building's sign, it finally fell to rest.

CHAPTER 27

Even though he arrived on the later side, Felix's office was empty. After some subtle enquiries with colleagues he hadn't contacted last night so as not to raise any premature alarm bells, he found a desk and logged on to the work network. He checked his emails. Nothing noteworthy. He pulled up The Cancer Man website. Nothing had changed since the other day. Yet this and the videos on it were all he really had to go on. After half an hour of thinking and working on a speculative idea, the empty office he'd been glancing over at now pulled too strongly for him to leave alone. He ventured over to it. The door was open, as it was much of the time. On the desk, the receiver of the Batphone was off its hook. Emet carried on in and upon changing his angle of sight, immediately noticed a mobile phone on the ground. He picked it up, only to find it was dead. He had a charger that would fit the phone but was sure, given the security lectures from other management he'd only ever partly paid attention to, it would only be unlocked by fingerprint or face ID.

'If you're trying to catfish somebody through my Tinder account, you're out of luck, I'm already using pics of somebody else,' said Felix, startling him.

As Emet turned, he noticed the grimace on his boss' face. 'Thank fuck for that. I've been at my wit's end. Are you alright? Where on earth have you been?!

'Woah there!' said Felix as he hobbled in with all the grace of an unoiled Tinman. 'One question at a time. Where've I been? At home. Am I alright? No. I feel like I got hit by a car-carrying truck and then rolled over by each of its cargo. Hence the tardiness. I must be coming down with something, but no rest for the wicked,' he said groaning with each agonising step. 'Apart from my phone,' he said, taking it back from his journalist, 'what can I do you for?'

Emet handed the phone over, seeing nothing but pain and amused curiosity on his boss' face. 'You don't remember, do you?'

Felix winced as he slotted his phone into his pocket and limped on towards his desk. 'I may if you tell me what you're referring to, young grasshopper.'

'Coming to mine last night.'

Felix raised an eyebrow. 'If you're trying to take credit for the state I'm in, I think I'd remember that. Besides, I have you down as a more tender lover.'

'Fee,' Emet snapped, trying to impart his seriousness. 'You turned up on my doorstep at tennish last night, looking like you were about to have a coronary, covered in sweat.'

'Have you been sniffing in the stationery cupboard?' asked Felix with a confused chuckle.

'I think you'd ran all the way from here,' insisted Emet. 'You were absolutely out of your mind; lights-on-nobody-home kind of thing. You said that Delancey O'Shea wanted to speak to me.'

'What are you talking about?' asked Felix, his confusion billowing into exasperation. 'And who's Delancey O'…what? That cancer guy you told me about?'

Emet nodded his boss' way.

Felix shuffled around his desk and gingerly lowered himself into his seat. When his grimace finally subsided, only concern remained. 'Em. I wasn't at your house last night. I was dead to the world with whatever this is, I assure you. Are you sure *you're* OK?'

'Don't go there, Fee,' replied Emet, shaking his head soberly. 'I'm perfectly fine. I swear, you were at my door. You'd ran all the way there. Once you told me O'Shea wanted to see me, you were off like a shot. You'd been activated like some sort of Manchurian Candidate.'

Felix sighed deeply. 'I know you feel fine. Would you just take the day off as a precaution? See if that clarifies things for you?'

Emet stopped himself from pushing back and thought for a moment. 'The Batphone. Check your last caller.'

Felix's eyes flickered to it, noticing that it was off the hook.

'That wasn't me, I swear,' said Emet. 'That was like that when I got here.'

Unconvinced, the editor picked up the receiver, hung the phone up, and dialled one-four-seven-one before hanging up a few seconds later.

'Well?'

'Private number,' replied Felix.

'Did it say when?'

Felix shook his head. 'Sorry, fella.'

'Why would upstairs call you from a private number?' asked Emet.

Felix shrugged. 'Who knows why they do half the things they do.'

'How about your phone? Check your calls list.'

'Come on, Em. Let's not draw all this out. Just take the day, see—'

Emet held his hands up. 'I'll take the day if you check your phone and there's nothing there, alright?'

Felix reluctantly nodded, plugged his phone in to charge, and powered it up. Emet watched him scroll to the recent calls list. He held it up for the journalist to see. 'Last call was yesterday afternoon. Nothing in the evening. A deal's a deal, yes?'

Emet stared his way, clearly holding back his words until finally he spoke. 'Yeh.'

'Get your feet up, your head down, get a good film on. If anyone can do that, it's you. Do whatever you feel you need. We'll pick up tomorrow if this thing hasn't floored me yet, alright?'

Emet reluctantly nodded, then turned and left.

Felix buried his mouth in his hands, shaking his head as he watched the journalist gather some things from his desk. 'Please not again,' he mumbled to himself.

More than an hour had passed when a knock at the door interrupted Felix from writing an email. 'Come in,' he said. As he looked up, his heart sank. 'Mate. You said you were going home.'

'I know I did, but you need to see this,' replied Emet, waving in George from building security, who was carrying a laptop.

Usually jolly, George looked stoic right now. After a quick hello, he set his laptop on the editor's desk for him to see, and pressed play. The time stamp said 21:17. After a few seconds, Felix's jaw dropped. He'd witnessed himself hurtling across the newsroom. George proceeded to show him further camera feeds from throughout the building, tracking his sprint along the corridor, down nine flights of stairs, and out of the lobby into the street.

'Derek left me a note to say you'd legged it past him last night but seeing as you seemed your chirpy self this morning, maybe except for looking in some pain, I didn't think it was worth asking you about it,' explained George.

'May I?' asked Felix, pointing towards the video. After playing it again twice, clearly flabbergasted, he thanked the security guard and wished him farewell. He took off his thick glasses, carefully folded their arms closed, and set them down on the table where he stared at them for a long while. Emet sat opposite him.

'I don't have any cameras at mine, so I can't prove you—'

'I believe you,' said Felix, his voice flattened by shock. 'How can I not remember any of that?' he continued, raising his wide eyes and his furrowed brow.

'I don't know,' replied Emet. 'But I hope you'll let me find out.'

CHAPTER 28

After Felix's search of his email folders and phone for anything from Delancey came up dry, Emet showed his boss what he had been working on. 'It's the only lead we really have. I know it's a slightly grey area, but these people were happy enough to appear on camera. I just want to know their names so I might find them.'

'Crack on,' said Felix, signing off without a second thought on the upload of Delancey's testimonial video into the paper's Fuusion account, which was a controversial new search engine currently in limited beta testing with search capabilities apparently light years ahead of existing search engines, and with scarily impressive facial recognition functionality. 'And keep me posted. I want to know what this creep did to me.'

Emet went back to his desk and hit upload. Judging by the speed the upload bar was moving at, this was going to take a while. After dropping Skye a few messages to let her know his boss had turned up just about in one piece, and that he could handle more very soon, he tried to turn his attention to a few new TV shows he had to review, constantly pausing them to check if the tool had finished yet. A few hours later just after he'd started the third show, it was done. It had returned names on four of the testimonial-givers. Now, the detective work began. Google, LinkedIn, Facebook, Twitter, and Wildfire – the Fuusion founder's original hit; a social media network that had taken the world by storm by incentivising popular positive content and progress towards life goals with hefty lottery-style cash prizes – were the first ports of call in modern journalism, although Emet didn't really consider himself a journalist, especially not an investigative one. Even armchair searching like this was tiresome to him. Of the four names generated, three had online presences, but only one of those had one open to messages from non-friends, and another was on LinkedIn, so even though not a personal connection, with Emet's premium account through work, he could message them too. Friends and connections requested, and messages sent, all he could do now was wait, and in waiting, there was no concentrating on a banal TV show. He needed a break.

Out he headed to the rooftop terrace; the mecca of the smokers on their breaks. He reached for his packet, immediately realising he hadn't picked it up off the sofa this morning. *Bastard.* Louise, surprisingly, was nowhere to be seen. He scanned around the other Globe workers, looking for a familiar, friendly face but came up blank. In truth, outside of Felix, there weren't many that warmed to him. His general prickly manner wasn't endearing. His success in gathering such a vast readership by writing such caustic reviews and commentary on such light topics had alienated him from many of the "real journalists working on real news". It wasn't his fault that they had chosen to write about energy-intensive topics that nobody gave two shits about, nor that their authorial voices were drier than camel's hooves. He didn't make the rules of the game. He just seemed to understand them and play it better than everyone else.

Nobody looked like a willing donor, and buying a single from a colleague somehow seemed undignified. He recalled Skye asking him to leave them for a moment. And how she'd held his hand as he'd breathed. He could breathe here now, almost feeling her hand against his, then her fingers against his cheek, as he wandered away from the second-hand smoke, treading gently so as not to disturb his reverie. As he arrived at the railings at the edge of the rooftop, he closed his eyes for a moment, the freshness of the breeze fluttering a feather and jangling those crystals in his mind's eye. He eventually turned his attention outwards to the cityscape. He couldn't see Rawlings's penthouse, but it sprang to mind. And then he looked at the gap across to the building beside his. It must be at least double the one Jim jumped if he'd been telling the truth. *Fuck that.*

Upon returning to his desk, he found a Wildfire message waiting for him:

Of course. I'd be happy to speak about my work with Delancey. It's criminal that such powerful methods aren't more well known yet. When would be good for you? I'll struggle to speak properly today but could make the time for a phone call or a visit tomorrow.

He typed his reply, stating that an in-person interview was always preferable, and asked for an address, before spinning his chair around and jumping to his feet. As he set his eyes on Felix's office, he gasped. His boss was manically scrawling on the inside of his main office window with a black marker, having half covered it. He trotted over, cognisant of not causing a scene as it didn't look like anybody had noticed Felix's odd behaviour yet. As he arrived in the door, it was as he feared; Felix sported the same spaced-out expression as he had last night. 'Fee,' he whispered loudly to no response. 'Fee!' The editor scrawled away. Emet grabbed him and pulled him away from the window, meeting a sleepy resistance for a moment before the marker fell to the floor. Felix froze. 'Fee!' Emet hissed, seeing the start of some machinations behind his eyes. The journalist yanked his boss further away from the window, snapping him out of his daze.

'Get…Em, what the hell are you doing?' asked Felix, utterly bewildered.

Emet pulled his seat over for him and shushed him. 'Just sit.'

In his utter confusion, Felix obeyed, with his gaze wildly darting around the room as if he'd just woken in a pitch black, strange place. Emet quietly clicked the door shut and pulled the blinds at the window half across.

'What…what's going on?' asked Felix, spotting the scrawlings on the window.

'I'm not sure. I just turned around and saw you scribbling that on the window like a madman, that vacant look in your eyes like when you turned up at mine last night.' Then he saw the Batphone's receiver on the desk and put it to his ear. Its howler tone still blared out. 'Mystery solved. This must be how he's triggering you.' He'd never seen Felix's eyes so wide. The editor's skin had lost all its colour and glistened in the sunlight from the exterior window. Emet pressed the hook switch to kill the tone and dialled one-four-seven-one. 'Private number,' he cursed, setting the receiver down.

From extreme stillness, Felix shot forward, grabbed the handset, and used it to rip the phone wire out of the wall. Startled, Emet turned to his boss, watching his anger recede only to then spike again. 'Motherfucker!' he barked, pointing to the window.

'Motherfucker.' Emet looked at it properly for the first time. The messy black scribblings were barely legible numbers, which if read from a zero could be a phone number with its area code. 'Where's that code for?'

'Umm. Somewhere out Hampshire or Berkshire way, I think,' replied Felix, trembling slightly now.

Emet took his mobile out, dialled one-four-one to withhold his caller ID, then dialled the number from the window. His thumb hovered over the green call button. He turned towards Felix. 'Have you eaten or drank anything in the last hour or so?'

'No,' replied the editor, his trembling worse now. 'Why?'

Emet hesitated. 'I'm just trying to figure out how the fuck he's doing this so that I don't hit dial and turn into some sort of hypno-sleeper agent.'

'Right,' said Felix, racking his brain. 'I'm pretty sure I didn't have anything. Are you thinking he can just be doing this with his voice?'

'Not a chance, but we don't know what game he's playing, so we have to be over-precautious.'

Felix reached into his desk drawer, pulled out a packet of wet wipes, and tossed one to Emet before scrubbing his hands, right cheek, and ear with it. 'Wipe anything that might have touched something, like that bloody phone for example.'

'Have you got any sanitiser?' asked Emet, receiving a shake of the head. 'Pass me a few more.' Upon receiving them, he set to work with them all, scrubbing his hands with the rigor of a medic or a chef, washing halfway up his forearms before wiping around each finger, each fingertip and nail, the backs of his hands, and all around his thumb, finishing with a general wipe of each hand with a fresh wipe.

'Bloody hell,' said Felix as the journalist binned the used wipes. 'If we ever have a serial killer in the office, I know who my prime suspect is.'

'You need to go properly wash your hands and face, and you need a cleaner in here,' replied Emet, ignoring the quip.

'I will after. Look, I'm fine,' said Felix, trying to calm his trembling as he comically raised his glasses off his nose twice by pressing down on the temple tips behind his ears. 'I'll do it afterwards. Shall we put him on loudspeaker so that I can listen in and keep an eye on you, just in case?'

'OK,' replied Emet. 'I fucking hate that some huckster has managed to put us on edge like this.'

'Em. I'm the one who has to explain going full Beautiful Mind on my office windows with a permanent marker. How do you think I feel? Call him.'

Emet sat down, laid his phone on the table, and hit dial. The phone rang, but only for one double ring. Then the call connected.

CHAPTER 29

'Hello, Mr Gordon. We meet again, so to speak,' said the velvety Irish voice down the other end of the line. 'How are you and Mr Riley this fine day?'

Emet and his editor looked at each other and then around them as if trying to find a spyhole in the office walls. 'I've felt better,' declared Felix curtly.

'I'm very sorry to hear that, Mr Riley,' replied Delancey. 'I hope you're feeling on top of the world again soon. If I'm ever under the weather and it's a beautiful day like this, nothing makes me feel better than some fresh air and a little stretch of the legs.'

'He'll be a lot better when you stop playing sick, probably illegal games,' replied Emet as he watched his boss try to keep a lid on his churning mess of emotions.

'Games? I love a good game, but Mr Riley and I have played none,' replied Delancey. 'We merely exchanged a little craic, and I asked him to pass along a message. There's nothing illegal about that, is there?'

'Is that really how you want to play this?' asked Emet, each word out of his mouth becoming sharper.

'I'm not playing, Mr Gordon,' replied Delancey. 'I really have no idea what you're talking about.'

'Look, we know this was you. If we find whatever you've been dosing Felix with, we won't hesitate to involve the police.'

'Dosing? I deal in words, Mr Gordon, not pharmaceuticals,' replied Delancey. 'They're a scourge of modern life, a chemical flail at fixing psychological and spiritual problems partially created by the companies and institutions that synthesise and prescribe them.'

'Save the anti-medicine spiel for your vulnerable clients, Mr O'Shea,' said Emet. 'I don't know how you got to Felix, but I assure you I'll find out.'

'Emet. May I call you Emet?' asked the Irishman to no response. 'There's no dosing gone on. I loathe London. It's far too busy for me. Our...*interaction* the other day was, maybe, only my second time there this year. You have the wrong end of the stick about me and my old acquaintance Jimmy Rawlings, which is why I thought you and I could arrange to talk properly in person, at a time convenient for the both of us, to clear the air.' Emet was just about to reply when Delancey continued. 'That is, if as a journalist, you would like the other side of the story, so to speak?'

Emet swapped a look with his boss. Felix nodded his way. 'When?'

'I'm fully booked with clients this coming week, but I can make some time for you to visit a week Saturday if that works for you?'

'How about The Dorchester again?' asked Emet.

'Oh no,' replied Delancey with a chuckle. 'I'm sorry but I've exceeded my yearly recommended dose of the capital. I made an exception for royalty that I won't be making again anytime soon. Even for the journalistic royalty you are. Besides, I'll have to schedule you around other client visits. How's one in the afternoon for you?'

'Where?'

'Not too far out of the smoke. I'll have my man drop you the address closer to the time.'

'No. You needn't call here anymore. I'll call this number for it the day before.'

'Very well, then,' replied Delancey, his grin almost audible. 'I'll see you a week Saturday. I hope you're feeling better and back running full steam ahead soon, Mr Riley.'

'Thanks,' replied Felix as he thrust his raised middle finger at the phone.

'Enjoy your weekend, gents. *Sláinte.*' The call ended.

The two men looked at one another. 'You need to get checked out by a doctor,' said Emet.

'I feel alright, but I will,' he said, taking off his steamed-up glasses and wiping the condensation from them. 'You remember you called the man a snake oil salesman?'

Emet nodded.

'He's much worse than that,' continued Felix. 'He's the snake too. And we need to defang the fucker and make a belt out of him.'

CHAPTER 30

They vigilantly watched the pixelated water, their guns at the ready. Then the giant alligator-esque dinosaur's mouthful of teeth snapped their way as it lunged out of the water at them. A flurry of trigger pulls, digital bullets, and blood red bite marks on the screen later, the reptile bobbed back beneath the waters, circling away before its next attack. Emet and Clyde fired off-screen to reload their digital ammo.

'Can we go on a motorbike or car game next?' asked Clyde.

'Let's dispatch this fucker, then we can play whatever you want,' replied Emet.

'You've been saying that for the last twenty—' Before he could finish, the deinosuchus was snapping at them again, them riddling it with shots to its mouth and body as it tore shreds out of their screen.

'Push 1P Start' blinked in yellow on Emet's side of the screen. 'Fucking *bastard!*' he growled as he dug his hand into his pocket, searching for another pound coin as Clyde kept shooting.

'Calm down, mate,' said Clyde, preoccupied with blasting the digital dinosaur back into extinction. 'I've got the scaley twat.'

Emet scoured the coins in his hand but all he had left were twenties and tens. Fingers and thumbs, he started ramming them into the coin slot, some of them passing straight out of the change slot. 'For fuck's sake.' The dinosaur dipped back beneath the waters, maybe about to make its big last circle around before its final attack. Emet breathed a sigh of relief, steadying his hands to deliberately feed the final few coins. But then it pounced again. Clyde hammered away on his trigger. After a frenzy of hits and gouges, he died just before Emet fed his last coin in. The reptile's jaws loomed large behind the bloodied screen. Emet shoved his gun back into the arcade game's holster.

'Mate. Watch it. They can't fix this retro gear too easily.'

Emet shook his head and shoved his change back into his pocket.

'What's up with you?'

'Nothing a few drinks won't take the edge off,' replied Emet as they climbed out of the arcade's *The Lost World: Jurassic Park* booth.

'Just the sort of talk I like to hear when it's your round,' replied Clyde.

'What's your poison?' asked Emet as they sauntered towards the retro gaming spot's bar.

Clyde examined the options, which all fed towards the bar from exposed pipes and unbranded kegs. 'I dunno, mate. Do you reckon they've got anything that wasn't brewed in a Shoreditch bathtub?'

Emet cast his eye along the bar staff and the drinks in peoples' pint glasses. 'It doesn't look that way. If you're fancying something a little more refined and don't mind a bit of a walk, I know somewhere with some mind-blowing tipples.'

Twenty minutes later, they swished in through the door of Crema The Crop. Unlike the night before, the place was abuzz with cocktail sipping customers bathed in its atmospheric, purple-tinged lighting.

'This doesn't look like your typical haunt,' said Clyde, scanning around as they walked towards the busy bar.

'Anywhere that does killer caffeine is my kind of place.'

'Do you remember that time revising for second-year finals you took so many Pro Plus your eyes were so sunken you looked like Skeletor and you fell asleep in your first pint after the exam?' asked Clyde, getting a chuckle from his friend.

'Whatever gets you through, right?'

Clyde shrugged. 'I wouldn't know. I didn't get through.'

Emet chuckled. 'Maybe, but you made it further than some.'

'Hello, you!' said Skye, her face lighting up, noticing Emet after just serving another customer. 'Long time, no see!'

'Too long,' replied Emet beaming back at her. 'Busy evening!'

'I told you. It's unrecognisable on Friday and Saturday nights.' She scanned the bar, aware more people were on their way to order. 'What can I get you?'

'It's not just me,' said Emet, pointing with his thumb towards his friend. 'This is my old mate, Clyde. Clyde, this is Skye.'

'Hello there,' she said with a cute wave.

'Nice to meet you,' said Clyde. 'And I'm actually a few months younger than Em, in case you're wondering.'

'You read my mind,' she replied with an amused grin. 'What can I get you two?'

'I'll have the martini again, please,' said Emet before turning to his mate. 'She does the best coffee and coffee cocktails in the land. The martini's superb.'

Clyde tilted his head uncertainly. 'It's not really my drink, that. I'm not sure if it's the taste of it or the links to spying and espionage that I have the aversion to. What else is good?'

Skye picked up a drinks menu and passed it Clyde's way. 'The specials are all popular.'

He scanned them and pointed at one. 'I've not heard of that before, so I'll try one.'

Skye grinned and nodded as she took the menu back from him. 'I'll set you up a tab. Somebody just left one of the tables in the alcove, so go grab it while there's one free. I'll bring it over to you.'

'Are you sure?' asked Emet, glancing both ways along the bar. 'It's a bit busy, isn't it?'

Skye radiantly smiled his way. 'I can handle it.'

The duo left the bar and sat down. 'Check you out, Mr Shaken Not Stirred. I knew this place was too cool for you to be coming in just for the vibes. You've got no chance, mate.'

'No?'

'Not a bat's. A, she's gorgeous and, let's face it, you're ginger.'

'Strawberry blonde.'

'Tom-ayto, tom-ahto. You still go as red as either of them if you keep the fridge door open too long. Gin-ger.'

'Maybe,' replied Emet with a smirk.

'And B, aren't you a bit…pedantic for her? She looks so smiley. So happy-go-lucky. And with all those crystals and feathers, she looks like she should be some *dude* with a vest and a headful of dreads, or a turtleneck and a topknot or something?' Clyde saw Emet turn his eyes away immediately. 'Mate. I'm sorry. I wasn't thinking.'

'It's OK. Honestly,' replied Emet, meeting his friend's eye for added assurance. 'You're not wrong. And he'd have liked her. But beyond the superficialities, you couldn't be more wrong.' He hushed his voice. 'She actually popped to mine last night. On her own initiative.'

'No?'

'Scout's honour.'

Half surprised, half impressed, Clyde nodded. 'Good for you, pal. If we'd have had pints, we'd be able to cheers that. Long may your good times continue. Did you meet her here?'

'No,' replied Emet. 'On that motivational seminar thing where I found out about all this cancer madness.'

'Ahhhhh,' replied Clyde. 'The crystals and feathers make sense now. Is she a bit of a crystal dangler?'

'A bit, yes.'

'Like, an evangelical one or…?'

'She doesn't seem too bad about it,' replied Emet. 'She's slightly magical in her thinking and a little out there, but happier for it than I am, so…' He finished his sentence with a shrug.

'Well,' began Clyde. 'If she's got the law of attraction, you can have your law of opposite's attraction. Maybe you can both manifest your heart's desires,' he jibed in a dreamy voice.

'Maybe you can manifest this,' replied Emet, giving his mate the middle finger.

'Medicine truly lost a bedside manner and a wordsmith with you, didn't it?' replied Clyde with a grin. 'Does she know you're going after them?'

'Going after who?' asked Skye, appearing with their drinks from around the alcove's corner.

Emet's pale skin flushed. 'That sensory sharpening's really paid dividends.'

She impishly grinned and shrugged as she set his martini down. 'So, go on then. Who are you going after?'

'Just some holiday company who haven't paid my mum back for a trip they cancelled on her ages ago,' replied Emet. 'She needed that holiday, and it's gotten beyond a joke now.'

Clyde nodded insistently. 'She's a proper grafter is his mother.'

Skye smiled confusedly as she set his drink down in front of him.

'Oh,' said Clyde, realising his statement sounded odd without context. 'I work at the same hospital as her. Biomedic.'

'You or her?' asked Skye.

'Me,' he replied. 'She does the properly smart stuff. Consultant oncologist.'

'Oncologist,' replied Skye with a squint, then a smile. 'Help me out a little.'

'A cancer specialist.'

She turned her gaze to Emet. 'Oh. How stupid of me.'

'It's just jargon,' Emet replied.

'Not that. I mean, yeh, not knowing that word is pretty ditsy, but not that.' She came over and laid her arm around his shoulder and kissed his hair. 'I'm sorry.'

He rested his hand on the small of her back. 'It's OK.'

She stepped away. 'I'd best get back to the grind. Coffee lols. I'll leave you hatch your plan of attack. Hope you like the cocktail, Clyde.'

'Thank you,' he said, raising it to her as she set off.

Emet watched her until upon reaching the crowd by the bar, she turned back and smiled sumptuously his way.

'Look at you two,' said Clyde. 'Nothing like some googly eyes to take your mind off the rest of the shit in your life. She's a beauty, mate. Cheers to her, and cheers to a long overdue Freckle and Clyde night out.'

They clinked their cocktail glasses together and each took a sip.

'You weren't joking. That's out of this world,' said Clyde, taking another sip of his creamy drink, which was sprinkled with hazelnut pieces. 'You wanna try a bit?'

'Go on, then,' said Emet, swapping glasses.

'Yep,' said Clyde after tasting the martini. 'That's sublime. What do you reckon?' he asked, gesturing back to his own.

Emet nodded enthusiastically as he cheekily took a second sip. 'That might be better than mine. What's it called?'

Clyde insisted for the cocktail back before Emet drank anymore. 'It's called a Nutty Irishman.'

Emet downed the rest of his martini in one sickened slurp.

CHAPTER 31

After the number of cocktails he drank last night – aside from a couple of sips, none of which were Nutty Irishmen – he needed the fresh air. Rolling down the window was a joy as the landscape only got greener every mile he ventured deeper into Kent. London didn't have one vineyard that he'd ever seen; "The Garden of England", as it was known, had many. As he rolled past a purple valley of lavender fields in late bloom, he inhaled deeply, hoping for its relaxing aroma to sweep him away. The fields were too far away to catch any scent, so feeling robbed of an olfactory delight, he quickly justified another one to himself and sparked up a cigarette.

His sat nav eventually bought him to an electric gate, but not that of a house. The road of houses was gated. He dialled in the number of his destination address, pressed call and a moment later, he was rolling down a road of private luxury. Each house he passed, or what he could see of them beyond their own gates and obscuring hedges down their lengthy drives, would ordinarily be considered a mansion but all side by side like this, he wasn't sure if that moniker would be accurate. *Terraced mansions?* Even the road itself was supersized; possibly wider than a four-lane motorway. With his grey Škoda Superb the only car currently on it, the busiest he ever guessed it could get was during the school run, possibly entirely with chauffeured vehicles.

After being buzzed into his port of call, he drove for another twenty seconds through a pristine topiary corridor until he saw the house in its full glory; five storeys, modernly built but timeless, perfectly melded with its surroundings.

Outside of the grand entrance stood a dainty, well-groomed woman in her forties. Upon Emet reaching her, she primly shook his hand and invited him in.

'I've never done anything like this before,' she said with crisp annunciation as they sat across from each other in the sprawling lounge. 'It's very exciting. I'm a bit nervous, to tell you the truth.'

'That's natural,' replied Emet as he put his recording dictaphone on the table between them, 'but there's nothing to be nervous about. Just treat this like a normal chat. Two people talking.'

'We both know that's not quite true,' she said, nodding to the recorder.

'You'll forget about that in no time,' he assured her.

'I could do with something to settle my nerves. Would you join me in a tipple?'

'No, thanks,' he replied with a raised hand. 'On the job. But feel free to have one if it'll put you at ease.'

She twiddled with one of her shawl's tassels. 'Hmm. It's never as much fun on one's own.' She twisted it around her finger. 'Do you mind if I smoke?'

Emet's brow furrowed in bafflement before spitting his words out too quickly. 'Uh, no, of course not.' He had to hide his horror as she pulled a black and turquoise pack of cigarettes from her pocket and offered one his way.

'Would you care for one? I don't believe these are professionally frowned upon.'

'I don't smoke thanks, Allegra,' he replied, still struggling to conceal his shock.

She pulled out an expensive-looking gold lighter, sparked up, and took her first drag. 'Yes. It was lung cancer. I can imagine the thoughts that must be running through your head right now. But you haven't seen what I've seen, and you don't know what I know.'

'You're right,' nodded Emet as the menthol-scented smoke reached his nostrils, transporting him back over a decade, making him lose his train of thought for a long moment. 'And that's exactly why I'm here. I want to know, and I want to let the world know.'

She took a long drag and began. 'It started with a tickly cough. My husband and I had just gotten back from a little winter sun getaway to the British Virgin Islands before he was due away with work. Whenever I fly, I pick up a sniffle of some kind, so I thought nothing of it. It got worse, the doctor prescribed me some antibiotics, but they didn't touch it, so she tried me on another, and that did nothing either. When I went back to her the third time, I saw her expression shift, just for a millisecond, as she removed the stethoscope from my chest. She said I should go for an X-ray that afternoon. It was a stage three neuroendocrine tumour in my lungs.'

'Did the doctor say what it might have been caused by?' asked Emet.

'Of course,' she said, smiling as she held her cigarette out between her two fingers towards him, 'but we'll get to that.'

'OK. So, what happened next?'

'Well, my husband had just gone away on this huge project that I couldn't have him come back from, not so soon anyway, so I didn't tell him and cried all night in my empty bed. I'd never cried so hard,' she said, pensively peering through the cigarette smoke spiralling up towards the high ceiling. 'I didn't know it was possible. The next day, they started me on aggressive chemoradiotherapy. It completely wiped me out, but I managed to get through three treatments before he managed to get out of me what was going on. He rushed home, cuddled me, held my hair back when I knelt on the bathroom floor for hours on end being sick in the toilet bowl. It's not until you're in a situation like that that you really understand the "in sickness and in health" part of your wedding vows.' She savoured another drag. 'Anyway, I went through the round of treatment and was just about to have a round of cranial radiotherapy, to eradicate any rogue cells that had found their way to my brain, when they found a small tumour in my other lung. I don't know how much you know about the types of cancer, but that reclassified me as stage four, which with small cell is, essentially, a death sentence. Radio and chemo and other treatments can slow the spread and growth, but the clock is ticking. My hair was already gone, and now I had to look myself in the mirror and watch myself grow more and more corpse-like every day.'

'I'm so sorry,' said Emet.

The woman nodded as she pulled out her phone and searched for something. 'So was I. For myself. For my husband. Yet we were so fortunate, really. We had the means for the best doctors, the best care. I didn't want to keep him at home with me, watching me wither away, while his project died too, so I insisted he went back to it, and he insisted I came with him.' She showed him a couple of photos of herself, hairless, skeletal, one of them with oxygen tubes in her nose. 'I carried on my treatment there while he worked at my request. But the treatments failed. I got worse. The cancer progressed. I was petrified every time bedtime came that it would be my last. Every time I woke up, I could see the relief in Joe's face. I hope you never have to watch somebody you love have to go through that. I knew when I'd be gone, my suffering would end, but from the look on his face that his would just be beginning. Anyway, we got to the point where they said I had a few months to live, that it wasn't long before a hospice would be the best thing for me. Joe wanted us to get people in so I could stay here, but I didn't want to turn this place we'd shared so much happiness into a crypt. I could almost feel myself fading day by day, cough by cough, but then we heard about Delancey.'

Emet fought to keep his expression neutral. 'Tell me about how you came across him.'

'It was Joe who heard about him through someone or another in his wider network. He knows so many people, the name's failing to come to me. I can find out if you like?' she asked.

'That'd be great,' replied Emet.

'So yes, Joe wound up in a conversation with somebody who knew somebody who said they'd used some sort of psychotherapy or hypnotherapy to cure cancer. Joe works with a lot of kooky people, and he hadn't said anything about my condition for fear of all sorts of odd dynamics, so it was purely by chance that it came up. He came back here utterly incensed having heard that. I had to calm him down.' She pulled in a long deep breath of mentholly smoke. '"What's worse than a snake oil salesman claiming to be able to cure something as hideous as cancer?" he said.'

Emet restrained himself from answering.

'But as much as I agreed with him – I mean, it's a truly abominable thing to claim – I was waking up every morning to the prequel to my husband's grief – I had to take a look. I was spending my days watching the seconds tick away, so it wasn't like I had anything better to do. I found Delancey online, applied, and spoke to him without my husband knowing. I knew what he'd say, and given I didn't disagree, what little energy I had wasn't worth spending fighting with him. Within a week, I made an excuse about going to see a cousin I hadn't seen for many a moon and travelled to Delancey's place for my session.'

'Where's that?' asked Emet.

Allegra tapped her cigarette into an ashtray in front of her, giving herself a moment to think. 'I slept most of the way there, but I think it was out Hampshire way, perhaps. I can dig the address out for you. It's a stunning property, very Gatsby, and the view out back over the valley is to die for. I got there, by that point wheeling along my little oxygen dolly trolley, and I actually recall having one of these,' she said, nodding to her cigarette, 'whilst I was outside waiting. I hadn't smoked for years, it was Joe's thing, really, but he'd stopped when I'd be diagnosed, horrendously guilty that this may have been some of his doing, and I'd began to miss the smell. So I'd bought a large carton, figuring at that point I shouldn't deny myself any fun I could still have, and snuck a few here and there, that evening being one I recall. I'd thought there was very little chance I'd get caught, as I'd been waiting quite a while to be called in, but there I was with one of these in hand when they eventually came for me. I thought I'd be castigated for it, but he really didn't care. Not only was it not going to make any difference at that point, but he said that even if smoking had contributed towards my condition, it hadn't been the major factor.'

'How long had you smoked for and then stopped?' asked Emet.

'Maybe fourteen or fifteen years on and then the same off.'

Emet neutrally nodded. 'So, what did he say had been the major factor?'

'My fear and doubt.'

Emet felt his teeth clamp together like a bear trap.

'He said there are people who live long, healthy lives smoking and that it ultimately boils down to how robust our internal workings are. Chronic fear and doubt riddle our defences with vulnerabilities, and so it's those that require cutting out. Once they're gone, your system has everything it needs to take care of the situation. It's not even like it's dealing with a virus or some sort of foreign pathogen. It created the cancer itself.'

'This is what Delancey said?'

'I know how it sounds, Mr Gordon, and I can see the look you're trying very professionally to hide from your face. And I get it. It sounds both logical and yet like a huge overclaim, doesn't it? And yet here I am, right as rain, having undergone what the doctors can only explain as a miraculous spontaneous remission. I went in there suffering from what I assumed was an incurable physical disease, and I came out having had a mental surgery I didn't even know I needed. My mind felt lighter right away and after a few days of feeling a little worse my physical suffering began to lift within something like a week. I had to use all my restraint not to go get a new scan earlier than the month he suggested, but when I did, my specialist couldn't believe his eyes. He actually sent me for a second scan to check against the first. The tumours had almost entirely vanished. He tried to make sense of it, even claim credit for it, saying it could be some sort of delayed reaction to the chemoradiotherapy, but he himself admitted he had never seen that treatment shrink tumours at this pace. A month later, I had more scans. They came up totally clear. Not those or my bloods showed even the slightest trace of anything.'

Emet chimed in. 'That everything receded so quickly is truly incredible. Do you by any chance have any of those scans?'

'Of course,' she replied. 'They're up in the attic, but I can fetch them shortly or send you some copies afterwards if that'd be helpful?'

'Thanks,' said Emet. 'So, what exactly did Mr O'Shea's treatment consist of?'

'I'm not sure I'd call it a treatment, exactly,' she replied. 'I sent him a video of my answers to a questionnaire, I went to sleep to some audio recordings of his for the week before I came to see him, we sat and did some sort of hypnosis for a little while, and that was that.'

'Do you remember much of the content of the session with him?' asked Emet.

Allegra shook her head. 'Not really. All I remember was looking at a large painting on his wall – that famous Dali painting with the melting clocks – and leaving, feeling quite confused. He looked so certain that something meaningful had happened, yet I had no recollection of any of it. To be honest, I feared it had been a massive waste of time. How could you have done meaningful psychological work and not remember a jot of it? But at the same time, I felt incalculably lighter. You know that refreshed feeling you get sometimes when you wake from a nap?'

Emet nodded.

'I felt like that multiplied by a thousand. As light as the oxygen I was inhaling through those ghastly nose tubes. It was a baffling experience of something and nothing. I remember rolling down my window and lighting up one of these on the way home,' she said as she stubbed out her spent cigarette, 'thinking to myself the whole thing had been a waste of time. It wasn't like I'd held any real hope for it, and at least I wasn't going to have to pay for it.'

'Why's that?' asked Emet.

Allegra leaned back from the ashtray. 'It was a no-win, no-fee sort of set-up. I'd signed a contract, I'd moved money into an escrow account which would only be paid if I had a significant reduction of my cancerous growths within three months of our session verified by a few independent consultants. I had nothing to lose apart from a few hours of my time.'

Emet was slack jawed. 'There was no fee upfront for your work with him?'

Allegra shook her head. 'Not a penny. There were some fees associated with the solicitors and medical scans and consultations, but nothing directly to Delancey.'

Emet couldn't help but furrow his brow. 'And the solicitors and doctors and the other third parties were all definitely independent?'

'As far as I'm aware. I did what diligence I could muster the energy to at the time. And payment only left escrow after I'd had the full works of scans and tests multiple times by three different specialists – the one I'd already been using and a couple of new ones I enlisted.'

Emet rubbed his nape. 'And, if you don't mind me asking, how much did you pay him?'

'Five hundred thousand,' replied Allegra.

'Pounds?!' asked Emet.

She nodded. 'I know it's a lot of money, and we're so fortunate my family is in a position to pay it, but they say you can't put a price on a life and it's just not true. I looked into it at the time. Behind the curtain of the NHS or private health insurance, do you know how much on average cancer treatment actually costs?'

'I know it doesn't cost half a million,' he replied.

'You're right, it doesn't,' she agreed. 'The NHS spends about ten thousand pounds per year on a lung cancer patient, but if you're paying out of pocket, it can be tens of thousands just for one course of chemotherapy. And that's with or without a result. And that's for months, more likely years of ghastly treatment that might save you whilst also making you feel so bad that sometimes you wish you were dead. I paid more, but I paid for a result with practically zero side effects. A few guided visualisations, one in-person session, and done. And this was beyond the point when cure by treatment was no longer an option, anyway. If you or somebody you loved were at death's door and you were offered a zero-risk chance to save them like this, wouldn't you take it?'

Emet saw nothing but sincerity in her face as he squirmed in his seat, trying to find the right words to answer.

'Honey?' came the call from the hallway.

'We're in here, darling,' replied Allegra before turning back Emet's way. 'My husband. Back much earlier than I thought he'd be.'

A few seconds later, a man appeared through the doorway, a huge smile on his face as he headed for his wife.

'I wasn't expecting you back so soon. How was the place?' she asked.

He shook his head, his mouth downturned in dismay. 'I don't know how these scouts imagine that it fit the brief. But anyway, it can wait for another day. How's your day going?'

She gestured to direct his attention towards their guest. 'I have my interview, remember?'

He glanced over his shoulder. 'Oh, sorry, there. Indeed, you do,' he said before planting a kiss on her forehead and turning to greet Emet properly.

It took a moment to dawn on him, but when it did, Emet flushed beetroot red. *Ground, swallow me now.*

'Joe, this is Emet…what's your surname again, Emet?'

He didn't want to say it. 'Gordon.'

Joe's eyes narrowed. Then Emet saw something he was praying not to see in them: recognition. 'Get OUT!' roared Joe, much to his wife's shock.

Emet raised his palms apologetically. 'I honestly had no idea. This is for a completely separate thing.'

'*Separate?!*' snarled Joe as his wife hung back at her husband's fury. 'Was your decapitation of my film and it dying at the box office separate? Was your demolition of me as a writer-director and my wife's terminal illness during the making of that film *separate?!*'

Emet began to stand. 'I'm so sorry, I had no i—'

'Do you have any idea what your cheap words cost me back then and how little value they have now?! Get the fuck out of our HOUSE!'

Emet grabbed his dictaphone off the table and met Allegra's gaze. 'I'm so sorry, I really didn't know.'

'It's best you go,' she replied curtly.

As he scampered towards the exit, Joe shouted after him, 'And don't you dare spew your libel in Delancey O'Shea direction, you hack. He did more for my wife than you've done for anybody in your entire life!'

CHAPTER 32

'Pass me one, sonny,' said Emet's father, Pierre, as they stood at the popcorn counter, watching the cornels explode into their delicious final form.

'I don't think we're meant to in here,' replied Emet.

Pierre grinned his way like he'd just said the most naïve thing in the world as the cashier put the full tub of popcorn on the counter. 'That'll be four pounds, please,' she said.

Pierre turned his grin towards her, dialling up its charm. 'The post-sex cigarette. Didn't that become famous on the silver screen?'

She flushed a little red as a grin broke out on her face. 'I think so.'

'Would you care to join me in one?' A cigarette, that is?' Pierre clarified with a chuckle.

She checked down the confections bar to see if any other employees were around, which they weren't. 'Go on, then.'

'You heard the lady,' said Pierre, gesturing to his son to get the packet out of his pocket. 'Let me give her what she wants.'

Emet pulled it out and passed his dad a pair of cigarettes.

'She's hot, son, but I don't think she can light them herself,' said Pierre, drawing a coy giggle from the cashier. Emet passed him a lighter before he passed the woman a cigarette and flipped open a flame. They leaned in towards each other, man and woman, flame and cigarette, until smoke rose, flirtatiously examining one another for a few moments through its ethereal swirls. Pierre stayed close as he raised the remaining unlit cigarette, touching its tip to hers until it smouldered too.

'Thank you,' he said, his eyes completely locked on hers as he took the bag of popcorn off the counter.

'You're welcome,' she replied.

'C'mon,' he said to Emet. 'I want to see the teasers.' He walked away from the counter, Emet having to make up a few steps.

'Da, we didn't pay for that.'

'Does she look short-changed?' asked Pierre before throwing a piece of popcorn into his mouth.

Emet checked over his shoulder. The cashier simpered his dad's way, enjoying her cigarette, not noticing the popcorn cabinet was starting to overflow. As he turned back to his dad, he shook his head disbelievingly. 'I still don't think you should be doing this in here,' he said, nodding to his cigarette.

Pierre took it out of his mouth, pointed it at his son's mouth, and playfully raised an eyebrow. 'But it wasn't my idea now, was it, son?'

Emet's gaze adjusted to the point of his dad's focus to find a cigarette smoking away in his own mouth.

'Come on in. I think they've just started,' said Pierre as he opened screen two's outer door for his son to go ahead. They proceeded until in the cinema at the top of the steep entrance stairs.

'One second, da,' Emet whispered.

His dad stopped, watching the onscreen trailer through his smoke as he chomped away on the popcorn. Emet knelt and untied the laces of his dad's paint-splashed plimsols.

'Ready?' asked Pierre.

Emet rose, took the bag of popcorn from his dad, and shoved a few pieces in his mouth. 'Ready.' He fixed his eyes on the trailers as he made his way to his seat and settled. 'Take some before I hoover it all up,' he said, offering the popcorn to his side. After a few moments of none being taken, he turned to find his dad wasn't beside him. Baffled, he scanned around the dark empty theatre, only to notice smoke and then a flicker of a flame coming from the bottom of the entrance staircase. His eyes snapped open as he flung the sweat-soaked sheets off himself.

The rest of the day was a write-off, as the rest of the last had been. After a hellish time getting to sleep and staying asleep, haunted by horrific, morbid dreams when he did, Emet couldn't bring himself to do much of anything. Lying under his duvet and gazing across at his front room windows when he eventually left his bedroom were about as much as he could muster. He couldn't even find the energy to eat a full meal. All he could do was sit and smoke his way through most of the rest of the pack he had.

He really hadn't known that Allegra was the wife of Joseph Parsons, the British auteur filmmaker whose last film, *The Winding Stairway*, he infamously savaged a few years ago with a one-star review that went viral, excerpts of which were plastered on a multitude of memes about the movie. "Untie your laces on your way in. A tumble down the cinema steps and a trip to A&E will entertain you more than this insipid drivel." Looking back on his review, one line made particularly bad reading: "To be an auteur guiding a story from script to screen, one must have the vigilance of an emergency surgeon over all aspects of its health at every point until it wheels out of the operating/editing room into cinemas. With a film this dead on arrival, Parsons didn't just misread a chart or get a dosage a little off; he was out on a ciggy break while all the monitors shrieked as it flatlined." He had found Allegra with the surname Baxenden rather than Parsons, even though Wikipedia listed Joseph as married to Allegra Parsons. No online photos existed of the couple together. With a little more digging, it turned out that Allegra Baxenden was from a low-profile, old-money family who had made their fortune generations ago in shipping. Emet's guess was that either her husband didn't want his success linked to the means of his in-laws, even though he believed there was a decent chance that much of the funding of his projects may be down to them, or that the highly private family didn't want their name brandished around any more than it needed to be, especially with some mediocre indie filmmaker. Either way, he understood Parsons's fury at him, and he'd blown the interview. There was so much more he could have learned from her about Delancey before meeting him, but now that would not happen.

He turned on the TV and scrolled through the streaming services. *The Winding Stairway* wasn't included in any of them and was only available for purchase or rental. He wanted to check how valid his slating had been but couldn't imagine it would warrant rewatching more than once, so he hired it, hit play, and lit his last cigarette.

Mediocre artists and their egos. They love our adulation, but they always play that same fucking "It's easy to criticise. What the fuck have you ever done?" card. I've known better than to put out a piece of rubbish like this. Granted, there were extenuating circumstances, but you just wouldn't make it, would you? At the end of the day, he made this piece of shit, which is only marginally worse than his other work, and he put it out into the world for people to pay to see, and the paying public, including Muggins here, have the right to have opinions about it. And my opinion, not just as a punter but as a professional, is still that this is dross. It's not just not to my taste. It's objectively bad. The narrative structure is poor, the acting is wooden in places, the rhythm of the editing is clunky, even the cinematography and lighting is shoddy, although I can imagine he'd refer to them as "artistic choices". They all want to have legacies, to be remembered. Well, this one will be. Just not by many and as a well-deserved Razzie nominee. Did I make it so that fewer people went to see this with my review? I hope so, I hope I saved them some valuable time and money, but also, they're adults. I didn't make them do anything. I gave them my honest opinion, they decided to respect it based on its own merits and my track record, and then they decided what to do. Would I have been slightly less acerbic if I'd known his wife was dying from cancer, if indeed she was? I'd have probably wanted to be, I'd have definitely used some different metaphors, but then he should have put some sort of disclaimer sticker on the *poster. <u>WARNING; Auteur going through some heavy shit at the moment. Cut him some slack.</u>*

Like an automaton, he reached for another cigarette even though he knew he'd ran out. And he'd ran out of patience with the film too. Off it went. He hadn't been out from underneath his covers all that long today, but they beckoned him now after his broken sleep last night. This time, he drew the blackout curtains, leaving no low-hanging fruit on his quest for a good night's sleep. After brushing his teeth, he plugged his phone in for charge, checking for one last dopamine hit for the day. Messaging a few times with Skye had been the only glimmers of highlight in the otherwise miserable weekend. Nothing was in his inbox from her but then a Wildfire message notification popped up. And another. And another. He swiped down his notification bar to look at the message previews. 'I'd say I'm sorry for his abruptness but I'm not' read the first fragment of Allegra's message. Then another message landed, and it didn't need reading. It was a photo. Then another appeared. And another. He wasn't going to sleep anytime soon.

CHAPTER 33

'Twice in a week!' declared Leigh as she relinquished her hug. 'It's not my birthday already, is it?'

Emet kissed her cheek. 'If it was your birthday, I hope you think I'd take you somewhere a little flashier than this,' he said as he pulled her out a seat at the canteen table.

'Thank you kindly,' she said with a little curtsy as she accepted the seat and put her Tupperware and cutlery on the table. As her son sat, she looked across at his cup of coffee. 'Aren't you grabbing a bite with your maw?'

'The food here looks like it might put me here,' he replied before nodding to her chicken salad, 'and I don't think you've got enough to go around.'

She opened her container. 'If you fancy some of this, we can get you a plate. You look like you need some protein in you.'

'You look fantastic too, Mum,' he said before downing a mouthful of the rank cafeteria americano.

'I didn't mean it like that. You just look a bit under the weather.'

'I've just had a few rough nights' sleep.'

'And you smell like you've just walked out of a nineteen eighties bookie's.'

Emet grinned but looked away. 'They really should reposition that smoking area on the way in. Or maybe these sick people should have the decency to give it a bloody rest while they're in here on taxpayer money.'

His mum gave him a disapproving yet compassionate look. 'Are you sure you're OK?'

'I'm fine, honestly,' he replied. 'A good night's sleep and I'll be right as rain.' He reached over the table and took her hand. 'And you really do look fantastic.'

'Thank you,' she replied with an accomplished smile. 'Another three pounds.'

'Incredible,' he said, squeezing her hand before letting it go. 'How many more left?' he asked, preoccupied, as he reached under the table.

'Maybe twenty-five or so.'

'At that rate, you'll be there in no time,' he said as he put his laptop on the table.

She eyed it and him, seeing his mind was somewhere else. 'Well, the less you have, the slower it'll shift, so hopefully a little while longer yet. What've you got there to keep me entertained in the meantime, Mr Mind Elsewhere?'

He stopped. 'I'm sorry. I just—'

'I know. It's probably something very important,' said Leigh, 'but so is being in the moment. And not just for the feelings of the people you're with.'

'I know,' replied Emet, struggling to meet his mum's gaze.

'Rein it in the best you can,' she continued. 'Be where you intend to be. Not somewhere else. Not the future. Not the past. Unless you mean to be.'

'I know,' he repeated, surrendering more this time. He finally met her gaze. 'I'm sorry. I'm here now.'

His mum weighed him up and nodded. 'Thank you. So, what've you got for your maw to cast her eyes upon?'

'Are you sure?'

'As sure as the day is long.'

He opened his laptop, edged his chair further round the corner of the table towards her, and set his laptop in a good viewing position for them. 'What do you make of this?'

She cast her eyes on the chest scan image onscreen and sighed deeply. 'Em. Is this to do with that snake-oil salesman?'

'It is,' he replied sheepishly. 'The paper want me to cover it.'

'Wouldn't this be best left for somebody else?' she asked, her face etched with a mother's worry. 'This isn't really your wheelhouse, is it?'

'I know you've always wanted me to do something that made more of a difference. *This* will make a difference.'

'But *this,* Emet?' she pleaded.

'Maybe *this* is exactly what I need. Maybe burying this clown puts more to rest than just this,' he said, nodding to the screen. 'Help me stop this. Please.'

She thought for a moment, then pulled the laptop towards her, and shook her head. 'Poor soul. She's not got too long. Maybe six months at a push with treatment. Is she one of his *clients?*'

'She is. But that's her before photo.' He reached over and clicked, swiping to the image of her next scan. 'This her after.'

Leigh sat up straight. 'No. It really isn't. People don't come back from being in a state like that. Very occasionally, people live well beyond what we expect, but that doesn't reverse itself. When were these taken?'

'One month apart. And there's more.' He clicked again, flicking to a third scan with no tumorous patches visible. 'Abracadabra.'

Leigh bit her bottom lip and shook her head. 'And this?'

'A month later.'

'And when were these supposedly taken?' she asked.

'A few years ago,' he said, flicking to the next image of Allegra in a wheelchair, her oxygen tank beside her feeding up into her skeletal face. 'And here she is now.' He scrolled to the next image of her, looking healthy, much like she did during their meeting. 'I met her on Saturday. This is basically how she looks now.'

'Unless she has undergone the most miraculous sponta…what am I even saying?' Leigh asked, annoyed with herself. 'I don't fully understand what I'm looking at, but somebody's playing sick games. These scans aren't legitimate or, at least, they don't belong to the same person. This woman either played up any state she was in for the camera or is a full-on stooge. All I know is she didn't recover from the cancer in that first scan, never mind how they're claiming she did. There's no way.'

'I know. Now do you understand why I can't leave this be?' he asked, to which his mum reluctantly nodded as he clicked again, flipping to the next image: a photo of a page of medical records.

'But I really don't understand what you can do about it,' she said as she scanned the screen. 'People like him lurk in the shadows around the fringes, never subjecting themselves to enough scrutiny to be found out, never allowing their "revolutionary methods" to be put to the test. You're too young to remember there was a professional debunker on the TV down the years – I forget his name, he was at war with that spoon-bending fella – anyway, he had a million-dollar challenge open to anybody who could prove they had paranormal abilities. That went on for years. Anyway, he died with that million in his pocket and all the famous paranormalists who said they'd be happy to take him up on his challenge just never did. They kept on saying they would but just went on with their unprovable business as usual. I'm guessing he's making a pretty penny out of what he's doing?'

Emet clicked through to the next image. 'You don't even want to know.'

'So, what reason does he have to expose himself?'

'I'm not sure,' replied Emet, 'but he's agreed for me to interview him next weekend.'

Her eyes turned to her son. 'You be careful with people like that. You have no clue what lengths a grandiose narcissist like that may go to to keep his game running.'

'I'll be alright. At least it's not like I've never been around one before.'

His mum heard him but said nothing, keeping her eyes on the screen. 'Is there any more?'

'Just one or two,' he said, clicking again, this time to a scan of a letter.

Her eyes widened. 'Bingo! The name there,' she said, pointing at the screen. 'Dr Shannon Richardson. I've met her at a few conferences. Can I send her this and check how much of it all ties together? There's no way it all does, but we should be able to get a much clearer picture.'

'Of course,' he replied. 'She sent me these knowing I might publish them, so this is just an advanced preview.'

Leigh shook her head. 'The arrogance of these people to think they can falsify some medical records they found online using Photoshop and get away with it.'

'I know,' said Emet. 'But they fucked with the wrong clan.' He grabbed her hand and smacked a kiss on the back of it. 'Cheers, Maw.'

She grinned and used her free hand to sandwich his. 'They fucked with the wrong clan, indeed.

CHAPTER 34

After knocking at the door and getting somebody to alert Clyde to his presence, his friend came out, balled up his nitrile gloves, and pushed his goggles off his eyes onto his head. 'Here he is. The autoclave assassin.'

Clyde grinned, then blew imaginary smoke off his finger gun. 'I quite like that. Do you reckon they'll put that on my name badge?'

'Yes,' replied Emet, 'but probably in microscopic text so only you and your colleagues can see it.'

Clyde grinned wider and tilted his head. 'I'd take that. Speaking of microscopy, what're you doing here, anyway? Penis enlargements are in urology on the north wing.'

'Funny how you know that,' said Emet with a feigned quizzical frown. 'Had to see Dr Leigh about something, so thought I'd see if you were free for coffee.'

'You and bloody coffee. I'm still gagging for a pint. But no, I'm chocka. Don't even think I'll get a lunch break. Unless maybe you wanna get on the centrifuge and run some tests for me?'

'I think you're fasting this afternoon, then,' replied Emet. 'It's good for you. Optimise that IGF-1. Dial up those neurotransmitters. Work some cellular magic.'

'Come on,' pleaded Clyde. 'You sound more legitimate than I do. And you could do it easily enough. It's not all that different from those arcade games. Bash a few buttons and it spits out a scoreboard.'

'What scoreboard? We kept getting munched,' replied Emet.

'Oh yeh,' replied Clyde. 'Scratch all that. Catch you in the next few days, then?'

Emet saluted with a finger gun, shot it his way, and then left the pathology lab. A few minutes later, a familiar winning, chiselled jaw smile beamed up at him from the magazine shelf in the hospital newsagents. "LEAP: Why the life you deserve is closer than you can possibly imagine."

'Next, please,' came the call from the cashier, causing Emet to step forward without realising it. 'What can I get you there?'

Emet was preoccupied with Rawlings's grin.

'If you'd like that one, sir, I need to scan the barcode.'

'Which one?' asked Emet, snapping out of his transfixion.

'The magazine.'

'Oh, no. *Definitely* not.'

'So, what can I get for you?'

'Sorry, yeh. Twenty of the Sterling Superkings, please.'

A few minutes later, Emet puffed away on one of his fresh purchases whilst watching the minutes roll down on the bus shelter's electronic sign to his bus being due.

'Excuse me, mate.'

Emet turned to find a man a little older and a lot larger than himself smiling warmly his way.

'Do you mind if I grab a light?'

He fished his lighter out of his pocket and passed it over. The man lit his cigarette, savouring its first sizzle and inhale. He offered the lighter back Emet's way but as the journalist went to retrieve it, the man wasn't letting it go. Surprised, he looked the man in his eyes, where he could see the warm smile had mutated.

'You should be careful with these flip models. They can get a little loose jawed and before you know it, all sorts is aflame. Keep an eye on that, Emet.'

The man let go of the lighter, causing it to recoil into Emet's chest. His smile was sinisterly slanted now. A bus pulled into the stop.

'I think this one's yours,' he said before his grin hooked itself onto his cigarette for a deep drag.

Emet's glanced round. It was his bus. He dropped his half-smoked cig to the pavement and stubbed it out under his shoe.

'A heart-breaking waste,' said the man, shaking his head before taking another draw.

Emet backed away, keeping his eyes on the stranger as long as possible before having to tap payment at the bus kiosk. He walked along the aisle of the bus and sat in one of the empty seats, situated right beside the bus stop. The man outside sidled over, smoking directly outside of Emet's window, deadeyeing him as he raised both hands up to his mouth. The bus's engine engaged. *BANG*. Emet jumped out of his skin as the window clattered. The man had thrust his cigarette and both hands into it, shaking the glass and scattering cigarette ash everywhere. As the bus pulled away and Emet looked over his shoulder out of the back window, the stranger was nowhere to be seen.

CHAPTER 35

Leigh pushed the box of tissues across the table. The older man, in his late seventies, gratefully received it from her, pulled a few tissues out, and passed them to his wife, who was crying almost inconsolably, her tears showing no sign of ending. As she dabbed the streams and struggled to keep in the sounds of her anguish, her husband held her tight. 'Buttercup,' he said into her ear. 'Just because this round didn't work out like we wanted, it doesn't mean the next won't.'

'That's right, Mrs Mullsworth,' Leigh chimed in. 'With a few adjustments to your treatment plan, we still have plenty of opportunity here. You caught this early. We're still in a strong position.'

'Did you hear that, buttercup?' he repeated in his most hopeful manner, stroking her hair. 'A strong position. And I'll be here with you every single step of the way.'

She cuddled in tighter to him, seemingly squeezing some sort of seal shut to slow the flow of her tears. Leigh swallowed the lump in her throat.

Five minutes later, the couple carefully rose from their seats, the lady gathering her bag as Leigh passed behind them to open the door for their exit. 'We'll be in touch over the next few days to begin round two, OK?'

'OK,' replied Mrs Mullsworth.

'You look after your bonny lady, won't you, Stanley?'

'In sickness and in health, it's my privilege,' he replied with the aplomb of a traditional gent, melting Leigh's heart.

'I just imagine you thought you'd be signing up for a little more of the health than I've managed so far,' replied his wife.

'Nonsense, my love. I signed up for the full shebang.'

Leigh raised an eyebrow. 'If you don't mind me asking, how long have you two been married?'

'I don't mind at all,' replied Mrs Mullsworth. 'We've been married four years.'

'Oh wow. Practically newlyweds,' replied Leigh with a grin.

'Still honeymooning,' said Mr Mullsworth with a twinkle in his eye, taking his wife's hand and kissing it.

'I can see. You just have the intimacy of a couple together many more years,' said Leigh.

'This is marriage number two for us both,' replied Mrs Mullsworth. 'We were both widowed. I think after the heartbreak and grief of it, having loved once probably made us both more able to love again, wouldn't you agree, Stanley?'

'I would,' he said with a staunch nod. 'And this time, we know more than ever how lucky we are and how we should put every single card on the table, because you never know which game of bridge will be a bridge too far.'

Leigh saw them out, closed the door, and rested her forehead against it. Eventually, she wandered back over to her desk, sat, and opened her top drawer. The framed photo of her teenage son and late husband smiled up at her. She reached down and stroked the glass covering Pierre as tears filled her eyes. Then the floodgates opened.

By evening, the tears had long stopped, having been replaced by streaming sweat. Drumma Mummas was underway and Leigh was hammering her weighted drumsticks together as if each song was her last.

'C'mon, Mummas!' shouted the instructor. 'I want you to hit those sticks like you're Lars Ulrich!'

The next song on the playlist began. The soft first few beats gave it away: *In The Air Tonight* by Phil Collins. The class fizzled with the excitement of a big song.

'That's right, ladies. A little change of tempo. I can feel it. Can you all feel it?'

'Yes!' they hollered back.

'Do you know what it is, Mummas?'

Leigh and the class-goers kept running on the spot, slapping a moving stick against a stationary one to the beat, a few of them shaking their heads.

'It's whatever you want it to be,' continued the instructor. 'Every moment you have the power to change your destiny forever, but this moment, this evening, this one's different. Can you feel it, Mummas?'

'Yes,' bellowed back a few of them breathlessly.

'As the music builds, I want you to let all the hurt inside you rise to the surface…'

Leigh pounded her feet against the floor harder.

'…I want you to decide that what's coming tonight is the end of that hurt in your life…'

The doctor clattered her sticks together with everything she had.

'…however long it's been with you, however well it's served you at times, I want tonight, this very coming moment to be the moment you take whatever lesson you can from it and promise once and only this once that this hurt is done…'

As Leigh wiped the pouring perspiration from her brow with her wristband, she used its underside to take some of the burning tears from her eyes.

'…that tonight, the burn we blaze through this song burns it all away, never to return, and that out of its ashes rises something beautiful. Are you with me, Mummas?'

'Yes,' Leigh bawled back with everybody else.

'Are you with me, Mummas?!' yelled the instructor from the depth of her being.

'YES!'

'Sing it with me, ladies!' the instructor yelled, her sticks raised overhead, signalling the next exercise.

In unison, Leigh and the entire group dropped into a ninety-degree squat and stayed there, tapping their sticks twice per beat as they sang along at the tops of their lungs.

'Yes, ladies! How long've we been waiting for it?' the instructor shouted quickly before the next line.

Leigh settled into the ever-more searing pain in her thigh muscles and whacked her sticks together perfectly in time as she belted out the words 'all my life' from the root of her being.

'Goodnight, ladies,' said Davide as the jelly-legged Drumma Mummas pottered past his reception desk.

'Bonne nuit, Davide,' one of them called back leading a chorus of poorly pronounced French goodnights and goodbyes.

He smiled. 'Rest well, ladies. See you next time.' As Leigh brought up the back of the group, he turned his attention to her. 'Rest well, Leigh.'

'And you when this long shift of yours finishes.'

'I had my taste of sweetness to get me through, thanks,' he replied. 'Goodnight.'

She stopped at his counter and passed him a small, folded piece of paper. 'Goodnight, Davide.' She turned away and strode off before he had a chance to ask her what it was. Upon opening it, he found a handwritten note saying *'If you'd like anymore sweetness'* accompanied by her number.

CHAPTER 36

8 it is. Looking forward to it, lightweight x

Emet alighted the bus with a perma-smile that outlasted the five-minute walk to the office, his eyes not even turning the way of the cigarette kiosk as he passed it and threw his empty breakfast yoghurt pot in the bin.

'What's up with you today?' asked Felix as they crossed each other at the water fountain.

'Wrong with me?' replied Emet.

'Yes,' said Felix. 'If I didn't know better, I'd say you were smiling.'

Emet sarcastically widened his grin.

'Fuck me. That warrants a front-page headline. Mardy critic gets out of the right side of bed. Or maybe somebody else's?' he asked, raising a comedic eyebrow.

'No comment,' replied Emet.

'There we go. That'd explain why you're not dressed like Wednesday Addams for once. You should do white more often,' said Felix, nodding at Emet's uncharacteristically stylish, bright shirt. 'Anyway, if I'm getting no details, you'd better have something else juicy for me.'

'I may have something on The Cancer Man. It looks like he may have left a loose end,' said Emet. 'I'm hoping to unravel half of his bullshit by close of play today.'

Felix raised the water cup he'd just filled. 'That'll be a story we can raise something much stronger to.'

Emet nodded. 'Let's see him *sláinte* that, the horrible fraud.' His phone began ringing in his pocket.

'Smiling *and* friends. What a day!' said Felix as Emet checked his screen to see the call was from a withheld number.

'Give me one sec,' said Emet before taking the call. 'Hello.'

'Maidin mhaith, Emet,' said Delancey in his dulcet tones. 'How are you this fine day?'

'Fine,' replied Emet coldly, his transformation of demeanour gripping Felix's attention.

'Not much of one for small talk,' stated Delancey, semi-amused. 'In that, we're kindred spirits.' Emet let the statement hang without interjection. 'Anyway, I was wondering if you would be available for our chat today? My schedule has changed suddenly and later in the week won't be possible. It may be weeks until I can free up the time again.'

'Who is it?' mouthed Felix.

'The Cancer Wanker,' whispered back Emet, covering his mouthpiece. 'He wants to meet today. But I can't pull on my thread yet.'

'Go anyway,' whispered Felix. 'You'll surely find more threads there, and your other one will still be there waiting afterwards for an almighty tug.'

Emet uncovered the mouthpiece. 'OK. I can make it. What's your address?'

'Laurel Canyon Manor. I'm sure your journalistic instincts can get you here. I'll see you this afternoon.' He chuckled to himself. 'The Cancer Wanker. I like it. Say hi to Felix from me.' The call ended.

Emet scanned around the newsroom to try to find anybody paying them particular attention to no avail and shook his head. 'This fucker really knows how to get inside your head.'

'You're telling me,' replied Felix. 'Best pack those ears with cotton wool.'

'I doubt there's any around, but we have plenty of newspaper I can try with.'

After a Tube across to Waterloo and a one-hour train ride out of London, checking occasionally for anybody paying him undue attention, Emet hailed a taxi at the local station and set out through the luscious countryside. Whilst relishing the fresh air through his rolled-down window, his phone rang. No private number this time.

'Good morning, Maw.'

'Good morning, my treasure,' she replied, her smile sounding evident. 'How are you?'

'Just on my way to the charlatan's lair,' he replied. 'He rolled forward a few days. Please tell me you have some good news for me?'

'Oh, well I do, but not that. I spoke to Dr Richardson, and it's sort of a dead end.'

'How do you mean?'

'Well, she did treat your interviewee, Allegra Baxenden, but everything stacks up. They are her scans, they are dated properly, and Mrs Baxenden underwent what she termed a "total spontaneous recovery". She said in all her years in practice, she has never seen anything like it.'

Emet raked his teeth across his bottom lip. 'So, what was her explanation?'

'She didn't have one. Treatment had stopped at the time it happened, and her condition was extremely advanced. You read about remissions like this in your textbooks and hear of the odd case study, but not many come across something like this in their career.'

'Have you?' he asked.

'No. I've seen developments speed and slow, and I've seen people survive months and years beyond their prognoses, but I've never seen anything like this.'

He scratched his head. 'And you're sure this doctor's being above board with you?'

'She's a legitimate professional. She has no reason that I know of to lie.'

'Hmm. I'll see about that.' He paused as something returned to his mind. 'Did you say there was some good news too?'

'I did, but it's totally off-topic. It can wait.'

'I'm just about to speak with the lowest of the low. I could do with something to smile about to buttress me from the bleakness ahead.'

Leigh hesitated. 'Well…tonight, your Maw has a date.'

'What? Like…a *date* date?'

'Ever my wee wordsmith. Yes, a *date* date. With a man.'

Emet was lost for words. 'Wow. That's…is he the first—'

'Aye. I figured there's life in the old girl yet and that it's been long enough.'

'No, absolutely,' he said, emphasising his eagerness to correct for his shock. 'What's his name?'

'I'll tell you if it goes well.'

'Fair enough. I'm sure it will.'

Leigh chuckled to herself. 'I'm glad one of us is. I'm thirty-odd years out of practise.'

'You speak to people every day, Maw. You'll be fine. Just be yourself.'

'Thank you, son,' she said with great tenderness. 'I've got to go. You look after yourself there. He sounds like a nasty piece of work you're dealing with.'

'Don't worry about me. Just enjoy your afternoon and have a lovely time tonight.'

'Thank ye, sonny.'

After the two said their goodbyes, Emet sat in a mild daze as the taxi driver harped on about the road up to the house and old trees. 'Super,' he replied, having not taken more than a few words of what had been said. As he rolled up the window, he felt a tremendous pang for some nicotine. 'You don't by any chance have a cigarette I can buy from you?' he asked the driver.

'I don't,' replied the driver, 'but you're not the first person to ask on the way up here. But we're here now, anyway.'

Emet leaned forward between the two front seats. Ahead of them loomed the gargantuan gates of Laurel Canyon Manor.

CHAPTER 37

They pulled up to the gates and the driver stopped the car. 'Old school,' he said. He eventually rolled down his window in response to a shout from the other side of the gates. 'What name is it?' he asked, turning back to his passenger.

'Emet Gordon.'

The driver relayed the name through his window, triggering two men to appear from out of sight and begin opening the enormous gates manually. 'You think he could afford the automatic ones.' When they were open sufficiently, he drove them in slowly, his speed and the angle of approach to the manor house giving Emet time to take in the entire scene. The pale stone building fit the English countryside perfectly while also looking, as Allegra said, like something ripped from the pages of 'The Great Gatsby'. Although clearly a period property, it was in near-immaculate condition. The courtyard between the gate and the house was lined with a pristine lawn containing a manicured hedgerow maze and two water fountains, both of which were currently dormant. All around the courtyard ran large iron railings and pale stone walls at least twenty feet tall. After what seemed a short eternity, the car pulled up outside the front steps. Emet passed cash to the driver, took a receipt and card, and waved away the change.

'Happy healing,' said the driver, prompting Emet to leave the car silently before it pulled away.

A man in butler's attire stood atop the stone steps by the house's main entrance. 'Welcome, Mr Gordon. How was your journey?'

'Scenic,' replied Emet stoically as he climbed the first few steps. The butler nodded. 'Wonderful. If you'll follow me, please.'

Emet followed him into the house, his head on a swivel as he entered the impressive atrium, its circular domed glass ceiling lighting the predominantly dark-wood-lined space flanked by a dual staircase. The stone, plaster, and staircase railings all bore the geometric patterns of the Art Deco movement. The butler carried on straight forward, ignoring both flights of stairs and leading them into a long dark-wood hallway. As he trod the black and gold marble underfoot, Emet regarded the bizarre Surrealist paintings lining the walls and the galvanised tin urns skirting both sides of the hallway every few metres. He'd seen these sorts of urns before but couldn't think what they were. All he was sure of is that they didn't fit the general aesthetic. Eventually they arrived at the end of the hallway, where the butler knocked on the pair of large golden railed doors ahead of them. No answer came from beyond them.

'Excuse me for a moment, please, sir,' said the butler before opening the doors just enough to step in.

Emet peered back over his shoulder. The brightness of the atrium seemed a pin prick from along this hallway.

'Mr O'Shea seems to have gone walkabouts,' said the butler, summoning Emet's attention back round, before opening the doors more fully. 'If you'd like to sit yourself down in here, I shall have him with you presently.'

Emet entered the room as the butler took off back down the long hallway, the patter of his footsteps quickly dying out. The journalist slowly made his way into the vast room, like a rodent cautiously exploring unfamiliar territory. The almost panoramic view out over what he assumed must be Laurel Canyon was stunning. As he walked towards the windows to look closer, he glanced over his shoulder, stopped in his tracks, and turned. A large replica of Dali's *The Persistence of Memory* dominated the wall and commanded his attention. He wandered over towards it, noticing as he got closer that it wasn't a print but a deftly painted replica. Authentic brushstrokes gave a painting a sense of movement and life that a print could never capture. He'd looked many times at images of this painting, scaring himself with the thought that if clocks could stop, maybe time could stop, maybe grinding the gears of the degradation of memory itself to a halt. *Some memories don't need to persist.* With the scale of the painting, his eyes were drawn to details he'd never focused on before. The barren ochre cliffs in the top right corner had two flecks of detail on them. *Are they figures?* The strewn-out white "monster" in the centre of the piece seemed more transparent than he recalled it. Then there were the melting clocks in the bottom left corner. At this size, the ants stationed on the face of the orange clock looked bulbous and grotesque. He could imagine the moist crunch they would make underfoot. Then, on the white melting clockface above it was painted a fly, the detail of which was incredible, with the accuracy of its shadow uncannily fitting. As he leaned in for a closer inspection, the fly's wings flickered open, causing him to jump out of its skin.

'Eternally disturbing, isn't it?'

Caught off guard for the second time in a second, Emet turned frenetically, regretting straight away that he hadn't been able to conceal his scare.

'I think that was the idea,' replied Emet, glancing back towards the painting, seeing that the fly was still there, painted and lifeless.

'Indeed. What superior way is there to be remembered?' said Delancey, his unsettling icy blue gaze holding on his guest. 'How do you like the place?'

Emet paused to consider his answer. 'I've not seen one like it before. I guess I'm still making my mind up on it.'

Delancey raised an amused grin. 'It is an acquired taste; not for everybody, I grant you. Still, I'd like to think more interesting than the Baxenden-Parsons's place.' His gaze lingered.

'Have you been following me?' asked Emet, measuring his tone.

'Following you?' echoed Delancey, his glee growing. 'I don't get out much, Emet. And I don't think I could summon the energy for such an act of espionage.' He continued thinly smiling his guest's way. 'They called me. Mr Parsons was rather ruffled. He thought I could do with warning about you, but I quite enjoy a ruffling.'

'No ruffling,' replied Emet, keeping his voice level. 'Just a run-of-the-mill interview.'

'Very well, although even that's a ruffle for me,' said Delancey, pulling his lapels to straighten out his patterned velvet evening jacket. 'I've not done an interview before. I'm not a public man, as I'm guessing you've found out.'

'Although not too shy of drawing attention,' said Emet, nodding towards his host's jacket.

Delancey peered down and looked back up, a grin creeping across his face. 'What, this old thing? This isn't for anybody's attention other than mine. What joy is there in life without a little panache?' He scanned his guest's plain white, grey, and black attire. 'Panache being a purely subjective phenomenon, obviously.'

'Obviously.'

'My butler should have brought you to the lounge, so please follow me,' Delancey said, opening up his body and gesturing with a hand towards the panoramic windows. 'Unless a more therapeutic meeting would be more to your liking?'

Emet's eyes turned to the armchair across the room on which he noticed a buckle. 'The lounge'll be fine.'

'Very well. We'll take the scenic route.' Delancey turned and set off towards the French doors. Emet followed at a distance, turning to check the painting as his host opened the door so that he wouldn't be noticed. Its vista remained lifeless. 'After you,' said Delancey as he opened one of the double doors. Emet cautiously passed by the imposing man, who he realised had disproportionately long legs now he was so close. He did not look directly at him, but coiled himself like a spring, ready to react if needed.

The sandstone courtyard outside stretched along the entire width of the back of the manor house, barren, without any of the embellishment from the front of the house. All the area contained was a few wooden benches that faced away from the house out towards the predominantly verdant scenery. 'Who needs topiary when you have a view to die for?' said Delancey, almost reading Emet's mind as he surveyed the sunlit valley.

The journalist walked out beyond his host, eventually reaching the edge of the sandstone. He looked over its edge expecting another ledge just beneath it, but instead he swayed, dizzied by the severity of the straight drop. It was an almost sheer cliff edge, with an eighty-odd degree gradient with the stony floor below around three storeys down.

'Careful, there,' said Delancey. 'Cancer, I can help people with. That fall, not so much.'

Emet refrained from responding, feeling like he was being baited with almost every remark by his host. 'It's stunning out here. Is this Laurel Canyon?' he asked.

Delancey arrived next to him. 'No. That's just the name of the house. And it is stunning until invaded. Speak of the devil.' He pointed down to a car slowing to a stop almost directly beneath them. 'I wanted to buy that land down there, but the owner wouldn't allow it. In retrospect, I shouldn't have bought the place,' he said with his first hint of a break from some sort of smile Emet had seen, his jaw mildly tense.

Emet examined the dusty track below where the car came from, its edges overgrown with greenery. 'It doesn't look like you get too much "invasion"?'

Delancey's gaze didn't even flicker Emet's way as he answered. 'I didn't know any level of invasion could be deemed acceptable.' He began to walk back towards an as-yet unexplored part of the house. Emet drew in a deep breath of fresh air, turned and grinned celebratorily at the annoyance he seemed to have stumbled across, and followed.

CHAPTER 38

Back inside, the pair headed silently along another steel-container-flanked hallway until they reached the library-esque lounge. Above the unlit fireplace between the walls of books, he was struck by the large photographic print of the man in shackles, partly because it was the first photograph he had seen in the house, and partly because the man it depicted bore a solid resemblance to his interviewee, sporting angular features and the same old-fashioned centre-parted hairstyle. 'Is that…is that Harry Houdini?'

'It is indeed,' replied Delancey, impressed. 'People know his name, it's travelled the last century extremely well, but seldom know the face that went with it. How do you know him?'

'I'm fairly certain I've seen some of his escape acts, but I know I saw 'The Grim Game' a long while ago,' replied Emet. 'By column inches, I'm predominantly a reviewer. There's not much I haven't seen.'

'Very good,' said the Irishman. 'If you ever care to see it in its truest glory, I have his full collection on original film in my projector room.'

Emet raised his eyebrows. 'Original?'

Delancey proudly nodded.

'There can't be too many reels of those lying around?'

'I doubt there are. I'm quite the collector, actually.'

'Of film?'

'Of Houdini memorabilia,' replied Delancey. 'The greatest showman there's ever been.'

A thought dawned on Emet. 'The tins along the hallway. Are they milk churns?'

'They are indeed,' said Delancey as he sat on one sofa and signalled for his guest to sit on the one opposite. 'I knew we'd get on. Harry Houdini himself escaped from all of those throughout his career. I don't have them all, but all I have were his.'

Emet nodded approvingly as he sat. 'They must have cost you a pretty penny?'

'A pretty penny indeed,' replied Delancey with a smirk. 'I have a good number of his other stage items too.'

'What's with the fascination?'

Delancey savoured the question, mulling over it as he crossed one leg over the other. 'On the one hand, I don't know if we ever know such things, such are the strength and opacity of our subconscious drives. My surface level answer is what I said before. He's the greatest showman there's ever been. A century on and he's still the most famous magician there's been.'

'Why do you think that is?'

'Because many of his tricks were real,' replied Delancey. 'Many of his escapes were from real containers and shackles before people's very eyes.'

'Wasn't he also a debunker of people who claimed to be able to talk with the dead?'

'He was indeed,' replied the Irishman. 'I have some of his books on the matter on these very shelves.' A thought suddenly dawned on him. 'Forgive me. Here we are gabbing away, and I've not asked if I can get you something? A drink? Maybe a smoke? I think we have some Sterlings lying around.'

Emet glared his host's way. 'What makes you think I smoke?'

Delancey shook his head and grinned with the expression of somebody who realised they had been misunderstood. 'Oh dear. I'm doing nothing for that paranoia of yours, am I? I just know you smoke because I can smell it on you.'

'And the specific brand?'

'Yes. I can smell it.'

'You smelled my *cigarette brand* as I passed by you?' asked Emet, trying to dampen his incredulity.

'I can still smell it now,' replied Delancey. 'I have what some have called the nose of a bloodhound. I can smell all sorts of things. Tobacco brands. People's last few meals. Cancer.'

Emet covered his face with his hands and blew out an almighty sigh. 'Mr O'Shea. What is this?'

'What is what, specifically?' replied Delancey earnestly.

'This interview. You said you wanted to straighten things out between us, but then you open with a ridiculous statement like that.'

'Emet. I understand my claim is unusual,' said Delancey, 'but it's known there are people with hyperosmia – I believe it's around two percent of the population with a heightened sense of smell – so how can you claim it's ridiculous without putting it to the test?'

The journalist knew his interviewee was correct about the existence of the ability. 'Go on, then,' he said reluctantly. 'What have I eaten today?'

Delancey let his eyes remain closed on their next blink and inhaled deeply, his face tilting towards the heavens as his spine arched backward and his lungs filled. After holding the breath for a short eternity, he let it go gradually, like the air escaping a tiny tyre puncture. As his thorax deflated, his head returned to its resting position, and his eyes slowly rolled open. 'Coffee, no milk, and some sort of yoghurt. Raspberry, I'm fairly certain.'

Emet remained impassive.

'And maybe some toast too.'

The yoghurt he'd eaten on the bus that morning had been raspberry, but he hadn't had toast for breakfast. That had been supper last night.

'Am I right?'

'Not entirely, but it's a cute parlour trick,' said Emet, 'but anybody on my bus this morning could tell you what yoghurt I ate.'

'And the toast?'

'Anybody with a good zoom lens could tell you that,' replied Emet.

'So, you did have some,' said Delancey. 'But you're insistent on finding an explanation more to your liking. And here you were asking what *I'm* doing with this interview. What's the point in us speaking if nothing I say or demonstrate has a chance of penetrating your pre-existing impression of me?'

'It has a chance,' replied Emet as he fished his dictaphone out of his jeans pocket and set it on the table between them, 'but after what you did to my boss and after I've had one of your men follow me, it's safe to say we're starting from a trust deficit.' He hit the record button, engaging the device's little red light.

'A trust deficit. That's a delightful turn of phrase,' said Delancey with an impressed grin. 'And an interesting method of rectifying that. I prefer analogue myself. Much more reliable. Plus, people are becoming so reliant on these gadgets, their memories are becoming so dim. Anyway, would some good news help us out?'

'If it's truly good, I can't imagine it'll hurt.'

'Not only do you have solid taste in tobacco, but you're cancer free,' said Delancey, tapping his nose, triggering a disdainful glower from his interviewer. 'What? Dogs can be trained to sniff out tumours, but I can't?'

'Dogs have far more powerful nose hardware than humans,' retorted Emet.

'That's a huge assumption you're making there,' said Delancey, a thin, sarcastic smile aimed his interviewer's way. 'But seriously, the blind learn to echolocate and read tiny dimples on paper, sommeliers learn to detect scent notes from fruit and the barrels they ferment in. With all my dealings with cancer over the last decade, isn't it feasible that I could become a sort of tumour sommelier?'

Emet shook his head in disbelief. 'There we go. The classic slippery slope setup. The snake oil salesman's speciality. Use a few truths to get somebody nodding, making statements like "hypnosis can reduce stress" and "chronic stress increases the incidence of cancer", then hit them with "so hypnosis can cure cancer", a logical leap that some, especially the desperate and vulnerable will miss.'

'I never claimed to be able to cure cancer,' replied Delancey, pulling an ornate golden cigarette holder from his inside jacket pocket and opening it. 'Are you sure I can't tempt you?'

'As good for your business as that may be, no thanks,' replied Emet. 'You call yourself "The Cancer Man". If you don't claim to cure cancer, what exactly is it you claim you do?'

Delancey lit his cigarette and made himself comfortable. 'Firstly, I didn't call myself that. It was a nickname that developed a life of its own that has commercial benefits it was recommended I take advantage of. Secondly, I'm not selling hypnosis. That label is so reductive and limiting. I've never found a sufficient label for what it is I do. Thirdly, I'm not talking about low-level chronic stress that, as your rightly say, elevates risk of all disease. I help people resolve their most destructive inner turmoils, which are acute drivers of disease. And ninety-five percent of the time, resolving these turmoils reverses their cancer processes.'

'I don't see the difference. You're just playing linguistic games to avoid taking responsibility, yet strongly implying that you are in fact responsible,' replied Emet curtly.

'That's a very cynical perspective, and I believe you're smart enough to see the difference clearly. Tell me, do cancer surgeons, the ones who use scalpels and lasers to cut malignant tissue out of their *patients,* claim to cure cancer?'

Emet dead-eyed his host.

'Even those who literally remove cancerous cells with their hands don't claim to be doing curative work. None of the vast array of treatments used in conjunction with surgery are claimed to be curative. Billions of pounds Sterling and of every other currency are spent every year on treatment, none of it is spent on cure. And they work directly on cancer.' The Irishman flicked some of his ash into a golden ashtray on the table ahead of him. 'I work on psychological trauma; spiritual sickness, if the stigma of the term doesn't make one balk. And even there, there are no guarantees. There is no direct causation. Do you really think that I can say words to a person that genuinely *cause* them to do something against their own self-interest, or even in it, for that matter?'

'I don't know,' replied Emet. 'I have an incredibly out-of-shape editor that nearly ran himself into an early grave to deliver a message on your behalf.'

'On my behalf?' asked Delancey with a smirk. 'Yes, I asked him to pass the message on, but you can't hold me accountable for another grown, capable man's overzealousness, can you? Maybe he just thought this would make a truly interesting story, or maybe that he should seize the day and that was the evening to start getting fit.'

'Or maybe you had him spiked,' replied Emet.

'That almost sounds like an accusation. Or like somebody playing linguistic games to avoid taking responsibility for making one,' replied Delancey before taking another long drag. 'I can reassure you that no such spiking has gone on, meaning that your boss either ran to your house completely of his own free will or he was caused to do something unheard of for him – maybe even extraordinary – through the power of my words, which begs a question, doesn't it?'

'What's that?' asked Emet, fed up with his host's smarminess but wanting to keep him talking for the recorder.

Delancey paused and locked eyes with his interviewer. 'What other extraordinary processes could my words affect?'

'You tell me,' replied Emet. 'These traumas you…help resolve. Do they help conditions other than cancer?'

'I believe so,' said Delancey with a slow nod.

'Like?'

'I can't say definitively, but if the nervous system can effect it, I can't see why not,' replied Delancey. 'But since specialising in helping those with the second biggest cause of global death, I can't say I've had much time to experiment with other conditions. Heart disease, even if partially caused psychosomatically, can't spontaneously clear itself up. Do you know why?'

'Go on.'

'For the same reason that hearts don't get cancer. They're the only organ in the body that whose cells don't divide or regenerate. Hearts can't mend.'

'Sounds like a Valentine's card.'

Delancey grinned and took another drag.

'So, given the demand, you have a long waiting list?' asked Emet.

'Like a hankie up a magician's sleeve.'

'That's hard work. A lot of responsibility,' Emet responded. 'Have you never thought of training some apprentices up to share the load and help more patients?'

'They're clients, not patients,' replied Delancey. 'And yes, I did try to train a group up to roll the work out further.'

'What happened?' asked Emet.

'Not everybody has the disposition for what I do.'

'How do you mean?'

Delancey tapped some more ash off his cigarette. 'Let's take your job, for example. Words on a page. Of the billions of people who have the ability to write in the most basic sense, how many of those can you teach to write at your skill level?'

Emet shrugged his shoulders. 'At my level, some would say a troop of monkeys and a few typewriters would suffice.'

Delancey grinned. 'Seriously. How many literate people, given the right education, could be professional writers, weaving their words and perceptions together with regularity at a high level to engage a wide range of readers? Half? Quarter?'

Emet shrugged again. 'Maybe something in that region.'

'And that is for writing, a fairly neutral affair for which the pedagogy has been developed over millennia. Yes, I learned some linguistic skills and therapeutic frameworks from books and various people, but nobody to my knowledge in modern times, has applied and combined those skills in such a way to achieve what I have with psychosomatically traumatised clients. I tried to teach others, but they fell into two camps. Those who were unable to psychologically deal with their own traumas and, therefore, the traumas of others, and those who were unable to grasp the complexity and nuance of the methods I use. To these people, my methods were sufficiently advanced as to be indistinguishable from magic, as the saying goes, even when I showed them behind the curtain. So, given their various inabilities to learn and the limited time I have on this earth, I thought it was best to dedicate myself to helping as many sufferers as possible.'

'How very noble of you.'

Delancey chuckled. 'We can't all help humanity reviewing West End plays and art exhibitions.'

Emet smiled wryly. 'I guess we can't. Was Jim Akachi-Rawlings one of these students?'

'You know he was, so why don't you ask your real question?'

'OK,' said Emet. 'Which camp of ineffectual learners did he fall into?'

Delancey could not contain his chuckle. 'Now, there's a loaded question I can't possibly answer. Apologies for the headline you'll never get to write.' He puffed on his cigarette. 'But I'm sure you can leap to your own conclusion on that.'

'Don't you rate Rawlings's work?'

'I've not been to one of his events – too many people for me. The most I've seen of them is a short video trailer, so I don't really have an opinion.'

'Given he's able to work with thousands of people at once, have you not thought about the same sort of format so you could help more people?' asked Emet.

'I'm working with very sick people and their deepest-seated troubles. We go to some extremely distressing places, so they need attending to too closely for the work to scale effectively.' Delancey took another draw. 'Besides, I don't think I'm one for the light show and the smoke machine and people up clapping and dancing in the aisles.'

'I thought you'd appreciate a good showman?' Emet asked, looking up at Houdini.

'I do when the interest they generate emanates from real stakes and not just from the confidence and patter that people mistake for charisma.'

Emet grinned, feeling like he'd found another sore point. 'Surely the financial allure of working with many at a time is strong?'

'You think I do this for money?'

'According to Allegra Baxenden, you charged half a million pounds for your few hours with her,' replied Emet. 'I think most would agree that's the pricing structure of somebody doing something for the money.'

'I can understand that superficial read of the situation, but I feel it's unidimensional. How often do we really know the degree to which somebody's motivation for doing something is purely financial and why do we selectively care about it? Collectively, society's not angry at menial workers for doing their jobs purely for the money because they have no real excess. It's only the high earners the masses judge that way because they have what some deem to be excess, and even that is selective. I hear that some of the athletes of today make comparable money. Nobody cares as long as they're performing well. Some film stars make tens of millions per picture. Nobody is angry at them despite the quality of the so-called *movies* they put out now, or cares about whether they made them purely for the payday.

Conventional cancer treatments, although free at the point of service for many, cost tens to hundreds of thousands, covered by taxpayer money. They're administered by teams of professionals with unknown, probably varying levels of love and commitment to any individual case, yes?'

Emet nodded.

'The treatment costs whether it works or not. The work I do with people, you may have heard, doesn't, and apart from feeling a little under the weather for a few days afterwards, doesn't come with a vast array of dangerous side effects. My clients only pay if there is a significant reduction in their cancerous symptoms, which thankfully there often is. I don't know of many professions that offer such deals. The regular tax-supported treatments are still available to my clients. I don't deter people from them. I'm not denying anybody anything, I'm purely offering a highly effective supplement or, if people wish to forego the conventional, an alternative.'

'And what about those who can't afford your no-win, no-fee fee?' asked Emet.

Delancey shrugged. 'The footballer doesn't play for the team who can't afford them. The movie star doesn't star in a budgetless film. The NHS doesn't give you the most effective treatment if they deem it to be too expensive. These are the ways of the world, Emet. I didn't create them. Would you do your job for free?'

The journalist locked his gaze onto his interviewee. 'The pieces that expose real danger to the world? Happily.'

'How very noble of you,' replied Delancey, smiling ironically. 'Maybe one day, your example will inspire such an act of philanthropy from me.'

Emet watched as his host stubbed out the last of his cigarette. How he craved one now. 'We've gotten all back to front here. Tell me about Delancey O'Shea. Where are you from and what road led you to destination Cancer Man?'

CHAPTER 39

Delancey sat back and surveyed his interviewer's lightened tone. 'There's not much to tell, really. I grew up in West Ireland in a tiny village that had only one road out that, for some reason, people seldom used. At my first opportunity, I left to travel the world, to see what else it had to offer.'

'What's your village called?' asked Emet.

'It *was* called Kilcairgnan.'

'Has it changed its name?'

'No. It doesn't exist anymore,' Delancey answered. 'Shortly after I left, the village was abandoned for the building of a reservoir nearby. It's one of Ireland's so called "ghost villages".'

'Where did your family go?'

'It was just my mother. She moved a few villages over but passed a couple of years later. Breast cancer, fully treated.' Delancey stared at his extinguished cigarette. 'Ripping somebody away from everything they know can cause profound trauma.'

Emet set down all of his hostility for a moment. 'I'm sorry for your loss.'

'Thank you,' said Delancey, lifting his gaze back to his interviewer. 'It's OK. It was a long time ago.'

'Regardless. Some pains persist,' said Emet wistfully.

'They do.'

The two sat in silence for a long moment. 'So, where did you travel?'

'It would be quicker to list where I didn't, but everywhere I went I sought out some sort of catharsis. Meditation in Nepal. Shamans and their potions in the rainforest. Hypnosis at multiple schools across the globe. I even studied a little with a descendent of Franz Mesmer himself, and also with an individual many consider to be the greatest hypnotist alive. And do you know what I came away with? Next to nothing. A bag of psycholinguistic tools that were meant to be able to fundamentally change what goes on inside of us, to fix what ails us, but that were capable of nothing more than soothing suffering momentarily. What's worse, over the long term, the temporary soothing actually makes people worse. If improvement is possible but I can't hold on to it or take it all the way, what is wrong with *me?* And that's when it dawned on me.'

'What did?' asked Emet.

'That *I* was the problem. A little breathing trick here or a reframe of a thought there, what's that going to do? It's like somebody clinging onto the side of the Titanic, paddling with their free arm, thinking they could steer away from the imminent iceberg. In our minds and hearts, Titanic and everything about it, from its rivets to its ballroom to its captain, only ever had one destiny: to sink. And we operate the same way with our own identities. I realised that our entire life experience, the way we perceive and create our reality, the sum total of everything about us brings us to this apex of suffering. It is part and parcel of who we are, and that is why these little tools seldom change anything, and definitely not over a short period. We don't need to change our breathing; we need to change who it is that breathes. We don't need to reframe the thought; we need to rebirth the thinker. The fact of the matter is that, based on the results in our life at that point in time, we are not good enough and the only thing positive about the person who got us to that point is that, by some miracle, they realised it. That suffering, that turmoil, that despair, they are the screams of a soul that wants one thing.'

Emet leaned forward. 'And that is?'

Delancey took a fresh cigarette from his holder. 'It wants to die. The person, deep down, wants oblivion. That's why they generate these illnesses. They are the protracted suicide attempts of people too cowardly to change or to kill themselves.'

His jaw wanted to fall open and his head wanted to shake, but Emet locked his impulses down. He knew that the best thing he could do was to let Delancey speak into the dictaphone, continuing to knot his own digital noose.

'And I recognised that in myself. My despair. My desperation. My cowardice. And it was then and there that I set about changing myself, taking parts of the methods I'd studied and applying them beyond my thoughts and behaviours to my very identity. Delancey O'Shea needed to escape the straitjacket of his old self, his previous life. I had to kill him to be reborn, psychologically and spiritually speaking.'

'And how do you psychologically and spiritually kill and rebirth yourself?' asked Emet, fishing for more explanation.

'Physically, you do it by depriving yourself of something vital or administering some sort of force on yourself that is beyond your capacity to tolerate,' replied Delancey. 'You hang yourself, or you slit your wrists, or you jump off something, et cetera. It's not all that different psychospiritually. You subject yourself to the most suffocating, sharpest, most bone-crushing psychospiritual force that lurks in your psyche until it can tolerate no more, until *you* are gone.'

'And what are these forces?' asked Emet.

'They differ in specific make-up for everyone, but broadly speaking they are people's worst fears, just not in the way we tend to think of them. Heights and spiders and the dark aren't people's worst fears, they're just external concepts and objects they project them onto. People's worst fears are the destructive, violent, disgusting things they know about themselves deep down but refuse to accept or acknowledge with their full being.'

'Can you give me an example?'

Delancey thought on it for a moment. 'Beyond childhood when the hardwired fear of falling is necessary to prevent children that don't understand the dangers of it yet from doing it, people aren't scared of heights. They are petrified that falling would leave them forgotten because they have led utterly pathetic and unremarkable lives. They are terrified of their loved ones struggling in their absence because they have woefully underachieved and failed to provide adequately for them. They are aghast that the lives they've created depress them so much that they look at a deathly drop and some part of them craves it.'

Emet, as much as he wanted to keep Delancey talking by communicating as little as possible, couldn't hide his horrified surprise from his face.

'Bleak, I know, but I've worked with a lot of people along the years, and this is what I've witnessed.' Delancey puffed his cigarette. 'You heard about me through Rawlings, so it would be natural to assume this would be all about sunshine, rainbows, and positivity, but meaningful change doesn't happen without profound suffering, both as a motivation to instigate it and as a necessary by-product of the means of doing it. He is a life coach. He affirms the way people live, and therefore limits them within the confines of their identity. If I were to be provocative, which I have no intention of being, I would say I specialise more in destroying the confines of the identity and killing the life people lead for rebirth to emerge.' He leaned forward and flicked some expired ash into the ashtray. 'Maybe that makes me a death coach.'

Emet inwardly smiled as his host leaned back. That was a readymade headline if ever he'd heard one. 'That'd be quite the business card title.'

Delancey wryly smiled. 'That it would.'

'Not so good for business, though.'

The Irishman shrugged. 'Forgive the cliché, but it's quality rather than quantity. The truth is most people are too boring to want to spend time with. Wouldn't you rather attract people who see the absurdity of it all, the surrealism of life?'

'Like Dali?'

'Yes, or any of his contemporaries. The people of that era, the Surrealists, Houdini, they saw life for what it is.'

'And what's that?'

Delancey took a long draw on his cigarette, crossed one leg over the other, and leaned back. 'You're all question and no content, and there's no fun in that. What do *you* think life is?'

'This is an interview,' replied Emet. 'I'm predominantly meant to ask questions.'

'I don't think it is, Emet,' said Delancey, taking his cigarette out and watching its smoke circle upward into the air. 'I may not've done one before, but I've seen and heard enough to know this is no conventional interview. And I've answered plenty of questions. You can answer a few of mine now. What do you see life is?'

Emet drummed his fingers on his thigh. 'I don't know. That's a pretty broad question. I can't say I have some succinct global philosophy ready to pull out of my back pocket.'

Delancey watched on expectantly.

Emet examined the floor for a moment. 'Life is just our experience of the passage of time. It's neither good nor bad in itself. It's us and the people in our lives who make them what they are.'

'And are people good or bad?' asked Delancey.

Emet pursed his lips in thought. 'People are capable of being both, and very few are all one or the other.'

'And me?' asked Delancey.

Emet paused. 'You?'

'Be honest, Emet. You've heard how candid I've been, possibly even to my detriment with your recorder sat right there.'

Emet's eyes glanced at the red light on the recorder. *There's some great stuff in the bank. Fuck it.* 'You…I just keep having to ask myself what sort of man sells false hope for disgusting prices to cure a fatal disease? And you're clearly smart enough to know what you're doing. The only answer I can think of is that you're the worst of all the snake oil salesman I've ever come across.'

'All?' asked Delancey, appearing concerned. 'Have you made a habit of coming across frauds?'

'A few,' replied Emet.

Delancey tutted and took a deep breath. 'Snake oil actually had healing properties, you know. Not the sort those bombastic Americans became notorious for fraudulently flogging, though. Chinese railway workers brought oil from snakes native to their homeland over to America with them in the mid-eighteen hundreds, which they used for various maladies. After analysis decades later, it turns out that their snake oil contained high amounts of omegas and had genuine significant anti-inflammatory effects. But the locals began using oil from their own snakes – a completely different breed with no such benefits – and before long, travelling hucksters were peddling their sham concoctions wherever they could get away with it. The most famous of all was caught selling potions completely devoid of any snake oil whatsoever, even the ineffective kind. Feel free to look that up.'

Emet glared at his host.

'I'm not one of these travelling flimflammers, getting out of dodge time after time before the rubes figure out I've sold them some pack of lies. I've been here for years providing my services, raising no complaints. What can I do to show you I'm not what you think I am?'

Emet sat up straight. 'Extraordinary claims require extraordinary evidence. Where is the evidence for what you do?'

'You've seen my testimonials.'

'They're not evidence,' snapped back Emet. 'They're anecdotes from, essentially, anonymous sources who could be anybody.'

'These people didn't sign up for public scrutiny or to be lab rats,' said Delancey. 'They wanted to heal themselves, they did, and now they have every right to get on with their lives in peace. But how about the source you met? The one who was good enough to provide you with the medical records you presumably worship? Is that not evidence?'

'Who knows what that is,' replied Emet. 'It's unclear what treatment she was receiving at what point. Real evidence would require real scientifically controlled, double-blind studies.'

'Pah!' said Delancey, puffing his cheeks out. 'I have one life and I will not waste it trying to explain and justify my methods to inferior intellects who have spent decades failing where I've succeeded. It wouldn't matter what I showed them, the medics would still go to their graves with their double-blind studied chemo still fed into them, waiting for it to work. I know what I do works, as do my clients. That's enough for me.'

'But if your methods have the effects that you claim, aren't you robbing the world of something revolutionary by not having them verified by the trusted institutions that would proliferate them?'

'Word of mouth will get me there,' replied Delancey. 'It just needs a little more time. But we digress. What about if I could arrange for you to follow one of my clients in real-time as a case study to see their entire journey?'

'How would I know they aren't a stooge?'

'Emet, Emet, Emet,' said Delancey, shaking his head. 'I thought what I was saying before was bleak. Where does all the cynicism come from?'

Emet dead-eyed his host.

'How about you provide the client, then?'

'Pardon?' asked Emet, more out of surprise than having not heard the question.

'Find me a cancer patient, so you know they're not a stooge, and I'll work with them.' He saw no response forthcoming from the journalist. 'Hell, I'll even do it on the house. A success story in a paper of record isn't a bad word of mouth. What do you say?'

'I say...I wouldn't want to waste their precious time.'

Delancey nodded his head with an air of regret. 'Well, then, Emet. I don't see that there's anything left to say, not that this was ever really a conversation in the first place. You've turned down every opportunity to truly test your beliefs. You can go write your preconceived piece with a few juicy quotes from me and push it on the suggestible, who have no faculty to question it or think otherwise and will think and act on it as instructed. Proudly brainwashing the gullible; it's not all that dissimilar from what you think I do, really,' he concluded, sardonically smiling.

Emet put his hands either side of his backside and went to push against the chair to stand, but then stopped and thought. 'Show *me.*'

'Pardon me?' replied Delancey.

'If you don't treat cancer but resolve turmoil, show me.'

Delancey took a drag of his almost-spent cigarette. 'You have turmoil?'

'Doesn't everybody?'

The Irishman leaned forward, stubbed out his smoke, and grinned. 'Excellent. Let's play.'

CHAPTER 40

Back in the glass-sided room, Emet scrutinised the insects on *The Persistence of Memory* painting. Delancey reappeared in the room with something in his hand, drawing his attention.

'I'm well aware this is unconventional,' said the Irishman as he approached his interviewer, 'but given the extreme nature of the reactions some people have to facing their inner traumas, I find it safest for them that they minimise their movement potential with one of these.' He opened out the item in his hand, showing it to be a straitjacket.

Emet guffawed. 'Are you taking the piss?'

'I'm not,' replied Delancey soberly. 'A minority of people react violently to their internal experiences, flailing around and convulsing, and there's no telling if you'll be one of them. It would be best if you did. For your own good.'

'There's no way I'm putting that on,' stated Emet.

'You're not epileptic or prone to seizures or a sufferer of night terrors?'

'Nope.'

Delancey leaned towards the dictaphone. 'And you accept full responsibility for any musculoskeletal injury you sustain during our session as a result of not being secured into the seat and not having your limbs fastened to your body?'

'I do.'

'Last chance,' said Delancey, offering the jacket. 'It's a Houdini original.'

Emet shook his head. 'I don't feel the need to escape.'

Delancey grinned sceptically and folded the straitjacket back in half. 'Very well, then.'

He perched on his wheeled chair, set the garment aside, and rolled himself close to Emet. This was the first time, except in passing, the pair had been so close. The journalist was struck by the perfect symmetry of his host's face and the unique shade of blue of his eyes. He didn't think he'd ever seen that exact colour in another person's. 'Why so close?' asked Emet.

'When things get intense, I sometimes monitor the client's condition via the carotid artery in their neck,' replied Delancey. 'We are only wanting psychospiritual death, after all.'

Emet's awareness flashed to the pulse in his neck as it quickened. *You're getting inside your own head, you silly twat. Just breathe and relax. You have control.* 'Wouldn't it be better to hook people up to heart rate monitors like Rawlings does?'

Delancey's gaze burned into him, but a polite smile and calm tone accompanied it. 'I'm not familiar with exactly what Jimmy does, but unnecessary gadgets and gizmos are a significant part of humanity's alienation from themselves and others and, therefore, are part of the problem. It's one thing a car to take us a long distance quickly or film capturing a scene we could never have seen. It's another thing entirely using some contraption to do something I can see with my own eyes or feel with my own hands superiorly if I haven't dulled my senses through technological reliance. If I put some monitoring machine on you right now, your attention would flicker between its screen and yourself, but right now, your attention is only on my words and your quickening pulse, isn't it?'

'You think I can be that easily led?' asked Emet, now even more aware of the accelerating throb in his neck.

'I don't think so, Emet. I know so. I can see that artery there, thumping like a drum. And the more you resist what you think is me, the more it will race.'

Emet felt it hastening further but tried to give no sign he was paying it attention. 'What I think is you?'

'You're not resisting my words. That racing heart, that warmth, that shallowing of your breath, that's you resisting where you're worried you'll go if you follow them. All I can do is encourage you to walk deeper and deeper into the undergrowth, but you're the only one who knows the exact direction because you're the one who knows the destination, don't you?'

Emet's heart thumped against his ribcage. 'I don't know what you're talking about.'

A hint of a grin appeared on Delancey's face. 'I know you don't…consciously. Yet you chose to experience my method. And you chose to come back through to my session room with me. And you chose to sit in that client chair with me, and you're still sitting there right now. All of this because you know there's a place deep inside you daren't tread, you daren't even go near. You know it's there, and you're worried if you let your guard down for just a moment, like you do when you sleep sometimes…' Emet's breathing stalled, unbeknownst to him, but Delancey acknowledged it with a tiny nod. '…that you'll be submerged in that place that's worse for you than Hell.'

'What the fuck am I doing here?' Emet asked himself out loud before turning his attention to his host. 'You're the worst type of conman, and I don't need to experience your method to write my piece.' He pushed himself up to standing.

'You're so close, you have to run away, don't you?' said Delancey, drawing a scowl from his guest. 'But you're so close, you owe it to the part of yourself that brought you this far to see this through.'

'I'd say thanks for having me, but I'll leave the lying to you,' said Emet, before reaching back down to the arm of his chair for his dictaphone.

'Emet.'

The journalist looked back his host's way. He watched Delancey's mouth move, but nothing came out, and with each missing syllable it seemed to move slower and slower. *Why do my legs feel like that?* flashed through his mind, then everything faded to black.

CHAPTER 41

'Da?' he called as he closed the front door behind him. Silence greeted him. He set his backpack down in the hall and continued into the house. The kitchen uncharacteristically smelled of smoke. *Maw won't like that.* With no sign of life in any of the downstairs rooms, he slid open the patio door and headed out to the studio, the door of which was open. The aroma of menthol and tobacco greeted him. 'Da?' Usually, a mess of half-painted canvases, easels, oil paints, and sketch books, the place was bare. Panic swelled in him. *Fuck. Have we been robbed?* He opened one of the paint storage boxes. It was tidily full. Then he noticed an envelope on the table. 'My wife and my boy' it said in unmistakably florid handwriting. His heart sank as a nausea rose. He grabbed it off the table and pulled the letter out. Before he could read it, his father's red handwriting immediately began to run down the page, making it illegible, but just as quickly, it stopped and began to reverse as if somebody had hit the rewind button. As the letters became clearer, his horror intensified. He could sense the pressure on the rewind button of his experience, and he couldn't bear it. He gutturally screamed, forcing every cubic inch of air out of his lungs against it. The letters stopped clarifying and began to bleed again. Then, as if on a bullet train passing from outside into a black tunnel deep underground, the very air surrounding him squeezed him from every angle, ratcheting up as if the train was delving deeper into the earth. Forced to swallow his scream, the letters began to unblot. He clenched his eyes shut, the pressure in his head building as the now-silent scream refilled his lungs, ballooning against his consciousness. The air pressure against his face began to shape itself. His nose and mouth were free as the pressure melded around his cheeks, parts of it spreading upwards and away from each other. As it crawled up towards his eyes and began to pull at his clenched lids, he could feel it was no longer air against his face; it was fingers. He let out a blood-curdling shriek as he tried to rip them off his face, ripping the railing out of the wardrobe, ripping the cannula out of the hand, ripping away the hand on his collar bone, the change of acoustics of the shriek starting to register with him as he flailed around with his hands in front of him.

After a couple of frenzied seconds, Delancey tore himself away from Emet's thrashing arms, wheeling himself back to a safe distance. 'You're here, Emet,' he shouted through the shriek. 'You're at Laurel Canyon Manor with a man you care very little for. It was all in your head. You're completely unharmed.'

Emet snapped fully back to the room and immediately shut up, mortified at the sound he'd heard spilling from his mouth.

'Don't worry. I've heard much worse,' said Delancey. 'I think, in hindsight, we should have gone with the jacket,' he said with a crooked smile.

Still catching his breath, Emet desperately gasped at his host, 'What did you do to me? What did you give me?!'

'Give you?' asked Delancey. 'I gave you nothing other than a talking to, Emet.' He curiously peered down at his hand. 'It's actually you who gave me something.' He raised it, showing Emet a deep, bleeding scratch mark on the back of it. 'And you kept a little souvenir for yourself,' he said, nodding towards his interviewer's arm.

Emet's gaze shot to his shirt sleeve, which was blotched with dark red blood. He felt heat shoot up him, then once again, everything faded to black.

A distant voice bled into his awareness as the feelings of up and down at the same time baffled him. At the same time as the light rose like a hood of darkness was pulled from over his head, he felt his entire world tilting downwards. Then he felt a hand pressing his shirt against his hot, sticky back. Immediately he resisted against it, forcing himself back upright.

'Relax, Emet,' said Delancey, pulling his hand out and wheeling himself back.

'Get the fuck off me,' snapped Emet, trying to focus his eyes.

'You fainted. I was just leaning you forward to get some blood to your head.' He watched as his interviewer tried to force himself back to normal consciousness and positioned his hands on the arms of the chair to push himself up to standing. 'I'd give that a minute or two if I were you.'

As Emet tried to heave himself up, he felt his eyes roll and his legs flop. He aborted his attempt, sat himself back down, and closed his eyes. 'What…what the fuck did you do to me?'

'You're like a dog with a bone,' replied Delancey. 'I did nothing to you. You saw the blood on your shirt and you passed out. My man is bringing you another to change into.'

Emet gulped in a few deep breaths, feeling his whole body clammy as he chanced opening his eyes again, mentally ordering himself to lock his gaze away from his sleeve. 'I don't need anything from you.' He paused for a few seconds before cautiously pushing himself to his feet, Delancey watching on hawk-like as he straightened himself.

The butler arrived at the doorway carrying a fresh shirt in his hand. 'Are you sure?' asked Delancey. 'You don't want to catch a glimpse of that and flake out during your journey home.'

Emet glowered at his host. 'I'll survive.'

'Very well.' The Irishman wheeled himself towards the table where the dictaphone laid and went to pick it up.

'No!' barked Emet, trotting over and swiping it away. 'Don't touch that. You're not doing a thing with it.'

Delancey showed his palms to his guest. 'No funny business, I assure you. You can even check my sleeves if you like?'

Emet turned off his recorder, barely taking his eyes off his interviewee, whose face still wore an almost perpetual smirk as he pulled on sleeve up, then the other. As he pulled them both back down, through seamless sleight of hand appeared a cigarette. 'Well, maybe a bit of funny business. Are we calling it a day?'

'We're done,' said Emet.

Delancey nodded and approached his guest, extending a hand to shake. 'It's been...fun. We should do this again sometime.'

Emet dead-eyed his host and left the hand hanging.

Delancey retracted his hand and fished out his lighter. 'Would you let my man drive you to the station?'

'I'll call a taxi.'

Delancey sparked up. 'Very well. Feel free to make yourself at home while you wait.'

'I'll wait outside.'

'Yes,' replied Delancey, turning to survey the sun-drenched panorama. 'Some fresh air will be good for you,' he said before taking a long draw. 'If you change your mind, the door is always open.'

His legs feeling sturdy underneath him now, Emet dared take a step forward. It held, so he continued to walk past his host, disturbing a cloud of his menthol smoke. As he reached the patio door, Delancey called after him.

'Will you write about me?

Emet looked over his shoulder. 'I will.'

'How exciting,' said Delancey before taking another puff. 'I don't get out to the shops much. Will you send me a copy?'

Emet glowered, knowing he had all sorts of damning quotes but still incensed by his host's amused attitude. 'I will.'

'Top man. *Sláinte,* Emet.'

The journalist stepped outside and welcomed the fresh air against his clammy skin. As he walked over the sandy ground and sat on one of the benches facing out onto the valley, he organised his taxi.

'To the station?' asked the operator.

Emet peered back over his shoulder. He couldn't see whether Delancey was still there due to the reflections. 'No. To Maida Vale, London, please.' The journey would cost a small fortune that he may not be able to claim back fully, but he couldn't wait to be away from this place and, more importantly, this man.

After paying the taxi driver, he burst into his house, almost treading on some of the Blu-ray-containing envelopes on his doormat, ran upstairs, and began unbuttoning his stained shirt. He knew he possibly couldn't smell the blood on his sleeve, but the sour, metallic odour of it, real or otherwise, had knocked him queasy the entire hour-forty-five journey home, despite him having his eyes closed almost the entire time and not looking at it once. His desperate fingers struggled with the last of the body's buttons, so he yanked the shirt open, popping two of them off. He took a few deep breaths before easily unbuttoning the clean cuff, removed his shirt from that arm and his body, then he closed his eyes, took a few deeper breaths, and locked his gaze towards the newly bare arm, with which he reached for his bloodied cuff, where his fingers fumbled at the button. Too chaotic in their efforts, he couldn't undo it. After a couple more seconds, the nausea burgeoning, he abandoned trying and began yanking at the rest of the shirt, trying to use it to rip the cuff open. The more he tugged at it, the more it dug into his wrist – *please don't fucking break the skin* – until finally the cuff bust open and the sleeve was off. He grabbed the wardrobe door, tossed the bloodied shirt into a storage box at the back, closed the lid on it, and slammed the door before running to the bathroom, where he peeled off the rest of his clothes without looking at the potentially bloodstained arm, and turned the shower on full blast. The relief when the warm water hit his sticky arm was absolute, but still as he lathered up his hands with soap, he wouldn't look at the arm he was scrubbing or any of the water below, where he feared seeing a pink tinge as it vanished down the plughole.

After washing his entire body twice, focusing more than usual on the soles of his feet, he finally felt cleansed enough to get out. After drying off and grabbing an outfit out of the other side of his wardrobe, he pulled the dictaphone out of the trousers he wore pre-shower. *What did you do to me, you fucker?* He turned it on and pressed play. Listening to the start of the recording, he quickly forgot about finding out what had happened to him, happy as some of the outlandish remarks flooded back to him. *I've got you.*

CHAPTER 42

As he stepped up to the door, he raised his right hand towards its bell, examining his forearm closely for any remaining blood. *You moron. You nearly scrubbed your skin off in that shower. There's none of it left.* He paused with his finger lightly on the bell's button, closed his eyes, and took a few deep breaths before ringing it. He was relieved when its tone was pleasantly gentle; wind chime-esque. After a few moments, he heard footsteps approaching the other side of the door. Thoughts of blood and the suffocating tension of the past few hours were instantly wafted away by the fluttering throughout him. He heard the chain come off and the door opened. Skye beamed at him, her face even more dazzling than usual with small gemstones adorning her brow, forehead, and upper cheeks. He'd only ever seen images of people like this at festivals, never in real life, and his face showed it.

'You don't think I look silly, do you?' she asked, her smile having dampened.

He shook his head. 'No,' he said, entranced by her. 'I think you're the most beautiful thing I've ever seen.'

Her smile shone wider. 'Well, I guess you can come in, then.' As he stepped forward, she met him with a full, plump kiss on his lips, then ushered him in and chained the door up behind. 'Make yourself at home,' she said, welcoming him to walk along the short hall towards the mellow light ahead. He entered the living room-kitchen. The space was tight but unsurprisingly cosy, with soft yellow lamps and candles illuminating the windowless room, and an array of unmatching yet complimentary woolly cushions and knitted throws covering the squeezed-in two-seater sofa and chair. 'It's little, but it's home,' she said as she watched him survey the place.

'It's lovely,' he said as he soaked in the ambience. 'I hope you like pink,' he said as he passed her the bottle of rosé he was carrying.

'Pink. Red. White. The full spectrum of colours is welcome here, in case you couldn't tell,' she said as she gestured towards the technicoloured sofa. 'Thank you,' she said, kissing him as she took it from him. 'Ooo. A cork. The posh stuff. Sit yourself down. This'll just be a jiffy.'

He sat himself on the two-seater, nestling amongst the soft furnishings as she wandered over to the kitchen. As he scanned around the room, something felt missing. It took him a moment to realise what. 'Oh wow. No TV?'

'Nope,' she replied proudly. 'No TV, no smartphone, no social media.'

'Wow. What do you do with your life?'

'Live it,' she said with a mocking smile.

'Hmm. Novel. But really. What do you do?'

'What *don't* I do? I go for walks, I do yoga, I meditate, I journal, I sit in the quiet sometimes. I work a lot at the moment, so there's never enough time to do all the bits I want. I mean, I have a laptop if there's ever anything I hear about that I desperately want to watch, but it's gathering dust most of the time. A big screen there can just eat your life, you know?'

He snickered. 'Only too well.'

'How was your day?' she asked over her shoulder as she opened a drawer.

'I've had better, but now I'm here, so my day right now is pretty perfect,' he said with a genuine smile. 'How was yours?'

She grinned back his way as she picked two wine glasses from a cupboard. 'It was nice. Americanos and agony aunt sessions. I mean, my customers are lovely, I'm glad they feel so comfortable confiding in me.'

'You're a gentle soul. It's a good thing,' said Emet. 'Trust me. People keep shtum around me. I like it that way most of the time, but sometimes I look at people who like people and wish I could.'

'But I don't know what I can say to help them,' continued Skye with a shrug as she rummaged through the drawer. 'What do I know about market fluctuations or R and D of live glucose sensors? I don't even look at the temperature gauge on my steamer.' She stopped searching. 'These won't do it,' she mumbled to herself before turning to Emet. 'Hey. If you reach down the side of the sofa there – maybe look before you do – is there a craft knife there? Maybe under the top book and sheets?'

Emet leaned over the arm of the sofa, picked up the book and sheets and put them on the coffee table ahead of him, then went back a second time, coming up with the scalpel-like instrument. 'I haven't offended you already, have I?' he asked, feigning slitting his throat with the covered blade.

She grinned and walked his way. 'The night's young…but no, it's for the wine. No corkscrew and all the sharp knives are too big.'

He passed her it, breathing a pretend sigh of relief. 'Sometimes people just like to vent with absolutely no expectation that anything'll change. It's just a pressure release valve.'

She took the plastic lid off the knife, sunk it into the bottle's cork, and re-angled it before trying to pull the cork from the bottle. 'Yeh, I know. I just see how much they suffer, and I want to do something more than just temporarily relieve some pressure.' The cork popped.

'Hey. There's plenty of value in temporarily relieving some pressure.'

'Oh really?' she asked with a suggestive smirk.

'Really. But I meant the wine.'

A giggle exploded out of her as her cheeks reddened. 'Well, we can tell where my mind is,' she said as she spun to pour a glass.

'Great minds,' he replied with a cheeky grin.

She poured two generous glasses, walked over and sat beside him, and handed him one. 'To great minds and temporary relief,' she said with a flirtatious smile.

'Great minds and temporary relief.' He clinked it, keeping his eyes locked on hers, his face already feeling the fatigue of smiling as he took a sip. Apart from a little activity these past few weeks, those muscles were long out of shape.

She took an ample mouthful and adjusted her tone back more serious. 'What good is temporary?'

'It's better than nothing,' replied Emet. 'And sometimes it's all there is.'

'Are we talking about people's problems or the other thing?'

'I hope we're talking about people's problems or else I'm going to have to give myself a one-star review. "Emet Gordon: Better than nothing".'

Skye chuckled. 'So what, you don't believe that people can solve their problems?'

'They can solve problems, sure,' replied Emet. 'But few seem capable of solving *their* problems.'

She playfully slapped his arm. 'You don't mean that.'

'I wish I didn't. I know people that have solved superficial problems. Got a better job. Solved their R and D issues. Optimised all sorts of tasks and routines in their lives. But the deep stuff? The intangible characterological stuff? I've seldom seen it. It took my mum, a competent, dedicated woman, a decade to lose some weight because it was tied to her sense of self. It was *hers*. She knew what to do, she's told hundreds, maybe thousands of patients to do it, and yet she didn't for the longest time. And she's one of a tiny handful of people I can think of that *has* actually managed it.' He looked at the gorgeous woman sat across from him, nursing her wine, the wind slightly out of her sails. He recognised he shouldn't be trying to criticise her beliefs. She wasn't an assignment. 'Sorry. Maybe that's just my experience. Do you know people that have sorted their problems out, that have changed?'

'Tonnes!' replied Skye.

'Super. What? Like friends and family?'

She paused and pondered. 'Well, yes. Mostly friends,' she said doubtfully.

'Good. Good friends?'

'Yes. People I've met on a few seminars,' she said, sipping her wine.

Emet nodded along. 'Like The Leap?'

'Uhuh,' she replied, taking another sip. 'Don't you believe me?'

'I believe you,' he said. 'I just don't know how much I believe in people making major changes to their lives in a weekend, and I haven't seen it myself. And I guess for somebody like me, it's hard to believe without really seeing.'

She gazed down into her rosé, deciding how she felt about what he'd said. 'I get that. But I made a pretty major life change in a weekend.'

'Oh yeh?'

She sighed, tilted her head, gave him a disbelieving smirk, then set her glass aside on the table, leaned forward, set his glass aside, and kissed him. 'Not the fastest on the uptake for a journalist, are you, lightweight?' she joked as she pulled away.

'One sip and my brain's packed in. I told you I can't hack it,' he replied as he reached for his glass again and took a sip, their smiles perfect mirrors of each other's. 'You think you've changed in us meeting?'

'Of course,' she answered. 'You showed me somebody can like me for quirky little me. Do you know how much that lifted me? I don't know if I'd have ever left without that boost. It's been a long time since I've been confident enough to make big decisions about what I want. I barely even know anymore.'

He shook his head.

'What are you shaking your head for?'

'I just can't believe you were with somebody who didn't like *you*. You're five stars through and through. And I don't give those out willy-nilly. Check my back catalogue.'

'Thank you,' she said, laying her free hand on his. 'And sorry for taking us there.'

'It's not a problem.' Seeing that she'd like to change the subject, he looked to the table. 'What's this?' he said, leaning forward to the books and sheets he'd picked up while fetching the craft knife.

'Just some doodles. Us talking about that lecturer gave me an urge to dust off the old sketchbook.'

'May I?' he asked, resting his hand on its cover.

'They're not finished, but knock yourself out.'

He flipped open the cover to be immediately faced by an intricate illustration of a geometrically constructed flower made up from many smaller geometric flowers. 'You did this?!'

'It's just a doodle,' she said with a shrug. 'Nice and relaxing to do.'

'Relaxing? I think if I tried to recreate that, I'd have a brain aneurysm.' He scanned around its detail, then zoomed out to a wider perspective. 'That's very mesmeric.'

'Yeh. It's sort of a mandala. Some people stare at them to meditate and go into trances.'

Emet paused, his entire demeanour stiffening. 'Do you?'

'What? Use them for meditation?'

'Or to go into trances?'

'No. Well, not, like, properly,' she said. 'I get into a bit of a zone doing them and colouring them in, but not, like, a *trance* trance.'

He nodded for an age. 'Have you been into a *trance* trance? With the lifelike hallucinations they talk about?'

'Why do you ask?' she replied with a grin.

'No real reason,' he said. 'Just you mentioned you've been to a fair few of these seminars.' He flipped to the next page in the sketchbook, where another intricate pattern, somewhere between the geometric and the naturalistic, awaited. 'At The Leap, I played along with the visualisation exercises and what seemed like hypnotic work. People made out like they were almost transported to alternate realities or back or forwards in time, the hallucinations no different from the real. I was just wondering if you ever experienced anything like that.' He turned the page again and found another sketch; a stylised array of feathers that almost appeared to move like an optical illusion.

'I don't think so. I can sort of loosely picture things in my mind's eye but they're fleeting images,' she replied, watching him regarding her sketches. 'I think I've been in a few trances, but I remember nothing about what happened during them.'

'Then how do you know you were in them?'

'Because I closed my eyes, and when I opened them again, stretches of time had passed.'

'Hadn't you just fell asleep at some…monotonous…voice?' he asked, demonstrating with a mocking flat, slow tone of his own.

'I don't think so. The people I'd been doing the exercises with said I'd been speaking back to them. Even acting things out.' She examined his expression as he turned to look at her. 'I know, that's not *proof* proof. But I believed them. They didn't have any reason to lie. And apparently, some of the best results come from trances like that, when all the conscious defences are completely down.'

He nodded sceptically. 'And did you get good results?'

She considered his question. 'I know you don't buy it, but I think so. It's all a journey and it brought me somewhere good.' She gazed at her sketch. 'And you?'

'And me what?'

'You didn't have any of those real visions or lapses in time?'

He staunchly shook his head. 'No.' He flipped to another page. 'These are incredible.'

She smiled and shrank a little. 'They're just sketches. They're not even done.'

'But they're so good. You should be an illustrator or something with this talent.'

She shrugged. 'I don't know what I should be, but it's not real art. It doesn't mean anything. It doesn't move anyone beyond maybe giving them a nice feeling of the aesthetic. It doesn't stay with them.' She took a swig of her wine. 'Not like that piece in your living room with all the floating men. Where did you get that?'

He slid his fingers along the blank page beside the sketch as his gaze persisted on it. 'My dad left it to me. *Nullconda*, it's called.'

She rested her hand on his thigh. 'Well, that's a beautiful piece to leave. Gorgeous and full of meaning. Do you know who did it?'

'He did.'

'Wow,' she said, taken aback. 'Your dad was a talented man.'

'He was. He knew it too. That's him in it.'

'What? All those men?'

'Yep. He was definitely in the mood for a self-portrait that day.'

'Oh wow,' she replied, almost lost for words. She looked across and noticed that a blueness had descended over Emet. 'We don't have to talk about it if you don't want to.'

'No. It's OK.'

'What was his name?'

'Pierre.'

'No wonder he could paint,' she said with a smile. 'Was he an artist?'

'Yes, he was.' Emet paused. 'Doubly so.'

'How do you mean?'

Emet picked the sketchbook off the table, set it on his lap, and turned another page. 'Well, he painted for a living, just about. His thing was photorealism. He was like a human Xerox. But beyond taking commissions for portraits, he struggled. The scene didn't seem to care about his work, as good as it was. I'd sit in his studio with him for hours sometimes marvelling at what he could create, but he was never rewarded for it. He got more and more bitter that his work was never going to be appreciated or remembered.'

'So, he changed to Surrealism?'

'Something like that. Just we didn't know he had until the police turned up at our door.'

Skye squinted. 'What do you mean?'

'My dad got arrested for fraud. He'd been counterfeiting some of the old Surrealist artists, selling what he claimed to be undiscovered pieces of theirs under some art agent pseudonyms over in Europe.'

'No!' she gasped.

'I know. We'd known absolutely nothing about it. He'd kept those pieces hidden and his trips away, which he'd always done even before the fraud, were under the guise of selling his own pieces. He did four years in prison for selling a few million pounds worth of art.'

She covered her agape mouth.

'He didn't even like Surrealism. He thought it was pretentious shite, one of the modern art forms that gave art a bad name, that let artists blabber their pseudo-profundities and grandiloquences, or at least that's what he'd always said to us,' Emet continued. 'It was so crazy to hear recordings of him in court, talking about the form like it was the second coming, running off his own bullshit, artsy fartsy spiel to potential buyers with a perfect Southern English accent. He was bloody Glaswegian, even if he did like to play up his mum being Swiss when it suited him. The fucker could Xerox accents *and* paintings.'

She moved both of her hands to the back of her head. 'You can't be serious?'

'I know. It's madness, right? But do you know the craziest thing? You should have seen how happy he was while he was waiting for trial and when he first went to prison.'

She squinted. 'Why was he happy?'

'Because his real pieces went right up in value. Because now his work was being appreciated and his name'd be remembered.'

'Wow.'

'Yep.' He paused, taking stock of his own story. 'So yes, he was two types of artist: a painter and a con artist. He nearly destroyed our lives, getting sued left and right while he was inside. His painting sales covered most of it, but if my mum hadn't had such a good job, we'd have ended up out on the streets.'

'Jesus. Did she divorce him?'

He shook his head. 'She loved him so much. It was hard not to. He was such a charmer. So charismatic. He could sell pants to a nudist. The man could make anybody feel like a million dollars. When he got released, he came back home. It was impossible to stay angry at him. Which I was a little angry about, to be honest. Anyway, a few years later, he winds up with stage three lung cancer.'

'I'm so sorry,' she said, mortified.

'Don't be. He didn't die of it. Not really,' he replied. 'The conman got conned. Even though my mum is a top oncologist, he got it into his head that conventional treatment wasn't for him. He wouldn't let her go to appointments with him, he wouldn't let her suggest doctors or approaches, nothing. Through her down the years, we'd heard of lots of death and, even in successful treatment, suffering. He couldn't get past all that. So, one day I got home and *poof,*' Emet said, exploding his hands open, 'he was gone. All he'd left were a few paintings, a handful of clothes, his book collection on how to make friends and influence-slash-manipulate people, cos he was right into all that shit, and a note telling us he adored us but that he had to follow his intuition and get these alternative treatments, and that he'd be back when he was better. A year later, we received a letter from some assisted suicide clinic in Switzerland. The *treatments* had all failed and the cancer had gotten too much for him. The only thing that came home were his ashes, and all I have left of him now is that painting, *Nullconda,* you saw; a sort of Surrealist knockoff. We had to sell the few originals he'd left to keep the house again with more litigation he left in the middle of. I left my medicine degree to make some money to help.' He closed the sketchbook and stared through its cover to the centre of the earth. 'At least he'd've been happy. The prices of his originals skyrocketed.' Emet felt Skye squeeze his hand, and she laid her head in the delve of his neck and wrapped her arms around him. He felt something miniscule land on the skin by his collar, then realised what it was as it rolled down his top. 'Hey.' She partially picked her head up, keeping her eyes down trying to hide her tears, but her sniffle betrayed her. He gently lifted her chin and looked into her glassy eyes. 'Don't cry.'

Her expression quivered. 'But that's so, so sad. What he put you all through twice. I can't even begin to imagine.'

He shook his head, scrunching up his chin. 'I wouldn't advise trying. No good comes from thinking of it.' He raised his hands to her face and wiped away her tears. 'Sorry *I* took us there.'

She gently shook her head and gazed into his eyes. 'You have nothing to be sorry about.' She rested her hands on his face. 'There's nowhere I'd rather be.' She leaned towards him and gently kissed his lips. His hands slid from her cheeks round to the back of her head as he kissed her back, their bodies meeting as their kisses intensified.

Ring. The gentle doorbell sounded. 'Leave it,' she whispered as she broke away a little for air. 'It'll be Deliveroo at the wrong number.'

'OK,' he whispered before pulling her back his way for another kiss, only to be pushed down onto the sofa where she climbed on top of him. They smiled ear to ear at each other and continued.

Riiiiiiiing. They giggled under their breaths and continued to get hotter and heavier. *Bang bang bang.* Emet broke away. 'Do you want me to go get rid of them?' he whispered.

'No,' she whispered as she pressed a finger against his lips. 'They'll piss off any second,' she said before switching to his neck.

Bang bang bang bang bang. 'I know you're in there,' bellowed a voice from outside, making them both freeze. 'Answer the door, Skye!'

CHAPTER 43

Emet read her anxiety-riddled face and knew exactly who it must be. 'You don't have to do a fucking thing he says,' he whispered even quieter than before. He could see her mentally cycling through a million different options and outcomes, every single one of them negative. 'I can go tell him where to go if you want?'

'No!' she gasped at the faintest of volumes.

'I've travelled hours to speak to you,' said the voice, calmer now but still forceful. 'The least you can do is look me in the eye and speak to me for a few minutes.'

Her brow contorted, the anguish looking too much to bear as she craned her neck up and towards the hallway, then she climbed off him. 'I have to,' she mouthed apologetically before raking her hands through her hair to straighten it out a little and grabbing a cardigan off the chair. 'Don't worry. I just need to tell him it's done to his face.' She trotted off out of the room. Emet sat himself up and shifted over to the chair, which was marginally closer to the door. He heard it open. The flat's walls were so thin, he needn't have moved; every word carried.

'Thank you,' said the man at the door.

'It's OK,' said Skye.

'Can we maybe talk through more than a crack?'

'How are you?'

The man sighed. 'I've been better. You?'

'I'm OK,' she timidly replied.

'Only OK?' He hesitated. 'Why be here if it's only OK? Surely home is better? Better than one of these pokey flats that you're probably having to work every hour at the first crappy job you could find just to afford.'

'Because it's mine and I needed space,' she murmured.

'I gave you space, didn't I? Didn't I let you go on all those seminars, even though they didn't clarify a thing for you? I did, didn't I?' Emet didn't hear a response. 'Please can we not do this out here? After all we've been through, can't we be dignified and have a proper conversation?'

'I don't know what there is to say,' she replied. 'I'm sorry.'

'Don't be sorry, darling. Just give us the opportunity to talk properly. That's all I ask.' There was a momentary lull. 'At least can you undo the chain? So I don't feel like I'm talking through cell bars or I'm some door-to-door salesman?' Silence fell again. 'Come on. Please at least chat to me fully face to face. Don't you owe me that much?'

Emet heard her undo the chain and sat up straighter.

'Thank you,' her ex said. 'You look stellar.' No audible reply came. 'I tried to look good for you. To show you you're worth the effort. That *we're* worth the effort…Look, I know you've felt lost in yourself, I know you don't know what you want to do with yourself, but don't confuse feeling lost about all that for not having found something real here. I love you, Skye, and I know you think you've lost that feeling for me, but I'm convinced if you find your direction, if you let me help you find your direction, that you'll find that love's still there. You did love me, didn't you?'

'Of course I did,' she replied.

'Good. Feelings like that don't just disappear, especially when nobody's done anything major. They just get buried under the messes in our heads and our hearts.'

Whirring away in Emet's mind were some of the influence tactics Jim Akachi-Rawlings talked about after his outburst at the seminar: asking strings of questions you knew the answer was yes to to create an agreeable momentum, reminding them through gentle questions of commitments they've already made, and what he called "striding and guiding", where you would conversationally walk with somebody at their emotional pace and direction before subtly steering them elsewhere. This was all happening at the door.

'I get how coming away was a good idea. I know you never intended to hurt me, did you?'

'Of course I didn't,' she replied. 'I just…I…I don't know.'

'I know you don't, and that's OK. We all don't know sometimes,' he said, "striding" in Emet's mind. 'But right now, I know. I know you opened the door to me, I know you wanted to give me the opportunity to speak, and I know as I look into those amazing eyes of yours that I've looked into so many times down the years that there's still something in there for me. You still feel something for me, don't you?'

'Of course I do. I'm not some sort of sociopathic monster, Joss,' she replied.

'I know you're not. You're the furthest thing from one I've ever met. I've never met somebody as caring as you. I think that's why you did all this at arm's length, partly because you didn't want to hurt me. But partly because you didn't want it to be real. You had a fuzzy idea that maybe some space would help you figure some of your stuff out, but you didn't really want to end this. Can you look me in the eye and tell me that every single cell of your being wants us to be over?'

'Joss…it's not that simple.'

'I know it's not, because the answer is no, isn't it?'

'It's not that simple,' said Emet as he appeared in the hallway behind Skye, 'because barely anybody ever feels that sort of certainty about any life-changing decision, so you're using that against her.'

CHAPTER 44

'Who's this?' asked Joss to his distressed ex.

'A friend,' replied Emet curtly to the tall, sturdy, bearded man ahead of him.

Joss looked him up and down. 'Well, maybe this isn't a conversation for "a friend" to be involved in.'

'Ordinarily, I'd agree,' said Emet, 'but you've used every manipulative trick in the book and not let her get a word in edgewise.'

'What are you talking about "manipulative"?' said Joss. 'I think you need to mind your own fucking business.'

'Look, I've not known her long, but even I can tell she doesn't like conflict, so you must know that, and you know under pressure very few people find the words they want quickly,' said Emet. 'So you just asked her loads of closed leading and rhetorical questions and put words in her mouth. Or at least that's my impression. Is that accurate, Skye? You can tell me if I'm way off the mark. I honestly won't mind.'

She paused for a moment, looking between the two men and then to the floor. 'Pretty accurate,' she said.

'How sure are you?' Emet asked.

She looked at him and then Joss, keeping her gaze on him as she answered. 'Fairly sure.'

'Skye,' said Joss. 'I don't know what your deal is with whoever the fuck this is, but this is between you and me.'

'I think she gets some say in that too,' chimed in Emet. 'Would you like me to leave you two to talk, or would you like me to stay?'

'Please stay,' said Skye. Joss's defiant expression fell.

Skye took a few deep breaths, raised her hand to her heart, breathed a few more cycles as she felt its beat, and sighed as she turned to Joss. 'I'm so sorry, but I'm not in love with you anymore.' Her mouth and cheeks quivered as she struggled to push the words out. 'I didn't want to say it to your face, to see it hurt you, but maybe we both need it.'

Joss's face contorted. 'What? Because of *this* guy?'

Skye shook her head. 'No. I'd already left. I said I was still making my mind up, but really I just didn't know how to say it. I was a coward. I'm sorry.'

'So, after everything we've been through, that's it?' asked Joss. 'You just don't love me anymore? All the promises, all the plans, they just count for fuck all now?'

'I'm sorry,' she replied, shaking her head. 'We could go through everything we've ever said to each other, every promise, every plan, and see who did what and who kept what, but it won't make a difference to how I feel right now. I didn't set out for it to be this way, but it went this way. I'm sorry for my part in that.'

'For your part in that?' asked Joss. 'Your part in that?! You change your mind like the fucking wind, Skye. All this bullshit about finding yourself, all the visualisations and the affirmations and the meditations about becoming a better person, about finding your purpose, about manifesting a path for yourself. Well, you succeeded, whoever you are now. You're going straight to fucking Hell.'

'Hey,' said Emet, stepping forward so he was almost level with Skye. 'I think it's best you go now.'

'Fucking happily,' replied Joss, a furious smile on his face. He locked his gaze on Skye, the corners of his mouth curling down like he'd smelled something putrid. 'You let me tell *everybody* I love I was going to marry the woman I love. And now, what? You get to use some bullshit mind trick you learned at one of your shitty seminars to forgive yourself and convince yourself you're a good person? Or brainwash yourself that on some subconscious level this is good for us both?'

'Joss...' she said.

'I don't want to hear your sorries,' he said as he stepped back. 'I'm just glad that none of that airy fairy bullshit works and that you'll carry the guilt of what you did as you wander aimlessly through the rest of your pointless life.' Emet went to step past Skye, but she tugged at his sleeve, prompting Joss to chuckle. 'And there we go. She's your problem now. Enjoy it before she manifests another purpose off the words of the next self-help guru and you're not in it.' He gave them a double thumbs up. 'Live your fucking best lives.'

Skye trembled as she watched him storm away. Even as he vanished down the end of the corridor, she didn't budge.

Emet laid his hand on her shoulder and grasped the door handle. 'Shall I?' he asked. She snapped out of her stupor and nodded, triggering him to close the door. He surveyed her face, watching her come down from what had just gone on. 'I'm sorry if getting involved wasn't the right thing to—'

She threw her arms around him and squeezed him tight. 'No,' she said through her sniffles. 'I wouldn't have been able to get that stuff out if you hadn't helped. Thank you.' They held each other for a long while, savouring the warmth and the feeling of each other's hearts beating against one another, before peeling away a little. For the second time that night, he wiped away some of her tears. 'I must look a state.'

'No. Not at all,' he said. 'I know it's an insufficient question, but are you alright?'

She wiped her own face, precisely squeegeeing under her eyes to try tidying any running mascara. 'I'll survive,' she said, trying to stop her sniffles.

'Would you like me to leave you to...I dunno...leave you to it so you can rest or whatever you need to do?'

She adamantly shook her head. 'Stay.'

'Are you sure?'

She gently rested her hands around his nape and drew him close, pressing her plump lips softly against his. Then every curve of her melded itself against him as she pulled him back for a barrage of passionate, breathless kisses.

CHAPTER 45

He wasn't looking forward to her skin leaving his. Since she kissed him last night, they had been in almost constant contact; their lips, their hands all over each other's bodies, their most intimate parts. They slept embraced despite the warm night, they showered together, and their fingers had been interlinked ever since they left her flat. His eyes were shattered, but his body felt the lightness of euphoria apart from this mild separation pang that had begun to build. It was daft. He knew he'd see her that night or tomorrow. It had just been pure bliss.

Her fingers lightly pulled against his. 'You got a minute more?' After he nodded, she steered him into the newsagent's nearest his office and opened a fridge. 'I'm parched,' she said, pulling out a bottle of water.

'I'm not surprised,' he replied with a proud, cheeky grin.

'You must be too,' she said, reaching into the bottom of the fridge and coming up with a much-larger two litre bottle, getting a chuckle out of him.

'I'll be alright with the regular, thanks.'

She swapped the oversized one for a regular and went to the till. 'Do you want anything else?'

His eyes habitually flickered towards the cigarette cabinet behind the cashier, its products hidden behind an opaque roll-down cover, then straight back to her. 'Not a thing.'

She grinned, turned and paid, and the pair left, cracking open their bottles. After a few mouthfuls and a few more paces hand in hand, they were outside his office. He let go of her fingers and paused, searching for the words he wanted. She cut him short, caressing the back of his hair and initiating a passionate cluster of kisses. When they broke away, she smiled as he began to search again. 'Save your words for the page today. I'll message you later when I know if I can do tonight, but it'll probably be tomorrow.'

As he went to reply, she playfully pressed her forefinger against his lips. 'For the page.' He grinned, then moved her finger aside and kissed her again. They backed away from one another, their eyes reluctant to part. She blew him a kiss and turned it into a wave. 'Go on. Get yourself to work, lightweight.'

'You tell him.'

Emet looked right and found Felix replying to her.

'Hopefully you have more success persuading him than I do,' the editor continued.

'And here we go,' Emet said to them both before waving Skye's way. 'See you soon,' he said semi-awkwardly before turning to fall into stride with his boss.

As they entered the building, Felix turned to Emet. 'So, how was it?'

'Fucking hell, Fee. We'll save those questions for the tabloids, shall we?'

Felix shook his head. 'Not your night, you plonker. Your interview yesterday. You gave me nothing in your text.'

'Ah,' replied Emet, reddening a little. 'Sorry. It was…I'll save it for the page. Can you hang on a few more hours?'

'Is it worth the wait?'

Emet pulled his dictaphone from his pocket and jiggled it his boss' way. 'You can have a sneak preview straight from the horse's mouth if you like?'

'It's OK. That smile on your face makes me want to wait for the full shebang.' The duo entered an elevator, the editor selecting their floor before catching his junior's eye in the mirrored wall. 'Look at you, you lovesick pup.'

Emet caught his own reflection, noticing the lightness in his own face even though his smile had damped a little with attention being brought to it.

'Hey, no,' said Felix, noticing Emet's smile losing some of its shine as the elevator slowed. 'It's a beautiful thing to see. You enjoy every blissful moment of it.'

Some warmth returned to Emet's smile as he nodded gratefully at his boss' reflection as the elevator stopped.

'And besides,' continued Felix as the doors opened, 'people think it's the permanently snarling dogs that have the worst bites. Their jaws are too tight to work properly, and what are they protecting in their miserable lives, anyway?' He turned to his journalist as they left the elevator. 'There's no stronger bite than from a happy dog, knowing it has something worth fighting for.'

Emet smiled bemusedly his boss' way.

'Go fucking get 'em, Fido.'

Emet nodded and the two peeled away from each other. He picked a desk, nodded over at Louise, who he was convinced had been evil-eyeing him ever since he bummed the cigarette from her, then logged on. After opening a new document, he plugged his earphones into his dictaphone, cracked his knuckles, pressed play, set his fingers on his keyboard, and smiled to himself. *Woof fucking woof.*

CHAPTER 46

I should know better. My mother is a consultant oncologist. For decades I have seen the burden her work places on her, and despite her utmost professionalism, skill, grace, and resilience, the toll it has taken on her at times. It is a testament to her and all those like her that they voluntarily bear that load, making tremendous sacrifices in their own lives and to their own health, without crumbling. I have heard many an anonymised story about the suffering of her patients and their loved ones. Even some of the success stories would make your heart sink.

I have some cobweb-covered rudimentary knowledge of cancer from the first few years of an abandoned medicine degree. Decades deep in the field, Mother is definitely made of tougher stuff than I. And then there is the most visceral of my knowledges of the disease: I lost my father to it a decade ago; a subject so raw my fingers prickle just writing those words.

I should know better, but I don't. For years, at the first sign of stress, my go-to crutch has been that long, thin one monikered the 'cancer stick'; the most smothering of all comfort blankets: the cigarette. I know the numbers too: one in two of us will have cancer during our lifetimes, four in ten cancers are preventable, nineteen percent of cancers are caused by tobacco smoke (a significant chunk of these for non-smokers), and twenty-seven percent of all cancer deaths are caused by it. And yet, I hadn't kicked the habit...until yesterday. Some use hypnosis to attach feelings of extreme nausea to the act of smoking, helping them quit. While hypnosis and nausea played a role in me stubbing out my habit, it was far from the common one.

I met with a man who claims to use a form of hypnosis to help people cure themselves of their self-destructive habits, but not smoking. No – he claims he can help them cure the specific thought and feeling patterns that cause cancer itself. In fact, he guarantees clients will be cancer free within a month of working with him, all while puffing on a menthol cigarette of his own. I met with a man who calls himself "The Cancer Man". And I will never smoke again.

Most cancer is treated in some form of medical facility: diagnoses and prognoses are made and treatment strategies are formulated in a doctor's office, tumours are extracted in surgical theatres, radiotherapy is administered in lead-shielded suites, chemo and immunotherapy is delivered intravenously in day units or via tablets from the pharmacy. These treatments are carried out by medical professionals with accredited training that took anything from three to seven years of full-time, scientifically based study to complete, and that doesn't account for their ongoing professional development. Even the person filling your prescriptions took a minimum of four years training to put the correct tablets in the correct sized bottle. And we are fortunate that when the tragedy of cancer befalls us in this country, the vast majority of treatment is covered by the NHS, costing us nothing at the point of service, and meaning our potentially fatal illness won't put us and our loved ones in a financial grave too. Half of all people diagnosed and treated by the health system survive ten years or more. That is how most cancer is treated. Most.

The figures on how many people use "alternative medicine" – practices like homeopathy, crystal healing, alkaline living, and reiki that are aimed at healing despite lacking biological plausibility, testability, repeatability, or evidence from clinical trials – don't reliably exist. Many of those using alternative methods are diagnosed by the mainstream system and use them as a somewhat harmless adjunct to their tried-and-tested treatments. But beyond diagnosis some abandon mainstream treatment or forego it altogether and rely solely on the unproven alternatives. Quackery has lurked in society's shadows since modern medicine began its major developments in the 1800s with the likes of Louis Pasteur and Florence Nightingale. I just didn't realise until a few weeks ago how close those shadows are to society's spotlights.

If you've flicked past an infomercial during the past few years, the odds are you've been momentarily blinded by the gleaming, winning smile of Jim Akachi-Rawlings, motivational guru extraordinaire. Over the last three decades, self-help, personal development, and life coaching have boomed, creating a multibillion-pound industry worldwide. The self-help and actualisation movement, or SHAM for short, an acronym coined by Steve Salerno in his excellent book by the same name, promises to help you make yourself happier, wealthier, and healthier through the power of your mind with secret methods detailed in its books, audio courses, seminars, and personal coaching. For just £795 (early bird), you can attend a weekend course and learn the secrets of creating a more abundant life forever...along with eight thousand other people. Then there are more secrets for taking it all to the next level for the bargain price of £3995 (early bird) at a five-day tropical resort. Then there's the ongoing video-call coaching for £199 per month minimum (early bird) with one of Jim's accredited coaches – the J.A.R.Heads, as they're affectionately referred to – for those that truly want to be held accountable for their development. I could go on, but I just wrote a word that brings me back to my original point: accredited. Who accredits the JARHeads? Jim. Who accredited Jim? Nobody. He openly says so himself. He barely scraped out of high school. He jumped across a gap between buildings to save a young girl's life (laudable) and that spawned a career of telling hundreds of thousands, probably millions of people how to live "better" lives. Jim is not alone. SHAM is mostly led by charismatic figures with no traditionally recognised training or qualifications to do what they do, who train and accredit others in their "methods", "systems", and "techniques" on expensive weekend and week-long courses. Similar is true in the "alternative medicine" space, although some of these "practitioners" do study full time for years at self-proclaimed "universities" for fees matching and sometimes exceeding those of real universities. The man I met claims to "help people resolve their most destructive inner turmoils, which are acute drivers of disease. And ninety-five percent of the time, resolving these turmoils reverses their cancer processes". He is totally unaccredited, has no university education, and operates in the greyest of all the shadows in which the SHAM, "alternative medicine", and wellness industries operate. He is also just one step removed from King JARHead himself, who he once briefly tutored in his methods before Rawlings leapt back to what senses he had and realised that some things are too dark for cheesy infomercials and the bright lights of packed-out arenas. The man I met is called Delancey O'Shea. He happily courts the nickname "The Cancer Man".

A far cry from the white coats, sterile surroundings, and technological tools usually adorning a cancer treatment centre, Delancey meets me, like he does his patients (who he refers to as "coaching clients"), donning an embellished evening jacket at his roaring-twenties-themed home office based out of his manor house in the home counties. Everything from the décor to the Surrealist art to the shrines to old-time magician Harry Houdini makes it feel like you're dreaming you're at a Vaudeville stage hypnotist's attraction where you'll leave having crowed like a rooster and having unknowingly handed over your valuables. The odd dream takes its first nightmarish turn when Delancey sparks up, with his deft swirling and circling of smoke possibly a part of his trance induction. At least he is kind enough to offer me one.

Generally, SHAMers are renowned for their winning smiles. They emit an aura of warm friendliness and extreme positivity. While a grin of some variety rarely leaves my host's face, I'm rarely set at ease by it. The hyperattentive, blink-shy gaze of his Arctic blue eyes adds to my apprehension, giving the illusion that he knows much more about me than anybody ever has at first glance. It's a trick used by the deftest of cold readers, that knowing look, to impart a sense of mystical power and secret knowledge, and he's exceptional at it. I can see how it sways people. But then he makes a claim of being able to detect an insight that breaks the illusion for me. Citing hyperosmia – a rare, heightened sensitivity to smell – he claims to be able to sniff out the presence of cancer. "What? Dogs can be trained to sniff out tumours, but I can't? The blind learn to echolocate and read tiny dimples on paper, sommeliers learn to detect scent notes from fruit and the barrels they ferment in. With all my dealings with cancer over the last decade, isn't it feasible that I could become a sort of tumour sommelier?"

Delancey informs me that I'm cancer free. That's usually welcome news, but in this instance, the messenger has changed its meaning. But at least he generously all-cleared me for free; a privilege given that a few hours work with him usually costs somebody with cancer £500,000, and his waiting list is as long as "the hankie up a magician's sleeve". He also says his medicine-less approach offers a unique benefit. "The work I do with people, apart from making them feel a little under the weather for a few days afterwards, doesn't come with a vast array of dangerous side effects."

I ask him about the affordability of his fee. "The footballer doesn't play for the team who can't afford them. The movie star doesn't star in a budgetless film. The NHS doesn't give you the most effective treatment if they deem it to be too expensive. These are the ways of the world. I didn't create them."

But one claim about his fee, substantiated by one of his clients, that I can't make sense of, is a money-back guarantee. "Conventional treatments cost in the region of tens to hundreds of thousands, covered by taxpayer money... The treatment costs whether it works or not... My clients only pay if there is a significant reduction in their cancerous symptoms, which thankfully there often is." He claims ninety-five percent of his clients resolve their own cancers; a figure unheard of for any treatment modality.

We move on to speak about the exact nature of his work. "I never claimed to be able to cure cancer," he continues. "I help people resolve their most destructive inner turmoils, which are acute drivers of disease. And ninety-five percent of the time, resolving these turmoils reverses the cancer processes." I point out that this seems to be dodging legal liability whilst implying strong efficacy. "Tell me, do cancer surgeons, the ones who use scalpels and lasers to cut malignant tissue out of their *patients,* claim to cure cancer? Even those who literally remove cancerous cells don't claim to be doing curative work. None of the vast array of treatments used in conjunction with surgery are claimed to be curative. Billions of pounds Sterling and of every other currency are spent every year on treatment, none of it is spent on cure. And they work directly on cancer. I work on psychological trauma; spiritual sickness."

Motivated to move beyond the grief of his own mother's death from cancer, he travelled the world to learn from masters of various spiritual and psychological techniques, coming away with "next to nothing", with methods "capable of nothing more than quelling our suffering in the moment". The central tenet of his own practice then dawned on him, "that *I* was the problem. A little breathing trick here or a reframe of a thought there. What's that going to do? It's like somebody clinging onto the side of the Titanic, paddling with their free arm, thinking they can steer away from the imminent iceberg. Titanic and everything about it, from its rivets to its ballroom to its captain, only ever had one destiny: to sink. And in our mind and hearts, we operate the same way. I realised that our entire life experience, the way we perceive and create our reality, the sum total of everything about us brings us to this apex of suffering. It is part and parcel of who we are, and that is why these little tools seldom change anything." He postulates we don't need to change our breathing or our thoughts; we need to change the core of us. If the conversation hadn't been enveloped by a dark mist so far, it now became pitch black. "The fact of the matter is that, based on the results in our life at that point in time, we are not good enough and the only thing positive about the person who got us to that point is that, by some miracle, they realise it. That suffering, that turmoil, that despair, they are the screams of a soul that wants one thing. It wants to die. The person, deep down, wants oblivion." O'Shea says that in realising this, he found his catharsis, splicing some of the tools he had learned into this philosophy and applying it to his "very identity". "I had to kill him to be reborn, psychologically and spiritually speaking." Causing what he calls "psychospiritual death" apparently isn't that different from the real thing. "You subject yourself to the most suffocating, sharpest, most bone-crushing psychospiritual force that lurks in your psyche until it can tolerate no more, until *you* are gone." These forces are people's worst fears, but not the common fears of creatures or heights most would cite. "People aren't scared of heights. They are petrified that falling would leave them forgotten because they have led utterly pathetic and unremarkable lives. They are terrified of their loved ones struggling in their absence because they have woefully underachieved and failed to provide adequately for them. They are aghast that the lives they've created depress them so much that they look at a deathly drop and some part of them craves it." This is a stark point of contrast to the usual philosophy of the SHAMers like Jim Akachi-Rawlings, who wholesale adopt more optimistic and humanistic perspectives, and who O'Shea doesn't rate the work of where deep change is required. "Meaningful change doesn't happen without profound suffering, both as a motivation to do something and as a necessary by-product of the means of doing it. Jim is a life coach. He affirms the way people live, and therefore limits them within the confines of their identity. I specialise more in destroying the confines of the identity and killing the life people lead...for rebirth to emerge. Maybe that makes me a death coach." I'll return to this remark.

When asked for evidence that his methods – which he refuses to pin down with a label, but most closely sound like a nightmare-inducing hypnosis – work, he points to video testimonials on his website, who only represent a small fraction of those he claims to have helped with a ninety-five percent success rate down the last decade. Only one of those individuals gave their full identity and was able to be tracked down for interview. "These people didn't sign up for public scrutiny or to be lab rats," says O'Shea. "They wanted to heal themselves, they did, and now they have every right to get on with their lives in peace." But is that really the extraordinary evidence required to verify such an extraordinary claim? If his methods are so world-shakingly revolutionary, shouldn't they be subjected to rigorous scientific scrutiny? He scoffs at the idea. "I have one life and I will not waste it trying to explain and justify my methods to inferior intellects who have spent decades failing where I have succeeded. I know what I do works, as do my clients. That's enough for me."

Where the lack of evidence is a red flag large enough to spot from outer space that would deter all but the most desperate individuals to engage in his service, it is not the only item of concern. Even if, and it is a preposterously large *if* O'Shea could do what he purports to do, trusting a man who works with people with cancer who also gleefully floats the idea he may be best labelled a "death coach" whilst puffing away on the most common carcinogen known to man seems unwise. Qualified people helpers like doctors and psychologists, whilst occasionally utilising humour, generally act with solemnity, recognising the gravity of the situations in which they deal. SHAMers plaster on enthusiasm with a trowel partly because they are joyful extroverts, partly because it genuinely helps lift their clients, and partly because lifting the corners of one's mouth makes it easier to keep lifting the seminar and session fees from their wallets. Delancey O'Shea's demeanour is altogether different. For somebody operating so closely to life and death stakes, although he denies this, saying that he doesn't work with cancer and doesn't encourage people to discontinue or avoid conventional treatment, he has the air of a man not taking any of this seriously. His almost ever-present grin, rather than seeming purposefully uplifting or happy for you, is sardonic, like he is smirking at a joke you aren't in on, probably about you. Absent is the warm bedside manner of a good medic or the unconditional positive regard of a psychotherapist. "The truth is most people are too boring to want to spend time with," he says when asked about why he doesn't work with more people given the power he claims his method has, indicative of a general disdain towards others. His probable motivation for this is hinted at during a passage of our conversation about Jim Akachi-Rawlings and the rest of the class of trainee Cancer Men he discontinued teaching. "To these people, my methods were sufficiently advanced as to be indistinguishable from magic". Delancey O'Shea has a superiority complex. He is not dealing with fellow human beings. He is a cat toying with mice, as one probably must be to sell what he does. But whilst not as smart as he believes he is, he is clearly still an intelligent man. Despite his lack of formal education, his verbal dexterity and the topics he can effortlessly float between demonstrate this.

And here we reach the crux of it. O'Shea should know better. He *does* know better. He is intelligent enough to know exactly what game he is playing and what the stakes are. He is even fascinated with the era synonymous with it. "The people of that era saw this world for what it is," he says of the early 1900s, the period when the term "snake oil salesman" was coined after quacks sold it fraudulently as an elixir in the Wild West for decades, with the most notorious of them being brought to the first instance of justice for it in 1916. The turn of the century and the scientific revolutions it saw brought in an age of debunking, with one of its most notable practitioners being the subject of O'Shea's fandom (and possibly his fashion sense), Harry Houdini. Primarily famous for his magic and escape artistry, Houdini was also a fervent debunker, having written books on the matter and testified at Congress in attempt to pass a bill that would ban fortune telling and spiritualism, acts he had warred bitterly with for years, who he claimed fraudulently and unscrupulously made fortunes delivering "messages from beyond the grave" to vulnerable, grieving relatives. It was shortly after the rejection of the bill that Houdini died, many believing caused by a blow to the abdomen by a man linked to the very spiritualist community he had been trying to drive out of business. O'Shea knows exactly what charlatanism is and how it can fall between the cracks of the law.

In the mind of a vulnerable person in a desperate situation, bad ideas that prevent or divert resources away from the proper treatment of cancer are cancers themselves, and false hope is the ultimate carcinogen puffed out by the charlatans that catalyse their unbridled, lethal growth.

I know better now, so I've stopped smoking and spreading my poison for good. Please do too, Delancey O'Shea. Or better yet, step up your Houdini imitation and just disappear.

Felix turned his eyes away from his screen.

'What do you reckon?' asked Emet.

Felix removed his glasses and gave them a wipe as he cocked his head to one side. 'I'll have to get legal to give it the once over and maybe have you trim some of the sharp, libellous edges off, but I like it, Em. It's a powerful piece. I dare say *meaty*. It shows him for what he really is.'

'I hope so.'

'You got a title for it?'

Emet nodded. "The Death Coach: He claims he can cure cancer. Would you trust your life with him?"

CHAPTER 47

The cursor blinked in the browser's empty address box. His fingers eagerly typed in 'thecancerman.com', bringing up Delancey's homepage. He peered disappointedly into the chilling blue eyes on the video's thumbnail. And then he noticed movement. The m at the end of .com disappeared. Then the o. The web address deleted itself letter by letter, each faster than the last. Then the text of the rest of the page did the same, and as it vanished, the thumbnail image started peeling away, pixel by pixel. With the rest having digitally disintegrated, Delancey's eyes disappeared into their own pupils, leaving nothing but blackness. An ecstatic grin spread across Emet's face. There was only one way to celebrate. He pulled out a fresh packet of cigarettes, lit one, and took a long, indulgent drag before blowing a circle of smoke at the black screen. 'Good riddance,' he said, flicking a few ashes into the empty ashtray by the keyboard. As he watched his smoke disappear into nothingness and caught his reflection in the laptop screen's blackness, he took another drag and sighed. *Gone and fucking forgotten.* He flicked some more ash down, only to notice a mound of it a couple of inches high. He looked back at the monitor. White letters began to type themselves. 'You can't delete it all that easily, sonny.' He slammed the lid down, the gust of air from it blowing the ashes up into his face. With a hacking, desperate cough, he jerked himself awake, spluttering for a few seconds afterwards. The shrill alarm of the fully lit sunrise clock screeched his way, triggering him to scramble across to silence it. As he caught his breath, grateful that at least his nightmare had let him sleep the full duration, he reached for his phone.

SKYE
Good luck with the big story today! See you tonight lightweight xxxxx

After replying to her, he propped one of his pillows up against the wall, sat himself up against it, fetched his laptop off his bedside table, and eagerly logged in. It was early, but he was keen to see the initial reader analytics. With the article running in the main paper, he was expecting to see much higher figures than usual.

'Morning, my boy!' said Leigh as she answered his call. 'Have you wet the bed?'

He chuckled. 'Not at all, Maw. I might've just got out of the right side of it for once!'

'The right side, you say? Ooo, do tell. As long as it's Maw friendly on the details.'

'It is, although there may be somebody I'd like you to meet sometime soon.'

She paused for a moment before answering through what sounded like the largest smile. 'Well, if that's to happen, I very much look forward to it. But go, what's the good news this morning?'

'I wrote it. The exposé about the cancer fraud. It's in the news section.'

'Oh my God. Well done, my treasure! That's marvellous.'

'Thank you. And I know it's early, but the online figures are flying. Tens of thousands, maybe hundreds or more if it gets picked up elsewhere, will have their first impressions formed by my piece and see him for what he really is.'

'That's great, sonny. Did you manage to find any of his disgruntled patients?'

'I didn't need to. He hung himself without too much rope in the interview. He called himself a death coach and said some pretty outlandish shit. Have a read when you get some downtime.'

'I'm off today, so I'll read it as soon as I get off the phone.'

'Excellent. You got anything nice planned?'

'Aye,' she replied. 'I've got class tonight and I'm thinking of treating myself to a not-so-wee shopping spree. I'd like some nice clothes that actually fit now.'

'Well, spree your socks off, Maw. You deserve it.'

'Thank you, son. Enjoy your first day as a news writer.'

'I will. Love you, Maw.'

'Love you too.'

They ended their call, and he refreshed the analytics page. Even just a few minutes later, the figures had climbed at a much faster rate than he was used to.

A few hours later, Jim spoke the final line of his guest speech at a City finance firm, kicking off a day of speakers. The auditorium broke into applause and carried it on as he waved gratefully their way and left the stage.

'Brilliantly done, sir,' said his assistant, giving him a Juggerjuice as he entered the backstage area.

'Thank you,' replied Jim before taking a swig as the pair strode towards his dressing room. 'Are you sure, though?'

'Sir?'

'I felt good, I did everything I needed to do before and during, but I ain't sure it was. That clapping didn't seem like it was turned to eleven,' he said as they entered the dressing room. 'Did it to you?'

The assistant hesitated. 'No, sir, it did not, but I don't think it was you.'

'C'mon now. This is always on me,' replied Jim with optimistic force. 'I'm only growing it if I'm owning it.'

'I know, sir, I know. Just there was something in the paper I became aware of just as you went on stage. I've left you a copy on your dresser. The page is Post-It'd. I'll leave you to your cooldown. Just holler if you'd like anything.'

'I appreciate you,' replied Jim, taking another swig as he approached his dressing table and his assistant stepped outside. He sat down and turned over the neatly folded newspaper. The Globe, just as he suspected. He flipped a few pages before arriving at the fluorescent makeshift bookmark. His eyes rapidly picked out his name in the small print. Then they hovered up to the headline.

CHAPTER 48

Wandering through the shopping centre, Leigh heard one of her phones ping. She sorted through her bag, rummaging past her paper copy of the day's Globe – she had read the article on the app but wanted the physical copy to keep – and took out the culprit: her work phone. An email awaited her.

Hello Leigh,

I'm happy to sign off on a three-month career break!

Would you like me to get HR to send you the appropriate forms? Are you heading anywhere nice?

Kind regards,

Susan

Joy overcame her, sending her weak at the knees. Unencumbered by shopping bags yet, she still needed to take a minute. She spotted a champagne bar in the middle of the mall ahead. *That'll do just the trick.*

One glass of bubbly and half a new wardrobe later, including new trousers and blouses for work, some elegant new outfits befitting a champagne bar, and some outdoorsy gear with a new pair of hiking boots, Leigh left the shopping centre, but the largest purchase was yet to come. She drove out of the regular retail areas towards the car dealerships, searching for the specialist she needed.

Jacked into the instrumental Lo Fi hip hop radio stream, nothing else existed to Emet as the words flowed unimpeded from his thoughts through his fingers to his screen. A tap on his shoulder snapped him out of his trance and he removed an earphone. Felix smiled his way, but this was not his ordinary piss-taking, mischievous grin. It was much more understated. 'The piece is doing superbly. Well done.' It was a proud smile.

Emet gulped. 'Thanks, Fee. I really appreciate you letting me take a stab at it.'

Felix nodded. 'Keep that knife handy. I might have to let you take a stab at a few more things outside of entertainment, arts, and culture.' He patted his writer on the shoulder for a job well done and took off before there was a chance to respond.

Emet pressed his earphone back in and sat for a long moment, basking in the warmth of the music and the feeling that he'd done something valuable. Between the barrage of approving nods and other types of congratulations he got, including a text from Clyde, the rest of the day flew by. After one last check of the reader figures, he flitted out of the office to the coffee shop.

Emet got to the counter and scanned around the place, which was surprisingly busy for six o'clock.

'What can I get for you?' asked the blonde barista, who he had seen working before.

'Is Skye in?'

'Emet, right?' she replied with a friendly smile.

'That's me.'

'She had to pick up some stock cos a delivery didn't turn up. She shouldn't be long. Can I get you a drink while you wait?'

'Ah, OK.' He checked out the menu, still deliberating when he began answering. 'I'll have aaa…'

'A decaf espresso martini, right?'

'Hmm,' he mused.

'You're celebrating, right? Big day at work?'

'I mean…I suppose so,' he answered. 'How'd you know?'

'Skye's proud as punch. Said you've written some big-deal article. Said she was looking forward to celebrating with you.'

He smiled, still deliberating.

'She won't mind you starting ahead of her, you know?'

'Go on, then.'

'Pop yourself there,' she said, pointing at one of the barstools. 'I'll have it with you in two.'

Emet sat, turning the stool a quarter so that he could people-watch while waiting. Contact with strangers was normally the last thing he craved, but today he enjoyed watching their expressions and trying to guess what they were saying and thinking. After a minute his drink arrived and he paid for it. As the barista returned to work, Emet ran his fingers around the base of the cocktail glass, savouring the notes of coffee emanating from his drink.

'Did I hear you say you're celebrating?' The voice came from a guy sat around the side of the bar, roughly the same age as him. With his tie loosened, his eyes red, and an empty glass sat beside his half-full one, it looked like he'd had a long day.

'Yes, sort of,' replied Emet.

'Work or personal?'

'Work.'

'Promotion?'

'Sort of,' replied Emet. 'I just did something that actually mattered for once.'

'That, my friend, is worth drinking to,' said the guy as he raised his glass. 'To doing work that matters.'

Emet raised his glass. 'To work that matters,' he said before sipping his martini.

His new drinking buddy downed the rest of his drink. 'And in my case, just to work that finishes!' He caught the barista's eye, pointed at his glass, and gave her a thumbs up. 'You want another, bud?'

'I'm good, thanks,' replied Emet, setting his glass down. 'Easing myself in.'

The guy nodded his slightly bobbling head, then interlinked his fingers behind it and sighed forcefully.

'Rough day?' asked Emet.

'Fucking brutal. Do you ever get it in your job where they just keep coming and coming at you with unreasonable request after unreasonable request and they just won't hear that the first thing they wanted is barely possible, never mind the fifth?'

'Thankfully for me, no,' replied Emet. 'I'm unbelievably lucky. My boss is actually quite reasonable.'

'You fancy swapping?'

'I can't say you're selling it all that well. What do you do?'

'I work for a tech start-up. Horus. You heard of us?'

Emet shook his head. 'I can't say I have.'

'You won't at this rate,' replied the guy. 'Anyway, here's me angling for a swap cos you're making your job sound cushty. You could be some Mi5 double agent for all I know.'

'Not quite.'

'What do you do?'

'I write for The Globe.'

'You're a journo?'

'I wouldn't really call myself that,' replied Emet before thinking for a moment. 'Well, maybe today.'

The barista handed the guy his next drink. Half of it was gone in the glug of an Adam's apple. 'To the newly crowned journo!' he said, raising it after he'd drank, drawing an amused grin.

'Thanks,' Emet said, raising his own and taking another sip.

'Eeeeevening!' Skye chirped, having appeared at the bar through the back. A chorus of greetings came back her way. She zeroed in on Emet, a radiant smile on her face. 'How are you?' she asked with a lowered voice.

'Excellent and yet somehow even better now,' he quietly answered.

Her smile spread even wider. She turned to the guy. 'How about you, Jason? Are you behaving yourself?'

'When don't I?' he asked before taking another mouthful. 'How are you?'

'Excellent and yet somehow better now,' she answered him, turning her eyes towards Emet.

'That's serving your favourite customer, that is,' he responded, drawing grins from Skye and her colleague as he finished his cocktail and pointed for another.

'That's probably just it,' she said as she reached for a fresh glass for him.

'It's alright, Skye,' said the other barista. 'You and Emet go and enjoy yourselves. Millie'll be here soon, and me and them out back can handle this until she arrives.'

'You sure?' asked Skye.

'Positively.'

'Thank you so much!' said Skye as she untied her apron. 'Do you need a few more minutes, lightweight?' she asked Emet, nodding to his drink.

He purposefully picked up his glass, giving her a jovial look before raising it to Jason. 'It was nice meeting you.'

'Likewise, bud,' he replied as Emet stood, downing his drink, and Skye took her apron off. 'Ah. Are you two a thing?'

Emet didn't know how to answer, so bobbed his head from side to side.

'Yep,' replied Skye, meeting eyes with Emet. 'We're a thing.' Warm smiles emerged on both of their faces.

'Aww,' Jason said. 'Look at you two. You make a nice couple. Have a brill evening celebrating. And congrats again, bud.'

'Thanks again,' replied Emet as a new drink arrived in front of Jason. 'Enjoy yours.'

'I will,' said the regular as he picked up his refill.

Skye came round from behind the bar and Emet followed her out into the radiant evening sunshine. A few yards away from the coffee shop, she turned, threw her arms around him, and planted a joyful kiss on his lips. 'Well done!'

'Thank you,' he replied. 'Did I mention its readership figures are through the roof?' he said, fishing for another kiss.

'Yes…' she kissed him, '…you…' kiss, '…did!' Kiss. 'But I won't kiss you because of that. I'll kiss you because I'm buzzing to see you proud of yourself because you did something worthwhile to you.'

He tightened his hold around her and the two kissed again, more passionately this time.

'So, how shall we celebrate?' asked Skye as the two parted their embrace.

Emet gazed into the blue sky, the sun from which was just beginning to appear a tinge golden. 'It's gorgeous out. Let's just walk.'

Skye smiled and took his hand, and the two began strolling along the street.

CHAPTER 49

Leigh trotted into the leisure centre late. After all the shopping and the good news, she'd been wiped out when she got home, fell asleep, and been out cold for a couple of hours, but she wasn't going to miss class and was at least, in theory, refreshed for her date with Davide afterwards. She slowed down to a power walk as she approached the reception desk, rummaging through her bag to find her membership card.

'Here's my sight for sore eyes. You look sensational, darling,' said Davide as she approached. 'It's OK. I think I know you're a member,' he said, pressing a button to let her through the turnstile without her needing to scan. 'I think they just started.'

'Thank you so much, you beautiful, beautiful man, you,' she said as she swept through the turnstile. 'Nine thirty?'

'*Absolutement*. Just make sure you save a little energy, yes?'

She stopped, skipped back a few steps, and leaned over the counter for a kiss. 'Don't you worry about that,' she said with a grin before jogging off to the studio. Halfway through their warm-up track as she entered, lots of the Mummas greeted her as she picked up some of the bright sticks and found a space.

'Ease yourself in, Leigh,' said the instructor, 'because tonight, we're going all in on some new routines.'

She wasn't joking. After the first few minutes, the routines picked up their pace, with Leigh unsure whether they were actually more intense or if she was just still sluggish after her daytime sleep. Her legs burned from the combination of seemingly never-ending lunges and squats with smashes of her weighted drumsticks interspersed between them in the current track, and a warmth also began to build at the top of her stomach.

'C'mon, Mummas. Keep those legs pumping,' called out the instructor. 'It's just discomfort for ninety more seconds. Commit yourself to squeezing everything you can out of yourself for ninety more seconds. Embrace the pain. Life gives us pain sometimes. Grow in confidence that you can take it and break it.'

Leigh pushed on, shoving herself back to standing from a lunge and whacking her sticks together overhead on beat with the other class-goers.

'That weakness you feel creeping into your thighs, keep feeding it. The weaker you make yourself now, the stronger you will grow. Aaaand squat.'

Leigh squatted down, counterbalancing herself by lifting her sticks out front. As she hit the bottom of her range, a pressure bulged in her under her ribcage, thankfully reducing as she stood back up. *Euugh. No more brunch bubbly on class days.*

'C'mon, ladies. Just over a minute now,' said the instructor, wiping her brow with a sweatband as she stepped into her next lunge. 'We're Drumma Mummas. We don't let things beat us. We're the ones who do the beating, aren't we?'

'Yes!' everybody chanted back tiredly, with Leigh so fatigued she wasn't sure how much sound came out of her mouth.

'We don't tire, do we, ladies?'

'No!' they boomed, stepping into another lunge.

'What do we do?'

'We bring the fire!' they yelled back in a gasping chorus. Leigh shoved herself back to standing, the momentary abdominal pressure spiking and falling again. As she banged her sticks together, the intensity of it all gave her a second of wooziness.

'We never stay down, do we, Mummas, because what do we do?'

In unison, they bellowed with all the might they could muster as they dropped into a squat, 'We stand back…' As they thrust themselves back up to standing, '…up!'

Leigh made it up, but the pressure didn't subside. Without time to even drop her sticks, she vomited all over the floor. The classmate to her right dropped her sticks. The one to her left screamed. Everybody turned the screamer's way in shock and saw what she had: a puddle of bloody vomit. But Leigh didn't see it. As if a black curtain fell before her, her vision cut out. Then with no awareness whatsoever, she dropped like a stone.

Hand in hand, Emet and Skye walked towards the South Bank, the golden evening sun on their skin. His phone began to ring. 'Sorry, I thought I had this on silent.' He pulled it out of his pocket. 'It's just Clyde. Fuck, I said I'd call him earlier. I don't need to take it.'

'It's fine,' she said. 'Tell him I said hi.'

He pulled her hand up and kissed it as he answered. 'Hello, mate. Sorry, it completely slipped my mind.' He listened on for a moment. The colour drained from his face and his hand fell away from Skye's. Her brow furrowed in concern. 'I'll be there as fast as I can.' He hung up and stared off into the distance for a moment.

'What is it?' asked Skye, grabbing his arm.

'My mum. I have to go.'

CHAPTER 50

Emet and Skye dashed down the hospital corridor towards Clyde.

'She's here, pal. I snuck in for a chat before. She's tired but stable,' said Clyde.

'Thanks, mate,' replied Emet as he washed his hands at the station outside the room.

Skye held Emet's arm and kissed his cheek. 'Get yourself in there. Send my love.'

He nodded and walked into the room. His mum was in bed, her eyes closed, looking every part the patient with a host of lines and wires running out of and off her. 'Maw,' he whispered.

Her eyes peeled open. She looked spent. 'Hello, sonny,' she croaked.

He walked right to the bed and took her hand. Up close, her skin had the slightest yellow tinge to it. 'Maw. How are you feeling?'

'Rough as old boots,' she replied with a weak grin.

'What happened?

'Apparently, I shopped till I dropped.'

He shook his head and squeezed her hand. 'Are you gonna be one of those difficult patients?'

'It's my prerogative,' she replied, a mischievous glint in her heavy eyes. 'Can you pass me that water, please?'

Emet passed her a beaker off the side table. Her hands shook as they tried to grip it. 'Let me. Just for now,' he said.

She sighed and let him take over. He lifted the straw to her mouth, where she slurped up a much-needed mouthful.

'You vomited and passed out in class?'

She reluctantly nodded.

He shook his head. 'Those fucking instructors. They push people too hard.'

'That's tosh, sonny,' she replied. 'They just encourage us. We push as hard as we want. But I can't say I was feeling grand when I got there.'

'Had you not eaten? Or eaten something bad?'

'No. Normal sort of stuff,' she said. 'I didn't eat for a good while before class because I didn't want it coming back on me. I had a wee glass of bubbly late morning, but that won't have been the culprit.'

He half grinned. 'What are you morning drinking for?'

'I was celebrating. You had your story out, and I'd just been granted a sabbatical. Apparently, I was a little late.'

He squeezed her hand. 'Better late than never. I can't tell you how happy I am you're taking some you time.'

'Aye. Well, we'll see.'

'Has anybody told you what's going on yet?'

'Not really. Just that they're running tests.'

Emet walked to the end of the bed and picked up her medical chart. 'Blood count…kidney and liver stuff…bilirubin. I must say, I thought you're looking a shade yellow. What's CA19-9?'

She paused for a moment. 'Can you do me a favour?'

'Anything.'

'Can you check if Davide is still in the waiting room? He's in his late fifties, wiry, good looking.'

'OK.'

'Tell him they won't let him in tonight, and please tell him I'm perfectly alright, that he should go home for a decent night's sleep, and that I'll message him first thing when I can sort out a visit.'

'Of course,' he replied.

'Go'n sort that for me now, sonny. I don't want him sat there all night for nothing.'

He immediately left the room, and, after a few quick words with Skye and Clyde, sought out Davide. After somewhat assuaging the Frenchman's fears after the hideous scene at the leisure centre, Davide shook his hand and left. As he walked back into the ward, Emet couldn't help but think how lovely his mum's new dating companion was, and that with his height and his lithe build, he bore a minor resemble to his dad. As he got back to the room, Leigh was being transferred from her bed into a wheelchair. 'Where are you scooting off to?'

'They're taking me on a magical mystery tour,' she said.

'Maw.'

'I believe I'm off for an ultrasound. Abdominal.'

'Are you ready, Dr Gordon?' asked the porter.

'I am.' She beckoned her son over and down for a kiss on his cheek. 'I'll see you in a wee bit, treasure.'

As the porter began to wheel her away, Emet saw her welling up. He wanted to ask her again what CA19-9 was, but he didn't want to upset her further. 'I'll be here when you get back, Maw.' He followed her wheelchair out into the corridor where she wiped away her building tears before thanking Clyde for calling Emet.

'And you must be the lovely lady putting such a wonderful smile on my laddy's face,' she said as she rolled past Skye.

'It's lovely to meet you, Miss Gordon,' replied Skye. 'I hope next time you're feeling much better and we're somewhere a little nicer.'

'Thank you, darling,' replied Leigh. 'I actually quite like it here. Probably one of the seldom spoken-of benefits of institutionalisation. We'll talk soon.' She waved at Skye and continued to be wheeled away down the corridor.

'She seems pretty chipper,' said Clyde as Emet arrived back with them, getting his phone out as he put an arm round Skye. 'Where are they taking her?'

'For an ultrasound, I think.'

'What for?' asked Skye.

'One second,' replied Emet as he typed 'CA19-9' into Google and hit enter. His insides plummeted. 'I think they're checking her for pancreatic cancer.'

CHAPTER 51

'This might feel a little warm,' said the nurse. Leigh smiled politely but before she could reply, the lady spoke again. 'Sorry. I'm such a moron, saying that to *you.*'

'It's absolutely fine, darling,' replied Leigh. 'It's one thing knowing it. It's a whole other thing entirely experiencing it.'

The nurse smiled, grateful for the understanding, then pushed the needle into Leigh's arm. After injecting the contrast material, causing a rush of warmth through the doctor-turned-patient's arm, she withdrew her needle and covered the tiny puncture with a taped-over cotton ball. 'We'll give that a little while to do its thing and get you in there as soon as we can.'

'No rush. Just whenever I'm good to go,' replied Leigh, looking down at her arm, imagining fluorescent purple blood running through her veins.

As she entered the scanning suite, the brilliant white circular mouth of the CT scanner dominated the space ahead of her. 'Hello, Dr Gordon. You know the drill. No metal on you?'

She patted her gowned body down. 'I hope not.'

'No problems with passing through small spaces?'

'No. My bedroom growing up prepared me well.'

The technician chuckled. 'It's nothing compared to the MRI scanner, but still, you never know what's gonna scare people.'

'No, I guess you don't. But I'm fine.'

The technician gestured for her to climb onto the motorised table.

'If anything,' she said as she sat, swivelled, and laid herself down, 'I think it's quite beautiful. Don't you think it looks like a halo?'

The technician tilted his head and chuckled in disbelief. 'I guess it does. You're the first person who's ever said that.'

'Do I get a lollipop?'

'I'll see what I can do. Are you ready?'

Leigh shuffled around a little. 'As I'll ever be.'

'Just relax,' said Emet. 'You'll be done before you know it.' The table began moving. 'Love you, Maw.'

'Love you too, sonny,' she said as her head inched closer to the heavenly white scanner. But on the backside of it, the glow became orange as it burst into flames. The cinder from the fire floated to the far wall, igniting it. It burned and melted and bubbled away, exposing a fiery hellscape beyond it.

'Ooo. That warmth really does spread through you, doesn't it?' said Leigh as her head began entering the scanner.

At the control desk, Emet turned the table's power off. It kept inching her forward. He hit the scanner's power button repeatedly. It remained on. He screamed out for her to get off the table, but all that came out was silence. He implored his feet to sprint forward so he could rescue her, but they wouldn't move. It would only be a moment before she began to emerge into the blazing side of the scanner now and he continued to mutedly scream in futility, clawing at the control desk in an attempt to make it stop. It was too late now. Her hair emerged, immediately catching light. Inch by inch, he would watch her burn alive.

He startled awake, and in jerking upright, Skye's head fell off his shoulder, waking her too. They had fallen asleep in the waiting room.

After a moment of orienting herself, Skye sleepy eyedly looked at Emet. 'What happened there?'

'I think I was sliding off the chair and jerked myself awake.'

'Oh,' she replied, draping an arm across his chest, encouraging him to sit back, and resting her head back on his shoulder.

'You can go home, you know. Get some proper sleep,' he said. 'We won't find out anything until late morning at the very earliest, and she's not in any immediate danger, so there's no real reason for you to be here.'

'Of course there is. That's why you're here. And that's why I'm here,' she replied, closing her eyes and snuggling her head into a good new position on his shoulder. 'So shut it and get some more sleep.' She relinquished the weight of her head and remained quiet. He rested his head back against hers and yawned but his eyes wouldn't stay closed, drawn to the ceiling's bright white strip lights.

When they woke a few hours later, Emet convinced Skye to go home, assuring her he'd contact her as soon as he heard anything. The receptionist for the ward let him go into his mum's room a few hours before visiting hours officially began. Despite the irregular beeping and occasional moans from nearby rooms, she was fast asleep. As he sat himself in a comfier chair beside her bed, the yellow tinge was unmistakable now. And she looked gaunt. *Surely, I'm imagining this?*

They both woke an hour later, and apart from a dull ache around her stomach, she felt OK in herself. Shortly after nine, she was wheeled off for an MRI scan – a much louder, more claustrophobic event than the CT scan she'd had the night before. Upon her return to the room, she forced herself to have a slice of toast, not hungry at all but knowing some energy would be a good thing. 'It's so surreal being this side of everything,' she mused.

Within the hour, a face familiar to both of them walked into the room. 'Hello, Leigh. Emet.'

'Morning, Amanda. Of all the rooms in all the wards in the hospital, you walk into mine,' said Leigh to her good friend; another consultant oncologist.

Amanda put her folder on the bedside table. 'How are you feeling?'

'Like I've had a punch to the stomach and a bigger one's coming.'

A tear of solidarity rolled Amanda's face. She sat on the edge of the bed and wrapped her friend in a hug before sitting back up.

'Let me see,' said Leigh, putting her hand out for the folder. After a minor hesitation, her friend passed her it. She flipped it open and turned through the results of her blood tests before getting to her scans. 'Oh,' she said, pausing long and hard. 'And here was muggins thinking I was doing so well.'

'You were, love. You were. So well it masked it,' replied Amanda.

Leigh turned to the next scan, eventually nodding. 'Righteo, then. Let's get me started on some capecitabine.'

'And gemcitabine?'

'That depends. Will you give me that to take on the road?'

'What's going on, Maw?' asked Emet.

'What do you mean "on the road"?' asked Amanda.

'I mean I had a sabbatical accepted yesterday and I fully intend to take it,' replied Leigh, 'so there's no way I'll be in and out of here like a Yo-Yo when I have things to see.'

'Can somebody tell me what's happening?' asked Emet.

Amanda was fully focused on her friend-turned-patient. 'Leigh…I'm not sure what you have planned, but you may want to rethin—'

'There's no rethinking this, Mandy,' Leigh said over her colleague, sitting up off the inclined upper bed. 'I can self-administer. You can put the central line in me right now if you like? Or you can just send me on my merry way with the capecitabine. I'm not staying here.'

Emet linked his hands behind his head. He could see from the stubbornness in his mum and the despair on her colleague's face that something like his nightmare was about to pass.

'I can't sign it off by myself but let me chat to Sanjay and see what we can do,' said Amanda.

Leigh laid back fully against her bed, relaxed her puffed up chest, and reached for Amanda's hand. 'Sorry, Mandy. I don't mean to be difficult,' she said as she welled up. 'I just need to go.'

Amanda raised her friend's hand and kissed it. 'Your apologies are no good here,' she said, her voice breaking towards the end of the sentence. 'Let me sort it for you.' She tenderly let go of her hand and left the room, closing the door behind her.

Leigh tilted her head up and gazed through the ceiling as Emet dropped his face into his hand. Silence reigned for a solid minute.

Without lifting his head, Emet eventually spoke. 'Pancreatic?'

'Aye.'

'Inoperable?'

'Aye.'

'Stage three?'

'No. Four?'

He lifted his head. 'How long?'

She paused. 'Without treatment, six months tops. With the GemCap, hopefully a while longer.' He finally dared to look at her. She turned her eyes to him. 'I'm so sorry, sonny.' Both of them burst into tears as he shook his head at her apology, got up, and wrapped his arms around her as she began to sob. 'I'm so, so sorry.'

CHAPTER 52

Emet walked out of the hospital's revolving door and over to a bench. As he waited for his phone to power up, he scanned the horizon. He saw the entrance he'd lied about passing through a few times before and the smokers congregated there; their carcinogenic clouds of comfort barely visible from his distance. He selected text messages, then Skye's name. He wasn't the sort of writer who ever experienced writer's block, but the words weren't coming. A few voicemail notifications appeared, all from Felix.

'Em. So sorry to have to call. How's she doing?'

The journalist deliberated for a moment, holding back his hot tears. 'They've still got a few more tests to run…thanks for asking. What can I do for you?'

'Fingers crossed for her, matey,' said Felix. 'Just a super quick one. Where did you save the audio file of your interview with O'Shea?'

'Umm. In the folder with the article in that I linked you to the other day. I made an audio subfolder.'

'Are you sure? I'm in the folder right now and I can't see anything.'

'Well, it's definitely there.'

'I'm not saying it isn't, it's just I can't see it,' replied Felix. 'Can you check at your end?'

'One sec,' replied Emet as he put his phone on speaker and navigated through his work drive to the relevant folder. It wasn't there. 'Hmm.' He clicked through all he folders he'd been using the last few days. Nothing. He clicked his recycling bin. It was nowhere to be seen. 'Umm. I can't see it at the moment.'

'Is it still on your recorder?'

'No, I emptied that when I transferred it over. It'll be somewhere. It's all cloud backed-up anyway, isn't it?'

'If you had the syncing turned on when you transferred it, yes,' replied Felix.

'OK, then,' said Emet, desperately clicking and scanning through more folders. 'What do you need it for?'

Felix drew a deep breath. 'Legal.'

'Why? They approved the piece before it went out.'

'They did.'

'So it's not libellous, is it?'

'Not the way we published it, no, but that's not the issue. Delancey O'Shea's solicitor has been in touch. He's saying the entire piece is libellous as the interview didn't happen at all.'

CHAPTER 53

He would have preferred a nightmare that night. At least it would have meant some sleep. Instead, he laid beside Skye in his pitch-black room staring at the ceiling as his mum's prognosis and an endless string of unanswerable questions somersaulted through his mind. *Why one of the most lethal cancers? Why had it been at the one time in the last decade when her weight loss wouldn't look like a symptom? Why didn't doctors, the people who save others from such conditions, have healthcare like athletes, with everything about their health tracked and monitored to help them stay as well as possible for as long as possible? And why, with their profession known to be one of the most stressful, illness-inducing jobs around, were they worked so long and hard? Would she respond to her treatment? How long would she have, and how much of that time would be of a worthwhile quality? She had no history of cancer on her side of the family. Did years of passive smoking around Da plant the seed for this? Did my smoking do this? Is some cruel, karmic joke for the story I've just written? Am I going to have lost both parents to it before my mid-thirties? Does it lurk in my future? Have I been a good enough son to her? How did she feel about all this? Is she lying awake like me, questions tumbling through her mind too? And most of all, why her? She had dedicated her life to extending the lives of countless others with this despicable disease. If anybody deserved a long, healthy life, wasn't it her?*

Now and then, he would study what he could see of the sleeping beauty beside him. She'd been a ray of long overdue shine in his life the last few weeks and had been so caring during the last day or so, but her light felt like a single ray being swallowed by a black hole now. Even her comfort couldn't make any of this feel remotely tolerable.

He didn't understand how he could go on without his mum, not now, not like this. But she was going to die. Unless some miraculous spontaneous remission happened. Or unless...

He needed to go in that morning but at no particular time. 'Without that clock lighting up, do you just sleep endlessly in here?' asked Skye, referring to the abject blackness of the room as she tried to find some energy in her slumbersome body.

I wish. 'I eventually stir,' he replied as he turned the light on.

'How'd you sleep?' she asked, draping an arm over his chest.

'I've slept better.'

After getting up and letting Skye shower first, he found her downstairs admiring his father's painting. 'You should start again if you really want to,' he said, alerting her to his presence in the doorway. 'Nobody knows how much time they'll get.'

She walked over to him and took his hand.

'Come on,' he said. 'Let's go.'

They walked along the passage, and he opened the front door for her. She pottered straight down the steps and stretched her arms overhead as she yawned, trying to get some fresh air in to wake up. As she turned back towards the house, she gasped. Emet was examining the red graffitied message across his door and the walls either side of it. It read "Take a leap you hack". He stood for a moment in silence.

'Emet, are you alright?' called Skye.

He looked over his shoulder, wearily nodded, and proceeded to close and lock the door, before turning and coming down his steps.

'Are you gonna call the police?' she asked as he reached her.

'In a bit,' he said apathetically.

'Are you sure you're OK?'

'It's those happy-clapping cunts that aren't OK,' he replied with an exhausted irritation as he began walking towards the end of the road. 'They think they're some sort of linguistic wizards, yet they can't even use a fucking apostrophe.'

After a quiet journey in together during which Skye repeatedly squeezed Emet's hand or thigh to bring him back to the moment, he thanked her for everything, and said he'd call her later with a mum update, before kissing her goodbye and entering the office. After a couple of hours of going through his computer and speaking with IT, he entered Felix's office.

'Em, you look shattered,' said the editor. 'What's going on?'

'The recording's gone. I checked everywhere. I clearly recall where I saved it, what I called it, everything, but it's gone. IT were no help. There's no trace of it.'

'I meant with your mum,' replied Felix.

'Right,' said Emet, resting his elbow on the arm of the chair and scouring his face with his hand. 'She's dying, Fee,' he said, his lips quivering slightly. 'Stage four pancreatic cancer.'

Felix covered his mouth in horror. 'Jesus fucking wept. I'm so, so sorry.'

Emet replied with something between a nod and a shrug.

'Do…do you know how long she has?'

Emet sighed. 'Months, maybe a year.'

Felix shook his head and expelled a guttural sigh. 'Fuck. I'm so sorry. Get yourself out of here, then. Go be with her.'

'What about the recording?'

'Forget that,' replied the editor. 'IT can look some more. I'll deal with upstairs and legal if needs be. Take some compassionate leave.'

'I'm better off writing, Fee.'

'Take it. I'm not asking.'

Emet's brow furrowed. 'I appreciate you looking out for me, but surely I can work if I want to?'

Felix leaned back in his chair, took off his glasses, and began polishing them. 'If you couldn't find your recording, upstairs wanted me to put you on administrative leave.'

'You what?!' asked Emet.

'O'Shea has a heavy-hitting legal team.'

'For defending him from claims, maybe.'

'You know how upstairs are. More spine in a pamphlet. Anyway, take the compassionate rather than the administrative. I want to keep you out of the HR disciplinary system for as long as possible.'

Emet stood up, shaking his head angrily. 'What sort of upside-down world are we in where this fraud walks around saying what the fuck he wants and yet I'm held to account for a recording of an interview *that definitely happened* going walkabouts? I have taxi receipts that prove I went there. As if I'd go all that way and not speak with him.'

'I know, Em.'

'How about they fucking back their journalists?'

'I know but forget it. You have real stuff to tend to. Go and spend some time where it's really needed.'

Emet let his rage subside a little. 'Sorry you're having to deal with this shit, Fee. I do appreciate it.'

The editor nodded earnestly, and Emet turned to leave.

'They asked me to ask you,' said Felix, 'you did definitely go there and record it, didn't you?'

Emet reached the door and looked over his shoulder. 'Are you sure it's them asking me?'

Felix hesitated. 'It needs to be known, Em.'

'You saw yourself Usain Bolting it out of this office a few weeks ago, and I offered to play you it in the lift the other day. You should be embarrassed even asking me,' the journalist said as he left.

CHAPTER 54

Ten days later, Skye snuggled in close to Emet as he opened his front door for her. 'Let me know you get up there safe,' she said.

'I will. If the Wildlings don't reclaim me before I get a chance,' he replied, gently taking hold of her waist before kissing her. 'I'll see you in a few weeks.'

'If you get good signal, video call me. I'd love to see some of the scenery.'

'I will.'

They kissed once more, then she left, leaving him to finish his packing mostly summer clothes, which he knew may well be a mistake given his destination's reputation. As he drew close to finishing, he ordered a taxi on an app and sat in the living room. The urge for a cigarette overcome him as he looked at the short pile of Blu-rays that had arrived over the few days after he'd been asked to take leave, and only intensified as he looked up at his dad's painting. He never had understood what it meant, what had been going on his dad's heart and mind as he'd created it, and given his visceral mourning whenever he studied it, he didn't think he ever could get close to deciphering it. His dad could spin a yarn with the best of them, so no doubt he himself could have pitched multiple interpretations of what it expressed, but maybe he himself didn't know either. All Emet knew was that it and the feeling it cast loomed large, and that as much as he treasured it, he was looking forward to not seeing it for a while.

The doorbell rang. *Hmm.* He hadn't had a text to say the taxi had arrived. Nonetheless, he rose, grabbed his bags, and headed to the front door. 'What the fuck are you doing here?'

Jim Akachi-Rawlings stood on his doorstep, shaking his head with his gleaming smile. 'Now there's a greeting! I still can't get used to it you Brits love to cuss more than we do, although I'm guessing we probably shoulder most of the blame for that with all the TV we send you.'

'And wank infomercials.'

Jim laughed. '*Wank.* I fucking love that as an adjective.' He noticed Emet's glower and continued. 'I tried you at work, but no dice. You got five?'

'You turn up unannounced at my home and you think I've got the time of day for you?'

'Emet. I know you don't trust me, and you don't think I've got much going on between my ears, but trust that I knew I was going to get a frosty reception and I came anyway. Don't give *me* the time of day, give what I'm saying the time of day. I think you'll like it.'

Emet weighed up his unexpected visitor's request. 'I have a taxi coming any second, so you're going to have to schedule something with me like a regular person would.'

'Where are you going?' Jim asked. 'I'll pay your taxi his fare for nothing and I'll take you. That way we can take our time.'

A few minutes later, Jim placed a fifty-pound note in the hand of Emet's taxi driver for what would have been a fifteen-pound fare.

'Sorry, mate. We don't take those,' said the taxi driver.

'What do you mean?' asked the perplexed American.

'We don't take fifties.'

'How come?' asked Jim. 'This is an English note, right?'

'It is, but we don't see them often enough to know if they're fakes or not.'

Jim turned to Emet with a disbelieving smile. 'Is this right?'

Emet nodded. 'Brits are very wary of being conned, at least the ones who haven't lobotomised themselves and ended up at personal development seminars.'

'You and that British wit,' said Jim before pulling out his wallet to find a smaller note.

'Ey,' said the taxi driver. 'Aren't you that bloke off those long adverts? What's it he says? Full belief...?'

Jim flashed his winning smile. 'Take the leap.'

As the taxi driver's face lit up, Emet's expression fell, partly because the driver recognised Jim and it looked as if he'd now accept the payment, but mostly because of what he'd felt himself do upon hearing the catchphrase. Reflexively, he'd almost jumped forwards and had barely managed to stop himself. Upon regaining his balance and checking that nobody had seen his wobble, he looked down at his hands. They were joined in the diamond-shaped viewfinder from the seminar. He juddered, yanking them apart and shoving them deep into his pockets.

'Bloody hell! My wife just ordered your audio programme,' said the taxi driver. 'Do you mind if we get a selfie for me to show her?'

'It'd be my pleasure,' replied Jim.

As the pair took their photo and the cabbie accepted the fifty having had a joke about it, Emet pressed his hands firmly against his thighs, freaked out at his act of muscle memory. *What the fuck was all that about?*

'Let's go.'

Emet snapped out of his anxious daze to find Jim carrying his luggage to his chauffeured car.

'We've got a train to get you on.'

A minute later, the car was on the move. 'Come on, then,' said Emet. 'The suspense is killing me.'

'I read your piece the other week. You mentioned me again.'

'And?'

'Well, Emet, I know you think you're doing the world a favour, associating me with somebody I had the briefest dealings with a lifetime ago, and I get it. He's making claims to vulnerable people, claims with nothing backing them up besides a few far-fetched stories. I'm guilty by association to you unless I show otherwise. And not so much for you, but for the world at large, I want to show otherwise, and you're uniquely placed to make sure the world gets the best from what I want to give.'

Emet disinterestedly gazed out of the window on his side. 'You people truly have a unique talent for speaking without imparting any meaning, and for making it all appear to be in the best interests of your blessed listeners, don't you?'

'My entire purpose in this life is to serve others, Emet.'

'Please,' interrupted the journalist. 'I'd have rather walked than listen to this shit.'

'I'll cut directly to the chase. I want to turn The Leap from an event that transports people to another level in their lives into one that elevates all society. I want to donate thirty percent of all profits from future Leap events to charity, I want that charity to be a legitimate cancer research charity, and I want you to help me select it.'

Emet disdainfully glared across at Jim. 'You're pathetically transparent. You think I'm going to write some sort of U-turn piece on how you're some sort of redeemed, benevolent saviour?'

'Not at all,' said Jim. 'I know you can't do that if you're involved with me. But I'm not gonna lie. I do want to redeem myself in your eyes, and everybody who believes what you do. I want to be a source for nothing but good, and I want no valid criticism of me to exist. You wouldn't publicly correct the record, but over time, if the record is straight in reality and in my soul, people are gonna know. I'll know.'

'And you want me to help because…?'

'If I can convince you, as sceptical as you are, that I'm a force for good, then I really must be,' said Jim. 'And there's nobody better to point me towards the best cancer research charity than you.'

'I'm a journalist,' replied Emet. 'Your guilt about what I exposed doesn't qualify me to help you.'

'I know, but I also know your mom is one of the top oncologists in the country. Will you link us up so that she'll consult on the matter with me?'

Emet glowered at Jim. 'Stop the fucking car.'

Jim showed his palms to his guest. 'Emet, rela—'

'I said stop the fucking car!' roared Emet.

Jim caught his driver's attention in the rear-view mirror and nodded. As the car slowed ahead of the next turn off the busy road, the speaker studied his guest's demeanour. 'I just wanted to involve you so that you know the money's going to the b—'

'Let me out,' Emet forcefully said to the driver. Before the car came to a full stop, Emet opened the door, dangling his foot onto the slowing tarmac. As soon as it halted, he was out, banging on the boot to get the driver to open it.

Jim rushed out of his side, avoiding the rushing traffic in the other lane. 'I don't know what I said, man, but please, get back in and we'll talk this through. I don't want you to miss your train.'

'Fuck my train and fuck you,' snapped Emet as the motorised boot took a short eternity to open.

'Emet, this is potentially millions a year towards helping extend lives and stopping people losing loved ones early.'

No sooner had he grabbed his bag than he dropped it and instead grabbed the towering Jim by the scruff of his neck and pulled him so close he could feel the searing heat of his own breath reflecting off the American's face. 'You keep her out of this,' he snarled.

Jim eyeballed him, a flicker of fury glimmering from deep inside his eyes as, on the surface, he remained largely unruffled. 'I don't know who you're talking about, Emet,' he stated in a flat, firm tone, 'but I'm sorry if you've lost someone.'

Emet surveyed Jim's face for a long moment and found nothing but sincerity. 'Fuck off,' he said as he shoved the speaker away.

Jim regarded the rage-filled man in front of him, who snatched his bag off the ground. 'Emet. Whatever it is you're going through, you need to speak to somebody. This isn't good for you.'

'Get fucked,' said Emet as he stormed away, hoping he would never see the guru or any of his infomercials ever again.

All his way back to his apartment, Jim cycled through a multitude of physiology hacks, from specific breathing patterns, to affirmations, to banded brainwave games, to clear his mind. Upon arriving home, he walked up to one of his gargantuan windows, took in the majesty of his view over the city for a long moment, then slid off the brainwave band he still had on from the car and flung it across the room. After a few minutes, he pulled his phone out and hit dial. 'Hey. It's Jim Akachi-Rawlings. Can I speak with Delancey, please?'

CHAPTER 55

After the blow up at Jim, missing his rigidly booked train, and having to pay a couple of hundred pounds for a replacement ticket, the six-hour journey provided Emet just enough time to calm down. He hated it, but the breathing methods he learned on The Leap had helped when he used them, though not as much as they did before his animosity towards their teacher had intensified. Swapping some light-hearted texts with Skye and the ever-greener surroundings had done their bit too.

After alighting the train and stretching the stiffness out of his legs, he could see his mum's new ride in the car park from the platform. He smiled all the way towards her and Davide and hugged her with every ounce of love he had. 'Hey, Maw.'

'Thank you for coming up, treasure. How was your journey?'

'Grand, thanks,' he said as they separated. 'Just nice to be away from the smoke.'

'Nothing but fresh air up here,' she replied with a warm smile.

'Nice to meet you properly,' Emet said, turning his attention to Davide, offering him a handshake.

'The pleasure is all mine,' replied Davide, disregarding the hand and hugging Emet. 'Your mother speaks so warmly of you.'

'Someone has to,' replied Emet. 'This is quite the set of wheels,' he continued, nodding to the small motorhome behind them. 'You can't believe how long she's been talking about one of these,' he said to Davide, before turning to her. 'Is it everything you wanted?'

'Aye, and a wee bit more.'

The trio drove off from the tiny rail station into the surrounding countryside, with nothing but hills, mountains, and lochs as far as the eye could see, providing a glorious backdrop to their chatter about the last week, with Emet finding out what they'd been up to in the parts of her motherland she'd long craved visiting. 'You didn't fill up on the train, did you?' asked Leigh.

'Nope. Saved myself for some of the local delicacies you always rave about. Do you have somewhere in mind?'

'Aye. We're very close.'

A few minutes later, they pulled onto a dirt track and eventually rolled to a stop by an expensive loch, shimmering in the late evening sun.

'Boozers can't get much footfall out this way,' said Emet.

'Who said anything about a boozer?' replied Leigh as she got out of the driver's seat and walked into the back of the van. 'Come and make yourself useful.' As Emet got up, the back of the van opened out and Leigh stepped out before pulling out what looked like a drawer, which opened and folded out to expose a small barbeque grill. Davide passed Emet with a large cool box and set it down by Leigh, who opened it and held up some of its meaty produce in delight. 'Native produce of the finest, freshest quality. Who needs a pub on an evening as glorious as this?'

Leigh began the grilling and fairly swiftly passed duties to Emet while Davide fetched some drinks. He emerged with some cold pressed green juice drinks for them along with one of Emet's favourite lagers. 'To the highlands,' she said, raising her juice.

'To the highlands,' repeated Davide in his silky French accent.

'To the motherlands,' said Emet, raising his bottle.

Leigh brimmed with joy. 'To the motherlands,' she replied, tapping bottles with her son and Davide.

As he continued grilling and chatting, Emet was transfixed by how happy his mother and Davide looked, sat side by side on their fold-out chairs, sipping on their juices in the heavenly evening rays.

A bittersweet emotion flooded his body, warm and painful in equal measure. Without him consciously realising, the smell of charring alerted him. It was then he noticed the smoke. The sausages, a little dark on one side, needed turning, and as he rotated them, his eyes followed their smoke as it dispersed into the sublime evening sky to be gone forever. His eyes focused through it, so the vaporous shapes veiled his laughing mum. She caught him looking her way, her smile dampening with a sadness mirroring his own. She chose to smile again, clearly hoping to lead him out of his emotional pothole, and mouthed two words to him. He mouthed them back. 'Love you.'

After food and drink, the light chatter continued. Emet found Davide to be a nice guy; colourful and easy to talk to, so much so that he didn't notice his mum slip away for ten minutes. When she sat back with them and Emet turned her way, she was sat on the back edge of the van rather than on the folding chair, rummaging around down the front of the neck of her top. Emet watched on confused until she pulled out tubes of the central line that had been fitted to the right side of her chest. Behind her hanging from a stand was a drip bag containing her intravenous chemotherapy medication, gemcitabine.

She saw him notice. 'Better than being sat in the ward, isn't it?' she said, nodding out towards the water as she began to connect the tubes to her line.

He looked out and back. 'Yes. Yes, it is.'

An hour after the sun set and the trio chatted around an electric lantern out the back of the van, Leigh almightily yawned. 'I think I'm going to have to turn in when this is done,' she said, examining her IV bag, which was almost empty now.

'Of course,' replied Emet, the conversation flowing so well that he had often momentarily forgotten the situation. 'I'm sure we'll all sleep well tonight. I only saw one double in there. I'm assuming I'm on a pullout?'

'No no,' said Davide. 'The double is yours.'

Emet raised an eyebrow. 'And you guys are…?'

'Stargazing,' replied Leigh.

'You can't sleep outside,' said Emet, trying not to look at her IV.

'We're not. Give me a wee minute with this and we'll show you.'

A few minutes later after the drip finished and Leigh disconnected and cleaned her central line connector tubes, she led Emet into the van. Sliding a panel on the wall aside, she revealed a ladder up into the ceiling, but there was barely two feet of space at the opening. 'That's a tad snug, isn't it?'

'A wee bit,' she said with a grin. 'But the highlands are a magical place.' She snapped her fingers and the ceiling began to move, part of it tilting up like an accordion, creating space at the top of the ladder.

'That's some snazzy shit,' said Emet. 'That seriously works with a snap?'

She grinned and removed her hand from behind a panel. 'Aye. A snap of the switch back here. Follow me.'

Emet followed her up the ladder and was breathtaken. The expanded ceiling had created a mezzanine bedroom with a double mattress on the floor. Better than that, the walls of the space were windowed with soft transparent plastic, giving the bed an almost panoramic view of the surroundings. 'Lay down. Take a gander.'

He laid, putting his head on one of the pillows and looked up to where a headboard would normally be. Instead, the stars of the clear night sky twinkled. 'This is stunning,' he said.

His mum laid her head on the pillow beside him. 'Aye. It's glorious.'

He peered at the twinkling above him, awestruck. When eventually he peeled his eyes away from the sky, the music was coming to a stop. His mum and Davide, dressed to the nines, finished their slow dance and softly kissed. The Frenchman stepped away, offering one of Leigh's hands to Emet. 'Your mother will dance the feet off me if I let her. Please, take the reins for one or two.'

Emet stood from his barstool, walked over, and took her hand. 'May I have this dance?'

'Nothing would make your maw happier.'

The instrumental music resumed, with mother and son gracefully waltzing away under the faux night-sky ceiling above the dancefloor. As the music quietened, Leigh laid her head on her son's shoulder, then kissed his cheek. He sighed, not wanting it to end, but soon enough it did. 'A drink?'

'A drink would be delightful,' she replied. They strolled over to the bar and took a stool each.

'What can I get you?' asked the bartender.

'Ooo,' said Leigh, admiring the plentiful selection of extravagant bottles behind the bar. 'What would you recommend for a gal like me?'

The bartender inspected her and nodded. 'I have just the thing.' He picked up a dazzling, pricey-looking bottle and just as he was about to pour, Emet looked up from the cocktail menu.

'No, not that one.' He turned the menu to the bartender and pointed at an item. 'We'll have two of these, thanks.'

The bartender frowned. 'Are you sure?'

Emet nodded. 'It's a classic. Two, please.'

The bartender leaned towards him, 'I know, but it's really nothing to write home about. Trust me. She'll love this. Let me make her one. If she doesn't like it, I'll make the other.'

'She's my mother,' replied Emet. 'I know what she wants. Just two of what I asked for, please.'

'Look,' replied the bartender, 'I'll do you my special on the house. I'm that sure she'll love it.'

Emet glared at the bartender. 'Jesus. Haven't you heard that the customer's always right?'

'I have,' replied the bartender. 'So, what does the customer say?' he asked, directing his question at Leigh. She glanced at Emet's menu, then at the bartender and all the drinks behind him. 'I'll—'

'Do I have to get your manager?' snapped Emet, stopping her sentence in its tracks. 'Just give us two classics.'

'Sorry, sir. Two classics coming up.'

As the bartender stepped away, Leigh smiled at her son. 'Thank you, sonny. It's such a relief sometimes for someone else to decide for you.'

'Exactly,' he said nodding proudly before seeing her wide smile change. *Is she being sarcastic?*

The bartender arrived back with two cocktail glasses and set them both on napkins, then began mixing their cocktail, but not in a tin shaker. It was in a bag. An IV drip bag. Happy that it was mixed, he flipped the bag up in the air as if flaring a shaker, catching it at arm's length overhead, and took the tube at the end of the IV bag in his other hand, opening its tap to pour a drink in each glass. Using the empty tube, he fancily swung the bag down into his other hand before bringing his free hand down to shield his mouth from Emet.

'Miss,' he whispered, still loud enough for Emet to hear, 'if you want the special instead, I knocked one up for you just over there.'

Leigh playfully shielded her mouth. 'It looks delicious. I might if sonnyboy here lets me.'

'Thanks,' said Emet, the word brimming with irritation. 'I think you have other customers waiting for you.'

The bartender looked along the bar, nodded, and left them.

'These look delicious, thanks,' said Leigh raising her glass.

Emet nodded pridefully and raised his glass too. 'Here's to a lovely evening and many more like it.'

'Aye,' replied Leigh, clinking glasses. *'Slàinte mhath.'*

An uneasy feeling gripped him as the words rang around in his head and he took his first sip, but he couldn't fathom why.

Leigh sipped hers too. 'It's a classic for a reason,' she said with a smile before taking another.

Emet shoulders lowered as he breathed a sigh of relief, knowing that he'd picked well for her. By the time he took another sip, her glass was dry.

'Wow. That went down well,' he said.

'Aye,' she said, 'it was…' She let out a tickly cough then went to speak again. A splutter followed. She banged her chest and went to speak again. A louder cough hacked out of her before a barrage of them followed. Emet jumped to his feet and banged on her back.

'Drink,' she managed to gasp as the ever-more painful sounding coughs continued.

'Can we get another here, please?' Emet shouted, waving his hand as his mum's coughing fit intensified.

'Here.'

Emet turned to find an appetising deep purple cocktail on a napkin beside his mum.

'It's just what she needs,' said the voice, which he now recognised. He raised his gaze in horror.

'No!' he protested. 'Give her another classic.'

'We've run out, and it wouldn't work, anyway,' said Delancey, a tight grin on his face. 'Have some of this, Dr Gordon,' he said, sliding his special cocktail her way. 'It'll sort you right out.'

'No!' barked Emet. 'Just give us some water,' he pleaded. Leigh pulled her hands away from her spluttering mouth. They were splattered with blood.

'The taps are out back. I don't think we have time for that.' He slid the glass closer to her. 'Drink, Dr Gordon.'

As more blood splattered into her hands, she gazed at the special like a desert wanderer at a watering hole. Her son swiped it away, smashing it into the bottles behind the bar, turning the possibility of drinking into nothing but a mirage. 'For God's sake, get her something!' he bellowed, turning to the Irishman, who was now lighting a cigarette.

'I did,' replied Delancey before taking a drag, his words barely audible over the choking. 'And now it's splashed all over the wall. Surreal,' he said with a sad shake of his head.

Emet set his fury aside and tended to his mum, putting an arm around her and helping her off the chair as she coughed so violently he was petrified it was damaging her. 'Come on. Let's get you something quick.'

She resisted him leading her away. 'Sonny,' she said through her spluttering.

'What, Maw?' he replied turning to her.

Tears ran down her pain-stricken face. Crimson ones. 'Save me,' she moaned, her bloody hands clasping either side of his face as just before she spat up a hefty, congealed clot. 'Save me.'

CHAPTER 56

Throughout the delightful following day, which was full of vibrant chatter and sprawling, stunning scenery, whenever he was out of conversation for any substantial period, he was haunted by his dream. The gruesome image of Leigh spluttering blood as she pled for a drink arose again and again, sometimes overlaying his smiling mum ahead of him.

Come the evening, they arrived at a train station. Emet handed Davide his bag and heartily shook his hand. 'It's been an absolute pleasure.'

'For me too,' replied Davide, pulling Emet in for a hug that he was much more receptive to than the one the day before. They parted and the Frenchman moved onto Leigh. Emet stepped away to give them space but saw the tenderness in their interaction and the happiness on his mum's face both sides of their kiss goodbye.

'I'd better get to the platform,' said Davide before giving her one last kiss. 'Have an amazing few weeks.'

'We'll try our best,' replied Emet.

'There is no try, Emet,' Davide replied with a warm smile. '*Vouloir, c'est pouvoir.*'

Emet looked at him with puzzlement.

'If you want it, you have the power to do it,' translated David. He blew Leigh a kiss and strode off to the platform, turning every few steps to wave until he vanished from sight.

Leigh linked arms with Emet and leaned her head on his shoulder. 'It's just us now, sonny. Well…you, me, and all his beauty.'

They drove ninety minutes to one of the lochs Leigh had on her extensive list and after tucking into a late picnic, the dark was upon them. Without the gregarious Davide there to keep the conversation flowing, the occasional quiet allowed Emet too much thinking time. After washing her evening capecitabine tablets down with water, she found her son looking straight through her. 'What's going on in there?' she asked, tapping her temple twice.

'Nothing.'

She sized him up and smiled. 'Or at least nothing a good sleep won't fix.'

He'd been in bed twenty minutes and although he was tired and the mattress was perfectly comfortable, he couldn't sleep. The cloud of last night's nightmare had hovered over him all day and he feared the moment he closed his eyes, its ghastly hell would fully descend upon him again.

'Emet. Are you awake?' came all call from above.

He sat up immediately. 'Is everything alright?'

'Can you come up for a wee minute, please?'

He swivelled out of bed and clambered up the ladder in double time. 'Are you alright? Can I get you anything?'

'Relax, I'm fine,' Leigh replied. 'I just thought this was a view for two if you were still awake.' She patted on the bed beside her. He crawled over and laid there, looking up to see out of the headboard-side window. The sky, which had been cloudy during their picnic, was now crystal clear. His eyes widened. 'Wow. I've never seen the stars like this before.'

'They are stunning. Do you want to see something even better?'

'Go on.'

'You see that there?' she asked, pointing up to the lower-left corner of the black expanded ceiling.

His eyes looked for what she was pointing to. 'The zip?'

'Aye. Give that a wee pull.'

He crawled over and pulled it, unzipping right around the ceiling panel until the blackout fabric that had covered it was completely pulled back. The entire ceiling was a window panel too. His mum patted the bed again, inviting him to lie down and marvel at the splendour with her. He rejoined her, awestruck at the scene. 'Wow. Why don't you have that unzipped all the time?'

'It's gorgeous to fall asleep to, but it's a bugger for waking you up so early with the light. And you know us Gordons need our beauty sleep.' She shuffled over to him and laid an arm over him, resting her head against the side of his chest. 'But I thought we could at least look for a while.'

He peeled open his eyes, surprised to find it was morning. He was still up on the top bed. The ceiling window hadn't been zipped back over, and yet he'd slept straight through. No nightmares. Nothing. The time was eight. The sky was dark grey, pregnant with an impending downpour, but he was still shocked the early light hadn't woken him. He looked next to him. His mum wasn't there, but she had left something on her pillow: a noticeable amount of hair. He got out of bed and climbed down the ladder. 'Morning,' he said to no reply. He opened the van door and stepped outside. 'Maw?' He heard her, but it wasn't a verbal reply; it was the sound of heaving. He walked around the van. She was vomiting behind a tree. She spat up the last of what she needed to and wiped her mouth with kitchen roll as she emerged. 'Here's the sleeping beauty,' she said, forcing a smile. 'How are you?'

'*I'm* fine,' he said, his face wrought with concern. 'How are you?'

'I'm grand now. It obviously needed to be out.'

He studied her washed-out complexion. 'Shall we take it a bit easier today?'

'Easier? Look around this place. There's too much to see!'

'There is,' he replied before pausing. 'But maybe today's not the best day.'

'I don't have too many to spare, sonny,' she said. Immediately she noticed that the truth of her statement had hit him like a gut punch. 'But it's just a little nausea. Nothing too serious. *Vouloir, c'est pouvoir,*' she said in her best attempt at a French accent.

And she did. The village they had mentioned visiting – done. The long hike they had planned – done. The restaurant they had found online that served traditional Scottish fare using the finest local produce – done. But after her starter there, she only had half of her main and even less of her dessert, sliding her plate over to Emet for him to finish the leftovers for her. That night, clearly exhausted but willing the smile to stay on her face, she asked her son to watch the night sky again with her on the top bed. A couple of minutes after lying beside her, drops of rain began to splash on the sky window.

'I love the sound of rain,' she said, closing her heavy eyes to admire it as the odd splash turned into a steadier drumming.

'Me too,' said Emet, 'although I think it's really going to start coming down any minute.'

'I wish it were the stars,' she said, sounding drowsier by the word.

'The stars?'

She nodded and cosied up under the duvet, relinquishing all her waking tension. 'Falling…so I could wish on one.'

Emet's lips quivered and even though her eyes were closed, he couldn't bring himself to look directly at her for the fear of emotion overwhelming him. 'What'd you wish for?'

'Health…'

Emet swallowed hard and tightened his brow.

'…for you…for Davide…for…Pierre.' With that, she was asleep. Emet watched her completely at peace for a moment. No nausea. No tiredness. No knowledge of what was coming. But he knew what was coming. As he looked to the sky and watched the raindrops bounce off the window, tears streamed down his cheeks.

After a hellish night of morbid, guilt-ridden dreams and broken sleep next to his serene, spent mother, the next day began in a similar fashion except with both Gordons wearier than the previous day. Leigh was sick again but then put some makeup and a smile on. 'The show must go on,' she proclaimed.

After a short drive to another village and some gentler walking than the previous day, she needed to sit down for a rest. An hour later, she was sick again. Knowing that she would need to refuel if they were to walk around another loch as planned that afternoon, she had tea and a scone at a local tearoom, taking half an hour to get the jammed and buttered treat down her. After sitting for the best part of an hour to let it digest, they set out into the nearby hills. Half an hour later, she brought her afternoon tea up. After the nausea subsided, they resumed walking around the mirrorlike mass of water, only for her legs to begin feeling wobbly. They sat on a large rock to see if it would pass. Emet suggested she drank some juice to increase her blood sugars but even the smell of it knocked her sick.

'I think this afternoon's potter ends here,' she said, gazing out onto the water. 'Tomorrow will be a better day.'

Emet squeezed her hand and nodded, sighing before joining her in looking out onto the glorious, overcast scene ahead of them. Getting back to the van was hard work, but Leigh's relief at having made it was short lived. She spent the evening on and off the toilet. Hollowed out but determined to sleep under the stars, Emet helped her up to the top bed. 'Would you like your space tonight?' he asked.

She shook her head. 'I'd like company.' She fell asleep fairly quickly, but Emet couldn't. He watched what he could see of her face in the moonlight. She appeared so much sicklier than the night before. He slept more than the previous night due to his sheer tiredness but awoke many times without memory of his dreams yet full of dread.

He awoke in the morning alone in the bed. 'Maw?'

'One minute,' she replied chipperly from inside the toilet.

He breathed a quiet sigh of relief, got out of bed, and climbed down the ladder before sitting at the little table they sometimes ate and drank at. She emerged from the toilet. 'Good morning, darling. How'd you sleep?'

'So so,' he replied, 'but how are you?'

'I'm actually feeling a decent bit better than last night, thanks. No more bad bowel movements, no more nausea for now, touch wood,' she said, touching the fake wood ladder frame. 'I probably just overdid it the other day. I'll take it *a wee bit* easier from now on.'

Emet smiled at her. 'I'm just glad you're feeling better.'

'A bit of brekkie to power our slightly pared-back plans?'

'Sure, if you're feeling up to it, but let me get it,' he said.

'What a lovely wean I raised, looking out for others.'

He chuckled to himself as he stood. 'I dunno about others. You're part of a very select group.'

'Well,' she said, 'I'm privileged, but I know you've got more caring to give.'

He let her comment pass him by, took her breakfast request, and returned with a cup of black coffee and a dairy-free yoghurt for her. He sat opposite her across the table as his eggs boiled on the hob. She eagerly tucked into the yoghurt with none of the hesitation of yesterday, savouring its taste, before looking at her son. 'What shall we do today, then?' she said aiming a bright smile at him.

It was only upon seeing the whites of her teeth that something caught his attention. It took a second or two to sink in. 'Maw. Your eyes are yellow. We need to get you to a hospital.'

CHAPTER 57

Emet put his foot down, getting them to the nearest hospital as soon as possible. Leigh knew the diagnosis – jaundice due to the blockage of a bile duct, common amongst those with pancreatic cancer – but also that she needed treatment. In her condition, surgery was not an option, so the lowest risk alternative was to have a stent endoscopically inserted via the mouth and down the oesophagus that would reopen the duct from inside. After the fairly routine outpatient procedure, Leigh knew she may experience pain when swallowing and at the top of her stomach, and that she needed to rest at home for a few days. 'Home is that van right now, so let me rest up in the motherland amongst nature.' After some minor objections from Emet, he agreed to it on two conditions: that they could make their way further south towards more hospitals or England if needs be, and that she would use the bed on the ground floor until all pain subsided. Three days after the procedure, having broken up her mostly van-and-bedbound days with short wanders by the new loch they parked near each day, Leigh's insides felt better. 'Maybe I can stretch my little legs a wee bit more tomorrow.' But when the next morning came, Emet found her shivering and doubled up under her covers.

Another trip to a more southerly hospital revealed she had an infection. After hooking her up to an antibiotic drip for a one-night stay, the next morning she was worse. A battery of tests and scans revealed the stent had also shifted and perforated the bile duct it was in, causing internal bleeding. In addition to this, a new CT scan showed that despite a few weeks of chemotherapy, the cancer had aggressively spread. 'For us to see some of the sights up here's been a dream come true, but I think home's calling now.'

A sleep-deprived wreck, Emet drove them back to London for his mum to consult with her colleagues about how to deal with her accelerated condition. Tweaking her treatment did nothing to slow it, and over the following weeks her suffering only increased between the cancer's development and the new chemotherapy's side effects. Random swells of nausea, agonising stomach and back pain, bouts of itching so intense she wanted to scrape her skin off, bone-deep lethargy, and further weight loss meant that just over a month after returning to the capital, her frailty was making it tough to maintain her independence, even with the regular aid of Emet, Davide, and other friends. 'I want to enjoy what time I have left with you, not watch you mopping up my sick and wiping my arse.' She wanted to end her days in a hospice.

Once there, she saw how wrecked her son was at seeing her slip away like this. 'Get yourself back to work, sonny. You could do with something to take your mind off this twenty-four-seven.' He reached out to Felix, explained his mum's situation, and asked if a return was possible; something he really wasn't sure of given he had no information on how the claim against the paper had developed. Felix said he could come back and, as long as he met deadlines, working flexible hours wouldn't be an issue. This was on one condition: he would stick to his wheelhouse of arts and culture reviews and criticism. He didn't want to add to his mum's worries, and the last thing he wanted to do was pick at the infected scab that was his last story, so he accepted.

Meeting deadlines wasn't a problem. Stacks of discs could be posted through his letterbox, and he would get through them with the extra hours in the day that not being able to sleep, or not wanting to, afforded him. But although he didn't sleep much, he wasn't really awake much either, especially when alone. Being at the hospice with his mum, Davide, and Skye pulled him out of his almost perpetual hypnagogia.

He had properly introduced Skye to Leigh at her house during the middle of her time at home, wanting to have done it at a better time but realising that there wouldn't be one. The two had hit it off and Skye, depending on her now-freer shift patterns, would sometimes even go to see Leigh independently of him. He quietly marvelled at how this woman, who had only been in his life a few months, had stepped up to the plate in such a morbid situation at a time when relationships should ordinarily be sunshine and rainbows. He watched in awe at how perfect she was with his mum. She could emotionally meet her in whatever state she was in and gently raise her, however bad she was feeling, much better than he could as he struggled to hold himself together. She could talk with her about anything, and when they ran out of chatter, their silences never seemed awkward. She was as caring, if not more, than the hospice staff, even sometimes with some of the other residents. If he hadn't loved her before the hospice, he certainly did now, although he had no clue when a good time would be to let her know. His eternal gratitude would do for now.

As he entered the hospice to visit that day, he said hello to the receptionist and made his way along the corridor. As he passed by one of the social areas, something caught his eye, up in the corner of the room. Two things, hovering, one slightly above the other. They were long helium balloons, perfectly still in the vertical plane, maybe a few days deflated. They began revolving at a snail's pace, revealing two characters on them. *No.* A cold chill surged up him. The higher had the painted self portrait of Emet's father from the painting in his living room. The lower one showed a similar style painting of his frail mum. Both hung there, unnaturally still now, peering at him.

'Call him while you still have the chance.' The Irish voice spun Emet's head. A care assistant was pushing a resident out of their room nearby. The assistant was Irish, but what followed in their conversation bore no relevance to what Emet had heard. Confused, he turned back to look at the balloons. No figures were on them. He palmed his eyes for a long moment and juddered before taking a few deep breaths and setting back off along the corridor. When he arrived at his mum's room, the door was open and she was in there with Skye. They both sat at a square table, engrossed in drawing something with rulers and white pens on black paper. He quietly stepped in, enjoying watching them and not wanting to disturb them. His mum eventually turned to the doorway, a large smile across her weary, gaunt face. 'Come in.'

'I don't want to interrupt.'

'You're not. We're nearly done with this part.'

He walked in, kissed his mum on the cheek and hugged her, then kissed Skye.

'What do you think?' asked Leigh.

He looked down to see a circular white-line mandala drawing almost as large as the table. While done in the style of a traditional one with almost architectural precision, the imagery wasn't the usual Tibetan Buddhist type. The beautifully balanced polyptych was a collection of images with meaning to Leigh; a tribute to her life and interests. There was a drawing of Emet, of Davide, of her late husband, and of Skye's crystals and feathers. There was the Caduceus – the staff of Hermes with two snakes wrapped around it that was the symbol of the medical profession. There was the folded ribbon, the symbol for cancer awareness associated with some of the charities Leigh had supported throughout her years in the field. There were symbols of her favourite bands and movies, as well as a pair of drumsticks for the class that had given her a new lease of life during the months before she found out she was ill. The patterns that brought the entire piece together were those of her motherland; thistles, tartan, the hills, and the lochs. The poignance of the whole thing overwhelmed Emet with emotion, which he tried to keep in as he kept examining the massive amount of detail embedded into the piece. 'It's incredible,' he said, struggling to keep his voice from creaking. 'It must have took ages.'

'We've been working on it this last week,' said Skye.

He kissed the crown of her head as his eyes kept discovering additional parts of the work. He recognised nearly everything there, but in the very centre of the piece was an almost circular band with tiny writing on it. Even with his glasses on, he couldn't make out what it said. 'What's that in the middle?'

'That's from the scariest but the best day of my life. That's your ID bracelet from the day you were born.' She turned to Skye. 'He came so early, they had to keep transfusing him for a few days. We're the rarest blood type, so when they ran low, they actually gave him some of mine.'

He couldn't hold back his tears anymore, so referenced them. 'So you're to blame for these.'

'Oh, sonny. Don't make me start. Come here,' she said. The two embraced long and tight.

When he let go, he took hold of Skye's hand. 'Thank you so much for doing this with her.'

'You can do it with her too…if you can stay inside the lines, the proper way.' Skye reached down beside the table, picked up an old small leather suitcase that she put on her knee, and opened it. Inside were several long, slightly conical copper pipes, some copper rods, and bags of brilliantly coloured dyed sand.

After Skye showed them how to rasp the copper funnels with the rods to empty sand out of them in a steady stream, she hit play on a playlist of Leigh's favourite music, and they set to work colouring the mandala in. They didn't go for long the first day, with Leigh tired from the sustained focus for the drawing but over the next week, little by little, slowly and carefully, with the help of Davide and even a touch from Clyde on a visit, they filled in and lined the entire design with radiant sand. From time to time during the process, Emet would lift his weary gaze to his mother's concentrating face, sometimes catching her smiling, other times grimacing. This may be the last thing of any substance he would ever do with her, and there was nothing he could do to stop her end. *Nothing. Not one thing. Null. Maybe that's what Nullconda meant.* He told himself over and over that there was nothing he could do. But it did nothing to cool the magmic heat bubbling up and scorching him from the inside out.

There was one last section of sand to pour – the oval inside of the hospital baby bracelet in the centre of the entire piece, which had been left to be the cherry on top of the sundae.

'What colour would you like it?' asked Skye.

At the most fragile she had been, Leigh brushed her wispy hair away from her face and considered the section. A weak, warm smile found its way out. 'The purple of heather,' she said, sharing a smile with Skye, Emet, and Davide.

Skye nodded at the perfect choice and prepared a funnel with some in. 'It's all yours.'

Leigh took the funnel in one of her weak hands and directed Skye to pass Emet the rod. 'Will you do me the honours, sonny?'

'Of course.' He took the rod, followed her trembling hands over the piece, and helped steady the funnel's end above the empty section. 'Ready?'

She took a long, deep breath in and scanned around the multicoloured circle beneath her. 'Ready,' she replied before tilting the nozzle down. As he rubbed the rod back and forth along it, the fine stream of purple sand began to pour out, their hands guiding it to fill in the entire gap, then slowly tilting it back to stop the flow. They held hands for a moment as they took it all in, then he hugged her, then Davide and Skye joined them. As they parted, they all stood back in awe of the coloured piece.

'That really is quite something finished,' said Emet, shaking his head in disbelief at how well it had turned out as he pulled out his phone and took a few photos.

'It's not finished yet,' said Leigh, a tear in her eye as she cuddled into Davide.

'What else is to do?' asked Emet as he moved around it, snapping a few more.

She looked him in the eye, her eyes full of love. 'Destroy it.'

Emet's jaw fell open. 'What for? You can keep that here. Have something beautiful to look at every day. At least for a while.'

'The beauty was in the doing,' she replied, 'and that will last longer than a while.'

As he clammed up, Skye squeezed his hand, then gently spoke. 'These sand ones aren't just about balance; they're about peace. Peace with the impermanence of even the most beautiful of things.'

His mum looked at him. 'There's a beauty in coming to peace with the ending of something too.'

All of his incredulous tension fell away, and he nodded.

Skye handed them all a brush three inches wide and showed them the way they would deconstruct the mandala, sweeping in a slow, smooth arc from the outside of the circle to the inside, then taking a small step around it and doing the same again. Even the manner of the destruction was serenely beautiful. They took one last look at Leigh's mandala; the representation of her perfectly balanced universe. 'I'm ready.' Then they swept and they stepped until the picture was replaced by a spiral streak of colours, before Skye swept the remains into a large glass jar, around which she fastened a purple silk ribbon.

'That's to go into water with a current, to impart the peace of it all back to the world,' said Skye.

'Sonny. After I'm gone,' said Leigh, 'will you take that up to one of the west coast lochs we didn't get to? The ones that connect to the sea?'

Barely keeping himself together, he nodded her way.

CHAPTER 58

Emet stared at the ribboned jar of sand, almost psychedelic in its multicoloured pattern, on his coffee table, then looked up at his dad's painting and burst into an uncontrollable fit of sobbing. Skye, on her way back from the toilet, heard him, trotted into the room, and wrapped her arms around him. 'No, darling, no. What's wrong?'

He sobbed so hard he couldn't catch his breath to get any words out.

'Breathe, darling, breathe,' she said as she stroked the back of his hair. The tears streamed inconsolably as he tried to get hold of his breathing, but he couldn't catch it. 'What is it?'

'It's…it's…all my fault,' he blurted out between his erratic breaths.

'No no no,' she said, tightening her hug.

'It is…it's my fault,' he gasped, fuelling his sobbing further.

'No no no,' she repeated more forcefully. 'This is nobody's fault, Emet. Not your mum. Not your dad. There's nothing you could have done for him and there's nothing you can do for your mum, so don't you think that. There's nothing anybody can do. These are purely tragedies of life.'

'They're not,' he blubbed. 'I should've done…better…I could've done…more.'

She pulled away from him and raised his hanging head by his chin, trying to get him to look at her. 'Emet. You listen to me. There is nothing you could've done better or more of. How you've been with your mum, going to Scotland with her, and being at the hospice every single day even though it's breaking your heart. You would go to the ends of the earth for her because you're an amazing man with a big heart, and that's why I love you.'

The words stunned him and pulled his gaze towards hers, but realising he was still crying, he covered his eyes with his hand.

'You don't have to hide from me. You can't love somebody as much as you love her and not be upset by what's happening,' she said, easing his hand away, showing him her eyes were welling up too. 'I'm with you in this, and I'll be with you right through it all. I love you.'

He wiped away some of his tears. 'I love you too.'

She gently kissed his lips, wiping away more of his tears. Her warm, soft lips barely left his before coming back for another. He wiped his face again and stroked her wavy hair, backing away to look at her. She gazed back with radiating unadulterated love. He set his hands on her waist, eased her closer, and kissed her more passionately. She met him in kind. From there, their passion only deepened, and he was happy to lose himself in it.

He awoke in the middle of the night to the distant sound of a phone ringing, maybe from next door, with a dry mouth, dehydrated from the throes of passion a few hours before. He reached for his glass of water on the bedside table. His hands searched for the solid vertical side of the tumbler, but instead met much thinner glass. *Huh?* As he turned on the glowing orb of his sunrise alarm a little to see what it was, the ringing loudened. The gentle golden light backlit the deep purple cocktail he'd reached for. 'No,' he said to himself as the ringing grew louder.

'You're an amazing man with a big heart.'

He rolled over. Skye was sat up in bed holding a ringing phone out towards him, the ring so loud it reverberated through his entire body, as blood spilled out of her mouth. 'And that's why I love you.'

He shook awake, feeling a hand on his shoulder. 'Emet. Emet!' Her words drowned out the ringing. 'Emet. It's just a bad dream. I'm here with you.' His sweat-drenched arm reached to turn on the light. There was no blood in sight. Aside from the concern on her face and in her voice, she was fine. She kissed his shoulder. 'I'm here with you.' He kissed her back and sighed. 'Can I get you anything?' she asked.

'No, I'm just parched,' he replied, reaching out for his water on the bedside table. After taking a swig, he knocked it against something as he set it back.

'OK.' She cosied up against him and kissed his cheek. 'Leave the light on for a bit if you want. I'm so shattered I'd sleep in broad daylight.'

He looked across at the lamp, the glass, and what he'd bumped with it: his phone. 'It's OK,' he said, dimming the lamp back to black. 'Get yourself back to sleep.'

She squeezed him and was dead to the world within a few minutes. The room was pitch black, his eyes were closed, but his mind's eye was wide open and all it could see was his phone. And in the silence, all he could hear was a distant ringing.

The next morning, he couldn't accompany Skye into central London. After barely any sleep, he had startled awake by his blindingly lit alarm clock and ever since that, had been puking his guts up in the bathroom. Skye offered to take the day off with him. 'I'll be fine. It'll just be a bug.' After convincing her to go, she reluctantly bid him farewell.

'Love you,' she said.

He mustered a smile. 'I love you too.'

Half an hour later, he dragged himself down to the living room. *Nullconda* and the sand jar loomed large. His sickness was no bug and the only medicine for what ailed him sat on the coffee table near the jar. Eventually, he leaned forward, picked up his phone, and scrolled through his contacts. He peered at the name long and hard. He couldn't do this. But he had to. The line began ringing. Part of him prayed it would ring out.

'Hello, Laurel Canyon Manor.'

Emet froze.

'Hello?'

He couldn't bring himself to say it.

'Hello. Is anybody there…?

He couldn't. But he did. 'Hello. Can I speak to Delancey, please?'

'May I ask who is calling?'

He hesitated. 'Emet. Emet Gordon.'

'Let me see if he's available, Mr Gordon.'

As the end of the line went quiet, nearly every fibre of Emet's being wanted to put the phone down, but he couldn't. And then he heard the voice that had plagued his dreams for the past few weeks. 'Emet Gordon. To what do I owe the pleasure?'

Emet held his tongue until he could no longer. 'You said that I could supply you with a case study to prove that what you do works. I have somebody for you. If you can reverse their condition, I will beg your forgiveness and sing your praises to the entire world. Will you work with them?'

The line went quiet. 'I wish I could, Emet, but you were right.'

'What do you mean?'

'What I was doing…without proof…you were right, it was irresponsible. I've stopped. The Cancer Man is no more. You win.'

Emet rested his head on his free hand. 'No. This is a lost cause, Delancey. There's nothing to lose and only credibility to gain.'

'I can't,' replied Delancey.

'You have to,' pleaded Emet. 'It's my mother. She has stage four pancreatic. There's nothing anyone can do.'

The line went silent for a moment. 'And there's nothing I can do either, Emet. You made me see that. I'm sorry. Goodbye.' The line cut.

Reeling, Emet set his phone down. He'd waited, and it was over. It was all over.

CHAPTER 59

After some more time on his hands and knees in front of the toilet, he couldn't throw up anymore. He laid on the cold, hard floor for forty minutes intermittently cursing himself under his breath before pulling himself together and heading out to the hospice.

A shell of himself, he mustered the greetings he could to the hospice receptionist and headed towards his mum's room, only to be stopped by one of her nurses on his way.

'Just to let you know, she had a bad night. We had to give her lots of painkillers. The last I saw, she was sleeping.'

Her thanked her and carried on in. He was horrified to see how much more ashen his mum looked than yesterday, her face still holding some of the pain she must have experienced last night. He crept in and sat himself by her bed as silently as he could, watching her chest rise and fall, wondering how many more days he'd be able to do so, wondering if when she drew her last breath, his breathing would give up too. His eyes were desperate to rest, but he didn't want them to, fearing where he would go if they did. *I need a coffee. Or a cigarette.*

After a while of fighting the drowsiness, he stood to perk himself up and Leigh stirred. Her eyelids peeled open, her dry lips parted, and her emaciated voice scratched out of her. 'Sonny…you look…like hell. Are you alright?'

'It was just a bad takeaway. I'll be fine.'

She suspiciously examined him but left it there.

'They said you had a bad night?'

'Aye,' she said, licking her congealed lips. 'Can you pass me a drink?'

He picked up the beaker from her bedside table and helped her slow, shaky hands direct it to her mouth. After a few mouthfuls, her eyes rolled shut as a wave of pain seized her.

'Your stomach?'

She gritted her teeth and nodded. 'Aye. The pain's…more boring than anything. I wish I'd have got on one of those…magic mushroom or LSD…end-of-life clinical trials. Must be hard to be bored…or anything, really…when you're off your wee face.'

'Clinical trial, shminical trial. You leave it with me.' He took hold of her hand with both of his, kissing it tenderly.

She poignantly looked at their hands together, then fixed a tired, loving gaze on her son. 'It's lovely to see you found…some happiness…with Skye. She's been an angel…with me and some of the…others here.'

'I'm glad you like her, Maw.'

'I do. And I know…she's a creative…and she feels a bit lost right now…but she'll be fine. She's a gentle soul but…I've met a lot of people going through a lot of tough stuff, and I can tell…she's got more mettle than maybe she knows.'

The way she spoke sounded like a summary to him, and a summary comes just before an ending. A tear rolled down his cheek.

'It's OK, sonny…I've had an amazing innings. I've helped lots of people.'

'You have,' he replied, another couple of tears rolling as he stroked her hand with his thumb.

'I had your da…'

The tears streamed now.

'I had you. And I get an opportunity many don't…to say everything I want…I get to tell you how much I love you…how proud I am of you…before I go.'

Redness rushed up his neck and face as he burst into a sob.

'Sonny, no no no.' She pulled his hand. 'Come here. It's OK.'

'It's not, Maw,' he blurted out. 'You shouldn't be proud of me. I've done terrible things.'

'Nonsense, Emet. You don't have a bad bone in your body.'

He covered his eyes with his free hand, unable to stop the tears falling. 'You don't understand. It's my fault, Maw.'

'What're you talking about?' she asked.

'It's my fault…' The words stuck in his throat like a dagger. '…Da died.'

She shook her exhausted head. 'No, son. Your da had cancer…and instead of getting proper treatment, he chose to chase a fairy tale told by people who bullshitted…just like him.'

'But I'm the one who told him…about spontaneous remission,' he said, more distraught by the word. 'He was railing against you wanting to control his treatment and saying that it was the only way. I'd just done a module on oncology, and being a young smartarse, I told him that it wasn't technically true; that in one in every few hundred thousand cases, the body reverses the disease process and heals itself without treatment. Who knew what was possible, I said. I saw a lightbulb go on in his eyes. I remember being proud about it, thinking clever little me had given him a sliver of hope; a thread of a lifeline. A couple of weeks later, I found his letter, and he was gone.' Tears and repressed rage spilled out of him. *'I* was the one who put that idea in his head. *I* gave him that false hope. His blood is on *my hands.*'

Her face drained of what little colour it had. 'Sonny…when you first passed out at that cannulation, how close was that to then?'

Emet lowered his gaze and turned it away.

'My God.' She winced as she tried to sit herself up in the bed. 'Now you listen to me, Emet Gordon. You are in no way responsible for what he did.'

'But I—'

'But nothing,' she said. 'Your da, I loved him so much…he made me feel like the most special woman in the universe…but there was so much going on in his head that I never knew about. He had…an entire criminal enterprise he hid from us. And all that lying and manipulating he did and got away with…I think it made him feel like he was special and smarter than everybody…like he always knew better…but it warped his sense of reality. Even though he had a wife who'd spent her life legitimately helping people with his very illness…he was a conman who became gullible to the most dangerous con,' she said as her eyes welled up. 'All you did was try to give him some nuance…and a speck of extra hope. Never feel bad for that. It was his ego…and his fantastical thinking…that ran with it in the wrong direction. Come here, sonny.'

Emet leaned forward and hugged her tight. She didn't hate him for what he'd done, but that wasn't everything. And he could feel the rest of the revelation bubbling up in his throat ready to be coughed out like the bloody mess from his nightmares. Just as he was about to spit out that she was his fault too, that maybe he had shut down the tiniest chance of her recovery, she spoke.

'The scars he left us with…to vanish like he did and let you think that had anything to do with you…' she said, shaking her head, '…and for me. I loved him. Even after all the lies. I stuck with him though his time in prison. I'd worked my entire career to be in the perfect position to help somebody in his exact position. He could have lived years longer…as my husband…as your da. It breaks my heart every day that instead of trusting me to help him, he chose to trust two-bit charlatans promising miracle cures. And as many years as I've helped people add on to their lives…I couldn't get through to him. That'll haunt me till the day I go. But at least I raised you, and you succeeded where I failed.'

Emet pulled back a little. 'How do you mean?'

'That horrid man you wrote about. His website's down. That must be off the back off your article.'

His eyes widened.

'You've stopped him exploiting the desperate…poisoning them with false hope. I thought there was no good to come from telling the public about him…opening the possibility for people to take the nuance and run in the wrong direction with it…but you were right. You beat him,' she said, buoyed and devoid of the pain that had been etched into her face on and off for the last few weeks. 'I can't tell you how proud of you I am, sonny. You've helped countless people.'

His entire body tremored as his proud mum squeezed his hand whilst burning tears streamed down his face. 'I really haven't, Maw. You don't understand. I—'

'Nonsense. I don't want to hear it,' she said, cutting him off. 'Doing good is in your blood, and as much as you say you're not a people person, I know when I go, you'll keep protecting them…because it's the right thing to do. Your Maw brought you up right,' she said, kissing his hand. 'So, by all means…keep fighting the monsters like him, just don't become one while you're at it. The world needs healers too.'

He nodded profusely, fighting back his tears, still wondering if he should say something.

'Keep doing me proud.'

He nodded, struggling to get his words out. 'I will, Maw.'

She choked up. 'I love you, sonny. More than a heart can hold.'

'I love you too, Maw,' he said, pinning his mouth shut as he hugged her tightly, trying to make her feel every scintilla of love he had.

CHAPTER 60

He knew it was coming and braced himself. He saw the first drop of blood begin to trickle down the wardrobe door's slats but no more came. Just one deep red drop sliding down the pristine white door. But then he felt a trickle down his chin. He wiped it. Blood was escaping from his pinned-shut mouth. The screech of the alarm startled him after a restless night full of dreams that he couldn't remember much of. They didn't feel nightmarish; more just unsettling. Skye had worked late last night, so he'd spent the night alone and although he felt deeply uncomfortable about not telling his mum that he'd tried to enlist Delancey's help on her behalf, he convinced himself he'd done the right thing. She was best spending the next few weeks or months proud of him, as she had much more energy and felt so much better after their heart to heart. He couldn't believe how she'd managed to energise herself in the state she was in to lift somebody else's spirits. But that was going to be who she was until the very end – a force for good.

He opened the blackout curtains to let the warm morning sunshine in. After a few duller, cooler days, it looked like he might get away with one layer for work today. He took a set of clothes from his summer selection, then took his phone off the bedside table. In addition to a few messages, he had four missed calls. They were from the hospice during the last hour. Dread-filled, his trembling hands hit call. The rings couldn't end fast enough. His heart was in his mouth when the receptionist picked up. He exchanged a few sentences with her, then crumpled to the floor, staring at the phone he'd just dropped. His mum was gone.

Swathes of people attended the funeral. Even though she didn't have any family apart from Emet, through over three decades as a gregarious doctor, she had such a network of work friends that people were standing in the church's aisles and at the back. Emet had been such a wreck for the last ten days that Clyde and Skye didn't think he would be able to deliver his eulogy, but he got through it.

At the burial, a few close friends crumbled some earth onto her coffin before it was due to be lowered. Emet brought up the rear, looked at her coffin for the last time, and raised his hand. 'I love you, Maw.' He opened his hand. Out fell a handful of the multicoloured sand from her mandala.

At the wake, he was a shell of a man, often stepping away from Skye, Clyde and his other friends, only to be found in the corridor or outside staring into space. At one point when he was sat across in the far corner of the room, zoned out, Clyde pulled Skye aside. 'I know he's barely with us today, but you've been with him the last few days, apart from being withdrawn, has he been odd at all?'

She frowned. 'Odd how?'

'Has he been saying anything that sounded weird, or has he been…speaking to himself?'

'Umm, no, I don't think so. Why?'

Clyde scrubbed his head before answering. 'I'm guessing he hasn't mentioned anything about his time in the hospital?'

Skye's eyes broadened. 'No.'

'I'm sure he would have at some point but there's been a lot going on. I know it's his thing to tell, but you need to know.' He paused, gathering himself. 'Last year, just after the tenth anniversary of his dad's passing, he came home to find he'd been burgled. Amongst all the stuff they'd taken were his dad's ashes.'

Skye's hand covered her gaping mouth.

'Fucking idiots probably thought it was an antique. Anyway, after that, he ended up in hospital for a six weeks.'

'He didn't try…?'

'No, no. But he was completely incoherent, and it was maybe going that way. I'm sure he'd have told you at some point.'

She took a while to say anything, trying to process the information. 'He would. It's not something anyone'd lead with, and this has been a rough, rough time.'

'Yes, so just keep an eye on him. If he starts not making sense, give me a shout.'

She nodded. They both looked over in his direction. He was still staring through the same patch of wall.

Although extremely down, Skye noticed no strange behaviour or utterances from Emet over the next week. 'Are you sure you're gonna be OK?' she asked as she put her jacket on, ready for work. 'If you leave it until Sunday, I'll come help.'

'I'll be alright. If there's any left to do by then, you can help me with the last bits.'

She nodded, kissed him goodbye, and left. A while later, he left too, with packing boxes in his car boot. As he pulled up at his first red light, he noticed the banner ad along the side of the bus letting passengers on across the road; he couldn't miss that winning smile if he tried. The Leap was back in town in six weeks. "Last few seats available". The red light wouldn't change fast enough.

Every familiar face at the hospital greeted him with warm sympathy as he made his way to his mum's office. "Dr Leigh Gordon: Consultant Oncologist" read the name plate. He slid it out of its holder and boxed it. Inside, he began sorting through her belongings, boxing any personal items. It didn't take long to come to the photo in her drawer of his younger self with both parents. He knew she had held on to her love of his dad but had no idea that her disappointment and anger at not being able to help him had remained so fresh for so long.

A knock came at the ajar door. 'I heard you were in,' said Clyde, poking his head around it. 'Am I alright to join you?'

Emet nodded and returned his gaze to the photo briefly before boxing it.

'How are you getting on? I've dropped you a few messages…'

'Yeh, sorry,' said Emet, breaking from his sorting for a moment. 'I'm…well, I'm whatever somebody is when something like this happens.'

'Course,' replied Clyde. 'Can I lend a hand?'

'I don't think there's much here. And it should be me,' said Emet. 'But I'm starting at her house today. I may enlist you with that at some point.'

'No bother. You just let me know when and I'll be there.'

Emet nodded appreciatively.

'Do you fancy popping out for a quiet one sometime soon? Raise a glass in her honour and give you a change of scenery?'

'We'll see.'

Clyde paused. 'She wouldn't want you by yourself through this.'

'I'm not. Skye's been there.'

'Good. Still, I'm here whenever you want me, yeh?'

Emet nodded.

'I'll leave you to it. I can hear the centrifuges calling me.'

They swapped a muted smile and Clyde returned to the door. 'I'll miss popping here. She was the friendliest face in this place. It's unbelievable given how consultants generally are.'

'I know,' replied Emet bittersweetly.

'She did a lot of good in here down the years.' He kissed his hand and pressed it to the door frame. 'See you later, Dr Leigh. And you. Much sooner though, yeh?'

Emet nodded and Clyde left. Soon after, Emet said a prolonged goodbye to the office he'd popped into from time to time over the last decade to see his mum, and left for the last time. His packing continued at her house, but he only got through a few hours of binning and boxing items before he was emotionally exhausted. Even the bathroom, devoid of anything with real sentimental value, had proved difficult when he opened the cabinet to be faced with bottles and bottles of painkillers and chemotherapy drugs and an unopened, old packet of his dad's Sterling Greens.

He pulled up outside his house, grabbed a couple of boxes out of his boot, and climbed the steps to his front door. As he put his key in the lock and turned it, there was no resistance against it. He looked down at it. There was a hole above the keyhole. *Fuck.* The lock had been drilled. He pushed the door open and ran in over the envelopes scattered on his doormat. As he turned into his living room, he halted in horror. The sand jar was smashed all over the floor. And his dad's painting was gone. He leaned against the doorframe and crumpled into a heap on the floor.

He laid there ruined for an age until he remembered that his front door was wide open and some of his mum's belongings were sat on the doorstep. He couldn't lose anymore, so mustered the energy to go get them, shut the lockless door, put the boxes on his coffee table, then fetched a dustpan and shovel. Upon returning to the living room and being faced by the bare main wall, he slumped down onto the sofa and gazed at the bright, sharp mess on the floor.

Eventually, he propped himself forwards and took the lids off the boxes. He rummaged through one and emerged with the tiny baby bracelet his mum had put at the centre of her mandala. She was gone. Everything was gone. His eyes were drawn back to the boxes. Poking out of the top of the other was one of her chemo drug bottles. He peered at it long and hard. Then he pulled a few bottles out along with the unopened cigarettes. The packet took him right back. His dad hadn't been a heavy smoker. He only really smoked to celebrate finishing a piece. Given Leigh's profession, that's as much as she'd tolerate.

Emet peeled the wrapper off and opened the ten pack. The menthol scent only deepened his nostalgia. He went to the kitchen, grabbed a candle lighter and a large glass of water, and returned to the sofa, where he sparked up and drew the time-transporting smoke deep into his lungs. He breathed it out and watched it swirl away like everything else in his life. After a while, he poured all the capecitabine tablets and painkillers onto the table and, four at a time, downed them with water between puffs of the cigarette. By the end of that cigarette, the two bottles were gone. The tears streamed down his face as he lit another. 'I'm sorry, Maw. In so many ways.'

Ten minutes later, his eyes had grown heavy. He was in a space between awake and asleep, but he could feel the chemically induced blackness slowly pulling him down. He was vaguely aware of something going on with his hand or something in that vicinity but couldn't feel it, so he strained his gaze there. His third cigarette, which he'd forgotten about for the last few minutes, was dangling out his fingers. And then it dropped onto the sofa beside him. Unable to move in his semi-sleep paralysis, he watched its orange and black tip smoulder against the material of the sofa. He tried with all his might to pick the cigarette up, but his body wouldn't comply. He was so numb, maybe he wouldn't feel it, anyway. *Let it go.* He let his eyelids fall closed. He let the black take him.

A low rumble crept into his awareness. And again, but sharper. More of a thud…*thud…thud.* Then a higher noise. The blackness grew darker in a patch. Then the loudest thud of all. He heard something indecipherable, but he knew it was his name.

Da?

It came again, clearer this time.

Da. I'm coming.

Then a blinding light appeared from nowhere.

Maw. I'll be there soon.

Clyde had pulled Emet's eyelid open and was shaking his friend's face, desperately trying to keep him alert as he spoke to the emergency operator on the phone. 'Stay with me, Emet!' he shouted, jiggling his face around. 'Stay with me!'

CHAPTER 61

'That's pretty.'

Emet looked over his shoulder. He guessed from the look in the lady's eyes she'd been in the hospital a lot longer than him and that she'd be in much longer still. 'Thanks. It should really be in sand, but this is the best they'd give me,' he said, lifting his crayon off the mandala in his colouring book.

'Sand, you say?' she asked, to which he nodded. 'I'm sure they'll give you some sand.'

'Yeh?'

'Absolutely,' said the dishevelled patient. 'When you ask for it, you just have to really believe.'

Yuck. As cringeworthy as he found her baseless optimism, he was shocked at the surge of aggression and the desire to forcibly get her away that rushed up inside him, but he smiled and nodded placatingly before returning to his colouring.

'Emet.'

He turned to look again. It was one of the ward's nurses.

'The doctor's confirmed. Do you want to get your things together?'

A few hours later, bag in hand, he thanked a few of the staff as he made his way to the exit. He'd seen Skye most days over the last four weeks but when the door opened, revealing her across the open threshold back to the outside world, the joy he felt was unimaginable.

She hugged him like a Boa constrictor and pecked his face with kisses. 'I love you.'

'I love you too,' he said, kissing her one more time, 'and I'll love you even more when we get the hell out of here.'

After a long taxi journey, they pulled into his road and parked up where there was space, fifty yards before his place. After getting out and walking for a few seconds, he stopped saw the van he'd journeyed with his mum in, having forgotten Clyde had moved it there a week ago for him.

'Are you alright?' asked Skye, linking her arm with his.

He nodded, and the two carried on to his front door. He examined the new lock with his thumb.

'That's top of the line. Nobody should be getting in again.' She paused as she passed him his key. 'Except Clyde. He has a copy for now. He said you can fight him for it.'

He half smirked and opened the door. Even with his time away and Felix knowing about it, there were still a few discs on his doormat. Other than that, the hallway was pristine. He stepped over them and made his way to the living room. Like last time, he was surprised to see what was on the main wall. The void left by the stolen painting had been replaced by a black square piece. It was the white line mandala they had coloured in with sand. 'One work of art for another,' she said.

His smile was laden with emotion. 'One work of art for another,' he repeated before wrapping an arm around her and kissing her cheek.

'Sit yourself down and relax,' she said. 'I'll get us a drink.'

He plonked himself on the sofa, admiring the drawing on the wall as he kicked his shoes off. It was strange to be back with the house reset but infinitely better than where he'd been for the past four weeks. He remembered the blackness from the last time he'd sat here and the call of who he thought were his parents' voices. Then he remembered the cigarette that he'd dropped, which drew his eyes to where he'd dropped it. There was a mark there, but again not what he expected. The burn mark had been stitched over with a small heart the same colour as the sofa.

'Love saved your life, so I thought that's a little reminder that you're never alone,' said Skye, half standing in the doorway. She then stepped fully into sight with a beaming smile, showing a large multicoloured sand-filled, ribbon-wrapped jar in her hands. 'I think I got it all. You can still take it where it needs to go.'

He welled up and waved her over. She put the jar on the table, sat, and snuggled into him. 'The words don't exist for me to thank you sufficiently.'

'They don't need to,' she said, kissing his cheek and settling back into his embrace.

'Will you come up with me to the loch?'

'Of course I will. Let's get you back feeling good, then plan it. Deal?'

'Deal,' he said.

'Speaking of plans…well, not plans as such, but an idea, I think I might know what I want to do beyond coffee and cocktails.'

'Oh wow,' said Emet, genuinely enthusiastic for the first time in weeks. 'Tell me!'

'Well, all that time I spent with your mum and some of the other people in the hospice, I loved helping them take their minds off some of what was going on and helping them make some meaning out of the time they had left. And then you'd said I should get back to more of my art, but I couldn't really see the point. Well, I see it now. I want to use it to help people. I want to become an art therapist.'

He tried to restrain his scepticism. 'Oh right. How does someone go about that?'

She looked him in the eyes and chuckled. 'I can see what you're thinking.'

'Oh, can you now?'

'Absolutely. You're thinking that's not a *real thing,* like life coaching or what Rawlings does. And that you can just call yourself it or do some one-week course ran by a self-proclaimed certifier and you're ready to therapise people. Am I hot or cold?'

He hesitated and smiled guiltily. 'You're Scotch Bonnet.'

She poked a playful finger into his chest. 'I knew it. Well, actually, they're regulated health care professionals like radiographers and physios, they're employed by the NHS, and you need a masters in arts therapy or arts psychotherapy to be one. So there.'

'OK, OK.' He hesitated again. 'But what does one actually do?'

'It's just like psychotherapy but with art replacing most of the words. There are people who can't speak. People who don't want to speak. Art is just another way to express what's going on inside. Sometime people can say more through it than they can with words. The therapist helps the person create something that really expresses what's going on for them to help them straighten out their head and then chats with them about it or gets them to refine or challenge what's going on with further pieces. Sometimes making something helps people solve problems. Sometimes, the problems can't be solved, and it just helps them come to peace,' she said, glancing up at the drawing on the wall.

A slow, earnest nod emerged from him. 'I'm sorry. I get it. I mean not fully, I don't get what they'll teach you, but I saw what you did and how positive it was. Even if they can just certify you to do that for a living, I can see its value.'

She grinned ear to ear and laid her head on his chest. 'Thank you.'

'So, how do you go about becoming one?'

'The masters is two or three years, full or part time, but I'd have to get onto one first. But I'm thinking before I go for one, I should go'n do a taster course. There's a world-renowned place up north that does ten-day residential things a few times a year. They've got one starting in a few days, then one in four months. I might see if I can get on that one in winter.'

'Why don't you see if you can go on this one?' he asked. 'There's no time like the present.'

'Work won't give me that time off so short notice.'

'If they won't, there are plenty of coffee shops and cocktail bars that'd take you on your return. Best espresso martini in the land!'

'I know,' she said, snuggling tighter into him, 'but there's money and stuff as well. It can wait a few months.'

She doesn't want to leave me alone. Not now. He looked down at the top of her sweet head and kissed it. 'Only if you're sure?'

'I am.'

'Hey.'

She took her head off his chest and looked at him inquisitively.

'Thank you.'

She kissed his chest and rested her head again. 'You're welcome, lightweight.'

CHAPTER 62

'Take it easy today, yes?' Skye asked.

'I will,' replied Emet. 'I might treat myself to a box set that I actually want to watch rather than have to.'

'That sounds nice. Maybe get some fresh air too.'

'That was a given,' he replied. 'A constitutional as a free man.'

She smiled and kissed him. 'See you at seven.'

He waved her goodbye and closed his front door behind her, finally picking up the Blu-rays near the doormat he'd walked over yesterday. He rifled through them as he made himself a cup of decaf tea to wash down his new morning antidepressant with – he'd reluctantly agreed to take them as it seemed his release from hospital was contingent on doing so – then went to the living room and turned on the TV. Within a second, he could tell from the music, the glossy, golden look of everything, and the cheesy smiles that he was watching an infomercial. Then Jim's winning smile appeared. 'So, if you wanna take your life to a whole 'nother level, join us and take The Leap.' The camera zoomed out to a full-length shot of Jim in the centre of the screen and either side of him it split into four, showing people of eight different ethnicities and ages. In perfect unison, they all thrust out their hands into that viewfinder diamond, seeing their perfect future out through it in Emet's direction, then swung back their arms in sync. As they launched themselves forward, all their camera angles did a fancy choreographed swivel, showing them taking off into the great unknown but not showing if they reached their ladder rung, instead cutting to seminar details and how to sign up for the last few seats in ten days' time. A burning rage shot up him, making every bone in his body want to throw his TV out the window but instead, he popped his medication in his mouth, washed it down with his tea, took a few deep breaths, and changed the channel.

A few episodes of a streaming drama series later, he went out for a walk. The nearby park, Paddington Rec, was a wonderful place he hadn't made anywhere near enough use of. At the beginning of her fitness kick, he took his mum there and between the running track and the sports pitches and all the people keeping fit individually and in classes, she adored it. Maybe he should take up jogging or yoga or tai chi, he mused as he relished the fresh air and sunshine on his face. He bought a posh salad from a local deli on his way back and put the TV on for some noise to eat along to. A few mouthfuls in and he remembered why he'd put a streaming service on – daytime TV was atrocious. He turned it off and scrolled through his social media feeds instead. During his time in the hospital, he'd turned off all notifications. When he got to Twitter, he discovered an inordinate number of mentions from within the last twenty minutes. Hosts of people had tried to send him the same link of what appeared to be a video hosted on Wildfire, but Twitter platform wouldn't allow him to view it and wouldn't even let him view enough of the link to have a chance of finding what it was. "I thought this snake had slithered back under his rock?" asked one comment. A sickening panic overcame him. He frantically navigated to Wildfire and typed in 'delanc' but saw there was no need. He clicked play on the featured video on the site's homepage, whose thumbnail in large capital letters said 'CANCER NO MORE'.

The video began, but it wasn't Delancey on it. 'Hello. I'm Jay Sharpa, founder of Wildfire. Cancer is a tragedy that touches the lives of many of us, way too many of us. It robs us of precious time with our nearest and dearest. And for me, it doesn't get dearer than this little dude right here.' He picked up a bald little boy, no older than six years old, holding him close. 'This is my son, Maximus. A few months ago, he was diagnosed with a stage four neuroblastoma. That's a cancer of some specialised nerve cells that has spread to other areas of the body, and it's one of the most lethal childhood cancers in existence. With it having spread by the time it was found, he needed radiotherapy and chemotherapy to shrink the main body of it before it could be removed and to slow the development of what had spread, followed by more radio and chemo. My little man is strong and brave, and we had the best medical team on the case, but the outlook wasn't good. Medical professionals are wonderful people with incredible expertise, but they're not miracle workers and we needed a miracle, didn't we, Max?'

His son nodded.

'And who was our miracle worker?'

'Delancey.'

'Yep. We were introduced to a man called Delancey O'Shea, and that's when everything changed.'

Various before and afters of medical imaging scans and blood test results showed on the screen, showing highlighted areas where tumours had cleared and that levels of HMA and VMA had fallen.

'In all my decades as an oncologist, I have never seen changes in a neuroblastoma case like this in such a short time,' said a man in a white coat subtitled as "Dr M. Yedlin – Consultant Oncologist".

'Max's scans here were taken thirty days apart, and what's more, they were both taken during a period of no conventional treatment, due to him having to recover from the last round. The only intervention that Max had during this time was from our new friend for life, Delancey O'Shea, or as I like to call him, The Remission Man.'

The video cut to Delancey, subtitled with his name and his new title. 'My name is Delancey O'Shea, and for many years, I've been helping people with cancer resolve the psychological and spiritual rifts within themselves. Ninety-five percent of the time, total remission of their cancer occurred within one month.'

A re-edited version of the testimonial showreel from The Cancer Man site played, shortened and with some new testimonials spliced in. Emet watched on with gaping eyes and a vein bulging out of his forehead, unable to believe what he was seeing.

Delancey appeared onscreen with Jay. 'Obviously, we realise these claims are bold, and many will believe them to be unsubstantiated and highly irresponsible, but Max and I as well as many others know otherwise through experience, so I wish to play my part in substantiating them so that the entire world can benefit. Until now, Delancey has had to work low profile for the fear of being penalised and prosecuted for sharing his unbelievable skills more openly. Now, I'm committed to helping him show what he can do to the world.'

'Ten days from now, he will give ten thousand people what is literally the opportunity of their lifetime. He will host an event here in London at the O2 Arena where he will work with an entire audience of individuals with stage three and four cancers to heal their deepest inner turmoils with the aim of reversing as many of their cancer processes as possible. Where he is not anticipating the same efficacy he's achieved in his one-to-one work, he nonetheless expects a high success rate.'

'We expect demand for the event to be extremely high and tickets are available by application only. To be eligible, applicants must supply evidence that they currently have a stage three of four cancer of some kind, they must be fluent in English given this works via talking therapy, they must not currently be engaged in any significant radiation or drug treatment, meaning they will not have had treatment yet, will be post-treatment or will be between treatment rounds and will have none scheduled for at least thirty days after the event, and they will agree to engage in a rigorous data-sharing and follow-up programme, including live blood monitoring, over the next year.'

'I realise how all this sounds; that this isn't the way research is normally conducted, but we know the baseline of survival statistics from the general population, and we know from a sample size of thousands what Delancey is capable of. Given my platform, I can't in good conscience sit in silence on this knowledge, regardless of how endorsing something so out of the norm makes my reputation look in the short term. I'm privileged enough to have engineered some of the most used technologies in the world today, but being able to lend my weight towards this man's work may be the greatest contribution I make to the world in my lifetime. I don't care about the short-term reputational damage this does, I don't care about the short-term damage this does to my businesses or my net worth, I don't care about the lawsuits that some of you may try levelling at me. This man and his method saved my son, and it could add years to the lives of millions of people worldwide every year.'

'If you are a sufferer who fits the criteria, apply now. The tickets are completely free. Delancey and I are covering the costs of the event and the study, so there are no hidden fees or anything of that nature. The potential downside is that nothing happens and you can have treatment one month later. The upside is that one month later, you could wind up cancer free with a whole new lease on life.'

'Where can people find out more about the event, Delancey?'

'Well,' said the Irishman, 'the event is called The Cathartic Unconscious Reprogramming Event, so they can go to—'

'Woah, hold it right there, Delancey,' interjected Jay. 'That's one hell of a mouthful. Do you think we can shorten that, Max?'

'I do,' replied his son with a big, cheesy grin.

'So, where should people go to sign up?'

He answered in his adorable little voice. 'w-w-w-dot-this-is-the-cure- dot-com.'

'Apply now,' said Jay. 'The world will change forever in ten days, and I want you to be part of it for the longest time to come.'

The trio smiled, Delancey more expressively than usual, before the screen cut to the web details.

Emet scrolled down with his trembling thumb. The video already had over half a million views.

CHAPTER 63

He puffed away on his seventeenth cigarette of the afternoon as he reopened Wildfire to check the video's views. It was at eight million. He tried Felix again on the phone to no avail. He wasn't sure if it was noticeable from the outside, but his entire body quivered constantly and had done for hours. Every muscle held tight, and their constant work had him burning up. Round the corner from the coffee shop now, he binned his remaining cigarettes and took a quick look at himself in his phone's selfie camera. His eyes were slightly bloodshot and sunken and even though he'd done his hair before coming out, it somehow now looked as if he'd been dragged through a bush. *Fuck me.* He walked thirty seconds back on himself to a pharmacy, bought some eyedrops and a travel-sized mouthwash, and tried to visually and olfactorily tidy himself up before heading back to the coffee shop. He stopped just short of the door, closed his eyes, and took a few deep breaths. *Calm the fuck down. There's nothing you can do. You don't want to end up back in that place.* He opened his eyes to find somebody walking out of the coffee shop door giving him a funny look. He'd been talking aloud without realising it.

'Hey, you,' said Skye with a radiant smile as he arrived at the counter. 'How's your chill day been?'

'Good, thanks,' he said, conjuring the best smile he could. 'How's it been here? Any news?'

'Pretty standard, thanks. Fairly busy. No news springs to mind. It's been nice to look at my lattes today and think that in a few years, all that frothing and pouring will actually mean something.'

'Yeh…yeh.'

Skye examined his face. 'Where are you, Em?'

'What do you mean?' he asked, pulling his attention back to her, giving himself a moment to replay what she'd said in his mind. 'It is nice. And it has meant something. You've brightened up many days. That matters.'

She examined him further. 'Are you sure you're OK?'

He lowered his voice and stepped even closer. 'I think they gave me a different brand of the meds. I'm not feeling one hundred percent.'

'Oh, darling,' she said, noticing a line building behind him. 'Well, I'll be done in a bit, and we'll have a nice evening together. Hopefully that'll help. What can I get you now? Flat white?'

'Please. Decaf, if you can.'

'I can and I will,' she said cheerfully. 'Find a seat and I'll run it over.'

All bar stools were occupied, so he headed to the main seating area and sat at the one small free table on the comfy upholstered bench-seat that ran all along the wall. He balled his fists as tightly as he could, pressing them into the velvety seat, then relaxed them. He repeated this a few times along with some quiet, deep breathing, trying to let go of some of his bone-smothering tension.

'Has that seating done you wrong?'

He looked across to realise he was sat across from Jason, the regular he had toasted doing 'work that matters' with before his mum was diagnosed. If last time Jason was tipsy, this time he was sozzled. 'No, no,' he said, manufacturing a smile. 'It's just a relaxation technique. Like a cat pawing.'

'Work'll do that to you, bud. Make you wanna press your fists into someone's face.'

'I've actually had some time off,' replied Emet.

'Nice. You been anywhere good?'

'Not recently. I did Scotland a while back.'

'So nowhere good, then?' said Jason, raising his half-empty cocktail glass with a smirk.

Emet smiled back. 'I dunno. They had some beautiful nature and lots of artisanal distilleries.'

'Now we're talking!' replied Jason before downing his drink and signalling to one of Skye's colleagues out on the floor for the same again. As he put his empty glass down, he knocked it, making it wobble almost to the point of falling but Emet shot a hand out and steadied it. 'Thank you kindly, good sir.'

'Are you sure you've got another one in you?' asked Emet.

'Me? I will have shortly.'

Emet sized up the inebriated man for a moment. 'Is it work still pressing on you?'

Jason picked up his glass and stared through it for a while.

'Sorry. I didn't mean to pry.'

'You're not,' said Jason, looking to the bar. 'I know I'm a mess. It's only normal to ask. That's what we do, isn't it? Good people? If we see people aren't OK, we let 'em know, don't we?'

'I guess so.'

'What's your name again, pal?'

'Emet.'

'That's right. Aren't you a journo?'

'Sort of. I write reviews on films, TV, and art.'

'Sweet. You seen anything good recently?'

'Honestly, it's been a while.'

Skye showed up beside them and exchanged looks with Emet while passing him his coffee, raising her eyebrows at how worse for wear his conversational partner was. 'You OK?' she mouthed, to which he nodded. 'Are you alright there, Jason? Can I get your bill?'

'You can, sweetheart, but I'd love my drink first.'

She checked the bar. 'Of course. I think it'll be with you in a jif. I'll sort your bill for when you're ready.'

'She's a good egg, isn't she?' he said to Emet.

'The best.'

Jason raised his glass. 'To the best egg,' he said before realising his glass was empty. 'When I'm refilled.'

'I'll leave you fellas to it,' said Skye, giving them a little wave before mouthing 'I won't be too long' to Emet and leaving.

As Emet sipped his flat white, Jason stared through his cocktail glass as he clumsily rotated it on his table. 'So, you don't do *news* news?'

Emet shook his head. 'Not really. I'm more of an opinion writer.'

'Must be nice being able to just say what's on your mind?'

'It has its positives.'

'Do you know journos who do the other stuff? You know, the investigative stuff? Like uncovering financial crimes and Wikileaks and stuff?'

'I mean, yeh. We all share the same office.'

'How does that stuff work?'

'What stuff?'

'Well, like the Panama Papers or Wikileaks. Does the paper find out about something dodge and go find a source or do they get contacted by insiders before they have a clue anything's happening?'

'Both happen,' replied Emet. 'Why?'

The waitress arrived with Jason's new cocktail and swapped him for his empty. 'To the best egg,' he said when she'd gone, raising his new full glass, initiating a clink with Emet's coffee cup before slurping half of it down. 'Would you do it?'

'Do what?' asked Emet.

'Be a rat. And end up living in some other country looking over your shoulder or in some embassy or jail for the rest of your life?'

Emet examined the froth of his drink. 'I mean, it's no fun being locked away, but I guess it depends what's at stake. For political truths, me, honestly, I doubt it. What's really changed because of what they did?'

Jason slowly nodded his head. 'What if it was more than politics?'

'Like what?'

Jason tapped on the base of his cocktail glass. 'Like life and death.'

'Then I'd really have to think about it. Depending on who it was.'

Jason grinned a wicked smile. 'Who it is matters, doesn't it?'

'Of course it does. Some people the world is better off without. But some people are worth fighting for.'

'The good eggs?'

'The good eggs,' replied Emet.

Jason stared into the rest of his cocktail for a long moment then raised it. 'To the good eggs and fuck the people who don't give a fuck about breaking them to make their omelettes.'

'Cheers to that.'

Jason downed his drink and stood. 'Especially Jay fucking Sharpa.' As he strode away from the table, his gait slightly unsteady, Emet's head whipped round to follow him and found Skye approaching.

'Are you ready?' she asked.

CHAPTER 64

'Emet.'

His attention snapped back to her concerned face.

'Are sure you're OK? If this is too much right now, we can go home and have a quiet one.'

He nodded. 'I'll be fine. Like I said, I'm just a bit groggy, and honestly, I've had a quiet one for the last month. Being around sane people…well, I'm praying for some osmosis.'

She grinned, reached for his hand across the table, and squeezed it. 'You're not crazy. What you went through…I can't see many coming out of all that unscathed.' She released his hand and stood. 'I'd best pop to the ladies' otherwise you're going to be getting more than sanity by osmosis.'

As she disappeared out of sight through the food market hall, he pulled his phone from his pocket and searched "companies jay sharpa has shares in". He selected the top result and read down the list of the entrepreneur's financial involvements. After Wildfire, Fuusion, and another two companies he was publicly known for, none of the long list of others rang a bell until the penultimate one: Horus Technologies Ltd. He searched for the company's website. Its homepage greeted him with the message "The future of live blood monitoring". He navigated to their personnel page, scrolled through the photos, and found him. The man from the coffee shop was called Jason Sekhmet. He then moved onto LinkedIn. There he was: Jason Sekhmet, Biotech Engineer at Horus Technologies. *Shit.*

'What's good in the world?' asked Skye, slightly startling Emet and causing him to close his phone.

'I…I don't know. But I'm sure there's lots to choose from.'

A waiter arrived at the table with the couple's food, providing Emet with a few moments to process his realisation.

'This is fantastic,' said Skye after her first mouthful. 'I've been waiting all day for this.'

Emet nodded as he chewed his food and watched Skye sip the green juice she'd ordered. *Waiting!* 'You shouldn't wait.'

She raised a curious eyebrow his way. 'Umm…I'm not anymore. It's just arrived, and it was well worth it,' she said as she chopsticked some more udon noodles into her mouth.

'Sorry, not that,' he said, putting his chopsticks down. 'I mean with your arts therapy taster. You said there's one in a few days. You should go do it.'

'I can't.'

'Why not?'

'Work…money…'

'Suicide watch?' he asked jovially before quieting his voice. 'Look, I might be a bit out of it with the meds, but I'm fine. I promise I'm not going to hurt myself. That was a one-time thing in an unprecedented situation. Nothing can possibly get that bad again, and I realise what it did to you and Clyde. I wouldn't put you through that again. Besides, now I've thought about it, if I met Maw in the afterlife having topped myself, she'd kill me.'

Skye shot him a disapproving look.

'Look. I can joke about it. I'm completely the other side of it. Regarding work, like I said before, if they won't give you the time off, you'll walk into another job when you get back. This is London. And money isn't a thing.'

'How'd you figure that?'

'It's a gift from me.'

She straightened in her chair. 'I can't accept that!'

'Of course you can. What you did for my mum those last few weeks, I can never repay you for that. The peace…the respite…the way you allowed her to pull the strands of her life together into some final meaning. I doubt there'll be anything I can ever do for you to parallel that. But letting me get this for you as a token gesture of my thanks, well, that'd be a start.'

'I didn't do any of that for repayment,' she protested.

'I know. And that's exactly why I want to do something for you. Just because it's a good thing to do. Maw said I need to focus on doing some good rather than just stopping bad. And I know for a fact she'd think of you setting about this new career as something purely good.'

She set her chopsticks down, stirred by the case he'd made. 'Emet. I love you, and I appreciate everything you're saying, and it's so nice of you to say your mum would approve…'

'I know one hundred percent she would.'

'…but it's too big a gift and I can't just leave work in the lurch.'

'I respect that you don't want to, but the fact is that you're on a zero-hours contract and they could give you nothing at all for the next fortnight if it suited them. This is the next chapter of your life we're talking about. The world needs a few more months of you as a therapist a hell of a lot more than it does of you as a barista. Please don't wait. The tragic truth is that none of us know how much waiting we can afford.'

Struck by his words, she sighed and drummed her fingers on the table as she thought.

'It's as if Jim Rawlings himself was here willing you on, and you know what he'd say, don't you?' he said as he gestured to her green juice, receiving a puzzled look back. 'He'd say *take the leap.*' As he humorously imitated the life coach, winning smile and all, a wave of pure revulsion washed over him. He couldn't even bear to speak the same words as even the weakest variety of these frauds. But he kept the smile pinned on and watched one grow opposite him.

'I couldn't accept it as a gift, but as a loan…'

'Whatever you want, it's yours.'

She brought her hands over her mouth as her smile widened. 'Work are gonna hate me.'

'You can guide them through some latte art therapy to heal the rift,' he said with a mischievous smile. 'What do you say?'

She bubbled with silent excitement until her hands exploded skywards in celebration. 'I'll do it!'

His hands shot up too in a delayed mirror of hers. 'Amazing!'

Her smile going nowhere, she lowered her hands and took his across the table. 'I can't believe I'm gonna do this. Do you really think I can be a therapist?'

'I have full belief you can!' he said genuinely whilst screaming inside at his word choice.

'Wow. I can't believe this. If they have space, I think it starts the day after tomorrow. I'll need to sort trains and accommodation and everything,' she said, slightly overwhelmed.

'We can sort it all online on the way home,' he said in a soothing tone. 'Nothing but a few clicks.'

'Wow. WOW. I can't believe I'm doing this.' Her loving gaze met his. 'Are you sure you'll be alright?'

'I'm sure.'

'What'll you do?'

'Get myself well. And if there's some light work I can ease myself back in with, maybe I'll take a look.'

'Light work for lightweight,' she said, sticking her tongue out of the side of her mouth.

'A match made in heaven.'

She joyfully squeezed his hands and kissed them. 'I can think of another.'

CHAPTER 65

After her supervisor had initially been put out, she changed her tune quickly when she realised upon Skye's return, she would get cover for a few days away she needed some for. There had been space for the course and a nearby pretty bed-and-breakfast at a reasonable rate, so quaint that Emet said he may join her there if he was still in full rest mode by the time she finished.

'You promise you'll take it easy?'

'I'll spend most of it right by that little stitched heart. The most exciting it'll get is a live show.'

'Is anything good on?'

'I very much doubt it,' he said, bringing her close. 'The best show in town's leaving. I'll miss you.'

'I'll miss you too.'

They kissed, already longing for their next, and he watched the crystals and feathers in the back of her wavy hair dangle and glide all the way through the barriers until she boarded the train.

As he walked out of the station, he got out his phone and replied to her heart emoji message. Then he dialled. 'I can head to you now…OK…see you at eight.'

He walked into the unfamiliar pub, bought a couple of drinks, and scanned around the booths, eventually finding Jason with an empty glass in the most tucked away of them wearing a cap and shades. 'Thanks for meeting me.'

'We're just two new friends meeting for a drink,' said Jason as he collected his pint from the middle of the table.

'That's right. And it's fine. Nobody knows I'm here.' He pulled his powered-down phone and its separate SIM card from his pocket to show. 'And even Wildfire can't track this.'

Jason let his shoulders lower a little and took his first sip of his drink. 'So, what do you want with me? You said you're just a critic.'

'I wrote a big piece, a news piece, a while back that I think is connected to your story. But I can't know for certain until you tell me what's going on.'

'And this is off the record? You're not recording me or anything?'

'It's off the record, and you can check my pockets if you like.'

Jason sized him up, then shook his head. 'I actually would but for it attracting unwanted attention. Especially with your recent track record.'

Emet flushed crimson red.

'Did you think I wasn't going to Google you? Why are you pursuing *this* of all stories given the fallout from that last thing you wrote? Surely, you're on a disciplinary or something?'

'I am, and I'm still here, probably for the same reason you're here,' replied Emet. 'But I don't know until you tell me.'

Jason reluctantly sighed and lowered his voice. 'Look. I'm just a fairly low-grade biotech engineer. But I know what's going on at work isn't right.'

'How so?'

'Our tech isn't ready.'

'Let's go back a step. The future of live blood monitoring. What exactly are you monitoring?'

'Horus has taken the idea of those wearable blood sugar monitors that are becoming more mainstream for the management of diabetes and is applying it to a myriad of different diseases and conditions so that people will know what medication levels they need and how they're responding to treatment without going to the doctors anywhere near as much.'

'And they're doing this for cancer?'

Jason nodded. 'For various tumour markers. CA15-3, CA19-9, CEA, loads of them.'

Emet shook his head. 'Surely they can't test those with a little patch with the right sensitivities?'

'Well, we've come on leaps and bounds with what we can do and we're getting there, but we're not there yet. We were meant to be launching early next year for less serious conditions, which was optimistic, but then, all of a sudden, upstairs announced this soft launch the other day, scheduled for two weeks' time. We couldn't believe it. Then I saw this advert with Sharpa. It's so fucked. We've only done very small-scale testing so far. It's not ready to go out to people with fucking terminal conditions for them to be our guinea pigs. And in collaboration with some faith healer or whatever the fuck he is,' he said, glugging a third of his pint down. 'I get that Sharpa's son has undergone some miraculous remission, and God bless him, but he's going to take a promising technology that could do lots of good in a few years and give it the kiss of death doing this. He's lost his marbles.'

Emet scrubbed the sides of his hair. 'And how exactly do you know the technology isn't ready?'

'Like I said, it's barely been tested, especially on cancer markers. Our blood sugar and ketone testing is rock solid. We have thousands of days' worth of data on CD4 levels in people managing HIV and on hormone levels in menopausal women on various treatments and our analyses have shown that we have, maybe, eighty percent reliability, but they're just a few conditions. Do you know how many different cancer markers there are, and do you know the tolerances we need to nail to get this right reliably?'

'How much data do you have on its efficacy with cancer markers?'

Jason swigged his drink again. 'Tens. Maybe over a hundred. And many of us have raised it with our superiors, but they don't want to hear problems. They just want solutions. It's all that raa-raa, the-sky's-the-limit, jump-and-the-net-will-catch-you bullshit. But there's no fucking net. Not for the people they're gonna be putting this on.'

'Do you have proof that it doesn't work well yet?'

'There are terabytes of proof, but they're scattered all over the organisation now. These last few weeks, they've segregated loads of our departments so we speak less and have less of a clue what each other are doing, and they've ramped up security in the building and on all the computers. There've been emails going back and forth for weeks, but they've really died down in the last few days. I'm sure a few of the older email chains have disappeared from my inbox.'

Emet sipped his pint as he pondered on all he'd heard. 'Do you think anybody there'd be willing to go on the record about any of this?'

'I very much doubt it. Everyone signed an NDA when they started, and I'm sure you're aware of how aggressive Sharpa is at defending his IP with the stories out of Wildfire. He will destroy anyone who even thinks about speaking out.'

'So, then, why did you come to talk to me?'

Looking like the weight of the world was resting on his shoulders, Jason swirled the rest of his pint and downed it. 'My brother. He died when we were at uni of thyroid cancer. Didn't even make his twenty-first birthday.' He peered into his empty glass. 'I got into this work to make it so that as few people die young as possible. And now I'm here.'

'I'm sorry about your brother. And he'd be proud of you for coming forward about all this.'

Jason shrugged. 'I dunno. This is about as far forward as I think it's wise to come. To let you know where to dig.'

'There's no time for me to dig, Jason. It's nine days until thousands of terminally ill people presumably put on this patch that you're a part of. I know you didn't choose to be in this situation, I know you'd rather it wasn't happening, but it is, and you chose to be brave enough to tell somebody about it. I can't do the digging. But if you can bring me some dirt, some real damning dirt, I will shout about from the rooftops so loudly that maybe we can shut this whole grotesque gig down and encourage thousands of very ill people to stick with the only treatment that has a chance, even if it's a miniscule one, of helping them.'

Jason took his shades off and looked Emet square in the eye. 'That's all very well and good, but it'd be me risking everything. If they find out I leaked anything, my life as I know it is over. How can I trust that you'll protect me when you couldn't even protect yourself from some modern-day witch doctor with a decent solicitor?'

'Look…you can't understand what I've already lost here,' said Emet. 'I'm on the hook already as far as this story goes. If anybody's coming for anybody, I'll make sure that it's for me and only me. I need to end this. But if you give me solid proof I can run with, even I'll be fine. And hopefully, so will all those people, relatively speaking. Ten thousand of them, Jason. Some of them the same age as your brother; some even younger. What do you say?'

Jason surveyed the black of his shades lenses and the white light reflecting off them before burying his face into his hands. He blew out an almighty raspberry before raising his face towards the ceiling. 'I say it's your fucking round again. I guess we've got some plans to hatch.'

CHAPTER 66

Computers with blocked USB ports. Online file sharing sites banned by the company network. Screenshots disabled on the computers. No paper in or out. No personal phones beyond the locker room. All paper waste shredded. Cameras everywhere. Random searches of employees and their bags on entry and exit. Emails clearly monitored. Horus was a fortress. But Emet had an idea. If it was going to work, it would take a few days which could scarcely be afforded, but he needed time to lay some groundwork of his own.

'Welcome back!' said Felix with a warm smile. 'How are you feeling?'

'Better, thanks.'

'Glad to hear it. What can I do you for?'

'I want to get back to it. Maybe not with a full load right away, but I'm better off adjusting back in slowly than being off for an age, then trying to resume full steam ahead. Plus, I want you to see that I'm still in full possession of all my marbles.'

'Still?' quipped Felix. 'The best creative writers seldom start with a full pouch. Anyway, I think starting easy, *only if you're completely sure*, sounds wise. Just let me know what sort of things you want, and we'll get you started.'

'Cheers, Fee.' Emet left his boss' office, found a desk, and wrote an email about pieces of work he'd be happy to take on. He didn't look at any of the paper copies of today's Globe or at their news site. He'd already seen the small story about The CURE in the day's paper before work, reporting on the general controversy surrounding the event and potential action brewing against Sharpa and Wildfire by advertising standards bodies, and he didn't want to be seen reading it by Felix.

After a productive day of viewing and writing, he headed to the hospital where he'd arranged to meet Clyde at seven thirty, but at seven, sat in its main coffee shop, Jason hobbled over to his table and sat, garnering a nod of approval. 'Bravo. And well done for coming. Can I get you a coffee?'

'I could do with an espresso martini if they have one.'

'I don't think that's on the menu, but they probably do cans of martini in the M&S. I could fetch you one if you want?'

'I'll survive.'

Emet slid the pair of crutches from beside his seat under the table to Jason. 'Stay at least an hour, probably more like two, and give me a shout with this when you manage to get something,' he said, putting a SIM card on the centre of the table.

Jason looked at the crutches and the SIM. 'Are we really doing this?'

'You know what'll happen if we don't. And they won't have a clue as long as you keep it up for a few days afterwards.' Emet saw the trepidation on his source's face. 'Are we good?'

Jason squirmed in his seat.

'None of that. You have to commit to make it work. Full belief,' he said, almost knocking his coffee off the table as he gestured to try to raise the energy of the man across from him, a hot flash of adrenaline striking him as he saved the cup. His plan was tight, but he knew that any course of action wasn't totally risk free and he hated that somebody else had to be involved. 'Are we good?'

After a moment of deliberation, Jason solidly nodded. Emet bought him a coffee, left, and spent the rest of the evening with Clyde, trying to act as normally as possible. The next few days were all about normality. He wrote a good number of reviews for the paper, made a slight effort to say hello to colleagues and smile around the office, and messaged and chatted with Skye whenever she wanted. He'd stopped the antidepressants as soon as he'd realised he may be able to affect the seminar but had started on sleeping tablets to knock himself out for a few hours a night. In the hours between work and his self-induced lights out, he frantically researched online trying to find any other leads that may help him stop The CURE. There was controversy all over the internet about it, there was pressure on the venue itself to pull the plug on the event, but there was nothing he thought an event with the backing of Sharpa couldn't deal with. But worse than all this were the videos that were being posted on Wildfire and other social networks; people with cancer from all over the world saying they were travelling to London for the gathering or begging others to donate to fund their travel. Despite the tickets being free, there were rumours of people offering immense sums of money for them. By the time the sleeping tablets kicked in each night, he had cried on and off for at least an hour.

Then on lunchtime three days after the hospital rendezvous, Emet's phone buzzed. It was from the burner SIM. Jason had something. That night they met in Jason's car outside a physiotherapy clinic.

'Where the fuck did you think of this?' asked Jason as he pulled the end off one of the crutches, tipped it upside down, and emerged with a tightly rolled bundle of papers which he handed over.

'You wouldn't believe me if I told you.'

'I know it's not much, but it's all I could get without alerting any suspicion. I hope it's enough.'

Emet finished unrolling the documents and started reading them. 'Me too.'

'That's it, then? We're done?'

'We're done. This is on me now. Go for your session, use the crutches for a few more days, and drop them off. If you do that and pasted the content of these into other documents to print off…'

'I did.'

'There's no way for them to know it was you. You've done a good thing, Jason. Truly.'

'I hope so,' he replied with a loud sigh.

'The only time you'll ever see me again is in the byline of this story,' said Emet, shaking the documents.

'And maybe the coffee shop.'

'Maybe.'

Emet put the papers in his bag, pulled his cap down, and went on his way.

CHAPTER 67

The next morning, Emet received a tap on his shoulder. 'Emet. C'mon. You know this is my space,' said Louise in her forty-a-day voice.

'This one?' he asked. 'Doesn't yours have your adjusted seat with that nice lumbar support?'

Irked, Louise scanned around the immediate area and spotted her seat the other side of the bank of desks down the row. 'It does,' she said through gritted teeth, 'I don't know who put that over there, but do you mind?'

'Of course not,' he replied, happily disconnecting his laptop from the display and wheeling himself a couple of seats away. 'Sorry about that. I slept awfully last night. I barely know up from down.'

'It's alright,' she said, slowly relinquishing the tension from her jaw. 'But I do sit here all the time.'

'Like I said, I'm still in dreamland,' he said before lowering his voice. 'I'm still getting used to some tablets they gave me, so I really am sorry.'

Slightly embarrassed, she accepted his apology and awkwardly away.

A couple of minutes later, he put something on the desk next to her. She looked and found a pack of cigarettes.

'For all the ones I bummed and then some. Sorry again.'

She thanked the back of him, feeling even worse for her earlier curtness.

He made his way across the office and gently knocked his knuckles against Felix's open door.

'Come in.'

After stepping inside, he quietly closed the door behind him, fully rousing his boss' attention.

'Good morning,' said Felix with a slightly arched eyebrow. 'That's been some exceptional work rate these last few days. You're not overdoing it, are you?'

'Not at all. I've actually got something extra for you,' replied Emet, putting an open folder on the desk and sliding it across to show its contents.

'What am I looking at? And whose bins have you been rummaging through?'

'No bins. What you're looking at came from a legitimate source at a company called Horus.'

'Horus…' Felix repeated to himself as if trying to jog his memory. '…are they a film distributor, a theatre company, or like Uber for prostitutes?'

'They're a medical biotech firm who make—'

'Something to do with blood testing?' Felix turned to the next page, froze, then fired Emet a searing look. 'I fucking knew it. All this productivity these last few days. You're still on this Cancer Man stuff, aren't you? You've been trying to butter me up.'

'Look, Fee. It's right there in front of you. Thousands of desperate, sick people are going to a "seminar" in a few days' time where a charlatan is going to "cure" them of cancer and this tech that doesn't work yet is going to help convince them of it. My source said that—'

'Emet!' snapped Felix. 'What are you thinking? You can't go after this. I told you to leave all this alone. Your credibility is shot as far as this is concerned. Do you think you can bring me a few documents from God knows where and who and we can do something with this?'

'Read them, Fee. There's data indicating poor reliability, email exchanges with people high up at the company ignoring concerns about the tech *specifically* for cancer screening. We *have* to do something,' said Emet, growing redder in the face. 'An arena full of people are walking off the edge of a fucking cliff if we don't tell them about this.'

'We are telling them about this,' replied the editor. 'We've published pieces on the event the last few days.'

'Surface-level pieces about what's happening, reporting on what others are saying about it, but saying nothing original or of any real value. We're a *news*paper. That on the desk is *news.*'

'According to you. The paper is likely going to have to settle the case O'Shea brought against it because of your lack of journalistic care.'

'I recorded that fucking interview.'

'So you say.'

'Just like you said you didn't Mo Farah it to my house.'

The comment gave Felix pause. 'Look. Upstairs won't touch this. Not from you. If you can pass on your source to someone else—'

'A proper journalist?'

'An investigative reporter,' replied Felix, trying to calm the tone of the conversation. 'And somebody uncompromised regarding this story.'

'Somebody who hasn't just emerged from the funny farm?'

'Emet. Stop. You're too emotional about this, and I totally get it. It's way too personal for this to come from you. If you can hand your source over to somebody else, we can look into it.'

'I don't know if he'll speak to anybody else but even if he will, by the time anybody else has managed to look into this, it'll be too late!'

'Maybe, maybe not,' replied Felix regretfully. 'I don't want that madness to go ahead any more than you do, but we have to follow a robust process, or it'll be the last immoral thing we stop.'

'It's not immoral, Fee. It's an atrocity.'

Felix gave his writer a sombre look and tapped the folder under his hand. 'Leave it with me, Em. And see if he'll corroborate with somebody else. You have to trust me. We'll do everything we can.'

Emet had known Felix long enough to know he wouldn't waver on his decision with real good cause, so he turned and headed for the door.

'Em.'

The journalist turned to his boss.

'You have to let this go. You've lost enough as it is. Don't lose this job too.'

Emet held the doorframe, gazing off into the newsroom away from his boss.

'Take the rest of the day. Take some more time off if you need to.'

He lowered his head and shook it, then sighed in resignation. 'OK. I'll go calm myself down. Maybe see you later.'

'Good man. No rush. Catch you soon.'

CHAPTER 68

Louise scampered out of the office just after six, almost immediately shoving a cigarette in her mouth. As she lit it, the tension melted away from her face as the scamper softened into a stroll, eventually carrying her out of Emet's sight, triggering him to leave the bar across the road and head back to the office.

There were still people in the newsroom, but it was at twenty percent capacity. With plenty of seats to choose from, he sat himself back in Louise's as he had first thing that morning, plugged his laptop into her monitor, logged on, and placed his phone on the desk beside him. He opened an app and scrolled through a ream of text until he found what he was looking for, then checked over his shoulders before sliding the desk's wired keyboard to himself. He followed its cable down to the desktop tower and unplugged it before pulling a small non-native device off its USB connector and pocketing it. He reconnected the keyboard, started up the paper's content management system and submitted a pre-prepared article for publication clearance, title: "Mass cancer event 'The CURE' using 'irresponsibly unreliable' tech to test thousands of vulnerable and terminally ill".

After logging out of the system, he returned the login page and typed Louise's email address in. He looked down at his phone, typed in her password collected by the keylogger device he had just taken off her keyboard, and hit enter. After a little navigation through the system, he came to the sign-off page. He reread the title of his article, then scanned the surrounding office, admiring 'The Globe' logo on the wall. *Thanks for having me.* He approved the article's sign off as Louise, then published it live to the paper's site, checking in an internet browser and on his phone that it had worked. After messaging the link to a few influential people on social media that he knew would be interested, he turned off all his social notifications, blocked the phone numbers of all of his colleagues, and shared it from his own accounts. He packed up, caressed the logo on the wall, and headed out. As he stood outside in the smoker's section and lit up, his phone rang. 'Hey. How are you?'

'I am wonderful, thanks! It's all so fascinating here,' said Skye, full of enthusiasm. 'How about you?'

'I…I'm wonderful too.

CHAPTER 69

Jim Akachi-Rawlings turned through the pages of the morning's Globe as his driver pulled up to the gates of Laurel Canyon Manor. Eventually the gate man came out of the main house and let them in.

As Jim was led through the long hallway towards the lounge, something was different about the place that he couldn't quite put his finger on. He arrived to find Delancey standing in the centre of the room, eyes closed, arms outstretched to his sides, smiling ear to ear, bathing in gramophone music. With no recognition of his arrival, Jim eventually sat on one of the sofas and intentionally rustled the paper as he put it beside him. The music played for around another minute before stopping. It was only then that Delancey opened his eyes.

'Good morning, Jimmy. How are you this fine day?'

'I'm doing great, thanks. You look like you are too.'

'I am. I feel on splendid form, actually. A little morning visualisation to get the juices flowing in preparation for my big weekend,' said Delancey as he took a seat. 'For *our* big weekend.'

Jim smiled his winning smile but scratched the side of his bottom lip profusely. 'Yeh, I hope so.'

'Don't hope, Jimmy. Know.'

Jim nodded at the correction.

'Can we get you anything while we wait?' asked Delancey, positively chipper. 'Some breakfast or a drink, perhaps?'

'I'm all ready to go, thanks.' The two sat in silence for a moment before Jim tapped the paper next to him. 'I know you don't pay a great deal of attention to what's going on in the outside world. I don't suppose you've seen this?'

'What's *this?*'

'Our mutual friend Emet Gordon.' Delancey's smile remained unchanged. 'He's published another piece about your seminar, but the paper pulled it pretty quickly. Rumour is he went rogue, managed to publish it without permission. It was only online for a few hours, and I don't know if it made many print editions, but it said that Sharpa's blood monitoring tech is bogus. I think it's wound up going pretty viral.'

Delancey chuckled to himself, causing Jim to raise an eyebrow.

'It's just the expression's such a curious one.'

'Right. So, you hadn't heard about this?' asked Jim, perplexed by Delancey's lack of significant reaction.

The Irishman shook his head.

'Jay or his team hasn't contacted you?'

'I don't know. I've had all my calls held since he wrote that first piece. People were occasionally managing to find my number, calling me and pleading for my help at all sorts of unsociable hours. I've not checked yet today.'

'Do you wanna go check? Maybe make some calls? I can wait a while.'

'No,' replied Delancey matter-of-factly. 'It's of no interest to me.'

'Woah. You really are ice cold, aren't you?' Delancey fished a cigarette and a lighter out of his jacket pocket as he just looked at him. 'When he wrote that piece about me, I had to do something about it. I had to at least try to set the record straight.'

'That, Jimmy, is because you care what people think about you.' He lit his cigarette and took a long draw. 'But don't worry,' he said with a smirk, 'even the worst habits can be overcome.'

Jim chuckled to himself bemusedly as a call came from Delancey's butler. 'Your client is here, gentlemen.'

Delancey nodded to acknowledge he'd heard. 'Shall we?' he said, standing and theatrically gesturing for Jim to lead the way. As the American headed towards the door, his host spoke again. 'Do you know the main reason you shouldn't worry yourself about what anybody says?'

'Shoot.'

'Because you know you're helping people. And if that's at the foundation of what you're doing, then, in the words of Phineas T. Barnum, "there's no such thing as bad publicity".'

After an ice-breaking chat, the test client sat in Delancey's therapy chair, nervously waiting with the straitjacket laid out ahead of her on the floor and the vast 'Melting Clocks' painting overlooking her as Delancey and Jim chatted outside, watching on through the large windows.

'You ramp it up until it looks like you've gone too far before you begin giving the commands about the allergen, you hear me?' asked Delancey.

'What's too far?' asked Jim nervously.

'Do you recall the first time you made a woman orgasm?'

'Umm, yeh,' replied Jim, perplexed.

'How did you know? Did you have a checklist of physiological markers?'

Jim half chuckled to himself and shook his head.

'I didn't think so. You just knew. And you'll just know here too. Come to think of it, this is essentially an anti-orgasm,' said Delancey, proud of his epiphany. 'Anyway, enough foreplay. Time to get down to it.' He opened one of the doors and invited Jim to go ahead.

'Are you sure you're OK with this?' Jim asked as he picked up the straitjacket.

'Of course,' said the client, holding out an arm for him to start putting it on. As he helped her into it, fastened it, and buckled her to the chair, Delancey sat in a chair in the corner of the room, lit a new cigarette, and turned his attention to the interaction.

'You comfy there?' asked Jim.

'It's quite comfy, actually,' said the client.

'Are you happy to make a start?'

'Let's do this!' she replied, clearly nervous but excited.

Over the next few minutes, Jim talked the client into an altered state of consciousness. Her breathing slowed and deepened. Her eyes, which she'd voluntarily closed a few minutes before, were heavily shut. All tension in her face had evaporated. She was almost entirely inside herself; his voice her only anchor to the outside world. He paused, covering his mouth for a moment before seeing Delancey move in the corner of his eye. 'Go on,' mouthed his mentor.

He uncovered his mouth and resumed. 'And as you feel that next breath fill you...that's right...I want you to feel how it expands you in every direction...how it makes you even lighter...and that lightness knows no bounds...feel it make you weightless and let it lift you like a hot air balloon, high above the here and now...so high that you can see your entire life laid out down there...now let the winds of change carry you back, back to above the first time that peanuts became an issue and then back above the hours just before it...'

A rustling distracted him. He turned to see Delancey pulling open a bag of peanuts and popping one into his mouth.

'...are you above it?'

The client nodded.

'Something unpleasant happened before the younger you had that first anaphylactic shock, didn't it?'

The client nodded.

'Now, you don't need to tell me what happened if you don't want to, but to resolve this potentially deadly overreaction your immune system has, you need to know what happened, and you need to feel those unpleasant feelings deeply, but it'll be for one last time. If you ever recall this again, you'll feel nothing significant. It'll just be another thing you got over. Does that sound good?'

The client nodded.

'Good. So, begin to float down into that scene…into that younger you…'

Her face began to flicker with anguish.

'Very good…let the sounds and sights around you clarify like a Polaroid developing until it's crystal clear and you *are there*…'

A frown gripped her. Delancey signalled from the corner, like a conductor, to escalate the tension.

'…until it's larger than life…' he said, louder and deeper now, '…and its shadows are darker than the blackest corners of Hell…and even the air around you presses on you like invisible walls closing in…'

She squirmed in her seat, her breathing shallower and more jagged by the breath. Delancey stood and began to walk over, his footsteps the only sound in the dead silence. Jim didn't want them to take her out of the building tension.

'…as you hear the footsteps of the Grim Reaper himself walking your way, ready with that scythe of his to turn the dial on that immune system of yours up to eleven so that death is lurking over your shoulder from this day on…'

Delancey smiled and threw a peanut up into the air, catching it in his mouth as the client grimaced, partly in anguish and partly in confusion.

'…let that feeling inside you build until it consumes you, until it takes you over…'

As the client tensed up more, Delancey laid his hand on Jim's shoulder and whispered to him, 'I'll take it from here.' He sat on the arm of the client's chair and bent to speak into her ear but spoke so quietly that Jim couldn't hear. Twenty seconds later, the client began to wriggle around in the seat. Her skin paled. Her frown deepened. Soon, wriggling turned to thrashing around, desperately trying to break away from the seat and out of her shackles. Delancey grabbed her around the sides of her face to keep her head from smashing into his as he kept whispering, faster and more menacingly. The woman's body convulsed, her back arching in violent waves as Delancey stood, using his weight to pin her down as he kept going until eventually her head whipped back out of his grasp. Jim saw her eyelids partially open, exposing nothing but the whites of her eyes, at the very moment that Delancey's entire demeanour changed completely. His whisper became steadier and firmer, and the woman slowly stopped writhing, seemingly focused entirely on the words entering her ear.

A few minutes later, Delancey roused her from her trance, all smiles with no traces of the terror she'd just endured. After removing the straitjacket and a little small talk sat back beside Jim, Delancey pulled the bag of peanuts from his pocket. 'As a kid, how good were you at catching sweets and the like in your mouth?'

'Pretty decent.'

He emptied a peanut into his hand and showed it to her with a questioning look. She examined it for a moment, then smiled. 'Go on, then.'

Jim's jaw clenched as the woman opened her mouth with a playful glint in her eyes. As Delancey lobbed the nut in the air, Jim had to stop the gasp audibly escaping him. The peanut bounced off the woman's cheek, prompting a laugh.

'Heads up,' said Delancey as he threw another, striking terror into Jim's heart again after a moment of relief. The peanut landed in her mouth. She pumped her fists in the air, sheer delight on her face. 'How is it?'

'Salty,' she replied, playing with it in her mouth.

'Just how I like them,' replied Delancey. 'Would you like something to spit it out into or is it going down the hatch?'

'Well, it's not burning or tingling, and I'm supervised, so what the hell?' she asked, swallowing it.

Smiling on the outside, the rest of Jim was frozen. He couldn't take his eyes off her.

'And you said you'd know within seconds of swallowing a trace of peanut that you were in trouble before?' asked Delancey.

'Yes. I'd feel it burning all down my oesophagus and in my stomach, then I'd start to feel it swelling shut.'

'And now?'

She waited a long moment, tuning into her bodily sensations. 'Nothing,' she said with a beaming smile.

Delancey nodded. 'Superb. Give it a minute,' he passed her the bag of nuts, 'then feel free to have a few more.'

The client had left, effusively grateful that she'd been able to eat a handful of peanuts with no allergic reaction whatsoever. Jim sat looking out over the natural vista behind the house. Delancey sat on the bench beside him. A moment of silence passed.

'Why did you take over from me?' asked Jim. 'I was getting there. I just needed more time.'

'You weren't, Jimmy. It was all too cautious.'

'She had a lethal allergy.'

'Which you weren't testing with the allergen at that moment, were you?'

Jim broke eye contact with his mentor and looked out over the valley.

'You lacked conviction in your entire approach. You constantly asked for permission, your pacing was all over, you didn't use any of the client's resonating metaphors, although I did quite enjoy the whole darker-than-the-shadows-of-hell-Grim-Reaper bit. You were never getting there like that. You couldn't elicit terror from her, Jimmy, because you were too busy eliciting it from yourself.' Jim lowered his head. 'And you don't need practise. I know you have the skills to do all those things. You routinely keep thousands of people mesmerised for days on end. You literally talk them into jumping off buildings. To quote a wise, wise man, what you need is "full belief". You need to take the leap, Jimmy. Fully commit to work fearlessly with no safety nets, especially now you've seen what too far looks like. No pussyfooting, no supervision, no silly gadgets, no failsafes.' He nudged his mentee, prompting Jim to look at him. 'Do you really think I had an EpiPen lying around?'

Jim processed what was being said to him.

'If you want to really help those riddled with fear and doubt, you must purge yourself entirely of them, Jimmy. I know you can do it.'

Jim set his face determinedly and nodded.

'And if you show me it with anaphylaxis, if you really show me it, who knows what else I may show you.'

CHAPTER 70

Emet checked his text thread with Skye. She'd said hi, but no response had come yet about how her day had been. He put the phone down, picked up his can of pre-mixed, fully caffeinated espresso martini off the table, cracked it open, and raised it to the mandala outline and jar of sand in front of it. 'Cheers, Maw.'

He took a few sips – it wasn't a patch on the freshly mixed, made-with-love variety – and picked up his half-smoked cigarette from his ashtray.

Bang bang bang bang bang. The violent knock at the door barely stirred him. He took another puff. The door rattled again. He flicked some ash into the ashtray. Then a head peeked into the corner of the living room window. It was Felix. 'The least you can do is let me in.'

Emet got up, opened up, and gestured for him to enter. Felix's perpetual smile was nowhere to be seen. He walked past him silently, eventually sitting across from him in the living room. Emet offered him one of the other cans on the table. Felix shook his head shortly.

'I thought you'd stopped,' said the editor, nodding to the smouldering cigarette.

'Old crutches,' replied Emet, sipping from his can.

Felix seethed for a moment. 'I wanted to come and see you face to face…to look you in the eye and see if you looked like you'd lost your fucking mind. I know it's been a rough time for you. I wanted to believe that it'd been too much for you and that you weren't in your right mind when you bugged your colleague's fucking keyboard and used a credible newspaper like your own fucking blog.' Felix glowered at him. 'But there's nothing wrong with you, is there?'

Emet shook his head and picked up the cig. 'I'm truly sorry at the mess I've caused for you to clean up at the paper, but I had to do it, Fee. It was either years off the lives of thousands of people or me destroying my career and inconveniencing an organisation I worked for and good people, like you, that I worked with. I know my apology doesn't clean up the mess for you, but I hope it means something. I had to try to stop this insanity.'

'But you haven't stopped anything, you fucking muppet.' Felix threw a plastic folder packet his former writer's way. 'You're an opinion writer, not an investigative reporter, and you failed to do the most rudimentary investigation.'

'I got documents and emails from an inside source at Horus,' replied Emet.

'But you didn't, Em' replied Felix, utterly exasperated. 'I don't know who you got those documents from, but it looks like they're forgeries.'

'What the hell are you talking about *forgeries?*'

'Horus contacted us. They opened their doors first thing this morning for our forensic computer analyst to go check their systems. Those emails and documents don't exist.'

'Not anymore they won't. They'll have deleted it all overnight.'

'They didn't, Em. He checked. There was no evidence of foul play.'

'You really think if a Jay Sharpa company wanted some data gone, they couldn't disappear it?' asked Emet.

'Maybe. But our analyst insists otherwise. Have you thought that maybe you've been had?'

'I haven't,' Emet replied, pulling out his phone and navigating to the Horus website's personnel page. 'I'm not disclosing their identity, but they're right he—' Jason's name and photo were gone. 'One sec.' Panicked, he opened LinkedIn and searched. Jason's profile no longer existed. He opened his contacts and dialled Jason's number. His stomach dropped at the dreaded tone. 'The number you have dialled has not been recognised.' Pale as a sheet, he lowered his phone.

Felix shook his head. 'Vanished without a trace, yes?'

Emet was too dumbfounded to speak.

'You should have left it with us, Em. We'd have checked the source. He's played you.'

Emet eventually snapped out of his daze. 'What makes you think it was a he?'

'I'm not talking about your source. I'm talking about O'Shea,' said Felix. 'He's an utter Machiavellian, Em. You let him get under your skin and he's turned you inside out. We could have got him together. I dare say we or somebody else still will. He's taken his game way too big for it all not to fall apart. He can't last long.'

Emet buried his head in his hands.

'I can't tell you how fucked off I am with you. You've left me a fucking nuclear clear-up to perform.' He paused and shook his head. 'Why the fuck did you have to do this? Who am I gonna break balls within the office now?'

Emet couldn't bring himself to look up.

'Hey. You've got a big following. Start your own thing. You'll be fine for work. Onwards and, well, maybe not too far downwards, yes?'

Emet mustered a nod.

'HR'll be in touch, but I want your pass now. I can't be having round two.'

'Fair enough,' replied Emet, utterly dejected. He got up, grabbed his cigarette, gave Felix his pass, and walked him to the front door.

His ex-boss turned to look at him. 'You fucking wank stain,' he said, shaking his head disbelievingly before offering a hand to shake. 'Look after yourself.'

Emet shook his hand. 'I'm so sorry.'

'I know. Just stay out of it now. You can't be the one to end this.' They let go and Felix set off down the front steps. 'Oh,' he said, turning back. 'And quit that shit,' he said, pointing at the cigarette. 'You don't need a crutch. You need to heal.'

Emet watched Felix off, closed the door behind him, slid down the back of the door, and smashed some Blu-rays beside the doormat to smithereens.

CHAPTER 71

After exchanging a few messages with Skye – she was busy socialising with fellow course-goers, which suited Emet just fine – and then drinking the rest of the cans of espresso martini, the doorbell rang. And then again.

'Fuck off,' shouted Emet. Half expecting another face to pop into view like Felix's had, he was surprised to hear the front door open. 'Hey! Get the fuck out of my house!' he yelled, his pronunciation loosened by the cocktails in quick succession for him. 'I'll call the police!' The front door closed and footsteps sounded along the hallway. Emet pushed himself half out his slouch, ready, at least in his mind, to pounce.

'Good luck getting them to do anything if I have one of these, dickhead,' said Clyde as he appeared in the doorway dangling his spare key. 'I saw your article and the paper's retraction. I thought you might need a drinking buddy. Look at the state of you off a few supermarket cocktails. You'd embarrass our younger selves.'

'Not just my younger self,' replied Emet, flopping down to supine.

'Well, we may be embarrassments but at least we're embarrassments together,' said Clyde, putting a bottle of ruby coloured vodka on the table.

'What the fuck is that?'

'It's Scottish and expensive and it's plenty good enough to help us forget our embarrassments for a night.'

Three quarters of their way down the bottle, Emet's defocused eyes stared through the red, shimmering drink in his glass. 'What the fuck am I gonna do? No paper worth a shit'll take me after what I just did. I've got a few months savings before I'm fucked with this place,' he said, gesturing to the room around them.

'Em. You're as smart as you are stubborn. You'll figure it out.'

Emet downed his drink, wincing as it scorched his throat. 'I'm fucked in the media.'

'Nah. You can surely ghost write or something.'

Emet shrugged, leaned back against the sofa, and shut his weary, uneasy eyes.

'Hell. Come back to medicine. That shit's in your blood. You're a thoroughbred, lineage of Leigh Gordon. Rest in power, Mrs G,' he said, raising his glass to the heavens.

'I don't think they give out medicine degrees based on who your mum is…was. Especially to squeamish fucks like me.'

Clyde knocked back his vodka. He tensed everything for a second, trying to make the sick feeling that overcame him pass. 'Firstly, you clearly don't remember all the toffs at medical school.' He closed his eyes and laid a hand on his chest, hoping its pressure would somehow keep him from vomiting. 'Secondly, it's not like you were always scared, is it?'

Emet looked away, not wanting to acknowledge the statement. 'And thirdly?' he asked, trying to move beyond it.

Clyde held up a finger, signalling he needed a minute. Eventually he opened his eyes. 'And thirdly, you're a grown up, mate. You can get over it. It's just a bit of red liquid. Look,' he said, picking up the remainder of the ruby vodka. 'Exposure therapy. Pass me your glass.'

'Here, you daft bastard,' Emet said, sliding his glass across the table. 'You can pour me another, but it looks nothing like blood.'

Clyde poured him a shot. 'It's red. Your imagination can do the rest, innit?' He picked it up, carried it over, sat on the sofa beside his friend, and put it on the table ahead of him. 'Stare into that.'

Emet leaned forward. 'If you stare into the abyss, the abyss stares right back into you.'

'Stop being so bloody maudlin and look at it before I confiscate it.'

Emet played along.

'Now close your eyes. Through the blacks of your eyelids, imagine it darker. Can you imagine it darker?'

'Yeh.'

'And thicker?'

'Yeh.'

'And alongside the smell of the booze…' Clyde raised his wrist so that his watch hovered just below Emet's nose, '…can you imagine that metallic, iron smell?'

Emet retched, shoved his friend aside, and bolted for the stairs with his hands desperately cupping his mouth.

'Fuck!' guiltily laughed Clyde as he sprang up and ran after him all the way to the bedroom, where Emet puked red just before he made it to the en-suite, then carried on spewing on the bathroom floor before he managed to get some in the toilet. Clyde grabbed a hand towel to mop up some of the red mess behind Emet, who was still on his knees heaving his guts up into the toilet bowl, then a used towel to mop up the rest in there. Emet finally stopped being sick.

'Jesus, mate, I'm sorry. I didn't mean to…'

Emet held up an exhausted hand to halt the apology, then rolled into a shattered heap next to the toilet.

'Have you got any other towels around to mop up this mess out there before it dries into the carpet?'

His throat raw from the vomiting and his mind barely functioning, he took a few seconds before replying. 'There are some old sheets and stuff…back of the wardrobe…one of the boxes.'

Clyde pulled out the first box he found and opened it. 'Jesus, fella. That's fucking rank. Murderers usually burn the evidence.' After a minute, Emet crawled out of the bathroom to find him trying to blot up the rest of the red on the light carpet. 'I think that's the best you're gonna get it without soaping it up or getting a proper carpet cleaner.'

'Cheers,' Emet replied, crawling past him towards his bed.

'Why the hell have you got that in there?' Clyde asked, pointing to a shirt with the bloodied sleeve on the floor.

Emet checked what he meant as he climbed onto his bed. 'It's my da's. I didn't want to get rid.'

'Have you never heard of dry cleaning?'

'I couldn't. The bl…'

CHAPTER 72

The windowless room was small and cramped. Through the hanging cloud of his cigarette smoke, he could see the walls were completely pasted with newspaper. The headline was the same from every direction: "Mass cancer event 'The CURE' using 'irresponsibly unreliable' tech to test thousands of vulnerable and terminally ill".

This is your muse now. Create something they'd be proud of.

He turned to one of the two canvases ahead of him and slathered it with oil paint, blackening its entirety in an uneven mess as he smoked his cigarette down to the filter before doing the same to the other. He examined both tarry backdrops as he lit a new smoke, pretty sure the paint was infinitesimally oozing down the canvases. *I'd best make a start.*

The only other colour on his easel was white, so he frantically pasted it onto one of the canvases, unaware of what his hand would produce. Soon, he was going back and forth between both canvases with the automaticity and speed of an inkjet printer but the jagged, chaotic strokes of a madman. It wasn't until the final few strokes that he realised what he'd created. He dropped his brush and marvelled at his violent, dark portrayals of *Nullconda* and his mum's mandala pattern.

Peering at the bottom corners of the pieces, he decided they needed signing. He needed a different medium from the oil paint. He took the cigarette from his lips and signed one of the paintings with its smouldering tip. *No. It needs more contrast.* He checked around the room for anything he could use for a bit of colour, but between the newspapered walls, the hanging smoke, and the paint, nearly everything was black, white, or some shade of grey. He rolled up one of his shirt sleeves, picked up one of the palette knives from his easel, and began sawing at his wrist with it. As he carved away with its blunt edge harder and harder, he didn't feel a thing but eventually he drew blood, dripping a pool of it onto his easel. He swapped the knife for a brush, dipped it into his new bright red paint, and signed both canvases. The colour was just what they'd needed. The signatures looked great. *Maw and Da. I hope you like them. They're the best I could do.*

'*You* could do?'

The voice came from below him. He peered down to find Delancey kneeling beside him, smiling thinly with his wounded wrist still oozing blood.

'*My* paint,' said the Irishman, directing Emet's attention back up to the canvases. The blood red signatures looked great, but they read "Delancey". '*My* masterpieces.'

Emet startled awake. The words hung over him like a thick tobacco cloud as he dragged himself out of bed and went to the toilet. As he sat there, reciting them to himself over and over, he noticed the reddish stain on the bedroom carpet from the night before. *My paint. My masterpieces.* He flushed, stood, and walked to the doorway, where he grabbed the frame to steady his hungover dizziness. Apart from the stain, the floor was tidy. The towels were gone. The shirt was gone. *The shirt!*

He darted over to his wardrobe, pulled out the storage boxes, and used a clothes hanger to rifle through their contents. 'Clyde!' he bellowed at the top of his lungs. 'Clyde!' When no answer came, he careened downstairs to the living room and grabbed his phone.

'Where are you?' he breathlessly asked upon hearing his friend's voice.

'On the bus, mate. I may feel rough as a badger's arse, but I've still got work to get to. You were dead to the world, so I just left you to—.'

Frenzied, Emet couldn't wait for him to finish. 'Where'd you put that bloody shirt you nearly mopped up with last night?'

'Chill, mate. I brought it with me. Thought I'd get it dry cleaned for you.'

'NO!'

'Whoa, Em. Calm—'

'Don't dry clean it. Don't dry clean it. That's his blood.'

'You what?'

'That's Delancey O'Shea's blood.'

'What are you talking about?' asked Clyde, full of concern. 'What have you done?'

'Nothing. It's from when I interviewed him ages ago. He got some blood on me,' replied Emet talking a million miles per hour. 'He's an absolute dead end. I could never find out anything about him, but maybe I can now. Can you get DNA out of that blood?'

'What? Me personally?'

'I didn't mean that, but yeh, actually, can *you* do that?'

'I mean, I haven't done it from blood like this before but yes, I reckon I could do it in the lab at work.'

'And if you can get his DNA, are there any ways it can be checked against some databases, like in the health service or in criminal databases?'

'Once you have the data, you can check it against any database you have access to. But I won't check it against anything in the health service. There's no chance I'm losing my job too.'

'Fair enough,' replied Emet, wracking his brains.

'But there are open databases,' continued Clyde. 'There are all these ancestry services now where people send off saliva samples and find relations they never knew existed. There've been plenty of stories of people ending up on the hook for child support for kids they never knew about, and crimes solved through DNA matches.'

'Can you do it, mate? Can you get his DNA out of that blood and send it to some of those services? I'll pay whatever they cost.'

Clyde paused on the other end of the line. 'As much as I love the thought of going all CSI, I dunno, mate. All things considered, this doesn't sound like the best thing for you to be chasing. Like, what good can come of it?'

'I don't know. But I know a conman when I see one. If there's even the tiniest chance I can find out anything about him that can stop him before he hurts people, I have to go for it. I'm fucked, anyway. What else have I got to lose apart from a few hundred quid to ancestry services and me owing you a pint?'

'Even if I can get something, there's no chance the ancestry sites would register anything before this event of his.'

'I know. I can't stop that. But I need to do what I can.'

The line remained silent for a moment. 'You'll owe me a lot more than a pint. CSI forensic experts are on espresso martinis and ruby vodka all the way.'

Emet smiled through his disgust. 'Don't ever mention that shit to me again.'

Clyde laughed.

'And if you can't get anything off the shirt, keep it. There must be services that do such things.'

'Thanks for your full belief, matey.'

A hot bile rushed up inside Emet like a thermometer under a flame. 'Anytime, matey.'

'Freckle and Clyde, out.'

The call ended and Emet plopped himself onto the sofa. All was quiet. He had nowhere to be. *What the fuck am I going to do with myself?*

CHAPTER 73

After half a day of nursing his brutal hangover watching some of the unwatched discs that had arrived during his time in hospital, he decided to get some fresh air and take in some art of a different medium, visiting a small gallery his dad's original paintings had appeared in many years ago before his stint in prison. Walking the same, smaller-feeling space, adorned completely differently now, felt dreamlike, a sensation which was only added to by the strange images hanging on the walls and embodied in clay and other media.

As the gallery closed, he set off on the long walk to his next destination and tried calling Skye, only for it to ring through. After an hour of walking during which he picked up a bunch of flowers and passed numerous billboards and bus sides advertising the upcoming weekend's Jim Akachi-Rawlings event, Skye rang back.

'Hello, you! How's your day been?'

'Hey. It's been a very quiet one. I may have gotten very drunk with Clyde last night, therefore unable to do much of anything.'

'That's my lightweight,' she said with gleeful sarcasm.

'I've even got some red vodka vomit stains to wash out of some carpet.'

'Wow. Red vodka. I thought Clyde was meant to be keeping you out of trouble.'

'I know. A debacle best forgotten. How has your day been?'

'In-credible. I'm learning so much. The people are *so* amazing. We've got an evening session in a bit, but I'm having the time of my life here. It's so wonderful to have found something that really means something to me and to be pursuing in what feels like the right way, you know?' Before Emet had the chance to respond, she spluttered a horribly chesty coughing fit.

His brow knit together. 'Are you alright there?'

'I'm fine. Just a bit of a throaty thing, probably from gabbing so much. Anyway, enough about me and my minor ailments. What are you up to right now?'

'I…have just been to a gallery my dad exhibited at once upon a time. I haven't been there since I was, maybe, thirteen. And now, I'm just about to arrive at Maw's cemetery.'

'So, some time with the parents?'

'Uhuh,' he replied, walking through the cemetery gate.

'Please lay a kiss on your mum's stone from me.'

'I will.'

'What was the gallery like?'

'It was surreal being back there after so long. Such a long time ago, and yet the feelings were so fresh. Uncanny stuff.'

'I can't even imagine. Are you OK, my love?'

In the middle of him replying that he was fine, she broke into another violent coughing fit. 'Are you sure *you're* OK?'

'Emet,' she said in her smoothest, most reassuring tone. 'I'm fine.'

He paused for a moment and peered down into the bunch of flowers. 'If it doesn't clear by the time you're back, will you go to the doctors?'

'Of course I will,' she said, her sympathy evident. 'I think it's time for us to head off. Sorry I can't stay with you longer. We can speak later?'

'Of course,' he said. 'Enjoy the company and the class. Tell me all about it later.'

'Thank you. Are you sure everything's OK there?'

'I'm sure,' he replied, walking up the long path towards his mum's grave.

'OK. Like I said, give Leigh a kiss from me.'
'I will.'
'Love you, lightweight.'
'Love you too.'
'Bye.'

The call ended. Emet carried on past the rows of gravestones, old and new, reading the inscriptions on them as he went. *I'm still above ground, and I still have Skye and Clyde. I need to grieve…to heal…to move onto something new, for them and myself.* He arrived at her plot and dropped his bouquet to the floor. Amongst all the flowers on top of his mum's gravestone was hanging an IV drip, its tube fed into the ground.

CHAPTER 74

Later that evening, he messaged Skye saying that his phone's microphone had broken, so he'd only be able to text. He also messaged Clyde to say that he'd had a day of sickness and diarrhoea and wasn't up for a visit that night. The next afternoon, he messaged both to say that the entire phone was faulty and that he was taking it to a shop for repair. A few hours later, he powered it down. Knowing that Clyde may pop over that evening, he booked into a hotel. He didn't want to speak to anybody. He was busy. And he didn't want to be dissuaded.

From his dressing room, Jim could hear the eight thousand Leaple being whipped up into a frenzy by his support act ahead of day two. Day one had gone perfectly to plan, and he felt on even better form than during his first London Leap. But instead of his regular preparations, limbering his voice and body for the day ahead, he was sat watching his tablet, viewing a live stream from outside The CURE. The massive crowd was growing, with way more people at the O2 than had tickets. Attendees from across the globe were being interviewed about their conditions and what they hoped for from the event, some evangelically confident that they would leave on their way to cured, others far more sceptical, saying they came purely because they had nothing to lose and everything to gain, no matter how unlikely that was. Jim felt his dressing room starting to rumble. The Leaple must have started their foot stamping. He imagined their excited faces when he walked out on stage. He'd seen so many throughout his career. But he refocused on the screen. Had he ever seen anticipation in his audience like on the faces of those waiting outside The CURE? Even those who said they weren't expecting anything were wide-eyed with hope. The rumbling was escalating, rattling items on his dresser. A head poked round his door. 'They're ready for you, Jim.' He turned the livestream off, swigged a mouthful of Juggerjuice, and went to grab a quick bite to keep him going for the next few hours. There was a myriad of options, but all he saw was the bowl of nuts. He stared at them for a short eternity before grabbing a handful and popping them into his mouth. He jumped to his feet, took a few slow breaths followed by a few rapid ones, then banged his hands against his chest and shot them out into the diamond viewfinder. 'Full belief!' he boomed, repeating the chest beating and chanting a few more times, louder each one before leaping towards the doorway and heading out to his fervent audience.

'Hey. I hope by the time you get this, you've had a brilliant morning session. I'm still having phone issues, but I just wanted to let you know I'm alright, that I love you, and that it'll all be sorted soon. Speak later.' Emet turned his phone back off and walked past North Greenwich station to see the bustling O2 Arena, which he had never seen so busy on a morning. It somehow seemed even busier than it would for a major concert. Half of the people buzzing around had the complex and gauntness of severely ill people. Many had bald heads or thin, wispy hair. Quite a few were using wheelchairs or walking with frames or sticks. The entire scene horrified him. So many vulnerable people, so much false hope. He tried to put a stop to it last night, but there had been no sign of Delancey at Laurel Canyon Manor. All he saw was a logistics truck loading up with large flight cases from the house, which he followed right to the Arena before he lost it. Was he getting ready to run away ahead of the backlash after the event? If so, why not just take the cargo straight to wherever he was heading?

As he strode through the slow-moving crowds, his horror only grew. Stood beside somebody in a wheelchair with a tracheostomy, a man in a carer's uniform held a placard overhead that said "Stage 4 throat cancer. Will pay any amount for a ticket". Ten yards later, a desperate woman holding the hand of a girl no older than eight begged passers-by, 'Please. Somebody. She has her whole life ahead of her.' She took one look at Emet in his venue security uniform and moved her attention on. 'Please!' she wailed. 'Some of you people have had a full life. She's just a child!' Emet upped his pace, unable to get beyond all the despair fast enough.

Having failed to get to Delancey the evening before the show as he suspected might happen, he was going with his other plan. In his time around entertainment, he'd heard of ticketless people getting into shows in various ways and was banking on one working that he heard had worked specifically at this venue. The security firm working the shows was always the same. He'd purchased one of their long-sleeved T-shirts on eBay and picked it up yesterday, and although he'd spent hours finding multiple images online of security staff taken from around the arena during the last month and forged a security pass from them, the man who he'd picked up the T-shirt from had only been too happy to sell him an old security pass for an extra fifty quid. 'Just flash that and you'll be in. They barely even give it a second look.'

As he walked into the outer ring of the arena which housed all the bars and restaurants, he heard a yelp of excitement. The arena doors were opening. He sped up, slaloming through all the bodies until he got to one of the staff entrances, where he paused and drew a deep breath before proceeding. Pass in hand, he approached the guard on the door and nodded firmly. His heart raced so hard it felt like the guard may be able to see his entire body pulsating, but the guard just nodded him on his way. He had to concentrate to keep the sheer relief in until he was the other side of the door. He pushed it and it went nowhere. He pushed it again. It didn't budge.

'Haven't you got your door card?' the guard shouted after him.

'Door card?'

'You haven't worked in the last few weeks, have you?'

'No. Holiday,' said Emet, trying to give as little away as possible.

'You should have got one in the post,' explained the guard. 'You need a card to tap in now.'

Emet froze.

'Who's your supervisor? I can get them on the radio, get them to come sign you in.'

Fuck. 'Umm. No, I did get one. I left it in the car.'

'What's your supervisor's name? It'll save you the trip.'

'No, it's alright,' replied Emet. 'I'd rather stretch my legs than get the earache.' He made no eye contact whatsoever as he made his way back past the guard and out of the staff entrance area. 'Fuck!' he cursed as he pulled off the staff top over his head and tied it around his waist. His head span as he wandered back along the restaurant concourse, watching the crowds disappear towards the arena entrances, looking for potential openings. After ten minutes of walking around the entrances, watching the ill audience members excitedly pour into the venue, he couldn't think of a way in without an official QR-coded ticket or a genuine staff door card. He watched the smiles of the participants as they headed in. He needed fresh air. He needed to think.

He walked back out towards the Tube station, sat on a bench, and lit a cigarette. The crowds were thinning. His time was running out.

CHAPTER 75

'Excuse me, mate.'

Emet turned to find a man, maybe five years his senior, pointing a cigarette his way.

'Can I grab a light?'

Emet nodded and passed his lighter over, receiving thanks as it was handed back.

'It's a mad one, eh?' said the man, nodding towards the arena. 'All that hope in one place.'

Emet nodded. 'It is,' he said, taking a puff of his cigarette to stop him saying anymore.

'Wha'd'ya reckon?' the man asked as he sat on the bench beside Emet. 'Do you really think he can do it?'

'I'm probably not the person you want to ask. How about yourself?'

'I dunno. All those people in there. They believe so much. Not because they know, you know? Just because they want to.'

Emet slowly nodded as the man blew out a large cloud of smoke.

'I mean, I obviously get it. They *want* to believe…who wouldn't in their situation? But hearing people speak so positively, so unquestioningly…well, when's something like that legit?'

Emet flicked some of his ash away. 'When indeed?'

The two sat wordlessly for a long moment, only the smoke from their respective cigarettes in dialogue.

'Do you work here or are you a carer or what?' asked the man.

'Or what,' replied Emet. 'You?'

'Me?' asked the man, grinning as he blew a plume of smoke into the air. 'Stage three-b bowel cancer.'

Emet immediately turned his full attention to the man. 'I'm sorry.'

The man shrugged. 'What you gonna do?'

'Were you trying to get a ticket?'

The man shook his head.

'So, what brought you here?'

'The miniscule chance, you know? But then hearing everybody going on like they were...well...I'm not one of those simpletons. Bloody hell, if I haven't got long left, I think I'd rather go to Lourdes than spend the day here. At least I'd see some beauty instead of a Frankie and Benny's and some bubble tea place.'

Emet chuckled inwardly and then squinted confusedly. 'So, you *were* trying to get a ticket?'

The man shook his head. 'No. I have one.'

Emet fought to keep his eyes from bulging.

'But it's bullshit, isn't it? If I go in there, I go to my grave knowing I was a mug just like all of them.'

Emet looked to the ground as he measured his response. 'I wouldn't call them mugs – they're in desperate situations – but yes, it's one hundred percent bullshit.'

The man rose to his feet. 'Thank you. Another sane voice. Fuck this shit. There are funner ways to spend a Sunday.'

'So, you're not going in?'

The man puffed his cigarette and shook his head. 'Nahah. Thanks for the light,' he said as he began to turn away.

'Where's your ticket for?'

'The floor section, not too far from the front. Why?'

'Can I have it?'

The man stopped and examined him. 'What do you have?'

Emet considered his answer. 'I don't have cancer, but I have two dead parents to it and a serious allergy to bullshit.'

The man raised an eyebrow. 'So, why go in?'

'To stop it.'

'How the hell are you gonna stop that? You're not some sort of suicide bomber, are you?'

Emet patted his T-shirt down. 'Nope. There's only one person who needs to be stopped for this to stop.'

The man lowered his voice. 'You're gonna kill him?'

'No,' Emet said matter-of-factly. 'Just stop him until somebody can legally stop him. Can I have your ticket and your documents?'

The man raised his chin and looked down on Emet. 'How much is it worth to you?'

Emet pulled his wallet out. 'I've got six fifty.'

The man laughed. 'That's not gonna get me to Lourdes or the Spearmint Rhino, is it? And you've sort of made me an accessory to something. What else've you got?'

'On me? Nothing,' replied Emet emptying his pockets.

'What you driving there?' asked the man upon seeing Emet's car keys.

'A Škoda Superb.'

'How old?'

'Maybe five or six years.'

The man pulled out his phone and Googled its value. 'That'd get me to Lourdes. Or Vegas. The car and the cash and the ticket and my documents are yours.'

Emet regarded the keys in his hand. 'Sold.'

The man shook his head with a disbelieving smile. 'You're mad.'

Emet nodded towards the arena and stubbed out his cigarette. 'Only if you call that sanity.'

Emet told him where the car was parked and swapped details with the man so that they he could sign over the car paperwork at a later date, then took a packet from him containing the ticket and photocopies of his medical records. They shook hands on their deal. 'Good luck,' said the man. 'I think.'

'Enjoy the healing waters of the Bellagio.'

Emet headed back into the arena, past a few sufferers still begging for tickets, and joined a shortening queue. A few minutes later, he was near the front. Beads of perspiration formed on his temples.

'Next.'

He stepped forward and presented his ticket. *Please don't let this be a fake.* The doorman scanned the QR code. A green light appeared on the scanner.

'Welcome to The CURE, sir.'

CHAPTER 76

Inside, the crowds were shepherded towards welcome desks. He saw participants walking away with workbooks, but as he grew closer he saw another souvenir: a pale purple patch donning the word 'Horus' on the back of somebody's arm. Once he saw the first, then he saw a sea of them. Then he saw the welcomers applying them, jabbing them to the arm of every person after cleaning the skin with an alcohol wipe. It was like watching cattle being branded. He walked along the queues, trying to find a way into the arena without having a patch attached, but there were none. He queued, downloaded the Horus app while he waited as instructed to by welcomers, and eventually reached the front. As his welcomer passed him his workbook and spoke to him, he answered on autopilot, preoccupied by the sight along the desks of so many people having these patches applied simultaneously as if on some surreal assembly line. The freshness of the alcohol wipe only fully brought him to.

'You might feel the tiniest of pricks, sir. Ready?'

He turned his head fully away and nodded. He felt the quick pressure, like a stamp, on the back of his arm, and then nothing.

'Excellent. Can you open your app and touch your patch to your phone, please?'

He did as she asked, still somewhat bamboozled by the whole scene.

'And can you show me your screen, please?'

He waved it her way.

'Excellent. It's paired. The readings won't operationalise until later, so you can focus on the event, but you're good to go. Remember your book there, sir,' she said, prompting him to pick it back up from the desk. 'Have a healing day, sir,' she said, sending him on his way with the same saccharine-sweet smile he'd grown familiar with from the assistants at The Leap. Feeling at his patch and navigating through the mostly inactive app, he pottered around the concourse, where unlike at the previous self-help seminar all sorts of merchandise, supplements, services, and other seminars were for sale, the only things to buy here were drinks and snacks. Including the carers, at least fifty percent of the people he moved amongst had mobility issues or looked extremely ill, but as bad as he assumed many of their conditions were, a sense of quiet optimism tantalised the air. After everything he'd been through since finding out about Delancey, from his mental short-circuiting outside of The Dorchester, to Felix's fugue visit and window-scrawling session, to his own bloody session with the Irishman, to everything he'd lost since, he couldn't stomach the hope surrounding him, being so certain of its falsity. It was all pinned upon incredulous, unsubstantiated claims made by a man overflowing with gleeful misandry; a man whom every bone in his body told him was a conman.

He entered the floor level of the arena and surveyed the vast space. He knew it had a twenty-thousand capacity but hadn't known until this moment why the event was only open to ten thousand. Whilst waiting outside, it had crossed his mind that the extra seats may be for the carers of many of the audience but that wasn't it. Everywhere he looked, every other seat was fitted with restraint straps, with the legs of the freestanding seats sandbagged down. The participants weren't going to be straitjacketed but they would be fastened to their seats, with space between them and their neighbours for safety in the event of violent flailing around. His blood boiled as he walked along the rows, watching the odd person curiously playing with the straps. *How the fuck can all this be allowed to happen?!* He took his seat – an aisle seat only a few rows from the front – and watched the arena fill as the lights began to dim. As he opened his workbook, a low sound began over the sound system: a slow, steady double-beating of a heart. The large screens above and either side of the stage slowly morphed out of blackness, a deep red pattern emerging on them. Eventually it clarified enough to show what it was: a video of cancer cells dividing. He checked the faces of those around him to see their reactions, which ranged from impassive, to unsettled, to outright fearful. After a while of new malignant cells appearing out of the cell soup, the growth halted and reversed until the screens returned to black. Blinding white text saying "This is The CURE" appeared. Another image began to emerge from the blackness. It was a clock, melting against a backdrop of dividing cancer cells, glooping more and more until just before one of its hands looked like it was about to drip off, then stopping and reversing, with the clock pulling itself back into a regular shape and the cells reintegrating until only blackness remained. "This is The CURE". The pulsating heart thump continued as he turned his eyes to the first page of his book. "Fear binds us. It consumes us. To live free, to live vital, we need to become aware of our shackles; of the parasites that strip us of our vitality. Search the deepest parts of yourself. You won't have to look or listen too far. They plague your dreams. They are the doubts that scream up from the basement of your subconscious every day. What do you truly fear?"

Emet looked around to see some people amongst the filling seats around him writing answers in the workbook as he turned the page.

'You need to fill those in, you know.' Emet turned to find an older wig-wearing woman in the row behind him. 'They said the more you start to pull this stuff up, the more effective the session will be.'

'Thanks,' Emet replied, turning back to face front and taking the pen out of the spine of the workbook, hovering it over the page to appease the busybody.

The screens flashed white with black writing, their message matching the simultaneous arena announcement. 'The CURE begins in fifteen minutes. Please make your way to your seat.'

Emet read the question again. "What do you truly fear?" He put his pen to paper and wrote *That there's nothing I can do to stop this*.

'I know this feels unstoppable,' said Jim, his face and the face of the audience member he was doing an intervention with gigantic across multiple big screens, the eight-thousand-strong audience dialled into his every word and microexpression. 'But that's only because you don't understand what's driving it. The moment you truly get that is the moment you can take control of the wheel. Do you want to take the wheel?'

The tearful audience member nodded. 'Of course,' he murmured.

'There is no of course. There's nothing taken for granted,' replied Jim. 'If you want it, you have to show this world you want it with everything from the conviction of your thoughts to the boldness of your actions to the certainty you speak with, whatever that emotion is that's spilling out of you right now. Now, use it all. Do you want to take the wheel?'

'Yes!' yelled the audience member through their tears.

'That's more like it!' said Jim, landing a strong hand on his subject's shoulder. 'So, tell me, tell us all here now, what is it that's driving you when you're doing the stuff the real you knows is falling short of your true standard?'

Tears streamed down the audience member's face as a thought took hold of them.

'I can see you've got it,' said Jim. 'Speak the unspoken. Let its grip over you vanish forever.'

The audience member swallowed. 'I...I'm desperate to help as many people as possible.'

'That's admirable,' said Jim, squeezing his shoulder, 'but you and I both know that ain't what's causing the pain at the bottom of this. Tell me, what's your intention in helping as many people as possible? What would that do for *you?*'

The tears continued streaming as the man's lips quivered. 'It'd help me…be remembered.'

'To be remembered.' Jim paused for a long moment, his eyes turning down momentarily before returning to his subject tearing up. His voice softened. 'And what would being remembered do for you?'

The subject thought long and hard, then the floodgates opened. He barely got his next words out. 'If people remember me…maybe that means I'm worth something.'

The words hit Jim like a sledgehammer, dislodging a tear of his own. He looked deep into the eyes of his subject. 'Let me tell you right now that you aren't worth something.' He paused, leaving his subject to fill with distress for a moment. 'You, brother, are worth everything.'

The audience exploded in applause, many rising to their feet.

Jim wrapped his arms around his subject, then backed away, gesturing to the intensifying ovation around them. 'Look. Listen. Everybody here recognises it, don't you?'

The audience whistled and cheered.

'And I know they don't know you, so maybe you think they're blowing smoke up your ass, but do you know how I know they ain't?'

The subject shook his head.

'Because they want to believe a deeper truth. They *know* a deeper truth. And that truth is that we're all worth everything.' Everybody was up on their feet now. The whooping and hollering forced Jim to pause for thirty seconds before continuing. He laid his hand back on the man's shoulder and looked him profoundly in the eye. 'Everybody here. We all have equal human value. We all have that magic. That spark. That boundless potential. The capacity to love and be loved. We can all change the world in the blink of an eye if we can remember what we are, then get out of our own way, and let our limitless potential flow out of us into actuality.'

The audience watched on in rapture.

'You have a beautiful goal. To help as many people as possible, but it was being driven by insecurity, right?'

His subject nodded.

'If you knew that you were worth everything and that the right people would remember you, would you still want to help as many people as possible?'

Callum wiped away some of his tears and nodded emphatically.

'So, your goal is independent of those insecure drivers and can be uncoupled from them. Will you commit to spending the rest of your day figuring out the link between that unlimited worth you have and your noble goal?

'I will,' his subject replied resoundingly into his microphone.

'Will you take the leap tonight away from doubt and a poverty mindset and into the certainty you have abundance within you?'

'I will.'

'And will you commit to leaping out of your bed tomorrow and many mornings for years to come to bring the abundance of you into actuality to help as many people as you possibly can?'

'I will.'

Jim wiped away his own tears, checked his subject's eyes, and nodded. 'I know you will, brother. What do we say?' He and his subject simultaneously banged their chests and thrust their hands out, yelling 'full belief', before jumping forward with the audience joining in their chorus of 'take the leap.'

'Give it up for Callum, Leaple,' said Jim as he backed away, bounding back to the stage amidst thunderous ovation. As he waited for the crowd to settle, he surveyed their joy. This was their reaction to a man committing to helping as many people as he could. Just as they quietened down, he jogged off the stage and ran back on, putting something on the little table holding his bottles of water and

Juggerjuice. 'To help as many people as possible. That's a hell of a goal, isn't it, Leaple?'

The audience boomed a 'yes' back his way.

'Truth be told, Callum and everyone here has inspired me. I'm blessed to be able to help a lot of people, but deep down, I know I can help even more profoundly. Today, I'm going to take a leap in my own evolution. It's one thing improving lives. It's another thing removing the very real risk of death.'

The Leaple put their hands together for their leader, some visibly unsure where he was going.

'What's inside us is more powerful than many of us can imagine. If we can harness the power within, we don't just have the ability to change our thoughts, feelings and actions. We can change the basis of it all, our truest abundance: our health. Many of the conditions that ail us do so because, on a subconscious level, we're at war with ourselves and it's pushed our immune systems out of whack. He reached down and picked up a packet of peanuts. 'For example, peanuts don't kill people. It's misplaced, overactive immune responses to them that do. Does anybody here have a peanut "allergy" they would like to use the power of their subconscious mind to resolve with me here and now?'

CHAPTER 77

The room bustled with excitement now. Five minutes ago, all carers had again been asked for a last time to leave the main section of the arena and head to the concourse. Event assistants checked up and down every row for anybody unseated or sat in a cordoned-off seat. The next heartbeat thump never came. Instead, a loud locking noise played over the arena sound system as the lights went all the way down and a countdown timer appeared on the screens. By the number eight, many of the crowd joined in with the visual countdown. A chill ran down Emet's spine as he bathed in the noise of ten-thousand suffering souls and the screen turned more blood red with every number that passed.

Eventually the count reached 'one'. The whole arena fell into abject darkness. Then blood red light filled the giant screens and flashed all over in a dazzling light show through mist pouring in from the ceiling above the stage and all around the arena, bright white messages shining through it all from the big screens, one line at a time in time with grand, ominous music:

> HEAL YOUR TURMOIL
> BECOME A NEW YOU
> THIS
> IS
> THE CURE

Down through the smoke billowing down from above the stage, something emerged. It was a pair of feet. The crowd went wild as more and more of a body descended. People were up on their feet screaming wildly, clapping their hands raw. Eventually, Emet stood just to see what was going on, disturbed by the hysteria he was in the midst of. Then it all became real. Out of the mist appeared that familiar thin smile. Delancey O'Shea outstretched his arms to the sides as if Jesus on the cross and lapped up the adulation long after his feet reached the stage. The applause remained ear-shatteringly loud as the Irishman released his harness and began to pace along the front of the stage, peering out into the mass of bodies celebrating him. Where most performers, given such a raucous welcome to the stage, wave and clap their audience, Emet watched as Delancey gave a few barely visible nods before returning to the front of the stage, his icy blue stare glaring through the spotlights until the audience simmered down and many sat.

'Thank you,' said the Irishman, joining his hands behind his back. 'Welcome to The CURE. Today, for the majority of you, is the first day of a superior chapter of your life. I know you will all have many questions, but talk is cheap. Let me show you the answers. Ilsa Schmidt, please raise your hand.'

Emet and everyone else in the arena looked around until all eyes converged on a spot-lit raised hand from the floor seating section across the other side of the arena.

'Enlist any help you require and make your way to the stage.'

A ripple of applause spread throughout the crowd as a group of assistants gathered around her and led her frail, spindly frame up to the stage.

'So lucky!' Emet heard a lady on the row in front of him hiss as the noise died down and the lady slowly made her way towards the host.

'Welcome, Ilsa.'

'Thank you so much,' said the lady in her thick German accent.

'Would you care to tell the audience of your condition?'

'I have type four breast cancer.'

'You've had medical treatment?'

'Yes. I've had a double mastectomy and four rounds of chemoradiotherapy,' she said, wiping a few tears away.

'And what's your current prognosis?'

'The doctors tell me I have three to six months to live,' she said, sniffling to hold back her tears.

'My panel of medical consultants here tell me that prognosis is accurate based on your blood markers. A normal level of one of the breast cancer markers CA15-3 in the blood is thirty units per milliliter.' He directed her attention to the big screen where the Horus app interface appeared. 'After all of her treatments and surgery, Ilsa's level right now is eighty-four point zero. In the context of her condition,' he turned to her, 'am I correct in assuming the doctors have been monitoring this, hoping that they could bring it down, indicating some efficacy of their treatments?'

'That's correct,' she replied.

'And over what period do they expect such reductions to occur?'

She pondered on his question for a moment. 'The best improvement I ever had was a reduction of about twenty points after my surgery. Apart from this, the best other result was a reduction of three units after three months.'

'A unit per month?'

'Yes.'

'What would you say if we could bring you down a unit today?' asked Delancey.

'I would say that would indicate a miracle.'

'What would you say if during the time you are on this stage, we could see your CA15-3 fall in real time?'

'I would say you are a magician or the messiah himself,' she said, her expression torn between hope and despair.

He smiled warmly. 'I'm neither, but to paraphrase the greatest magician who ever lived, *your* brain is the key that sets you free.' He turned to the audience. 'Let me show you that you all have the keys for the most incredible of escapes.' He turned back her way. 'Please sit.'

Ilsa sat on the armchair from Laurel Canyon Manor and Delancey produced the straitjacket off the seat of his plush wheely chair, then spoke between her and the audience. 'As explained in your pre-seminar materials, a safety precaution, overkill for many but an absolute necessity for the minority.' She nodded and he put it on, buckled her in, and fastened her to the chair. 'What's about to follow isn't much of a spectator sport, but it will give you some idea of what's to come for yourselves and hopefully that score changing up there will provide ample excitement. There are lots of very ill people here today, but Ilsa's marker levels are amongst the highest, hence her selection for this demonstration. A round of applause for her, please.'

The audience clapped resoundingly.

Delancey eventually shushed them. 'Now, I must insist on quiet, please. What Ilsa is about to experience and what you're about to witness can be deeply disturbing for a few minutes, but on the other side of it is a new life free of one's deepest turmoil. However distressing it looks, please remain quiet and calm. Ilsa, are you ready to face your darkness?'

'I am.'

'And would you like the audience to leave us to our business, no matter what?'

'I would.'

'Then let's play.'

CHAPTER 78

Emet shuffled closer to the edge of his seat, ready for the trance induction to begin but then *snap,* Ilsa's head fell and her eyes closed at the click of Delancey's fingers, drawing a gasp from thousands. 'Very good, Ilsa,' he said in the bassiest of voices before turning to the audience and speaking normally. 'From the pre-work, it was also apparent that Ilsa would make a swift demonstration subject, being high in what a hypnotist would call "suggestibility".' As he turned his attention back to her, thousands adjusted in their seats and sat forward, then silence fell. The numbers upon the screen glared brightly at them all.

'Let any sound that isn't my voice fall away, Ilsa. It's just you and I. You filled in your workbook, didn't you?'

She nodded.

'You know what you truly fear, don't you?'

'Yes,' she said monotonically.

'Would you care to tell us what that is?'

Her blank face began to flicker with anguish. 'That I am powerless.'

'That you are powerless. Describe to me what powerless feels like in your body right now.'

'My body trembles…it feels empty…my chest feels tight…my face, the cheeks, they are warm.'

'Yes. And as you tremble, emptying, tightening, warming a little more with every breath you take, do you know where this feeling comes from?'

She gulped and a tear trickled down her cheek. 'I do.'

'That's right. And for all the places you've been in your life and all the time that's passed, you never really left that place, did you?'

She shook her head, more tears falling now.

'And it's eaten away at you, slowly cannibalising your peace of mind, picking the soul from your bones, hasn't it?'

She nodded; her brow tightly furrowed.

'It'll be done with you once and for all soon unless you face it. Unless you resolve it. I know it's never left you, but that's because until now you've always run from it. Are you ready for the first time ever to truly face it?'

Ilsa shuddered, then eventually nodded.

'Good. That tremble is ready to take you there, isn't it?'

Ilsa's flaccid body began violently tremoring.

'Let it rattle you right out of the here and now,' said Delancey, louder and with menace. 'Feel your chest tightening as the fear grips you…as it lifts you…as it pulls you back to where it all began…your face burning now as you get closer and closer to the furnace of fear that started it all!' he said, half out of his seat as Ilsa's face turned crimson red and she began to writhe and tremble, trying to escape the jacket and the seat. Wheeling closer and laying his hand across her collar bones, he pinned her thrashing body back against the seat. 'You can see her now in front of you…the younger you…when all of this started.'

Tears coursed down her face, which looked more in pain than upset.

'How old is she?'

'Six,' sobbed Ilsa.

'When I snap my fingers, you will be her, six again, seeing through her eyes. Three…' Her face contorted in horror. '…two…' She heaved with her entire body, striving to escape her shackles. *Snap.*

Emet thought he'd been disturbed, but now his horror knew new bounds. The audience gasped as Ilsa shrieked and shrieked and shrieked, trying to escape the chair with the strength of ten women fighting for their lives. She was going to rip her way out of that straitjacket or rip herself to shreds trying.

Delancey was on his feet, using all his power across her chest to keep her in position. 'What do you see and hear, Ilsa?'

'Runter von mir, Papa! Runter von mir!' she screeched at the top of her lungs.

Horrified looks passed around the audience. Emet heard somebody behind him whisper to their neighbour, 'It means "get off me, Daddy".' His stomach turned.

Delancey grabbed Ilsa's head and spoke rapid-fire into her ear as she turned brighter and brighter red, still frantically trying to claw herself away from her hallucinated hell, which only seemed to subsume her more with every second. Then the audio feed disappeared. All that filled the arena were Ilsa's traumatised screams and pleads in her mother tongue. Every bone in Emet's body wanted him to run to the stage and stop this but Ilsa was so deep into it now, he had no idea what interrupting them would do, plus there were a few assistants staged between the end of his row and the stage.

Her body convulsed so hard against the seat it looked like invisible forces were flinging her in all directions. Delancey shoved her chest back one more time and with one final sentence, her body arched in a way it didn't look like its frailty could survive, then everything went quiet and still. Delancey removed his hand from her chest. Audience members swapped concerned glances. She was so still, was she even breathing?

Delancey returned to her ear, said a few words, and then swivelled to the audience, and tapped his lapel mic, triggering it to turn back on. 'And now we wait.'

Ilsa was breathing and over the next forty minutes, Delancey spoke softly to her, sometimes with a full thirty seconds between sentences, remarking on her breathing and heart rate returning to normal, on her tension falling away, and on the products of all that turmoil she'd held inside for so long blowing away like dandelion seeds in the wind. Even though the obvious drama was gone, everybody couldn't take their eyes off Ilsa, unsure if she was OK after such an emotional ordeal. And then, as Emet studied her face, wondering if such fright had taken time off her life, it happened: the number on the screen behind her dropped from eighty-four point zero to eighty-three point nine. Emet heard ten thousand people stop breathing simultaneously. He watched his neighbours look to each other, eyes wide as saucers, mouths agape, wondering what to do. Then a tentative applause began. Delancey snapped out of his locked stare on his subject, looked over his shoulder at the audience, and then up at the screen. 'Do you hear that?' he asked as he turned back to Ilsa. 'That's for you. I think you should open your eyes and look at the screen behind you.'

After a few seconds, Ilsa's stretched her spine and legs. Slowly, her eyes peeled open as if awakening from the deepest of sleeps. It was only after her eyes refocused that she could make out all the bodies out in the blackness ahead of her. Emet saw the moment where she remembered where she was.

'Ilsa,' said Delancey, pulling her attention his way. 'The screen.'

She turned and looked up at it, then turned back towards the audience and Delancey with her jaw hanging wide open. The applause escalated and her shock turned into the widest of smiles, fuelling it even further.

'That was you, Ilsa. *You* faced your demon and now *your* body is healing itself. This is only the beginning. You will be free,' said Delancey, unbuckling the jacket from the seat and undoing the jacket as the ovation became raucous, with all the audience on its feet and Emet having to follow in suit just to see what was happening. 'We're going to keep revisiting your figures over the next few hours to check on your progress. If you start to feel a little off with some nausea and a temperature, don't worry, it's just the healing response.' Delancey slipped one of her arms out of the jacket and kissed it. 'Thank you for coming up and for your bravery.' Delancey pulled the jacket entirely off her and flung it to the floor. 'Live free, Ilsa.'

The arena went berserk. Emet had been here before for concerts with twice as many in the audience as this, but he had never heard commotion like it. A greatest hit was no match for a life saved, and that was what they were bringing the house down for. He panned around the audience, observing the sheer, unbridled joy on their ill faces. They were so hopefully happy, they might never stop clapping.

But it's just a fucking number on a screen. Are these people mad?! They're not mad, Emet. They're just desperate to believe and they don't know those figures can't possibly change that quickly, and they don't know that a little patch can't read those blood markers with that sensitivity in real time. But you know. You know. He fed a fucking drip into her grave. He zeroed in on Delancey's grin as the Irishman handed Ilsa off to some assistants at the far side of the stage, then looked ahead of himself down the end of the rows. There was only one assistant between him and the stage, and they were applauding Ilsa with everything they had. He took a tiny smiley-faced paper tab of LSD out of his pocket, a quarter of the size of a postage stamp but dowsed in enough lysergic acid diethylamide to send somebody on a psychedelic trip for six to twelve hours, began clapping as he edged out to the aisle, and then he took off, running faster than he ever had. He didn't watch the crowd, he didn't watch the assistant, he just ran. Although the stage front wasn't guarded by security every few yards like it was at concerts, there was going to be a hell of a leap to get up high enough to clamber onto the stage quickly. As he approached his take-off steps, only one passing thought invaded his supremely focused mind: Jim Akachi-Rawlings jumping between those rooftops. He accelerated into his last step. *Bang.* He flew through the air, everything in him willing itself onto that stage. *Thud.* He hit the stage's ledge waist high and shoved himself up, scrambling to his feet. As he pushed off like a sprinter out of the blocks, his ears filled with the gasp of ten thousand reeling onlookers. A few steps into his sprint, his target, having sensed something was going on from the audience, turned his way. As he hurtled towards Delancey, gearing up to tackle him, there was no fear on the host's face. Not a flinch or blink either. Purely glee. Emet tackled him hard, bringing them both tumbling to the floor as screams shot up from the audience. Emet clambered up Delancey and tried to pin the host's head still as he readied the tab between his fingers to aim for the Irishman's mouth, but then came the hit. A hefty security guard bundled Emet off Delancey and five others were metres away. Before they descended on him and had any chance of restraining him and finding the tab of LSD he tried to spike the speaker with, he popped it onto his tongue. The other guards descended on him and the next thing he knew, everything was black.

CHAPTER 79

'This ain't gonna be no pretty visualisation. You ready?' asked Jim.

His demonstration subject, a woman in her late forties, nodded. 'Fully.'

The eight-thousand strong audience clapped, Jim eventually hushing them. 'OK. I want you to close your eyes and breathe with me.' Jim audibly breathed at a normal pace, then faster, then faster still, matched all the way by his demo subject. 'Now, you continue, forcefully in, shallowly out, forcefully in, shallowly out, and as you do, I want your mind to blow back like you're in a hot air balloon overlooking a time when the younger you down there had a mild allergic reaction you had. Nod when you're above it looking down.'

After a few moments of her eyes flickering behind their lids, the demo subject nodded.

'And as you speed up that breathing,' he said, demonstrating a few quicker breaths, which the subject followed along with, 'let all that air you're pushing in and out fly you above another time in your life when you had a stronger reaction, maybe even a full anaphylactic shock, where you can watch all the way from up here, completely safe, away from it. Nod when you're above it.'

A few seconds later, she nodded.

'You're a pro. Now, as you take that breathing up a notch and you recognise you're perfectly safe as an observer, watching those events back, I want you to understand that all your immune system is trying to do is keep you safe, but it's taking things way too far. You weren't always allergic to peanuts, were you?'

The subject shook her head.

'Something happened at some point in your life that caused you a significant emotional disturbance that threw your immune system out of whack, and you never resolved that disturbance, therefore your immune system keeps overreacting in the same way. It's not actually the peanut that hurts you. It's your immune system's overreaction, flooding you with histamines, et cetera, that does. Are you ready to find that emotional disturbance and resolve it?'

The woman nodded enthusiastically.

'Excellent. So, I want you to make that breathing faster still. Let it blow you like the winds of a storm back above where you need to be.'

The woman hyperventilated almightily, but her face flickered with no emotion other than confusion.

'That's right. And you may not even consciously know when that moment was, but eventually it'll pop into your mind, and you'll see it down there below you. Tell me when you're there.'

She kept determinedly hyperventilating, going on long enough that Jim began to hear the audience becoming restless. A bead of sweat formed at his hairline. Then her face transformed. Fear gripped her and the hyperventilation became jagged and uncontrolled.

'There you are. Feel your breath running away with itself as the air starts to disappear from your balloon, bringing you lower and lower towards the experience.'

She began to squirm in her chair, her expression becoming ever more disturbed.

'On the count of one, you're going to be in that experience, living it like you did for the very first time, just even more intensely, with all the settings turned up to eleven.'

Her entire body trembled.

'Three. That's right. Feel that tremble pulling you down into it. Two. Almost fully there.'

Her eyes still closed, she turned her head away from facing forward.

'You can turn your head whichever way you want, but you can't escape it. One.'

She involuntarily yelped as she dug her fingernails into the arms of her chair, her entire self bracing as her breathing sped up to a pant and veins popped out of her neck and forehead. The entire audience sat forward in their seats.

Jim turned up his energy. 'You're there now, and let it be realer than real can be. It grows to tower over you. The sound of if reverberates through you like a tuning fork. The smell of it saturates your lungs.'

Her body quaked now as her lungs heaved to pull more and more oxygen in.

'It surrounds you. Overpowers you. You see it and hear it and feel it all. There's nowhere to run from it. Face it in its worst form!' he bellowed, half on his feet out the chair by now, fuelling her unbridled terror. He turned quickly to an assistant off stage and gave them a nod to bring the packet of peanuts back onto the stage before hearing a collective gasp. He turned back to his demo subject. Gripping the left side of her chest, the anguish on her face took on a dimension of pure pain. Jim's eyes widened. He hesitated for a minute, then sprang into action. 'And now you can float back up to a completely safe distance above the experience,' he rattled off in a soothing voice, 'and leave all those feeling with her back down there as you relax just like anybody watching a movie would.'

But she didn't relax. Her agony intensified. Then it completely stopped. Her entire body fell limp. Jim's eyes bulged. Screams sounded around the audience. He dove over to her and checked for a pulse. 'Medics!' he bawled. A curtain quickly descended to hide the stage as the sound of footsteps sprinting onto it was drowned out by the seminar's signature music.

CHAPTER 80

'Emet,' said the whisper.

Blackness surrounded him. A hand gently combed through his hair, but his head was throbbing.

'Emet.'

Groggily, he opened his eyes. He squinted confusedly as they slowly pulled into focus. 'What…what are you…?' He cut himself off and closed his eyes. *You're tripping, you dickhead. Just breathe.* But the hand persisted stroking him as real as anything he'd felt. He reopened his eyes. Skye's face pressed against his, and one of her tears rolling down his cheek.

'Are you OK?' she asked. 'That must have been a nasty bang.'

'What…where are we?'

'We're in London, darling.'

'What about your course?'

She peeled away from him.

With clear eyes and space between them, he barely recognised her. Her usually wavy hair was die-straight and scraped back into a tight bun. She wore dark, metallic make-up and crimson lipstick. Her nose ring was gone, and she wore a smart, dark dress and designer heels. Suddenly the chair he was sat on lifted in the air. Freaked out, her tried to escape it but realised he couldn't. His hands were bound to it and each other behind his back, and his legs were shackled to it too. As he was carried past her, he scanned over his shoulders to find two men moving him forward. 'What the fuck is this?' They abruptly planted him at the front of the room ahead of a drawn pair of curtains.

Skye reappeared ahead of him, kissed his cheek and caressed him again, another tear rolling down her cheek as she set her hand on one of the curtains. 'I'm on my course.' She opened the curtains. They were still in the arena, looking down from a corporate box onto the stage and the crowd, watching Delancey. He was briefing the audience on the last stages of securing themselves to their chairs. His jaw fell wide open as his pale skin washed a deeper shade of white. 'What the fuck is going on?'

'He's going to save their lives, and millions more because of you,' she said, her heart breaking as he tugged against his restraints with all his might. 'I know you'll never forgive me, but I hope when nearly ten thousand people are cancer free, you'll understand what I did.'

'What the fuck are you talking about? When did he get to you?!'

'He didn't get to me, Emet. I didn't learn art at uni. I taught myself in hospital and a hospice while I was dying of leukaemia. I was one of his first cures. He saved me.'

He was utterly gobsmacked. Their entire relationship flashed before his eyes.

'I'm so, so sorry it had to be this way,' she said, wracked with guilt, barely able to get the words out. 'He needed exposure, and you were uniquely situated to give him it.'

He couldn't believe what he was hearing. 'So what? You whored yourself out to play some sick game with me?'

'I didn't whore myself out. You have to believe me. I had genuine affection for you.'

He sneered at her. 'You whored yourself out.'

'I had to!' she cried at him. 'It was the only way.'

'Fuck you! There are a million different ways to get publicity.'

'Not like you've given him with all the controversy. And this was the only way he said he'd teach me.'

Her sentence knocked the wind out of him. His disdain deepened. 'Forget that he's selling bullshit for a second. Didn't you think that maybe somebody who insists doing such despicable shit isn't the man to cure cancer?'

'He said I had to show I could be somebody else. He said to do this work, you have to be willing to wade into the darkest waters of yourself and others. I had to show him I could. And it's not bullshit, Emet. See for yourself,' she said, nodding towards the stage.

He glowered at her, refusing to pay any attention to the show. 'You said you loved me. You watched my life crumble. You stole my dad's painting and nearly had me ki—'

'No! That was nothing to do with us!' she interjected.

'Whatever!' he said with pure disdain. 'You watched *my mother die* while you played some twisted game with our lives!'

'No, Emet!' she blurted out. '*You* watched her die. You had every opportunity to reach out to Delancey for help and you chose not to. There was no fee. She didn't have to stop treatment. It would have cost you nothing but a bit of face.'

He could barely force the words out. 'But I did reach out. I asked him and he said no. He said he'd stopped being The Cancer Man.'

'No, you didn't.'

'I did,' he regretfully insisted.

She scrutinised his face. 'You didn't, Emet.'

'I fucking did!' he bellowed at the top of his lungs. 'Don't you see what this man is? He's a deranged sadist and he'll fuck you over too!' A pair of hands grabbed his head. As he wrestled against them, the other guard duct taped his mouth shut. He looked up at him. It was Joss; Skye's supposed ex.

She wiped away her tears and stiffened her chin. 'You're wrong. I know you can't see it yet, but he's going to help so many people, and I'm going to as well. I really am sorry I lied to you,' she said, cupping his face only for him to thrash his head to bat her hand off. 'Watch. This moment is going to live through the ages.' She gazed admiringly out of the window down at Delancey. 'He's willing to go so much further than everyone for what he wants, and that's why he'll change this world forever,' she said. 'While lightweights just talk.'

She walked beyond him, her high heels clip clopping until the door opened and they were gone. He tugged again at his restraints for a full thirty seconds before he gave up, realising his efforts were futile. The tape was impossible to work off his mouth. His heart was pounding out of his chest, his mind was doing somersaults, and sweat was pouring off him. But now an odd dizziness overcame him. As he looked out of the large window ahead of him, its flat surface began to warp like a pond's surface. He looked down into the audience, who looked all strapped in now, but saw movement. At first, he thought people were standing from their seats, but actually, they were rising with them. From the arena floor section, tens of people were floating up into the air, eventually settling to hover at different heights above the audience like balloons. *Like Nullconda.* He closed his eyes. *It's just the trip. It's just the trip.* He prayed for the floaters to be back on the floor when he reopened his eyes, but they remained suspended, unnaturally still, with more starting to rise. The sound of the heartbeat from before the show resumed over the sound system. The entire arena throbbed. And as foreboding music built behind the heartbeat, Emet looked down at centre stage where Delancey stood, arms outstretched to his sides, looking double his normal size. His bassy voice boomed louder and deeper than ever before. 'Let us begin.'

Along with all the lights, the image of Ilsa's live blood readings on the big screens faded to blood red, casting the entire audience in their horrifying hue.

'Take that colour with you as you close your eyes.'

Emet daren't even blink as the rest of the audience closed their eyes. He tried to stand out of his chair and tear the restraints away, gaining an extra few inches of height momentarily which allowed him to see down to the back of the room. Bathed in blood red, some of the faces looked as if their eyes had swallowed themselves.

'Feel it coursing through your veins and arteries, every beat of your heart…' he said as the double beat played over the sound system, '…pushing it faster and faster still…'

No! Emet's awareness of his own heartbeat magnified, only intensifying it further still. He heaved at the restraints behind his back.

'…your heart pushing against your lungs, forcing them to pump faster and faster and faster. Your whole body swilling and gushing and flowing with air and blood and disease, every breath and beat taking you closer towards your last one, towards the end of everything you love, towards the climax of your ultimate failure. Feel the chaos of that fear now. It's been silently gnawing away at your insides for an age, just whispering at its presence, but now it will overrun you. With every breath you take, you lose more control. With every beat that frantic, cowardly heart of yours makes, the fear swells, larger than you, larger than everything you love, larger than your life itself.'

Red mist began to appear in the aisles and billow down from the ceiling, making the arena appear like a ghoulish circulatory system with gaseous blood seeping between its human organs.

'It consumes you…it fills your lungs…it blinds you. You saw Ilsa get dragged to her past…to the memory of the most traumatic incident in her life…the one devouring her insides…'

The music grew, its base making Emet's ribcage vibrate, as the audience, more drifting up into the air now, was hazily submerged deeper in blood red. He yelled in vain, the little sound leaving his taped-shut mouth being swallowed by the ambient noise.

'Well, you needn't go anywhere as your trauma has come for you. You know what you've been running from. It's eaten away at the edges of your consciousness for too long. It's hung off the back of you like a shadow. Now you must face it. On the count of zero, you're going to open your eyes and see it all coalesce into a hellish, inescapable existence around you.'

A few terrified screams filled the arena momentarily.

'That's right. You should be scared.'

From amongst the mist under the red spotlight, to Delancey's shadowy, angry smile glinted demonically. 'This is worse than your worst nightmare. This is real, and if you don't end this now, it will end you. Five…'

Emet yanked again at the rope around his wrists as many of the audience began to writhe and moan.

'…four…'

He desperately pushed his shins against their ties as more screams bounced around the arena.

'…three…'

With all the might he could muster, he pushed back against the chair and out with his shins to try to bend its frame as he started to see droves of the audience struggling in their seats.

'…two…'

He rocked from side to side, trying to get the chair wobbling only for one of the security guards to pin a hand on his shoulder. Half of the audience was yelling and shrieking now.

'…one…'

Through the floating, screaming bodies, a plume of deep red mist rose and twisted, travelling directly towards Emet's box. His heart almost pounded out of his chest as he watched it close in on him through the rippling, molten glass. On stage, Delancey was growing out of the red, casting a dark, dark shadow over the mist-bathed audience ahead of him. With every ounce of fight he had left, he screwed his feet into the floor, stood a few inches, and then rocked to the side, toppling the chair and landing on one of the guard's feet.

'For fuck's sake!' hissed the guard, grabbing his foot, then grabbing the chair and dragging it away from the window. 'Let's get this piece of shit out of here.'

As the other guard picked up the chair and they carried Emet towards the box's concourse door, Emet heard the music crescendo. '…zero.' As the door closed behind him, it halved the ear-piercing volume of the cacophony of shrieks left behind.

CHAPTER 81

His ties cut, the tape ripped off his face, and the patch pulled off his arm, Emet was unceremoniously thrown out of an arena door. He half-heartedly shoulder charged them for a while but knew it was too late, so he gave up and headed out past all the bars and restaurants. The Sunday afternoon smiling crowds gave him a wide berth, their bodies morphing and bending in odd ways as they gave him space. 'Oy oy! You started early!' a bunch of youths shouted his way as he swayed on the tilting floor. Halfway to where he'd parked his car, he remembered he no longer owned it and U-turned back to the Tube station. As he reached it, he took one last look at the arena. Its usually smooth white dome bubbled and blackened like tar. He threw his guts up.

The Tube ride and walk home were hellish with the warping and bending of most floors and walls making him dizzy and nauseous, but there was nothing left to spew up. He was empty.

He opened his front door and fell to all fours, then rolled to his back and used his foot to pull the door closed behind him. As he looked up at the corner where the ceiling met the walls, the junction rippled and pulsated. Needing to get away from the visual unsteadiness, he closed his eyes. The plume of red mist from the arena was just about to swallow him as they snapped back open. His body felt leaden as he rolled his head off the pool of drool he'd created. Hours must have passed as the light coming in from the window above the door was just starting to glow golden. As he pressed himself up to sitting, his hand found a padded envelope on the floor. News of his sacking apparently hadn't stopped the discs yet. There was also a note in Clyde's handwriting that said one solitary word: "Wanker". He stood, steadier on his feet than before with no wall warping but still feeling odd. He poured himself a glass of water, plonked himself on the sofa, lit a cigarette, and gazed at the mandala and sand jar below it. It would never mean the same again. He couldn't wait for the sand to be in a Scottish loch now. The black backing paper of the mandala sketch felt like a portal to a part of his past he wanted as far away from as possible. As he took another drag on his cigarette, he opened the padded envelope. The disc read 'One In Two: The Other Half Of The Cancer Story'. His heart ached. He pulled out a note. 'Dr Leigh was a remarkable woman. We're sorry for your loss. We thought you might like some of the extra footage we got with her. Regards, WeiszGuy Productions.' He put out his cigarette, got up and put the disc in, and hit play. And a few seconds later, there she was from months ago, her big, beautiful smile filling his screen as she played with her lapel mic. 'One two, one two,' she said, grinning straight down the lens. 'This is all so exciting. Have you got my good side?'

'There are only good sides,' replied the cameraman, widening her smile.

'In my line of work, we call that an exceptional bedside manner,' she grinned. 'So now we've established I only have good sides,' she continued with her tongue firmly in her cheek, 'I have to take the opportunity to ask somebody in the industry: is it a myth that the camera adds ten pounds? I'm asking for a wee friend, of course.'

'Of course,' replied the cameraman. 'You tell your friend that it is indeed a myth.'

'She'll be *very* glad to hear that,' said Leigh, blowing out a mock sigh afterwards.

Everything inside Emet swelled with emotion as he soaked in the infinitesimal details of her smile and the playful glint in her eye.

'And there's much more to looking good for the camera than that,' said another voice from off camera.

Emet's blood ran ice cold.

'Charisma is ninety-nine percent of the game,' said the bassy Irish voice, 'and you have that in spades, Dr Leigh. Have you ever done anything else in front of camera or any other public speaking at all?'

Emet leaned forward in horror. *No. It's just the trip.*

'I've spoken at the odd medical conference down the years,' his mum replied.

'No entertainment background at all?'

It wasn't the trip. It was the unmistakable voice of Delancey O'Shea.

'No,' she replied, clearly flattered.

'Well, your exceptional bedside manner would have stood you in good stead for a career in front of the masses. You have real charisma. We meet many bullshitters in our line of work, desperate for attention, feigning confidence, but you have the inimitable gravitas of somebody who knows their onions.'

Emet watched his mum take the compliment to heart. 'That's lovely of you to say.'

'It's lovelier to witness, so thank you. And before I finish with the compliments and we get some work done, do you mind if I ask you a question?'

'Not at all,' replied Leigh.

'What is that delightful fragrance you're wearing? I'd love to pick some up for my partner.'

Leigh tilted her head in slight confusion and shook her head. 'I'm not wearing anything today. I think your nostrils are mistaken.'

'No no no. Not mine, doctor. I have many short comings, but my friends say I have the nose of a bloodhound and it tells me that *you* are wearing something truly sublime.'

No. Aghast, Emet raised his hands to his mouth as his mental gears whirred. *No. This must be at least six months ago. It can't be...*

Leigh smiled bemusedly in Delancey's direction. 'No. I'm fairly certain I'm not wearing anything. I think that's just plain old *Eau de Leigh.*'

A small pause passed. 'Well, if that's the case, you should find a way to bottle it and take your perfume show on the road because it's an exquisite scent that could change your entire life.'

'Hmm,' she replied, deciding what to make of what he'd said. 'That might be the oddest compliment I've ever had, but I'll take it,' she finished with a smile. 'Maybe along with a shower in the staff changing room.'

Emet paused the video. His blood boiled like magma. His entire body trembled. Then he exploded up to his feet, ran into the kitchen and fished some keys out of the drawer, before running out of the house and across to his remaining set of wheels, the motorhome.

CHAPTER 82

Washed out, Jim stared into the murky water of the Thames as the voice on the other end of the phone reassured him. 'They obviously can't guarantee anything, but they're doing everything they can for her.'

'And she's at the best hospital?'

'The very best.'

'And her family. You're taking care of them?'

'We're making them as comfortable as they possibly can be. We've got suites for them in a hotel on the same road if they want them.'

The words went past him, only registering a few moments later. 'Good. Thanks.'

'Jim. Cardiac arrests just happen. This isn't your fault. The timing was pure coincidence.'

Again, the words didn't register for a few seconds. 'Uhuh.'

'If she'd have been somewhere else, the odds are she'd be dead. You acted quickly. You saved her life.'

Silence hung on the line.

'You saved her life. And she signed a health waiver, so what we know morally is backed up legally.' No response came. 'Jim. Are you still there?'

'I'm here.'

'It's been a long day. It's only natural to be unsettled by seeing what you saw. But it's done now, and everything is being done for

Sandra to return to peak health. There's no point in any more suffering than there's already been, is there?'

'No,' Jim eventually replied.

'Good. Get a good state change in you tonight, sir. Go for a walk. Get some fresh air. See some of London.'

'OK, Justin. Let me know if you need anything else from me.'

'You're good, sir. You've done everything you can.'

Jim paused. 'Goodnight.'

'Believe, sir. Goodnight.'

He ended the call and stared at his phone's home screen. His background image was a photo of him amongst tens of adoring fans overlaid by the message "Serve and deserve". He listlessly put it back into his pocket, then aimed his gaze back past dancing reflections on the water's surface, deep to the darkness beneath. Five minutes passed before he lifted his gaze and turned it along the river. A few hundred yards away in all its majesty stood Tower Bridge.

'Mr Rawlings! It's such a pleasure to meet you!' said the Tower attraction manager as he welcomed him in. 'I'm just glad I was running late. I was hoping if you were going to come through, I'd have had a chance to roll out the red carpet for you.'

'No need at all,' replied Jim. 'Getting to see this while I'm in London is all the blessing I need.'

'I hope you don't mind me asking, but are you OK?'

Jim swallowed, took a deep breath, and nodded. 'Just wiped out from delivering The Leap.'

'I'm not surprised! I've seen how much you go for it. You really leave it all out there. I really want to get to your next one.'

Jim politely smiled and nodded.

'Anyway, enough of my wittering. Follow me.'

The pair ascended the staircase of the North Tower and the manager opened the main doorway at the top of the stairs. In front of them was the East Walkway with its Victorian steel frame, its incredible views out onto the Thames and the parallel West Walkway, and its spectacular glass floor that stretched out most of the sixty-one-metre space between both of the bridges' towers.

'Wow,' gasped Jim.

'I know. It's quite the feat of ingenuity, isn't it?' the manager said as they walked a few metres out onto the transparent floor and looked at the bridge and the water below. 'This walkway was built through the late eighteen hundreds and was first opened for the public to cross in eighteen ninety-two when—'

'Do you mind if I just take it all in first?' asked Jim. 'Maybe you can fill me in on the history after I've had some time to explore?'

'Of course, Mr Rawlings,' said the manager apologetically. 'I'll leave you to take a good look around. You can come find me when you've absorbed all the beauty she has to offer. Just before I go, can I be really cheeky and ask something of you?'

'Ask away,' said Jim, forcing some life into his smile and his eyes.

'Do you mind if we get a selfie together up here?' the manager asked sheepishly. 'Your audio courses have changed my life. You're literally a hero to me.'

Jim lifted his gaze from through the floor and sighed. 'I'd love to, but I'm guessing we ain't strictly meant to be up here, right?'

The manager nodded.

'But maybe outside.' The manager nodded, a little crestfallen. 'Tell you what. How about we share something really human up here that you can't get in trouble for?'

'Like what?'

'I hope it don't sound weird, but how about a hug? I'm a million miles from home, so you'd be doing me a real favour.'

'It doesn't sound weird at all. It'd be my honour,' said the manager. The two embraced, Jim wrapping his arms around his tour guide, giving him the fullest hug a stranger would ever give. The manager went to let go but could feel Jim wasn't finished, so retightened his hold. 'Are you sure you're OK, Mr Rawlings?'

'Better for this, brother,' he said as his muscular hands patted the manager's back so firmly as to jangle every coin and key he had on him. 'And the view will cure the rest,' he said as they parted.

'OK then, I'll leave you to soak it all in. I'll just be in the stairwell in the South Tower on the other side if you need anything.'

'Thank you.' Jim reached a hand towards the glass floor. 'You mind if I start with a lie down?'

'By all means. Rest well, Mr Rawlings.'

'I will,' said Jim as he got onto the floor and laid out. He remained there for a few minutes after the manager disappeared, then stood and ambled along the walkway, admiring the view out along the Thames. The dark waters shimmered even more through the glass under the red evening sky. *This* was beauty. He walked along the glass floor, watching the traffic pass by far beneath, until reaching the North Tower again, where he made his way into the stairwell. Instead of descending the stairs, he observed the other doors into the tower itself. He walked over to one and laid his hand against it. His eyes worked their way down to the keyhole. Out of his pocket, he pulled the set of keys he had picked from the manager's pocket and tried them one by one until one unlocked the door.

CHAPTER 83

The van hurtled along the roads out of London as a gale began to rage. Emet powered his phone up. As messages and missed call notifications galore poured in, he hit record on a voice note. 'Mate...I'm so fucking sorry. I shouldn't have fucked off and left you worrying about where I was. I just had to go try to stop him delivering that seminar, and I didn't want stopping, and that's what you'd have done because you're my mate. And in the end, I didn't stop it.' He didn't notice the red light as he sped through it. 'I fucked you over and I didn't even make it pay. You're the only one who's had my back. Skye's a psycho lying bitch. He fed a fucking drip into her grave!' He teared up and put his foot down, the pedal feeling like it was wrapping round his foot, pulling itself down to the floor. 'I can't explain it, but I think he knew she had cancer before she did. She could have caught it earlier. She should still be here. He has to pay! He has to be stopped!' Tears rolled down his burning cheeks. 'I love you, mate. You're the best friend I could've possibly hoped for. I had to do this. I hope you underst—'

The phone rang in his hand. The call was from Clyde. He deliberated on answering the call, then eventually hit accept. 'Mate, I'm so, so sorry.'

'Fuck that, you dickhead. We got a hit.'

Emet squinted. 'You what?'

'A hit, with the DNA.'

As the van sped along the road, Emet watched as the lampposts unraveled into double helixes. 'What, with O'Shea?'

'Yes! One of the DNA databases turned up a familial match from some distant cousin. I don't think his name's O'Shea, Emet. I'm not even sure he's Irish. I think I have a name for him.'

'Go on.'

'I think his name is Erich with a c-h. Erich Weisz. I think he's English.'

Emet slammed on the brakes and pulled over into the hard shoulder. 'Have you searched his name and found anything on him?'

'It's a nightmare to search, Em. That's Harry Houdini's real name.'

'You're fucking kidding?'

'I wish I was,' replied Clyde. 'It swamps the search results. There might be stuff on him, but I can't find it. The sheer number of results is wild.'

Wild…Wildfire! 'Clyde. You're a genius. I'll call you back.' Emet hung up and scrolled to the app store. A few minutes later, he'd set up a Fuusion account, which was now open to a wider test audience. Five minutes later, he found a hit on an Erich Weisz of around O'Shea's age. 'Ho-ly fucking shit.'

CHAPTER 84

The motorhome ripped around another sopping wet corner, with a gust of wind catching it and lifting a wheel, but Emet's feelings and sensations were so all over the place, he didn't notice and wouldn't have cared if he had. Laurel Canyon Manor was just minutes away and all he knew was he had to get there. Now under the cover of corridors of trees, Emet raced the van around corner after corner until finally he slammed down on the brake. A huge, old rotten tree had fallen into the road and there was no way around. Unsure whether or not he was hallucinating it, he inched the vehicle forward to see if he could drive through it. That wasn't happening. He swung the van around, drove back on himself to the last junction, and rather than continuing the drive up the hill, he drove down into the valley and parked. The rain calming and the sky clearing now, he tilted his gaze up the sheer cliff face, which bowed and buckled to his tripping eyes. Without being able to spot from this angle, he was fairly certain Delancey's house sat atop it, and ran to a nearby footpath back up the hill.

Gasping for breath, the gigantic gates finally came into view. He didn't fancy his chances climbing them, but there may be no other way. He stayed close to the tree and bushes as he spied for any gatemen or security guards, but none were in sight. He had to go for it. He ran to the gate, grabbed a railing and hoisted himself up but the whole thing moved. The gate was open. He jumped off, pushed open a gap just wide enough to squeeze through, shut it behind him, and scanning as he went, sprinted over past the hundred-year-old

Rolls Royce to the house. The oversized door and its gigantic knocker loomed. He reached for it as it reached for him and they knocked the door together, the sound reverberating around his head. When no answer came, he put his ear to the door and could hear music. He waited a while longer to no avail. Eventually, he tried the handle. The door creaked open. He took a cautious few steps in. Barring the music, there were no sounds of life. 'Delancey!' he yelled. 'Delancey!' He wandered through the main atrium, the straight lines of the grand Art Deco house flexing and disorienting him with every step. As he entered the long hallway to the lounge, the haunting music grew closer. The Surrealist paintings on the wall swirled and reached out to him like living nightmares as he passed. There was something else different about this hallway too, something missing perhaps, but he couldn't put his finger on what it was. He reached the room and pushed open the heavy door. The twenties' music crackled away through the gramophone and the fireplace was ablaze. He walked over to the table where a half-drunken glass of red wine sat beside a half-smoked cigarette in an ashtray, its vapour still spiralling away. The music finished, leaving nothing but the sound of the shellac record rotating on the turntable and a feint telephone dial-tone. The receiver of an antique candlestick telephone laid on the side table off its hook. 'Delancey! Delancey!' He thought he heard a muffled shout back, so trotted out of the room in its direction, back along the surreal hallway, dodging the tendrils and tentacles reaching out of the walls. 'Delancey!' He heard a less muffled response this time. Somebody was in. Their voice called back. It led him to the therapy room and more music. As he entered, sat by a stack of film cans an old-fashioned projector whirred away. The music was the soundtrack of the movie it was playing onto the wall, 'The Grim Game' starring Houdini. As Emet gazed at the black and white face of the iconic magician, the colour seemed to drain from the rest of his surroundings until it flushed back in, all in shades of red.

'Emet Gordon,' called Delancey's voice from through the French doors. 'Check the clocks in there.'

Emet's eyes instinctively travelled across the wall. The only clocks they found were painted on the Dali replica.

'You're right on time. Come join me out here. It's a beautiful evening.'

Emet headed outside. The sun burned almost white gold just above the horizon in the spectacular sky adorned with every shade of red imaginable. Delancey stood near the cliff edge, facing out onto the valley, a plume of cigarette smoke rising above him into the ether.

CHAPTER 85

'Quite the sky, don't you think?'

Emet's nostrils flared as he walked out towards the edge. 'What sort of sick freak are you?'

Delancey turned to face his guest, wearing the widest of smirks. 'You tell me, Emet. You've been certain all along, haven't you? Which of your terms fits best? Snake oil salesman, shammer, or charlatan?'

'You fucking knew!' screamed Emet. 'How did you fucking know?!'

'How many times have I told you?' replied Delancey, tapping his nose. 'But you wouldn't believe. No matter how much evidence I provided, you just didn't want to believe.'

'I didn't believe you because you're a fucking con artist, not a magician, but *how* did you know?' growled Emet as he stormed closer.

Delancey took a draw on his cigarette. 'Any sufficiently advanced method is indistinguishable from magic, Emet.'

Emet poked his finger in Delancey's direction. 'Cut the fucking shit, Erich!'

The ever-present grin and all the colour vanished from Delancey's face.

'That's right, you evil prick. I know who you are. You think you're smarter than everybody, but your PhDs in virology and pharmaceutical sciences didn't stop a second-rate journalist finding you, did they?'

'How…how do you know that name?' stammered Delancey.

'Tell me how you knew about my mum!'

Delancey took a moment to compose himself. 'I...have,' he replied curtly, as if sick of repeating himself, before taking another drag and burrowing his frosty gaze into his interrogator.

'You somehow got her blood and had her tested, didn't you?'

Delancey shut his eyes, his nose and mouth furrowing in abject disgust. 'It doesn't matter. It doesn't matter,' he affirmed to himself. 'If they're anyone's problem now, they're his.'

'It doesn't matter?!' bawled Emet with incredulity. 'Answer my fucking question!'

Delancey took a couple of deep breaths and opened his eyes, his smile resurrected, and took another drag. 'I cured it, Emet. *I* found the cure. In my lab. Years ago.'

'Bullshit!' snapped Emet, but the longer he looked into those icy blue eyes, the more an unfamiliar, uneasy feeling inside him grew. That the man in front of him was telling the truth.

'I cured it. *Me.*' Delancey looked Emet squarely in the eye as he took another drag. 'Yes...there it is. Your belief. Try to deny it all you want, but I see it just like you saw my lies.'

'No,' gasped Emet. 'You can't have cured pancreatic cancer?'

Delancey tilted his head gleefully. 'I didn't.' With a slick sleight of hand, he made his cigarette disappear. 'I cured *all* cancers.'

'No...' He studied the man across from him for any sign of mistruth, praying for it, but he saw none. 'You can't have.' Overwhelmed by the ramifications of what he'd heard, he stood agape for a long moment as the grinning man ahead of him reproduced the cigarette. Then a question burrowed its way into his consciousness. 'Did you...did you say years ago?'

Delancey puffed out some smoke. 'Coming up fifteen, yes.'

Emet's horror grew. 'Then why...why haven't you said something in the proper way? Do you...do you know how many people you could have saved?'

'About ten million a year globally, correct?'

Flabbergasted at the casualness of the response, Emet barely even nodded.

'Exactly. That's why I said nothing. You asked me once what I thought life is and you said it's the people that give it meaning. I guess I largely agree with that. The truth is, as special as you "people" try to convince yourselves you are over and over again with inane self-help seminars and therapy and solipsistic navel gazing, talking about your pathetic self-constructed problems until the cows come home, as much as you try to cling on to your miserable existences that you yourselves want to escape half of the time with any mind-altering substance you can get your hands on, most of you are nothing more than boring malignancies sucking the life out of your society and the planet. Life can be precious, but most of you deserve to die.' He took another puff on his cigarette as Emet stared his way like a deer in the headlights. 'Your mother was a decent woman, trying to do good for morons who didn't deserve it. Maybe that makes her a little simple. But *you*. What are you? Wallowing in your self-pity; a walking, gaping psychic wound, your guilt and anger making you more gullible than her morons and even Jimmy Rawlings's happy-clapping simpletons. You earn your living doing nothing of value, just taking the work of others and tearing it apart for the entertainment of the masses. And what's worse is you're smart enough to know exactly what you're doing. You look upon me with contempt, but deep down you know that even though I withheld my discovery from the masses, I've done more for the world by *your own* definitions in the single hour-long session I could be bothered to do each week whilst hiding amongst the wishy-washy charlatans and fake gurus, than you have in your entire life. *You* and your kind are the real cancers.'

'You…you're beyond insane.'

'No, Emet. My mind is crystal clear. I saw the solution to one of the biggest plights in human existence, then I saw what most of you are, and now I see what I have to do.'

'And that is?'

'To be celebrated like I should be forever, like my namesake.'

'So what? You're going to share your "magic" with the world?'

'No. I'm going to die shrouded in mystery and take all my secrets with me,' said Delancey, taking a step back towards the cliff edge.

'Stop!' yelled Emet, slowly stepping forward and holding a palm out. 'You can't kill yourself. The world needs your cure. Tell me what it is.'

A mischievous smile spread across Delancey's face. 'You really want to know?'

'Yes!'

Delancey took a long drag on his cigarette and puffed out three rings of smoke. 'You're looking at it.'

As the smoke dissipated ahead of him, Emet's mind flashed back to the red mist at the event. 'It's...it's airborne?'

'Bravo. But what makes it is in *my* blood.' A prideful, wicked smile unfurled across Delancey's face. '*I* am the cure.'

Emet edged further forward and held both palms up, begging. 'Please! The world needs you. It needs what you've done!'

'Yes, because my life is precious. But I don't need it. You're all so tedious, clinging on to your pitiful lives, devoid of dignity. I'm going out exactly as I want, in a blaze of glory. Thank you for helping with that,' he said, pointing with his cigarette past Emet, inviting him to turn his head.

Emet turned to see the therapy room ablaze, the fire spreading to the rest of the house. 'What are you talking about? That wasn't me.'

Delancey chuckled. 'That mind of yours is really playing tricks on you. First, deleting that recording of our interview, then dumping that cigarette from the study into those film cans on your way out here. You really should be careful who's whispering in that wind to you as you go beddy-bye.'

As Emet turned his mind inside out, trying to remember if there was any truth to Delancey's claims, a wailing entered the periphery of his hearing. Suddenly, memories flashed to mind. He *had* deleted the interview recording. He *had* thrown the half-smoked cigarette into the film cans. He had heard Skye's voice at night. He had heard Delancey's through his phone.

'That's my cue, Emet. It's been a hoot,' said Delancey, sliding his heels right to the cliff edge, kicking sandy dust of its edge, swirling into the void below.

'Don't!' begged Emet.

'I won't. There's not much of a story in suicide. There's just one last thing I want to say to you before I go.' He grinned at the former journalist. 'I have belief you'll be alright, Emet. *Full belief.*'

It was done before he could stop it. He'd felt the rise of rage on hearing those two words a few times over the last few weeks, but never like this. As if his hands weren't his, the eruption of white-hot hatred inside him had propelled his hands in their diamond shape out full force into Delancey's chest, sending him flying off the cliff edge. Horrified, he watched the gigantic man fall through the air, the widest smile on the Cancer Man's face until he smashed with a blood-curdling crunch into the motorhome roof below. He stood in abject shock, only realising he hadn't yet retracted his hands after ten seconds of staring down at Delancey's motionless body. The wailing that had entered his consciousness a while ago was now louder. From across the valley, it was a police siren growing closer. He peered down again. Delancey moved. *I have to try to save him.*

He sprinted around the side of the house, calling for an ambulance as he ran. 'Laurel Canyon Manor! Somebody's fell off a cliff edge! They need urgent medical assistance!' He dashed out through the gates and careened down the footpath through the woods. Arriving at the van as the sirens grew ever closer, he clambered up the van's side ladder towards the caved-in roof. His grip on the rung lost nearly all its power as the copious amount of blood came into sight. He managed to hang on but couldn't look at the hideous scene ahead of him. Then the metallic stench of blood hit him. Sick to his stomach, he hung on, his mind racing as the sirens grew closer. He could see the flashing lights through the trees now. He had to try to save the gravely injured man beside him but was utterly paralysed. The police car emerged from the woodland road. It screeched to a halt.

He thought of his dad's letter. His mother's smile. Her mandala. He wondered whether there was even the tiniest chance that any of the craziness that Delancey had spewed was true.

The police car doors flew open. 'Stop where you are! Slowly get down from the vehicle and put your hands above your head.'

Emet raised one of his hands overhead from the rung, showing its empty palm to the police. 'I didn't do it!' he yelled.

'Make your way down slowly, sir.'

'He needs an ambulance!' cried Emet.

'One's on its way, sir. Now, make your way down slowly.'

'There's no time!'

'Make your way down slowly, sir!' one of the officers hollered back.

Emet took a foot off the rung but then, bracing himself, turned back briefly to see the bloody mess behind him. He slowly lowered his overhead hand to the rung, then edged it onto the crumpled roof.

'Make your way down, sir!'

He took a couple of slow, deep breaths just like he'd learned to at The Leap as he peered at his hand, then averted his eyes as he dragged his palm along a crumpled, jagged piece of the roof's metal shell.

'Make your way down, sir!!'

He daren't look but he could feel it across his palm. The stinging burn. The hot liquid trickling along it. He took one quick glance at the horror of the roof and plunged his gashed-open palm into an oozing pool of Delancey's warm blood.

The police ran his way, shouting for him to come down, but he wasn't hearing them. He gawped at his blood-bathed, dripping hand, and then red faded entirely to black.

Follow the next part of Emet's story in

THE CANCER MAN: METASTASIS

Available for pre-order
(hopefully faster than the announced date)
at your region's Amazon store

Arton's next book, the Christmas thriller

ALL I WANT FOR CHRISTMAS IS YUYU

is available for pre-order at your region's Amazon store

For exclusive updates on Arton's work and a free copy of this book's companion novella,

THE ART OF THE CON

sign up to his mailing list at

www.artonbaleci.com

If you enjoyed this book, please leave
a review on its Amazon page

Printed in Great Britain
by Amazon